The Good Patient

The Good Patient

A Novel

Kristin Waterfield Duisberg

St. Martin's Press

New York

www.stmartins.com

ISBN 0-312-30039-5

10 9 8 7 6 5 4 3 2

For Erik

Acknowledgments

Grateful acknowledgment is made to the following people, without whom this book would not have become.

Margot Livesey and C. Michael Curtis were among the first to believe in and champion my story and encouraged me through the early days of my first draft. Peggy Slasman, Anne Dubitzky, and Dan Ginsburg let me out of my "real" job at Massachusetts General Hospital gracefully, leaving me to write with very little guilt. Leslie Epstein at the Boston University Creative Writing Program told me my work was publishable and made it more so; Chris Castellani, Michelle Chalfoun, and Sarah Towers provided endless enthusiasm and kind support at BU and well beyond. Michelle, in particular, deserves a special place in heaven, not only for introducing me to Mary Evans, my agent, but for reading repeated 650-page drafts. Mary Evans had the faith and vision to take on all 650 pages and make them better—and fewer! Linda McFall of St. Martin's Press gave remarkable care and attention in bringing this book into the world while nurturing a new life of her own. Eva Schoenfeld helped me work through some of the story's most difficult spots. She provided a model for Dr. Lindholm and a great deal more.

Years ago, Peter Smith was the first person to tell me that, while I could do many things, I should be writing; if he had been more impressed with my first job out of college I would likely still consider editing equity research reports for JP Morgan a fine career. My entire family has been enthusiastic and encouraging through the many years this book has taken to write; I thank Grace, in particular, for sharing "her" computer and often too much of my time. Finally, and most important, the sacrifices my husband made to allow me time and space to write are many and unquantifiably generous. My deepest, highest, and greatest thanks to him for this book and so much else.

One

Chapter 1

From the inside out, these are my layers: bad, good, bad, good, and now—new—again bad. They attach beneath my skin, nested one inside the other like Matruschka dolls, anchored with a pin through each skull at the top. They ring like a bell, scream and peal, complain, when layers and outsides clash. Beneath the layers, there is nothing: unbounded emptiness like the equation of the universe inverted so that one equals zero.

I was born with just bad, in New York City in August, a twin, half dead, half orphaned. My mother told me the story once, in the hospital, how she'd gone into labor early on a Queens-bound F train, in the dead heat of the Summer of Love. When the first contraction came, a tightened belt beneath her skin, she dropped her purse and grabbed hard on my three-year-old brother's hand. He screamed, and people crowded in to help; she announced she wasn't moving, and I likely would have died somewhere between Prospect Park and Far Rockaway if an off-duty EMT hadn't been there to hustle her off. At Bellevue, the attending obstetrician cut a clean line up the front of her peasant blouse and told her he was going to do the same thing to her stomach: her baby—her *babies*—were in serious trouble. Both babies were in breech, the one closer to the cervix in extreme distress. The umbilical cord was caught. It was a matter of minutes before one or both of us was dead.

"Well, you can imagine my shock," she had said to me. Her fingers trailed through the air like water. "Your father had left us without a word of where he was, I had your two brothers at home and no job and no money. Babies—*zuh*, plural? It was the first time I heard the word. I told him I didn't want you, naturally, in the heat of the moment I didn't want any of us. I told him just let me die, me and my babies, but by golly you were determined to be born."

By golly, indeed; you might even say, My stars. I pushed my way right past my dead sister, bottom forward, dragging that umbilical cord like a piece of toilet paper stuck to a shoe. Broke my collarbone and tore a hundred-stitch hole in my mother, just to get into the world.

"Hey—check this out. Do you suppose if a hemophiliac cut himself accidentally and didn't bother to stop the bleeding, it would be considered suicide?"

Twenty-eight years later, another dying August New York day, and I'm attempting my own ass-backward introduction to the world once again. This time I'm already at the doctor's office, however; an imposing mahogany-and-leather suite filled with furniture that looks like it would be at home at the Harvard Club on 44th. Today is my first appointment with Rachel Lindholm, MD. She's a psychiatrist, and she is late. The source of my question is a pamphlet I'm reading on chronic depression in hemophiliacs. The audience is my husband, Robert, who's looking awfully uncomfortable for a guy who's pretty used to sitting on $5,000 couches. I repeat the question—"Get it? Bleeding? Hemophiliacs?"—and tickle his thigh with the pamphlet. It's a joke.

Robert gives me a baffled, uncomprehending glare and doesn't even glance down at the pamphlet. Have it his way, I suppose, but for my dollar, why not enjoy yourself if you're going to have to wait? I go back to my reading and think that's one thing I can add to my short list of advantages psychiatrists hold over psychologists: better waiting-room literature. I should know. I'm a junior account manager for Pharmaceuticals at Boylan & Westwood, which is New York City's premier public relations company, if you're willing to believe our collaterals, and plenty of this stuff crosses my desk. I also should know because I've spent a goodly portion of my life doling out fifty-minute dollops of my mind to head doctors—PhDs and MSWs, even an EdD, one time. Dr. Lindholm is my fifth. She's my first psychiatrist, though.

Shall I give it all away, right up front? I'm here to see her because of the splint on my right hand, a hard shell of plastic that protects three broken metacarpals and two dislocated knuckles, which throb dimly even though it's been two days and a half-dozen schedule four drugs since I hit the bathroom wall. It was a screwup, a momentary indiscretion, a judgment lapse. I admit it, freely and adultly, with full cognitive rationality, and I suppose I'd beat myself up for it if that wouldn't constitute overkill. But I should have known better than to pop a wall with my right hand, of all things, with bones so fragile and used to this routine they crack like stale cookies. If I had to hurt myself—and it seems, at least in the moment, that I had—I should have done something less ostentatious, like burning my palm on the stove, or tripping in front of a subway. Not breaking my hand again. Not something so token, so recidivist.

Out on the street, a car alarm goes off, and I take a second to rearrange myself on the couch, unfurling the pamphlet across the top of my splint like a sommelier's towel. Briefly, I think about what's awaiting me and consider carrying myself into the inner sanctum thus disguised. I can almost laugh at the ridiculousness of it, the sight gag, but the truth is I hate the idea of walking into Dr. Lindholm's office, any doctor's office, with malady so obviously declared. Why tip the balance beyond where it inherently starts? For a semester or two in high school, I saw a male therapist, Dr. Zobel, a bald and bearded

Freudian, and the very first thing he did at my first session was point his chin my direction. "Why don't you start by telling me what's wrong with your chest," he said.

"My chest?" I was there for the ever-disappearing Bourbon in the kitchen drawer, a tendency to fuck my brothers' friends. "You mean the size of it? Or lack thereof?"

"Do you think there's something wrong with the size of your chest?"

I'd looked down to assess—are you kidding me?—and then I saw. I was wearing a scoop-necked T-shirt and I was covered in hives, scarlet roses blooming from sternum to clavicle. Panicky heat prickled my throat and my palms went damp. "I have a rash."

"Ah?"

"A necklace. From my boyfriend. I'm allergic to electroplate."

After that first hour, I made a point of wearing high-necked shirts to his office and, in the winter, turtlenecks, and while he was quick after five or so visits to point out the change, it made me feel better, as if I had won at least one small victory against myself, and therefore, by association, him. Stupid, treacherous body. It's forever giving me up like a weepy john in a raid.

Today, I'm wearing a slate blue silk pantsuit, high-collared and wide-sleeved, to give the impression that I just dashed over here from the office. I tried to pick something that would say quietly expensive, suggest that I was an impossibly well-put-together young woman. The purply-blue of the fabric almost matches my fingers, a detail Robert didn't comment on when he swung by home to pick me up. Instead, he just winced a little and patted my hair, as if that was the one thing on me he could be sure wasn't about to break. He's not here because we're doing marriage counseling or because he thinks I couldn't make it here on my own (though *wouldn't* might be another story), just in case you were wondering. He has taken a few hours away from his still seventy-to-eighty-hours-a-week-after-a-decade job—corporate law, for Adelstein & Kravitz; M&A services at your service—because

I have a bad habit of lying, and he is here to make me tell the truth, to this doctor, and to him.

Easier said than done. I'm a terrible liar, impulsive and indiscriminate. I try not to be, but a good lie is just too much fun to resist. The patterns and protocols, the sheer superfluity, extravagant as an Elizabethan dance—

Robert sighs loudly and shoots his left cuff. His thumb rubs the face of his watch a couple of times, then both hands lift and rotate against the orbits of his eyes.

I clear my throat. "Time is it?"

"Four-ten. Four-eleven." He sighs again.

"Sorry about that."

He squeezes my good fingers once, a quick pulse like a farmer's hand on a cow's full teat, and half-smiles at a ficus tree across the waiting room. It's just us and the ficus, the swanky sofa, a pair of club chairs, and a spring water dispenser that emits occasional burps. At the other end of the room, Dr. Lindholm's receptionist sits with her profile to us, typing industriously away. She is middle-aged, the mother of college students, perhaps; still styling her hair in the Dorothy Hamill she chose when the eldest was born. She has on glasses and brick red lipstick; her back is Miss Porter's School, I'm-not-listening straight. She yanks a sheet of paper from her typewriter and rolls another in.

"So that's—what? Like, thirty-three bucks, huh?" I tip my head to the side, toward Dr. Lindholm's door. "Think she'll give us a discount if we complain?"

"Goddammit," Robert says quietly. He pulls his hand away and tucks it under his arm. His other hand comes up and clamps itself around his biceps, the naughty fingers that had tried to socialize with mine now locked securely away. The tips peep out from under his armpit, his fingernails reproachful. That's not funny, they say to me. You're not one bit funny at all.

"Sorry," I say again.

Robert stares straight ahead.

"I'm sorry, Robert."

Not like this has to be such a big, freaking deal.

I refurl my depressed-hemophiliacs pamphlet. *"Like many other of the 'silent diseases,'"* I read, *"the emotional effects of hemophilia on adolescent males, in particular, can be invidious."* On the cover, there's a picture of a neurasthenic young man sitting on a bed, his chin in his palm. He's wearing a Nirvana T-shirt and a pair of enormously wide-legged jeans with ratty, frayed cuffs, a compromise between grunge and hip-hop circa 1993. He is definitely not some ad company's stock photo. He is pimply-faced and weak-chinned; his hair has only recently begun corkscrewing into coarse curls. His upper lip is sooted with scraggly growth and for a second I take pity; he needs a lesson from his father. He needs to sneak open the medicine cabinet and squirt the pile of Foamy in his hand, *Now where did I see that razor again?* One stroke across his cheek, another along the naked boomerang of his jaw . . . Would a single nick, a dull, crusty blade do the trick?

Briefly, I'm taken back to my earlier question to Robert, my joke. A little of my Nirvana-boy pity comes along for the ride, however, changing something of its shape along the way, and this time the whole thing strikes me as less funny. After all, I never mean to hurt myself, either. My injuries usually evolve from a minor bump or bruise that I nag into a major medical issue. I guess I've always thought it was okay to hurt myself because if something really horrible came of it—an amputation, say, or something fatal—I could blame the original, unintended wound: I didn't do it to myself; it just happened to me. Years ago, when we used to talk about this stuff, Robert told me he would never forgive me if I killed myself, and you wouldn't think that was the kind of statement that allowed for wiggle room, but I suppose if anything could provide it, unintended injuries might just be the ticket.

[8]

But it's no longer a negotiable topic—it hasn't been for years; bad me, to have brought it up—and so I sit silent and studious, waiting for Dr. Lindholm, and Robert sits locked behind his angry arms. This is the way she finds us.

"Darien Gilbertson?" She smiles.

That's me. I stand up.

Dr. Lindholm's eyes fall briefly, assessingly, to my blue fingers, and then skip back up to my face. "Pleased to meet you. I'm Rachel Lindholm." A quarter turn. "And you must be Robert." Robert agrees that he is. "Shall we?" Dr. Lindholm takes a crab-step in the direction of her office, and Robert and I follow her in.

"So, Darien. Robert." Dr. Lindholm fixes each of us with a brilliant, competent smile. We take our places on furniture carried over from the Harvard waiting room: Robert and me thigh-to-thigh on a burgundy leather sofa with such a high polish you could probably see your reflection in it; Dr. Lindholm in a gray leather easy chair with one foot tucked up under her, casual-like. Two vanity-sized boxes of tissues mark either end of the coffee table that separates us, his and hers in neutral ecru. "Gilbertson? Do I have that right? I look at my notes and I can barely read my own writing." Dr. Lindholm screws up her forehead and frowns down at a leather portfolio in her lap, turning it to one side and then the other, an Etch-a-Sketch. She shakes her head. "Gilbertson. I'm sorry you had to wait."

We both nod mutely, awaiting the explanation. Dr. Lindholm beams at each of us a little more. "So, let's get down to business, then," she says. "Can I get either of you coffee? Coffee? No? Okay." Her eyes shift meaningfully to my hand. "Where should we start?"

I measure Dr. Lindholm before launching in; there's no way this is going to work. Already, I hate this woman too much. Dr. Lindholm is tall and willowy, and Aryan to the extreme: corn silk hair in a chin-length bob, pale blue-gray eyes and skin with an enviable translucence

I swear you can see bones and blood vessels through if you catch the light right. She's dressed in a sage green suit, discreet letter Cs stamped on the buttons, and heels that actually match, Garanimals for the professional set. I look for a run in her stockings, lipstick on her teeth, nothing. She looks like somebody's wife, a social trophy with a standing date for tea in the Oak Room and a box seat at Lincoln Center. She looks nothing like a doctor to me.

Robert got Dr. Lindholm's name from a nurse in the emergency room, who said that she was the best for self-mutilation cases. We apparently were lucky to get an appointment so quickly, though *lucky* wouldn't exactly be the word for how I feel at the moment. With Dr. Lindholm sitting across from me like some giant bar of Ivory soap, I feel dull and grubby, and suddenly ludicrous in my suit. I'm five foot two and tend toward skinny, pasty-skinned, Elvira-haired; I wear makeup and keep my hair long as much as anything to minimize the chances of being mistaken for a boy. For a second, I shift my gaze to Robert and then back again, mentally pairing the two of them, Robert and Dr. Lindholm, she's a little old for him, RobertandLindholm, but then again, he's a little old for me, thirty-five in October. I wonder if he finds her attractive.

As if pondering this possibility himself, Robert leans forward, his elbows on his thighs. "We start right here, with this hand," he says. "I think I told you all of this on the phone yesterday, right? We're here because Darien needs some . . . needs a whole lot of help. She's always had this self-destructive streak, but for the most part she's been okay. We've kept it under control." He pauses and glances quickly at me. "But then Monday night she broke her hand while I was at work. Actually broke her own hand, and won't tell me why. It's something that she used to do when she was younger, and that's just—it's just a big freight train we need to put a stop to right now. I'm scared as hell. I'm really pissed off. And I just—I don't know what to do."

Good Lord. He makes it sound as if breaking hands was a regular habit of mine, like collecting stamps or Barbie dolls, an extracurricular activity. I wait for Dr. Lindholm's alarm, but she only nods and says okay. All very reasonable and clear. "Thank you," she tells Robert. "That can't have been easy for you to say. Now," she turns to me, "Darien. What about you? Why do you think you're here?"

"Why do I *think* I'm here?" After five doctors, I have the first visit procedure down and can go through the routine on autopilot, laying out the relevant data points like setting the table for a five-course meal. Anorexia at age ten, bulimia at twelve, alcoholism and sexual promiscuity with the onset of puberty; lying, nightmares, and self-mutilation for as long as I can remember. Everything from the knife rest to the fingerbowl. "I know why I'm here. I'm here because I broke my hand, and because that's really just emblematic of a whole host of other things that are wrong with me, or that at least have been wrong with me in the past." I throw the last of that out there, eager for her to ask about what those other things might be. Starving, puking, binge drinking, sluttiness, pathological lying—did I mention these before? I don't mind talking about them.

Dr. Lindholm doesn't bite. She just nods and waits for me to continue. "So I guess I'm here to deal with some of those things before I become the personal target of my insurance company." When neither she nor Robert as much as smiles, I add, "And, of course, because I love my husband, and I know what I did, what I do, is hurting him, and it needs to stop."

Shit. I can hear how insincere, how careless it sounds, even though I mean it. I open my mouth to backpedal. "I do love him," I say again, and when I can't think of anything further, I join in the silence of the room, punched with tiny, regular holes by the *tick-ticking* of a pendulum clock set on the wall like Switzerland between Dr. Lindholm's chair and the couch. I study the diplomas on the far wall and feel her

[11]

study me. Wellesley College, 1979; Columbia College of Physicians and Surgeons, 1983. It figures. Robert smiles down at the square of carpet braced between his shoes, thumbs at his temples.

"I'm glad to hear that," Dr. Lindholm finally says. "That gives us the very best base to work from." A pause. "Whose idea was it for you to come here?"

"Mine, obviously." Robert looks up from the floor. "As you can see, Darien sometimes has trouble taking things seriously. Hurting herself is about as serious as she gets. She hasn't done anything in a long time—well, just little, clumsy things, like running into things by accident. By accident?" He turns and looks at me. I shrug. "But this thing on Monday really came out of nowhere. It just sounds too much like—" He stops. "I just want to know what it is I can do to help. I'm willing to do whatever it takes to make her better. I just need her to tell me the truth."

Acting out is what they used to call it, when I saw my first therapist back in Philadelphia. With Robert here playing the parent role, pushing me to tell Dr. Lindholm what happened, the scene takes on a perverted sense of déjà vu, history revised and improved. Haven't I sat through this lesson before?

At that first session, at the tenderized age of eleven, my mother hustled me in by the elbow and sat so close to me that I could feel her knee burrowing into my thigh. "This is nutty," she had announced to Dr. Gladys Flynn, combing maroon-tipped fingers through her Ann-Margret bob. "I have no idea what we're doing here, why this is any business of the school's. Did you know Darien's teacher said they were going to send Social Services to investigate me if I didn't bring her here to see you? Not that it's any of your business, but there's nothing wrong with her. Girls just go through these phases. Being attractive is important to them." She shook her helmet of hair, plastic bangles clattering noisily to her wrist. "I'm a good mother," she said. "I do the best I can."

Now, as I study the diplomas, try to see if Dr. Lindholm graduated Phi Beta Kappa, wonder if she had to choose between field hockey and tennis for the fall varsity season, I hear her say, "Darien, would you be willing to talk a bit about what happened Monday night?"

"Monday night?" I straighten in my seat. "Oh, yeah, sure. Well, I broke my hand, which you know, and I did it by hitting a wall, which you also know. But it was really more an accident than anything else. It pretty much happened by accident."

Robert turns to look at me, incredulous, and I feel my face grow hot at having been so quickly caught. It's a lie, of course, but what a clumsy, obvious one! A cow patty, a turd of the tongue. I really am out of practice with this therapist crap.

"Accident?" Robert and Dr. Lindholm speak in unison.

"Okay, so maybe 'accident' is pushing it, but it wasn't exactly deliberate, either. There must be some semantic nuance in between that would cover it. You know, sort of a deliberate accident. Is there a word for that?"

Dr. Lindholm shakes her head and says she doesn't know. "It's an interesting question, isn't it? Why don't you just tell me what happened?"

"Right, well, it's just, there's not that much to tell. I was standing up in the bathtub, shaving my legs, and I lost my balance and fell onto my hand. It hurt, so I was sort of pacing around in the bathroom, waving my hand in the air, trying to kind of shake it out, and when I was shaking it I inadvertently hit the wall. It actually made it feel better, hitting the wall, so when it started to ache again, I hit it again, this time on purpose, but only because when I did it the first time it made it feel better and I figured that maybe something had gotten dislocated or out of place. You know, reducing it, maybe.

"Anyway, I guess I hit too hard because that's when I broke it, just then, on that second hit. As Robert said, I broke my hand a couple of times before when I was younger, so it wasn't like it took a lot of effort. I think my hand is really just pretty fragile from having gone through that before. There wasn't much to it at all." Telling it this way to Dr. Lindholm, I almost believe it myself.

Dr. Lindholm looks at me, not writing. "Actually, broken bones tend to knit stronger."

I look back at her. Neither of us blinks. Her eyes are an unreal blue. Like a sled dog's, husky's. "That's right, isn't it?" I finally say. "They do. Must be maybe I have osteoporosis."

"At any rate." She glances down at her notepad. "We can talk about this more at a later session. Why don't you tell me a little more about some of the things that have been wrong with you in the past, as I believe you described it."

Robert shifts on the couch, making little protesting noises, but Dr. Lindholm cuts him short. "Robert, I think I heard you say earlier that you're here to help Darien, and pushing her on something she's not yet ready to talk about isn't going to help her at all. Now, I know that's hard on you and I know it doesn't seem fair, but you've come to me for advice and for the time being my advice is to drop it. What we need to do today is establish a baseline, and I know Darien appreciates that you're here for support in doing so. When Darien is ready to talk about the rest, I'm sure you'll do so, either in privacy or perhaps back here with me. But unless she has more to say, I think we're done with the topic for now."

And suddenly I like Dr. Lindholm. She's my favorite person in the world. I settle in next to my slump-shouldered husband and begin with all the rest. He's heard this part a thousand times.

Forty-five minutes later we are back in the waiting room, me conferring with the receptionist from behind my splint and a half-chewed fingernail, Robert bent over his checkbook. I've found that most doctors like the first payment up front—which, to the uninitiated, can be even more traumatic than the causal first-time shock of having your soul split open and laid on the table for inspection—though after the initial go-round, waiting for the insurance to come through never seems to be a problem. Maybe they figure after two visits you're emotionally entrenched and can't help but return, and you'll make the money work one way or another, but for me, I have to admit the entrenchment begins the minute I walk through the door and settle in on the couch: today's burgundy drawing-room number; Dr. Zobel's naughty black leather; the slip-covered sofabed at Dr. Flynn's. I've never done a Freud-style analysis couch, though, and when I was in college that disappointed me. Whither the crossed ankles, the upturned gaze, the solicitous *Mmm-hmms* from above? I later came to appreciate the irony of regular, everyday, you-could-buy-it-at-Ethan-Allen couches, and to this minute, there's something to the notion of sitting arranged like a couple of genteel ladies having cucumber sandwiches while discussing stuff that could get you arrested if it weren't for patient-doctor privilege that sucks me right in. As long as I don't think about it too much, therapy is tremendous fun.

I think part of my fix is the sheer pleasure of embarking on a routine, a ritual, and God knows I need something new to do with my time. But the greater part is the unacknowledged pitting of intellects. Today's session was just the warm-up, and Dr. Lindholm and I both sailed right through. She asked questions and I knocked the answers back; easy lobs, Wiffle-therapy. She nodded and took notes as I spoke.

She impressed me, if only for not latching onto the broken hand business or any other single malady right out of the gate. My junior year in college, at Swarthmore, I spent six futile months with a social worker who pounced on bulimia within half an hour of our first session and clung to that as her focus throughout our entire, useless relationship. It was an issue I was somewhat bored with by then, eight years into the habit and more or less on the wane, but she, so freeze-dried thin that she couldn't endure a whole hour in her chair without cushions (and even then she would shift, painfully, from one buttock to the other, cupping the resting glute in her hand), managed to drag each discussion back to bingeing and purging with great avidity. She pronounced it "byoo-leemia," like bugle or beauty, and I would counter with "buh-leemia," like button. Our differing ideologies on pronunciation was only one of the things that fated that particular therapy to failure, and eventually I felt bad for her as I came to realize that my issues fell well outside the scope of her interest and experience. When I told Robert about her, years later, he observed that she was well compensated for her ineptitude and discomfort, and this afternoon, despite—or maybe because of—Dr. Lindholm's early rebuke, Robert's confidence in this new doctor seemed to grow as she digested each new piece of information with equanimity.

"So, I'm sorry," Robert's voice comes to me. "The co-pay will be twenty-five dollars when?"

"Sessions five through eight," Dr. Lindholm's receptionist replies.

"But today it's ten?"

"Today, it's nothing. It will be ten dollars next time, sessions two, three, and four, but today you're paying it all up front, no co-pay." The receptionist hands Robert a pink form. "You'll send this to your insurer for reimbursement. Do you have the address?"

"Umm, somewhere. If you could put your hands on it, though, not too much trouble, that would be great." Robert smiles encouragingly and the receptionist reaches for a massive Rolodex with color-coded cards. Robert frowns down at the pink claim form in his hands. "And what happens if Darien needs to be seen more than eight times?"

"Robert." My voice comes out more sharply than I intend, but this is taking far too long, and though I don't want them to, the events of the last hour, of the last forty-eight hours, are beginning to find their places in my brain. I shake my head, pull on Robert's hand. I am back at Dr. Flynn's office again, an undependable, unhinged child, and a voice whispers in my ear: *My God, Darien, what are you doing?* I can't do this. I swallow. I just can't.

Robert closes his checkbook and slides it into his breast pocket. "Sorry," he says to the receptionist. "I suppose this all makes sense to you."

"Nothing about health insurance make sense to anyone these days." She turns back to me. "Can you come in on Wednesday nights? Six o'clock?" Her voice drops a discreet note, though Dr. Lindholm's door opened minutes ago, inhaled her five o'clock patient, and closed again.

Robert nudges me with an elbow. "That's fine, isn't it?"

"Yes," I say. "That's fine." Then we smile and the receptionist and I wish one another a very good rest of the day, a very good rest of our lives, and finally, Robert takes my healthy hand and steers me back in the direction of the ficus tree. We open the door to the street, and we are gone.

Robert expels a long breath as we make our way up Park Avenue, and after a brief consultation with his watch, suggests an early dinner before he heads back to the office. He looks a little weatherworn, sad around the eyes, and I try to mirror his expression, stamping down on the sudden, inane joy that fills me at the prospect of being out on the New York streets.

Dinner? I'd love dinner! The sunlight, the commuter hour makes the idea seem decadent, so I hop over the cracks in the sidewalk and yip, "Yes, yes, yes!" Robert mutters, "For chrissakes, Darien," and I subdue myself until we reach the restaurant, a tiny Italian bistro on 74th and Second, not far from our first apartment. We haven't eaten here for years, though, and by the time we sit down, I have forgotten again that I am supposed to be lugging around our visit to Dr. Lindholm like a doped-up hippopotamus. I address the back of Robert's menu happily.

"Wow! That wasn't so bad, was it? God, that angel hair pasta thing-amajig looks good. Did you see it? It must be new, or at least relatively speaking. It's loaded with mussels. Probably got about two heads worth of garlic in it, though." I take a few preemptory practice breaths against my hand, *hah-hanh,* and reach for the list of specials, lobster fra diavola, two different risotti. "You know, Dr. Lindholm was *really nice.* And smart as hell! She may be the first doctor I've seen who I didn't think needed help more than I did. And her suit! God, that was beautiful. I've never actually seen someone live, in person, wear Chanel. And to think if I'd stuck with that psych major, I could be in her Guccis now."

I laugh, aiming for self-deprecating, though in fact I've returned to mentally congratulating myself for the choice of my own slate blue suit. Dr. Lindholm and I could have been girlfriends on the town, practically; an aunt and niece. I look up from the second risotto and find Robert studying me, his face set in serious lines. A tic pounds in his left cheek. "But I guess a psych major wouldn't do it, since she has an MD and all . . ."

"Darien. Sweetheart." Robert reaches through a maze of glasses and candles to grasp my left hand. "I want you to talk to me. I mean"—he rubs his chin with his free hand and shakes his head, the gesture effortful, laborious, patronizing. "What's all this about? I mean, I sure didn't walk out of that office and just—just *forget* everything we talked about. And I know you, sweetie. You didn't either. So can we drop the manic charade and talk about this? Please?" His eyes are begging.

Goddammit, I think, *Godfucking dammit.* Impatience—panic—wrenches my stomach. I don't want to talk about this; I don't. I want to forget about it; put it on the shelf until next Wednesday night. Tonight I wanna—well, play.

"Yes, sir-*ruh,*" I say, as MacGruff deep as I can. I knit my brows together and squinch my face up. "Your wish is my command. Life is a very serious business, nothing at all like a game of charades. Okay, then, I'll start. First word, three syllables. Rhymes with banana. Montana?"

Robert's eyes skid away from mine and he starts to draw his hand back, but I clutch it harder. *I know he's—I understand but I—I can't.* I will get a smile out of him if it kills me. "Ro-*bert*." I tickle his palm with my finger. "Work with me here. Okay? Okay. It sounds nothing like banana."

Dinner passes in almost complete silence, save the most perfunctory small talk—the food, the weather—every time a waiter drifts into earshot or a busboy rounds with the water jug. At one point, we agree with no little irony that the air is starting to feel like fall. I order the mussel and angel hair pasta dish, not so worried about the garlic, after all, and by the time I twist the last spaghetti strand up, Robert and I are into a limping dialogue about the mountain of paper awaiting him back at work. Will he be late? Absolutely. Will he have to work the weekend? He hopes not. He pays the check and tucks me into a cab before he heads back downtown.

"Listen, Dee," he says, smoothing my hair through the cab window, "I'm sorry. I've been angry, and I know that makes you defensive, but I'm scared to death right now. I just don't know where this thing came from, and I'm scared of what's behind it. I really need you to talk to me about what's going on in your head. We've been through so much stuff together, you know? I just don't understand where this is coming from now, and why you won't talk to me about it." Robert pauses and passes a hand through his own hair. "You don't have to be your mother's daughter; you don't. I know you don't believe me, but—it's a choice you're free to make, and I really hope you won't choose— Anyway. I love you more than anything. Please don't shut me out. Okay?"

He steps back from the cab with a pained smile, his sad eyebrows knitted together. Only for a second do I think, *Aye-aye, sir.* It's been a long time since I've looked at him, really looked at him, and I am shocked now by the deep lines around his eyes. He still looks like a college guy to me, tall and athletic. I hadn't noticed the little boy's tummy that now sways his swimmer's build or how heavily the gray laces his messy brown hair. He looks like a little boy, lost. He needs a haircut.

I want to reach out to him, kiss his forehead, breathe his soap-and-shave-cream smell, but I can only smile back and nod as the cabbie pulls into Second Avenue traffic and watch him as he grows smaller and melts away to nothing in a pool of city streetlight, and by the time I can form a kiss and throw it to him from my cast, he has already turned away, and it falls amid the garbage and tired soles of a late summer night.

This is what happened.

Monday night I was home alone with our dog, Walter, whiling away the time where I usually spend it when Robert is working late, or as he was that night, at a client dinner: in the bathroom. Waxing my eyebrows, painting my toenails, reading; it's all useful, more virtuous, somehow, than watching TV. Monday night it was time to shave my legs. Being perpetually behind the eight-ball in the mornings, I tend to sprint out the door on a to-the-knees dry shave, and since I often take a bath at bedtime to subdue my insomnia, I usually save the soap-and-Lady Schick routine for then. On Monday, despairing of my scratchy thighs but not quite disposed to sit in the tub, I turned on the taps and stepped in in my underpants. I was going to shave stork-style, one leg at a time, and it would have worked fine except halfway through the right leg I lost my balance and fell sideways out of the tub, onto my hand. Very glamorous. Very easy to do.

The razor took a good chunk out of my ankle en route, and I thought, *hmm,* some potential there, but it was the hand that came between the marble floor and the rest of my body that sent a delicious knife of pain through my arm and to the top of my skull, full of bittersweet promise. *Ouch,* it said to me. *Rats.* It cleared its throat and added, *Oh, my.* After a few bemused, inverted minutes on the bathroom floor, however, it became clear that my hand, while mildly abused, would take a good deal of work before it even approximated broken.

It's a routine, actually. After giving my hand a few hours and every opportunity to swell up of its own accord, I wander back into the bathroom, pressing my knuckles against the wall, fist stumbling over the towel bar. Start with a couple of practice swings: just light pops that bounce off the wall benignly; experimental, restrained, set to the soft music of Walter's whines outside the door. A slight jolting sensation, a pleasant little buzz of pain up to the elbow, then nothing. The next hit is harder; maybe not so girly. Once again, I have forgotten to take off my Swarthmore ring, and this hit breaks the skin between my pinkie and fourth finger. That's better. The next hit's the beginning of the mental game: can you do it? Hit just as hard, or harder, without taking off the ring or easing off the punch at the last second? Usually, and tonight, I can, and a number of these, strung together by brief intervals of squatting on the floor with my elbow squeezed between my knees, follow. This is prime time, when speed becomes of the essence, when the offended limb or digit begins to expand furiously, frantically, in an effort to protect itself. This is the game at its best. Now, each hit wins you less and hurts you more: you either gotta go over the edge and break the fucker or back off, a bruised failure.

For the most part, nothing goes through my head as I play this game. It is a soothing blank, green and cool as a kindergarten chalkboard; the pain is amazingly peaceful. Calming. But the final hit comes from a voice in my head, a grotesque parody of a Nike commercial, pushing me to love the pain; kick the final quarter mile, land the triple axel. This is my finest sporting event, mortal combat with a voice that hisses and sneers, "Pussy—chickenshit baby bitch—what are you so fuckin' afraid of? You can't do it? You can't do it?" Not once has the voice beaten me, not even the time when I was fifteen and crammed into the corner of the bathroom behind the toilet, legs drawn against my chest, gripping the hammer in trembling, terrified hands as the voice sneered, "Whassa matter? you can't take it? you can't take it? jesus, this is nothing. you can't take this pain? you can't take shit . . . okay, okay, okay, this is it!" and then the hammer lunged like a badly shanked golf swing and chipped a neat shot off my right kneecap, over the sandtrap and onto the eighteenth fairway through a lush jungle of pain. I dislocated my patella on that one and, rather embarrassingly, wet my pants, a fact I was only dimly aware of as I passed out, flopping back onto the black and white linoleum like a 4:00 A.M. catch at the Fulton Fish Market. But now—or, rather then, I should say—the voice is perfunctory, a cigarette-edged snarl of "Oh, come on, you know how to do this shit," as I pace a few excited circles into the bathmat and throw my shoulder and my passion into the wall and am rewarded with the delicate snap of bones like old chalk as they give against the plaster, and knuckles, familiar with this now thrice-visited routine, obligingly shift from their sockets and out of harm's way. The screaming is externalized, in counterpoint, in Walter's furious barks. Yes, indeed. Much better. Ten-fifteen and all is well.

Once I had finished my routine and was sure I wouldn't throw up, I took six Advil and headed for bed, hoping that by tomorrow my hand would be functional enough to heal without Robert ever discovering what I'd done. I surrounded myself with pillows, one for my pounding knuckles; put on my favorite nightgown and some Debussy. I drifted off to a vision of us on our last vacation. Anguilla, sunlight spanking off turquoise licks of ocean, me hanging onto Robert's shoulders, treading water thirty feet from shore.

At once, Robert is jerked out from under me, dragged to impossible, nightmarish depths by some unseen monster, disappeared in an instant, forever gone, and I bolt to full consciousness with a cry. It's a sign. I know it's a sign, and I sit shaking and brace myself for the call from the police. I look at the clock: almost 2:00 A.M., and terror washes me cold. Of course. Why didn't I know before? Selfish, selfish, caught up. Robert gone, shot through the heart, stripped of identification, knifed in the kidney in a subway tunnel, life gasping out of him in slow leaks. Oh, Robert! I leap out of bed and reach one-handed for my clothes. Should I call the police first? No. No. I should just go.

As I scrabble over the problem of where to bury him—with his father, in Winnetka? in Eastman, out in the apple orchard, with a rolling blue view of the Berkshires? would he want to be buried at all? cremated? I'd really like him embalmed, like Evita Perón—sobbing and steeling myself for the funeral and kindness to follow, he walks through the door, a little drunk but very much alive, and wearing a lopsided grin that suggests he's happy I waited up. Until I throw a shoe at him, which, launched from my right hand, misses his head by a mile.

"Jesus Christ!" I scream. "Do you have any idea what time it is? You said you'd be home at eleven. Eleven! It's almost two o'clock now. That's three hours. I thought you were dead. I thought you were dead!" Each statement comes out in a vicious bite, and Robert stands in dumb amazement as the assault continues. "Where the hell were you?" I grab another shoe to heave. "Who were you with? Why didn't you call?"

"Dee," he finally says. "Hey—"

I thrust my hand in his face and shrill, "And I think I broke my hand!"

Admittedly, it's a cruel thing to do. An evening of swelling and a couple of cursory attempts at holding things have left me with a hand that looks like it's made out of Play-Doh. It is swollen beyond its normal size again, a down mitten, ill-defined by a seemingly random arrangement of bones. The back side is highlighted with a mottled rainbow of bruise: reds, purples, and blues. The elephant wrinkles on all my knuckles have turned themselves inside out.

[23]

"Look, it's about the size of my head," I say. I point to the pinkie side to draw Robert's attention to the craze of blood that spreads out between my fourth and fifth fingers. In what now appears to be something of a tactical error, I neglected to take my class ring off before the final punch, and it is buried in bloated flesh.

Robert's briefcase drops to the floor. He falls to his knees in front of me, locks his arms around my waist, and drags me to him. He burrows his head in my stomach and cries. He shudders like a horse, rocking, pushing himself savagely against my pelvis. The words that come from him are unintelligible, the sound is something primitive, unearthly. A Guernica of grief. *"Darien! Oh, God. Oh, God. Darien."*

"Hey. *Hey,*" I croon, stroking the top of his head with my good hand. He keeps crying, so I keep stroking. "Robert. Robert. It's okay, sweetie, it's okay. I'm sorry. Everything's going to be okay."

His crying stops. He looks up at me, his face a ruined mask. "No, Darien, it's not okay," he says. He captures my broken hand by the wrist. "There's nothing okay about this at all."

Aside from guilt, I feel nothing, but I have the grace at this point to be ashamed, and silent, just as he is silent on the ride to the hospital, holding my good hand hard. He flinches only once, as the doctor positions my arm in the air and begins the artful, papier-mâché process of setting my hand. He watches, furrowed in concentration, and as I catch his eye in the quiet room, I give a one-shouldered shrug and say in a facetious singsong, my very best Groucho Marx, "Oh well. Ya hits plaster, ya gets plaster."

My mother's daughter, indeed. It's a voice I learned from her.

Chapter 2

I suppose that's what started the fight, that stupid Groucho voice. My mother used it all the time when I was little—when Santa Claus forgot to bring me a "Baby Alive" doll, leaving a Raggedy Ann I spotted at the New Beginnings thrift shop instead; when I asked her how my little brother, Logan, could be growing in her tummy if we didn't have a father; when I would come home from school at three o'clock to find her sitting alone with the shades drawn, smoking in the dark. When I pulled the shades up and climbed into her lap, burying my head into her soft abdomen, she'd put on that voice and call me "schweet-aht," tip the ash off an imaginary cigar into my hair. The act would send me into fits of giggles, assure me that everything was okay. It took me a long time to figure out that the voice was a blind alley, a smoke screen. A lie.

One of the first things—one of the only things—I told Robert about my mother was that if he ever heard me use the Groucho Marx voice he should hit the door running, because if I used that voice I might as well be her, and our relationship might as well be over. As I heard my voice come out in the hospital cast room, I lunged forward nearly off the table in his direction, as if I could reach out into the antiseptic air and intercept the words before they reached his ears. *Fuck.* I knew at once I'd made my earlier declaration prematurely, naively, believing too sincerely that once I'd met Robert, I'd never have reason or need to lie again.

The doctor thought he was hurting me and assured me that the worst part was almost over, and, righting myself, I pretended to be utterly occupied with the business at hand: a little antiseptic for my cut knuckles, the careful molding of my hand in a half-fist. He was a resident, a Howdy-Doody type—orange ringlets, faint stubble of the same—who looked barely my age. "Dr. Bruce," the patch on his white coat said, and I asked myself, First or last name? Was it an indication of rank, or had I perhaps been pawned off on a pediatrician? Dr. Bruce gave me a smile and explained that actually I wouldn't be getting plaster at all.

"I'm going to put you in a splint to keep those knuckles in place until the swelling goes down, and then when you come back in a week we'll give you fiberglass."

"Is that right?" I asked, the voice my own.

"You bet. Plaster hasn't been the standard for casts in years, at least not in the big tertiary hospitals. If the last cast you had was plaster, you must be coming off quite a string of good luck." Dr. Bruce glanced quickly at Robert, glowering in the corner, and gave me a wink.

"You said it," I said. I winked back.

"Of course, *luck* is a relative term. Most people wouldn't consider a break this bad from a bathtub fall to be all that lucky." Dr. Bruce busied himself with a roll of cotton batting, unwinding the length and then rewinding it more tightly.

I took a couple of slow breaths, in and out. "Of course not." I watched Dr. Bruce's fingers work the batting, tuck and knead, roll. "But then again, not everyone's as lucky as I am to live on the Upper West Side, with exposed brick wall in not just the living room but the bath. I kind of fell into the wall, you see, fist-forward, when I slipped."

I spent the cab ride home trying to make it up to Robert, saying serious things, saying honest things, but although the sky had begun to lighten by the time the cab drew up to our building, my husband's mood had not. In the apartment, Robert locked the door behind him and then leaned against it, rubbing his face with both hands. I made my way across the living room, to Walter. Robert addressed me directly for the first time since I had cracked wise in the emergency room. "Kites, Danyon," is what it sounded like he said.

My husband's singlemindedness has never ceased to amaze me. On the ride up, I had prayed for some small disaster—dog crap in the foyer, say, or a robbery—to forestall the confrontation that I knew awaited me, but the fates hadn't chosen to play along. Nothing greeted us but a forgotten overhead light and a frantic, leaping dog. Briefly, I'd thought Walter might hold potential for detour—a trip to the dog run, a few minutes of compensatory attention—but Robert was, apparently, well beyond that. He had nearly knocked Walter backward as we came through the door, he was so eager to move things along.

"What's that?" I said. I crouched down behind Walter, who stretched his chin across my hand. "Sorry, buddy." I kissed the dog's wet nose. "Daddy didn't mean it." Robert's suit coat was still collapsed on the floor where he'd dropped it hours earlier, and I risked a hand to point it out. "You want me to take that suit to the cleaners?" I remembered it had smelled of smoke, Smith & Wollensky's. There was a shoeprint, mine, I thought, on one sleeve.

"No," Robert said. "I don't."

"Oh." I pulled Walter tight, trying not to pace. "You sure?" I didn't want this—didn't want to start talking, apologizing, explaining myself yet again. What I really wanted was to pop a couple of painkillers and then grab a little sleep. Dr. Bruce had been nice enough to prescribe Percocet. I had a meeting at nine.

"Yeah. I'm sure. I said, *Christ, Darien.*" Robert dropped his hands from his face and shook his arms out. "As in, Christ, I'm tired. Christ, I'm angry. And Christ, I don't like the direction this is heading. I really don't have any intention of becoming your partner in crime in this, standing there like an asshole and backing up your lies."

For a moment, I considered a bulldog defense: *I see. This is all about vanity, isn't it? I let Dr. Bruce think we lived some kind of tenement existence when I should have been waxing rhapsodic about the white marble walls of our tub.* But I found myself suffering a rare if temporary prepossession of self-control and managed to settle for a subdued nod instead. It wasn't the point. It wasn't the point at all. "I know."

"I'm serious, Darien. Take a look at yourself. It looks like somebody crushed your hand in a goddamn vise."

"I *know*, Robert. I'm sure Dr. Bruce is on his way to call the Department of Social Services right now. After that maybe he'll order up a couple of police dogs to sniff out where you stash your hand-crushing machine."

Robert stared at me for what felt like forever, his face twisted with anger, confusion, exhaustion. I held the stare as long as I could, jerked away as I felt a smile start to form. The sucking whine of an elevator in motion hummed behind him. I could hear his breathing from the far side of the room.

"Do you actually think this is funny, Dee? You really think this is a joke?"

"No, no, I don't," I said quickly, too quickly, trying to keep ahead of a sudden, awful giggle leaping up against the back of my throat. And the truth is I didn't think it was funny at all. The truth is there's something wrong with my wiring that makes me smile at the most godawful things, at the most inconvenient times. Not a smile of pleasure at all, it's a sort of sick, leery lurch that rises from my stomach and through my chest, pulling every muscle in my face up into a panicky rictus, an idiot's grin. It's the smile I smiled when my friend Jenny told me her little brother was hit by a car, and when my secretary, Isabel, told me she had cancer. It's the smile I smiled when my mother told me she was divorcing my stepfather, Charlie, on the grounds of sexual abandonment, and when she told me she was marrying Tony instead. Maybe when you have no depth, like me, you simply don't get the full complement of emotions; maybe the smile's the first menu option on the humanoid's if/then list.

"Bullshit, Darien, you do. First you pull that Groucho Marx crap in the emergency room—or did you forget you told me about that?—and now you sit here laughing, like it's some kind of goddamn joke. Jesus."

"Are you kidding me?" I never told him the Groucho Marx thing meant my mother thought something was funny. I told him it meant something terrible that was too painful for her to be honest about. I told him about the smile, too, the only person I've ever confided in. The school nurse, shaking her head over the cigarette burns on my arms, the dentist, confronting the eroded enamel on my teeth . . . "Do you really think you want to get into this right now? Because I certainly don't. I said it was an accident. I said I was sorry. And as far as I'm concerned, you're on mighty shaky ground with this emotional attack you're trying to launch."

Robert had been moving toward me in a hurry but stopped dead at the last of this. He grabbed at his head with both hands. "I didn't hear that," he said. "Tell me I did not just hear those words from you. Darien, sweetheart, you—I— We've got some serious talking to do." Robert dropped his hands and started back toward me, a few dazed, bewildered steps. My heart squeezed, unbidden, for him. He crouched down and snapped his fingers for Walter, now shoving his nose against my palm. "Here, Walter, here boy, attaboy. Here, fella." The dog looked uncertainly at him and then me. I uncurled my fingers from Walter's coat and nudged him gently away.

"Robert," I said, softly, "look. I'm sorry. You're right. We need to talk about this. I want to talk about this, just not right now." I swallowed hard, processing the lie. "But the thing is, you know, it's not even five-thirty. If we put it on the shelf until tonight, we can both go back to bed now and still get in a couple of hours of sleep before work. You're tired, I'm tired, and I'm afraid we're both going to say stupid things we don't mean and it's just going to be a waste of time. We'll talk about it later. Tonight, I swear. But please, just give me a little time to think."

Robert had both arms around Walter, hugging him and rubbing his whole body. Walter wagged from nose to tail, his mouth lifted in a big, canine grin. Robert pulled him a little closer and buried his face in his coat. "Old boy, good old boy," he crooned, muffled, his brown curls mixing with Walter's gold. He lifted his head, finally, to speak to me. "I'm sorry, Darien, I'm really sorry. But I just can't do that." Walter grunted softly as if in assent. "Giving you time to think about what you want to say to me and how you want to spin it is pretty much the last thing I want to do."

Once I was done with laughing, Robert and I fought, or something like that, until eight o'clock, when he stopped to take a shower and change for work and I made a beeline for bed. He kissed me on the forehead and I held his hand in my good one when he stopped in the bedroom to say good-bye, and I nodded seriously when he asked me if I'd be okay. It was our version of a truce, and as I snuggled down under the covers, buoyed on a wave of Percocet, I said the word to myself over and over, *truce, truce,* to remind myself that it was not a victory, that the situation was not one to which the word *victory* could appropriately be applied. In a little over two hours, though, I had gone from young hysteric to ace negotiator, arguing Robert from a voluntary hospitalization to a two-week leave of absence to a day or two of R&R. That much I could handle, I thought, that slow I could make myself, forty-eight hours of bonbons and bad TV. *Truce, truce.* I couldn't help it, though. It felt like a victory.

Chapter 3

Somehow, it is Friday by the time I make it back to work.

At the office, the first person I run into is Carl, who is one of our marketing associates, and probably the last person I want to see. "Well, looky here," he booms. "If it isn't the Lady Gilbertson, back from her mystery vacation. I see Robert finally got smart and started beating you." And then, somewhat more quietly, when I don't respond, "Good Lord, woman, what happened to you?"

Carl is gay and insists on playing to his own brand of stereotype. He's one of the most impossibly handsome men I've ever met, a Ken doll come to life, and when he first started working here, I couldn't look at him straight. Even though our cubicles adjoin, I used to have to call him whenever I had a question, because it was inconceivable that I could look on that face—improbably green eyes, hair a careful tumble of Sun-Inned curls, teeth capped like Feen-A-Mint tablets— and not start laughing. Once I got inured to his looks I started noticing his caustic, irreverent sense of humor, and we became good friends. I've always had a thing for gay men. I sometimes suspect I have more in common with them than I do with other women.

"Mister Carl Edwards," I finally say. "Nothing terribly glamorous, I'm afraid. I just fell out of the bathtub and landed on my hand." I spent most of the trip downtown working on my story before coming to the entirely novel conclusion that the truth would serve me best. I've left some room for embellishments, though, should they become necessary.

Carl snorts with laughter. "I won't even touch that. No, wait; on second thought I will. Didn't anyone ever tell you to hold onto the faucets when you're taking it up the ass?"

"Silly me. And there I was, holding onto my ankles."

"No, but seriously. A whole week for a broken hand? Did you have to have surgery or something?" He lifts my hand by the tip of the pinkie, holding it out away from him like a fisherman with a particularly unimpressive catch. Most of the swelling has gone down, and the livid purple bruises have begun to fade to green and yellow, but it's still relatively unattractive. Something makes a loud snap, most likely a tendon, and Carl releases the pinkie with a shudder. A faintly sour odor hangs in the air.

"It wasn't a week, Carl," I say. "It was only a couple of days." He takes a step back and offers me a skeptical grimace, and my presence here feels instantly justified. Robert hadn't understood why I couldn't just wait until Monday to go back, take the weekend off; what was one more day home? I had suspected there'd be something like Carl's curiosity to be addressed.

"Anyway, I should jet, because I'm sure Duncan is already looking for me. Stick your head over later and we'll grab a cup of coffee. I want to hear about all the good dirt I missed."

I drop my bag next to my desk and flick my PC on and almost immediately the aforementioned Duncan is in my cubicle. Duncan Killcoyne is manager of the Pharmaceuticals group, a man who has fostered a unique and unintentional sense of camaraderie in the department by inspiring communal hatred in those of us who work for him. He's very tall, very muscular, and very bald—one of those guys who took to heart the old sop about how bald men were more masculine because they had more testosterone. From what I've been able to determine from my professional and social interactions with him, Duncan is of the unenlightened opinion that I am attracted to him, and that my marriage to Robert is simply a barrier to be surmounted. The turnover in our group is high, even for PR, because he's such a bozo to work for.

"Welcome back, Darien," he says. "I trust you're feeling better."

"Yup," I reply. I put my splinted hand out and tilt my coffee cup toward me. It is lightly crusted with the dregs of Monday's final fill.

"Not female troubles, I hope."

"Oh, no." I frown into the coffee cup. "At least not anything that a call to human resources wouldn't cure. Thank you for asking, though."

Duncan inhales deeply, thrusts his hand in his pants to resettle the two inches of shirt his breathing has uprooted, then coughs. "Why don't you take a few minutes to, ah, *reorient* yourself," he offers.

I raise an eyebrow and look around myself to suggest that that's precisely what I'm in the process of doing. "Okay. Thanks."

"Why don't you come and see me when you're ready. No rush, though; no rush. You need to take it easy, I know. Just stop by when you've gotten yourself together." He holds his hand out in a peace sign as he turns and walks away.

I spend almost an hour scrolling through my e-mails and listening to voice mail before I wander over, sit myself down, and listen to Duncan tell me how my unanticipated absence has directly influenced the lukewarm reception of my last project. "Mia was on calls and we got nothing," he says. "Two inches in the *Journal*, a blurb in *Press Weekly*. Did you see the piece in the *Times*? Of course you didn't. And the stock didn't budge."

"Wow," I say. "Damn." I refrain from opining that perhaps the problem is that the product is crap, fourth to market in its class, with little to distinguish it from the competition other than our exaggerated claims of its virtue.

"Damn is right," Duncan replies. "Gibson was ballistic." *Tappita, tappita, tap.* Duncan fingers a pencil, then drums it against his desk. "The good news for you is you haven't blown it just yet. I'm going to give you a chance to redeem yourself on Pharmax. There's a meeting at their midtown offices this afternoon, if you think you're up to joining us." He cocks his head to the side, blinking rapidly. "But do think about it, Darien. Think about it carefully."

He spends a few minutes describing the new project, emphasizing the role his goodwill has played in this opportunity, and all I can do is stare. Pharmax has been my account since before Duncan joined the firm; I've already put together three successful pitches for them. Duncan emphasizes, absolutely innocent-faced, that he will be leading the project, and that he will be available at all hours to offer me support if I'm unsure of myself, if I don't think I can handle the stress. After ten minutes of this performance, I find my voice and my feet and I thank Duncan for his magnanimity.

The rest of the morning passes without event. I wade through the pile in my in-box, dividing trees' worth of correspondence into stacks of urgent, undecided, and headed-for-the-circular-file. Nothing strikes me as particularly urgent, so I content myself with an article about programmed cell death that I vaguely remember ordering a month or so back but now don't know why. As the clock nudges its way toward twelve, I stick my head over the partition and ask Carl if he's buying coffee.

While I drink mine he sucks down three cigarettes and obsesses about his weight, lobs the occasional grenade designed to scare out more information on my broken hand. Manhattan worker bees hurry by with coffees in takeout cups and Carl tips back his espresso shot. He smiles at me and says, "So anyway. Robert called this morning and I grabbed your line. We had a nice chat." A long drag on his cigarette. "He told me what really happened."

My heart stops. "Oh really?"

"Yeah. About your broken hand. He said you were hanging from the showerhead and in his own selfish pleasure he dropped you on your ass. Have you thought about suing him? There's gotta be precedent."

On the cab ride up to Pharmax, I put as much distance between myself and Duncan's splayed thighs as possible and stare out the window at New York. Corporate wonks clip by, Hartmann briefcases banging against their legs, messengers weave through the traffic on Rollerblades and beat-up ten-speed bikes, homeless men shuffle down the sidewalks, wearing wool sweaters despite the heat. New York street sounds and smells filter through the rolled-up windows and fold themselves into the white noise of my brain. *I'm all right, I'm here, I'm okay,* I say to myself, reach out to touch the window. *I'm all right, I'm here, I'm okay.* I say it over and over, like it's a magic phrase or the key to a riddle, without even knowing why.

It's six-thirty by the time I am finished with my meeting: much too early for dinner in New York on a Friday—there's only so many times in a week eating at the senior hour is a thrill—but too late in my book to do much else by way of work. If these were the old days, the life-before-Robert days, there would be no question about what I would do next: I'd already be at a bar if not on it, skunk-drunk and smoking, and a whole lot stupid, to boot. Even now, in the abstract, there's something appealing about the idea, but I do emphasize in the abstract. The first few years Robert and I were together I was a teetotaler, out of necessity as much as to reassure him, but we're finally at the point now where I can pick up a glass of wine at a party or order a bottle at dinner without provoking any soul-searching discussion. Getting drunk tonight, particularly by myself, would just be an exercise in masochism.

Unable to come up with much else by way of happy-hour options, I decide to brave the commuter crush and head home. I get on a subway without air conditioning, wedged in among impatient businessmen headed for Grand Central. Cuffs shoot, watches and train schedules are consulted repeatedly. Wool sleeves and lapels tickle my nose. At Grand Central, suburbanites and locals trade places, and I spend the latter half of the ride smashed up against an enormously large-breasted woman with cottage cheese arms and the sartorial gall to be wearing a tube top. By the time I emerge from the 72nd Street station, I am so sweaty and disheveled you'd think I'd spent the half-hour doing something virtuous, like running. I make a reservation at one of my favorite restaurants for nine-thirty, change my clothes, tussle a bit with Walter, and settle in with a book until Robert gets home.

I assume that despite the fact that Robert called me a very un-Robert-like three times today for interim reports, the dinner topic du jour will be how my day went, so I consider it a bit before I get too engrossed in *Anna Karenina* again. The word that best describes it is *uneventful*, but that hardly makes for good dinner conversation. The truth is, what I do is somewhat hard to describe and nebulous even on an eventful day, a fact that only feeds my general suspicion that I don't contribute all that much to the world. Today's meeting up at Pharmax was with one of the few clients I genuinely enjoy, no qualification, no ulterior motive, and Maggie and I sat in her office just shooting the breeze for about an hour after our meeting ended. She'd commented on my broken hand, then dismissed it more or less with a wave of her own. She confessed that she had undertaken a medical "accident" herself recently: a pregnancy, just about eighteen weeks. "No kidding!" I'd said. "Congratulations!"

Maggie had patted her stomach and smiled. "One kidding, actually."

As a rule, procreation is dangerous territory in the Gilbertson household, but it is ice I'm willing to venture out on when Robert, over dinner, asks for the rehash; when it's clear he's relaxed and we are happy, laughing, and fine.

"Oh, hey," I say, leaning toward him. I've already given him the

Cliffs Notes version of the day, going easy on Duncan's smarm, eliciting a rather unexpected leer describing Carl's bathroom scenario. "Do you remember me telling you about Maggie Fischer, my client at Pharmax? She told me today she's pregnant. Four months or something. I think she's pretty excited but she was totally hilarious about it, making all these wisecracks like she was embarrassed."

Robert is halfway through a bite of steak when I spring this, and his whole face rises and falls in a vigorous effort to finish chewing so he can respond. "Why would she be embarrassed? She's married, isn't she?"

"Yeah, but she and her husband are in their mid-forties and she's the original *über*-career woman. I don't think they were planning on having kids. She made some crack about how she must have been holding her menopause handbook upside down."

Robert just looks puzzled.

"She thought she was going through menopause." I don't bother to finish my own mouthful before continuing. "It was a mistake. Anyway, she decided not to tell people until she had amniocentesis and 'knew it was a keeper,' as she put it." At this, Robert's eyebrows shoot up and his jaw drops, revealing stray bits of steak, the good Catholic boy raised to think the very word *abortion* a sacrilege. "Robert, honey, swallow that. Anyway, it's a boy, and I think she's pretty psyched, but you should hear her going on about dick care." I stop to laugh, and snort instead. A sharp sting of tuna and cilantro makes its way up my nose. "She kept saying that: 'I mean, holy cow, Darien, there's dick care to be done, here. Dick care! I don't even have a penis. I don't know the first *thing* about maintaining one!' I told her the alternative wasn't much better—what would you call that, beaver care?—except for the circumcision thing."

Robert now looks horrified, which wins me over utterly. One of the things I love most about my husband is that he is so completely earnest, and that, in his book, things like abortions and babies' penises are subjects not to be handled lightly. It's one of the reasons we're so good for each other, like a matched set: to me, nothing's sacred. To him, everything is, including me.

He sets down his knife and fork and sputters, "Christ, Darien, that's a little twisted, wouldn't you say? I mean, she actually told you she would have aborted her baby if it hadn't been healthy?" He looks as concerned as if it's his own child we are talking about.

I just smile and say, "She also said something about asking the pediatrician if she can hang on to the foreskin in case the kid decides he wants it back someday." I reach across the table and, using my good hand, push a renegade lock of hair up out of his eyebrows. "Robert, honey, life isn't all heavy, you know? She was only joking. Sometimes it's good to look at things that way."

He sighs and shakes his head. "You know I don't get you sometimes, Darien. I just think there are some things that should be off limits, but whatever you say."

"It's not what I say, Robert. It's what I believe."

Ever the good lawyer, he frames his counterargument, pushes me with logic. "Would you have thought it was okay if she'd told you that she *had* been pregnant, but that she'd had an abortion because the baby had, I don't know, Down syndrome or something, and wasn't a keeper? Would it have been okay to look at things lightly then?"

I'm sure Maggie wouldn't ever have broached the subject if the baby hadn't been a keeper, but it doesn't seem a point worth debating with Robert. I smile at him and pat his cheek. "You silly man," I say. "Lighten up."

We linger over coffee and walk the long way home, behind the Museum of Natural History, holding hands. It's late summer muggy, but an undercurrent of cool cuts the heavy air and I am sweating and shivering both. Robert wraps his arm around my shoulders and kisses the top of my head. "Are you okay?" he whispers, and I can hear him perfectly even though cacophony rises off Columbus and an unseen drunk on the museum steps is singing loudly, tonelessly to himself.

"Yeah, I'm great," I whisper back. I know he is not asking about the weather. "Really, I'm fine. I'm going to be fine. I really like Dr. Lindholm. I think she's going to help me."

He squeezes my shoulders so they roll together and my face rotates into his chest. He stops and hugs me hard. "I was so scared, Dee. I thought I lost you, or was losing you. All that stuff you told me about when you were younger. I just thought you were going back." With his face buried in my hair he gives one big snuffling, snorting cry. His whole body is shaking, and, as stupid and improbable as it sounds, in that instant I understand for the first time that what I did is something that happened to him, too, and that what comes next also will happen to him.

Pressed against his chest like that I can't see anything, but I screw my eyes tight all the same. I push my nose and cheek into the waffle of his shirt so I can see the words, feel them seep past me and up to him as they come out. "I know, Robert. I'm sorry. I just lost it, for a minute. I promise it won't happen again." I want desperately for it to be true. And then I hold my breath, waiting for him to push me again, but after a minute he kisses the top of my head and we move on. I exhale slowly, surreptitiously, and am breathing normally by the time we reach our block.

At home, I make the first move, stroking his hips and tracing my fingers lightly over his buttocks, though little convincing is required. We haven't had sex in over a week, since before I broke my hand, and I know he has been patient. He hesitates only once, as his tongue makes slow circles over my breast, to ask me if he should stop, if it is okay. I unclench my teeth and nod hurriedly, yes, yes, of course. I need it to be okay.

Chapter 4

For starters," Dr. Lindholm says when I come in for my second session, "I want to write you a prescription for Paxil. You'll need to be very careful about your drinking."

She is sitting on the gray chair, one leg folded under her, her portfolio on her lap, as if she hasn't moved since Robert and I left her here a week ago. Without changing her position, she reaches behind her to fish around in the lab coat hung over the back of the chair. Her head thrusts forward and the cords on her neck stand out like cables or hemp and for a second they suggest they are the only thing that keep her head from snapping off and rocketing through the air toward me, ass over teakettle, something my grandmother used to say but I never understood. *Ass over teakettle, ass over teakettle.* I repeat the phrase to myself silently, imagining Dr. Lindholm's head rotating through the air with its blond bob spun out in twin Viking horns, landing in my lap with a ripe *plop*, eyes unblinking and surprised. I swallow a giggle. Dr. Lindholm's body relaxes and her hand returns, triumphant, bearing a prescription pad.

"Wow," I say.

She looks up from where she already has begun scribbling. For the moment, her writing stops. "Wow?"

"I can't believe you just keep your prescription pad there. So accessible. I mean, don't you worry about patients swiping a few while you're not looking—maybe rushing around for your four-point restraints or something—writing themselves a few scrips for morphine or Valium? All it takes is a few PRNs, 150 milligrams, throw in a t.i.d. or two for good measure . . ."

"Mmmm." She smiles. She returns to her pad and begins muttering to herself, under her breath. *Let's see, start with 20 milligrams for four weeks, p-o, increase to 30 for two more.* Her lips move slightly as she does the calculation, and her pen scratches the corner of the pad. It figures. For Pete's sake. A shrink who can't do basic math.

"Was that all, Darien?" she says.

In fairness, I should tell you right now that I have revised my opinion of Dr. Lindholm since last week's visit: I hate her, and read mannerism and intent into her every gesture. She reminds me of too many women I have envied in my life: popular girls in high school and college, Junior League wives I meet at Robert's office parties, all of whom possess a sort of remote external perfection to which I have long strived and in which I have consistently fallen short. It puts me on the immediate defensive, a condition exacerbated by my general antipathy toward Wellesley alumnae. I work with a couple of Wellesley women and can spot 'em a mile away. Cashmere kittens, dykiest dykes, it doesn't matter; there's something about them that's always the same. An aura of expectation, entitlement.

"For starters," I finally say, "I'm not taking Paxil, or anything else for that matter, so don't knock yourself out trying to come up with a dosage for me. I wasn't one of those kids who wandered around sucking their thumbs, trailing a blankie, so I'm not about to take up the adult equivalent of that habit now. *Paxil.*" The name has a nice spit to it, and I work it. PACKS-ill. The cheapest of the selective serotonin reuptake inhibitors, no doubt approved on every shrink's formulary. I can't believe I don't even rate Prozac.

"You don't believe in drugs?" Dr. Lindholm asks.

"Not of the prophylactic variety, no."

"May I ask why?"

She can ask all she likes, but I'm not sure I want to get into this with her just yet, the fact that I'm against the idea of treating mental illness with medication, in much the same way I'm against treating colds with Sudafed. I knew Dr. Lindholm was a psychiatrist, and assumed the issue of medication would come up, and indeed she'd asked me a bit last week about whether I was on any medications—MAO inhibitors? anti-arrhythmics? for Pete's sake!—but I hadn't expected her to be so prescription-happy so soon. Break out the sad family stories first, you know? It seems a bit ill thought out, if nothing else.

"It seems kind of hasty, impetuous, don't you think?" I say. "Like that whole overprescribing Ritalin thing with kids. You've only met me once."

"I'm a medical doctor," Dr. Lindholm replies. "It's a medical diagnosis, and unfortunately we don't have the leisure of deliberating a great many courses of action before deciding on one." She gestures toward my splinted hand to make her point. "If you came to me with a fever and sharp pain in your side, you would expect me to diagnose appendicitis within an hour, wouldn't you?"

"I don't know," I say. "Would you do a CT scan? Hate to have you jumping in there and carving me up if it was just psychosomatic or gas or something." I think a second, *What else, what else?* "Or what about an ectopic pregnancy?"

"Well, of course you'd still need surgery for that."

I nod. "Oh, right. Of course you would. Could you do it the same way, though? Laparoscopically?"

"Darien." Dr. Lindholm pulls her tucked leg out. "You told me last week that the therapy was Robert's idea. Is that the only reason you're here? Because your husband wants you to be?"

I smile. "Not really. I'm not that much of a pushover. Just because he's the one who came up with the idea for me to come here now doesn't mean he's the one who thinks I can be helped by therapy. My husband thinks there are no problems in this world that can't be solved through hard work or exercise. When he's upset, he runs five miles—or six miles, whatever; whatever that loop in Central Park is— or butts heads with guys on the soccer field or pulls an all-nighter for some client. I think he's sort of indulging me in this because he got kind of freaked out. Not that he thinks it's anything I couldn't solve for myself with a little self-control."

"Really?" She looks surprised. "I saw Robert in here last week. It didn't look that way to me."

"Well, you know. He's got a good game face."

"And you?"

"Me?"

"What do you think?"

I shake my head and study the floor like this is hard for me, but now the conversation is going exactly my way. "I don't know, really. Do you want me to put a label on it? Give it my oh-so-professional differential diagnosis? I think I'm a high-functioning, high-functioning— I'm struggling for the right word, here; hang on a second—emotional hypochondriac. I don't know. Maybe I have some obscure personality disorder, like histrionic personality disorder or narcissistic personality disorder, or something, but that would account for only some of what's wrong with me. It's probably a lot more complex or maybe simpler than that."

"What do you mean when you say you're an emotional hypochondriac?"

What I mean is that I'm like a walking catalogue of every mainstream disorder or syndrome known to humanity; a veritable *Merck Manual* of neurosis, if you will. "Did you ever see that Woody Allen movie, *Zelig,* where he keeps popping up in all sorts of random places and takes on the personality of every person he's around?" I ask Dr.

[43]

Lindholm. She nods. "It sort of goes like that. I read about a disorder, I have it. Bulimia's in vogue, I start puking. Donahue does a bit on nymphomania, I become a sex fiend. Self-mutilation's very popular these days. Somebody prints an article called 'The Cruelest Cuts' and bam, baby, I'm there." Actually, cutting myself isn't something I'm particularly big on, but it seems beside the point. The one time I did try to cut off my toe after reading an article about women who amputate their own digits, I failed miserably. I was mad at myself for weeks.

Dr. Lindholm looks at me and says, "I wonder if you hear yourself, the tone of your voice, when you say that."

She refolds her legs and waits and I think absolutely nothing at all.

"There's a very common phenomenon among first-year medical students that goes like that, when they first start studying disease processes," she says. "But I don't think that's what we're talking about here. Students only think they have the diseases they're studying; they don't actually develop them."

I actually don't either, I don't think; I'm able to give them up far too easily. I think I just try them on for size. Mutilation's not my thing; it's just my latest thing. So far, I haven't found the malady that fits exactly right. "No, I suppose you're right," I say. "I think whatever's going on with me is more basic than that."

I hesitate. This moment is a decision point, the moment at which I can choose a course for this therapy. In the past, the choice has usually been clear: move forward with blatant contempt and outright opposition, which is the only way to go when you're being treated by someone who has more problems and less brains than you do. Dr. Flynn, for example, lived on Nicorette and hung her walls with no-name diplomas, and I knew from day one that I didn't need to take seriously advice on eating compulsions from someone who couldn't control her own addictive behaviors. Why not spend the hour spinning fabulous tales, describing miraculous giant steps toward cure that make her think she's the best doctor in the world, if that's what she wants to believe? Dr. Zobel wore his beard enormous and bushy to compensate for his Ben Franklin–bald head, and whenever we discussed sex he would stroke it, his lips parted in a wet, deflated O. Why not devote countless sessions to made-up sex stories, bathroom quickies and locker-room blowjobs, compulsive sessions with a stolen dildo; leave him to battle it out by himself alone? Dr. Lindholm is a tough read, though, displaying no obvious flaws or perversions, which should by now be in evidence. Giving her something real will be the safe bet, as long as what I give her is small enough. The trick is one of proportion. I start with this:

"What I really think is at issue is I'm just not normal. I don't respond to the world in a normal way. Where anyone else would drink three beers and turn into a giggling fool, I see it as an opportunity to pick a fight with the biggest guy in the room. I never cry. I don't like to feel good. I don't think I've ever had a spontaneous, genuine emotion in my entire life. I feel like I'm a robot; like I have access to this menu of normal responses and I always have to think a little before I choose the right one."

Dr. Lindholm scratches something down on her notepad and pushes her lower lip out in a frown. "Tell me more about what you mean by that," she says.

It's the weirdest thing, really, like my emotional surfaces have all been blunted, maybe, dulled with those orange sticks you get at the dentist in advance of the Novocain. Like there's some huge disconnect between events and their implications. It's something I can usually hide from the real world at this point since I've been in enough situations to have ready access to the right responses fairly quickly. Every now and then, though, it fails me in a rather noticeable way—like just the other day, when I almost got hit by a car and didn't realize I was supposed to get upset until the woman behind me did, or like the time at Swat when a guy I'd slept with died. He was one of my suitemates' boyfriends, a guy I'd slept with one drunk night or another; he had jumped from Clothier Tower and killed himself during final exams. One of our other roommates, Liesl, told me, sobbing hysterically, and as she finished gasping out the tale, I wondered if he'd jumped toward the dining hall or away. I busied myself counting the tissues piled around her to keep myself from laughing outright at the image of Swatties at Paces, winding down between exams, startled shitless as Jim fell like some ponderous, flightless bird, a limp ostrich or a dodo, into their plates of lasagna and tofu stir fry. I counted tissues first starting with the one balanced on the top of her bare foot, and then backwards from the one halfway between the garbage can and the couch. Seventeen in all, pink and snotty and wet.

When I looked up and realized Liesl was waiting for some response from me, I struggled to look properly aghast and said, "Wow. Bummer. That, aah, that's really bad. Anyone check his pockets for goofy stamps?" The only thing I could recall with any certainty about the night I spent with this guy was that he was hellbent on dropping acid and had actually dragged his roommate out of bed to see about borrowing his girlfriend's car for a trip to Philly.

. Liesl's reply had been stiff. "Jesus, Dare. I'll give you the benefit of the doubt and assume that hideous response means you're in shock. You might want to think of something more human to say before you see Stephanie, however."

Shock might actually be the right word for it. If that's the case, then I've spent my whole life in shock.

"I think that's maybe why I hurt myself, you know," I say. "I hurt myself so I can feel something, anything. How's that for an explanation worthy of Phil Donahue?"

I have made a mistake. Dr. Lindholm's voice is gentle when she answers. "What do you think you were feeling when you did that to yourself?" She indicates my hand. The tone alone is cause for alarm.

"Pain, I suppose," I say dryly.

"What kind of pain?"

[46]

"Physical pain. Ow-I-just-slammed-my-fist-into-a-marble-wall-with-all-my-might pain." I deliver this in a tone that says this is the most obvious thing in the world, as if I have enough conviction about it, Dr. Lindholm will, too.

"Mmm-hmm," she says. "What else?"

I frown, pretend to concentrate. I look just to the left of her shoulder and study the bookcases that flank the far wall. I spot all the usuals: a *Diagnostic and Statistical Manual,* edition IV, a *Physician's Desk Reference,* a *Gray's Anatomy,* all the typical books on sexual abuse and incest, alcoholism, and eating disorders. There's also a book on post-traumatic stress disorder and something called *The Mutilated Mind.* A print that looks like an original bridges the blank between the cases, a chalk drawing in unexpected blues, pinks, and greens that could be of Central Park, or maybe not. The walls are wainscoted in a Paris blue that echoes the print nicely. My eyes run from the frame to the lip of the wainscoting, back and forth, back and forth, as I answer.

"Nothing else. Just pain." I understand that I am being stupid, that I should give her something—anger, fear, pleasure—to gnaw on, but they all lead to roads I don't want to traverse. The kind voice makes me too wary; it's not something I've yet built defenses against. Better to piss her off, build some friction I can work with.

"I'd argue that you were feeling a great deal when you did that to yourself," Dr. Lindholm continues. "Often, when people hurt themselves, there's a trigger event, a confrontation, perhaps, or a frightening memory, that initiates the hurt. The person feels very out of control emotionally and uses the mutilation to redirect her emotional energy, distracting herself from the trigger issue and in a way answering the emotional pain it inspires." She waits. "Do you think it's possible that that's what happened here?"

Print, wainscoting, printwainscoting. "Possible? Sure, it's possible. Anything's possible. But it isn't what happened. I hurt myself for sport, sometimes. I really do. Maybe I just have a higher threshold for pain, or something, or maybe I get a big endorphin high from hurting my-self. But it's mostly recreational, I guess, which probably makes it much worse."

"Darien," she says, still kindly. "With all due respect, I don't believe that. I heard what you said earlier, and I understand accessing your emotions is very difficult for you. But it's my job to help you do just that. I need to understand the emotional mutilation, if you will, that lies behind the physical act. And I can see it in you, see that it's there. But I need you to help me help you. If this is too hard for you to do right now, tell me, and we'll go somewhere else for the time being. But I do need you to level with me. We can't make you better if you can't be honest with me."

Damn straight. I move my eyes reluctantly from the wall to her face. It is gentle and open, not jittering for a square of Nicorette or struggling to subdue its guilty, voyeuristic arousal. It gives off maternal patience, empathy in waves. "Maybe I have Munchausen's syndrome," I say.

Dr. Lindholm's expression doesn't change. "Is that a serious question?"

"Mmmm, no; probably not."

"A person who suffers from Munchausen's imagines their illnesses or diseases in an attempt to create sympathy. Any symptoms they present are typically feigned. Your symptoms are quite real."

"Huh. Interesting. I never knew that about Munchausen's, that feigning thing. Then I guess that makes 'Munchausen's by proxy' something of a misnomer, since all the 20/20 coverage says these people actually do poison or otherwise harm their kids to get attention for themselves. I read one time about this woman who actually injected her son with his own feces, and he got all septic and nearly died, and then when he got better, she cut him with upholstery scissors and put coffee grounds in the wounds. Now there's someone who's messed up. Two someones, actually."

An expectant silence follows my summary statement, and Dr. Lindholm's voice is soft when it finally comes. "Did your mother hurt you when you were young?"

I laugh; my mother couldn't have cared enough to bother. Absolutely not, I tell Dr. Lindholm. My mother never touched me. We face off like that for a few seconds, unblinking, and though I want to, I don't laugh again. Finally, I give Dr. Lindholm a pleasant, professional smile and glance up at the clock. It is only six-thirty.

"I don't know anything about you that you don't tell me," she says, and it is a thought that is at once comforting and, oddly, sad.

She begins flipping through her notes. "So you recall nothing specific happening at the beginning of last week that upset you. No trigger."

"No, I'm telling you, I was shaving my legs and I fell out of the shower onto my hand. That's how it happens. I start out with a stupid little clumsy injury, and I turn it into something else. Something bigger, something better." I start free-associating on this, relieved by the shift in course, the tack to shallower waters.

"Nothing out of the ordinary? Within the last two weeks? Stresses at your job? A fight? Bad dreams?"

"Nope. Nothing. Oh—just my birthday. I turned twenty-eight on August 19."

She writes that down. "Was that hard?"

"Was what hard?"

"Your birthday. Turning twenty-eight."

"Only in that Robert called for reservations too late and we couldn't get a table at Bouley."

"Mmm," Dr. Lindholm says. "I can see where that would be hard." She flashes me a smile and then takes a breath. "Darien, last week you told me about a lot of the things you have done to yourself. I'm going to tell you what I have written down and then you can tell me if I've missed anything."

"Fire away," I say, and settle back to hear someone else describe to me how very screwed up I am.

. . .

When the hour is over, I have to tell Dr. Lindholm it's time to stop. She seems prepared to go on all night. And why not? We've talked about the times I've punched walls, slammed my hands in doors, swung at my knees with pans, hammers, baseball bats. We've discussed in exacting detail the patterns I've carved into my legs with broken glass and box cutters, or tattooed with burning cigarettes. We've conferred over the time I hacked at my toe like a stubborn chicken wing and failed, how I shoved it into a shoe and limped off to work without telling anyone or seeking treatment when it began to swell and ooze. We've even touched on my sexual proclivities, the drinking and fucking of my youth, the fact that Robert is a missionary-style, as-many-nights-a-week-as-he-can-get-it kind of guy. Who could possibly want to cut such conversation short?

I glance at the clock repeatedly, pointedly, as we approach seven o'clock, and finally Dr. Lindholm takes the hint.

"I think we'll stop for tonight, if that's all right with you," she says, and I push myself forward on the couch like a second grader who's finally heard the recess bell. Dr. Lindholm smiles. "One more thing, please, before you go," she says. "Do you have another minute?"

I slump back. "Of course."

"How did this go for you tonight? Do you want to continue?"

This catches me off guard; I wasn't aware there was a choice. I briefly consider the options—telling Robert Dr. Lindholm said I didn't need therapy, just dropping the whole thing outright; not telling him but working late every Wednesday, let him assume I'm coming here. Or shopping. After all, that $200 a week would still need to be spent. But then I remember Robert's stricken face, the jerking of his shoulders as he fell in front of me, and I think, *I can do this for him.* He deserves it. What the hell. She's not going to throw anything at me I can't take.

"Sure," I say grandly. "Why not? I think this went well."

She ducks her head in a way that almost looks shy and says, "I'm glad to hear that. I wasn't sure. We need to create a place here where you can feel safe about letting some of your defenses down, and if you don't feel like that can happen, is going to happen, I want you to tell me that." She stops for a deep breath. "In some ways, you're the one in charge in here. You control how fast or slow we go, what we do or don't talk about. You decide what you want me to know. I think it's important that you understand that, so if you ever feel like you're not in control, you can tell me to slow up. Does that make sense?"

It makes sense, all right. The deal is she gets to sit in her chair and look all calm and professional and in control, and I get to sit on the couch, sniveling and squirming like an earthworm on a pin, and if I fight it she gets to throw up her hands and claim I'm in control. Her little speech is a nice attempt to create the illusion of equality, of partnership, but you only need to take a single step away from it to know that isn't true. She's the doctor, I'm the patient. I am sick and she is healthy. Only one of us really needs anything from the other—money doesn't count— it's a power imbalance any way you slice it. For a second, I resent her for underestimating my ability to see the logic through.

She doesn't wait for my answer. Her eyes go to her lap and her fingers trace the edge of the prescription for Paxil, still clipped to the corner of my file. "In light of that, I won't push the Paxil on you right now. I still feel very strongly about getting you started on medication, but let's agree that you'll take a couple of weeks to think it over. It's not my preferred practice, but I want this to be your decision. I can get you some information on it, efficacy, side effects, contraindications, to take home with you if you think that would help."

She must have forgotten what I do for a living. I have a whole Paxil file at work. Early on, when they were first marketing it, I even got a few free samples (amusingly addressed to Darien Gilbertson, MD), which I immediately passed on to Carl. "No, no, I know all that," I tell her. "I know it's considered to be among the better of the SSRIs,

I know it can cause constipation and lowered sex drive, blah-blah-blah. It's not that. It's much more philosophical. I just need to be sure that all of this is a step forward—that I'm going through this for a reason, and not just the chance to become some lobotomized, tranquilized marionette."

"I promise you we won't go so far as lobotomization," she says. She tries a smile. "This is about finding an acceptable level of pain."

"Oh, okay," I say. I don't know what the hell she's talking about. I reach for my bag. Time's up. Time's more than up.

"Do you understand what I mean by that? I mean that right now you use physical pain as a substitute for emotional pain that's too hard to feel or that you won't permit yourself to feel, and that as we do this work, if we do it right, that pain is just going to get harder. Medication can help moderate it. Just take the edges off a little, to enable you to handle it safely. I sometimes tell people it's as if their emotional spectrum is a high-end stereo, with really high treble and really deep bass. The medication just narrows the range of the stereo, temporarily, to cut off those extremes. It won't change who you are, fundamentally. It will just protect you from those extreme highs and lows that lead you to hurting yourself. Okay?"

"Yeah, okay." I'm a stereo, whatever. I look at the door. It's almost seven-ten, for Christ's sake. I stand up. "I'll think about it. It makes sense, what you're saying, at least in theory. I just need to think if it makes sense for me."

Dr. Lindholm stands, too. "Good. I'm glad to hear that. I respect your concerns, and I'm sympathetic to them. But I can't tell you strongly enough how *helpful* I think medication can be to aiding you in moving forward on this safely and well. There's some big pain there, Darien. Don't sell yourself short on it."

I find the doorknob, twist it open. My brain rejoices—*yes!* Home free, and too hard earned. I repeat myself, dumbly, as I step through it: "I'll think about it, Dr. Lindholm, thanks. I really will."

Chapter 5

But I won't.

What Dr. Lindholm doesn't know is that all the drugs and therapy and behavior modification techniques in the world aren't going to make me normal. I'm just not designed that way. There's only one thing in this world that has ever allowed me to be normal, and that is my husband, that is Robert. I love him. I need him. I owe him my life. I know it sounds crazy—impossible—I know it wouldn't hold up under medical rigor, that it's not an explanation that Dr. Lindholm could ever accept or understand. But Robert has been my lifeline, and that is the closest thing to a fact I have ever known. He's been my oasis, my talisman, a single stroke of luck I never believed could be found. And I'm scared to death that he's losing his magical power over me: his ability to keep me sane.

We met in a bar, which is funny in an ironic sort of way because that's probably the last place you'd find either of us these days. Even from the beginning, Robert was rescuing me.

It's a Friday night, and I'm out drinking with a couple of people I work with: Hillary Nixon, who is probably my best friend, and then only because she's amenable to ditching work at three on a Friday for five-dollar pitchers at the Bear Bar; and Porter Hendrie, who's some milk-fed momma's boy from Marketing who only has this job and a second-rate Ivy League degree because his father's a bigwig at Johnson & Johnson. Porter lusts after both me and Hillary in the most adolescent, unfocused way, a condition we've happily taken advantage of by manipulating him into paying for our beer supply. He's only been with us since six o'clock, but the pitcher he now returns to the table with already represents his fifth five-dollar investment.

"Thanks, *Porter,*" I snicker. I drag the pitcher toward my glass with one hand, helping myself to his half-smoked cigarette with the other. "Porter. What the hell kind of name is that, anyway?"

"It's a *fam*-ly name," he whines. He bats his eyes at me, trying for cute and somewhat soulful.

"Oh yeah?" I reply. I take a swallow of beer. "What family? The Carrington family, from *Dynasty*? The Walsh family, from *Beverly Hills 90210*? Or maybe your father was a baggage handler at the airport. Isn't that what they call those guys, porters? You know, those guys with the little airliney uniforms and the stupid caps?" I laugh so hard at the thought of Porter's big, bad, chalk-striped father in a polyester uniform that beer starts coming out my nose. I cough and gag loudly for a few minutes, then stand up, knock my chair over into the table of drunk guys sitting behind us, and stagger toward the bathroom.

Inside the bathroom my blurry, moving reflection grazes off the mirror and a stall reels toward me. I collapse on the toilet seat, fully clothed, and continue laughing, talking to the still-burning cigarette clenched between my fingers. "Oh, Jesus, Darien, you are such a drunk, stupid bitch. Get a grip on yourself, drunk off your ass and taking potshots at the little rich boy. Purty tuf ta get a piece of that J&J action iffen yer makin' the big boy's son cry."

I drum my fingers on my numb face, sigh, push up my sleeves. Lay the cigarette in the crook of my left elbow and close my arm over it fast. The pain cuts a searing swath through my anesthetized brain and I start laughing again, butting my head lightly against the stall door and moaning, "Ow, ow"—sort of dreamy and lackadaisical. A woman waiting to use the toilet peers at me through kohl-lined eyes as I stagger back out of the stall.

"You all right?"

"Oh, yes, I'm fine, thank you, lovely of you to ask. All yours. Careful 'bout all the shmeg on the floor. Wouldn't want to mess up them nice shoes." I wave a hand in the approximate direction of her red stiletto heels and make my way for the door.

One of the drunk guys I knocked my chair into is standing just outside. "Hey." He grabs my upper arm as I reel by. "Hey. Dollface. C'mere."

"Name's not Dollface, asshole, it's Eunice. Eunice Doppelganger. And you can let go of my arm, thanks." The response is automatic, an uncharitable, intellectual snob reflex housed deep in my brain. When I am drunk, as I am now, and find unworthy people hitting on me, as I do now, I like to make up names for myself—the more ludicrous the better. With one instant, inebriated, passing glance I have determined that the guy who has grabbed my arm is a big, dumb, gold-chain-wearing, hockey-playing fuck, and I am going to mess with him.

"Yeah? Well it's nice to meet you, Eunice. What say we—"

"Oh, but you can call me Eunie," I interrupt, pronouncing it "Yoo-nee." "All my friends do. I went to SUNY–Stony Brook, so it's kind of a joke. You know—Eunie from SUNY." Trying to see how many ridiculous, irrelevant facts I can pack into the story all at once, how many fabrications I can concoct, is part of the game. My level of aggression in doing so must correlate somehow to the measure of disrespect I feel for my target, how insulted I am by his attentions. This guy looks like a Jersey boy, with his greased-up buzzcut hairdo and Chess King tie. A dumb fucking asshole, probably graduated from CCNY or some local community program, who inexplicably feels he has the right to hit on me.

"Oh, okay, Eunie, I'm Mike. What say we grab one of those tables in the corner? Things were getting a little crowded back over there." He gestures over to our tables, where Porter has transferred all of his toothless lust over to Hillary and where Mike's own buddies watch us like a spectator sport. One has the temerity to give Mike a two-handed thumbs-up, which I enthusiastically return.

"Naaw, Mike, what say we stand right here so your buddies can get a good view as you try unsuccessfully to pick me up?" I smile as I say it, openly imitating his broad accent.

"Now, who said anything about picking you up? You happened to make me spill my beer when you got up from the table. I thought for sure you'd want to buy me a new one."

"Oh you did, did you?" I fold my arms over my chest and put on a look of utter fascination at this news. "Now, why on earth would a big 'ole business guy like you need to turn to a little working gal like me to get his beer money? You look like a guy who does pretty well for himself. I mean, *nice* gold watch, some pretty spiffy looking shoes—looks like gen-u-ine vinyl to me. Heck, you must be pulling in, what? Twenty-five K? Maybe thirty, wit' commish? Whattayou, Mike? A brokah? A bankah? Betcha work down on Wall Street, take the ferry in from Hoboken every morning."

"Aaw, fuck you, bitch," Mike says, choreographing a manly, disgusted swing into the air between us. He turns to walk away.

"Hey, Mike; relax, man, I was just kidding. You just scared me is all, grabbing me like that. A girl likes to be courted a little, you know?" This is all part of the game: stringing him out and then reeling him in. I have no idea why I'm wasting my time with this jerk other than I'm dead drunk and can't think of anything better to do.

"And you are a broker, though, right? Let me guess—Bear Stearns?"

"Yeah, well, Bear Stearns is midtown, okay? I work for Solly. That's downtown. World Financial Center." He hikes up his pants as he talks and glances quickly at his pals.

"Oooh, SALomon Brothers. Very impressive. I'm a DLJ girl, myself."

"Is that right. Know Jimmy Pexton? In corporates?"

"No, no, I'm in munis; trader's assistant. I really don't know anyone on that floor." I don't know what the hell I'm talking about, but it's what one of my Swat roomies' older brothers used to do. I suffer from a new bout of choking laughter when I realize that now makes me Eunie from SUNY in munis; decide to take it as an opportunity to move the game up a level. "Hey, Mike, I'm dying here of chokealation or something. How about you buy me that beer and we can continue our conversation at the bar?"

Mike is completely at ease again, and confident that his considerable charms are winning me over. "I'd be happy to follow you to the bar, sweetheart," he says, "but I do believe it is you who owes me a beer."

"Yoo oze me? Owe me," I say. The grammar fix goes unnoticed. "How about you buy this one and I'll pick up the next?" I don't have so much as a dollar on me, but offer him a promising leer as he obediently turns and heads for the bar.

I climb up onto the chair next to him, nearly falling into the lap of the guy on my other side as I do. "Uh. Sorry. Almost ended up in your lap, there." I sort of push myself off my would-be seat cushion and aim for the empty stool, noticing in a flash how stunningly beautiful he is.

"More than happy to share with you," the seat cushion says with a Pepsodent smile.

The guy sitting next to him swivels to see what the commotion is all about, but he's no match for his Pepsodent friend. Not ugly, mind you, a little dopey-looking maybe, the kind of guy brought along to make other people look good. He says to his buddy, "Easy going there,

Marlon" (or something like that—Harlan? Snarlin'? My hearing is going). "Heather's got us all on strict orders. The bachelor party's still a few months off."

Mike starts forward with both fists clenched, a portrait in testosterone, but he doesn't need to bother, nor does the dopey guy with the less than kind words: good-looking guys always give me the creeps. I give this one a seasick smile and turn away, lightly pushing Mike back into his chair. "Put it back in your pants, there, Menelaus," I slur. "Nobody's gonna steal your milk money."

It all goes downhill from there. I think I remember counting four Jaegermeister shots and beer chasers, some conversation about the fall of Troy ("You know, Menelaus. Helen's husband. That poor sorry bastard who was cuckolded by Helen and Paris—or did you never hear of the Trojan War? Wassamatter—that one never made it to video?"); another conversation that has something to do with Trojan condoms. The heat and the noise and the beer are finally getting to me and my shirtsleeve is starting to stick to my arm. I don't feel so good; am having trouble forming complete sentences as I hoist another beer mug toward my face, feel it crash into my teeth, beer pouring all down my chin and pooling in my lap. I am on the verge of blacking out when Mr. Jersey Boy jerks his chair closer and, working his fingers intimately toward the inside of my thigh, suggests I wait to pass out in his car, so he can fuck the smirk right off my smug little preppy-girl face. It is with great effort that I drag my leaden lids open long enough to savor the brute sneer on his lips. Then I lean toward him, mutter, "Iwuzzactually thinking something more like this," and disgorge the contents of my stomach down the front of his shirt in a single toxic heave.

The next thing I know, painful light is streaming through a window that isn't mine. I am lying on my right side on an unfamiliar couch, propped in an awkward half-sit with what feels like a bean bag but upon closer inspection proves to be a dog bed. Even more mysterious, I'm clutching a soggy sweat sock in my left hand. Somewhat familiar with the phenomenon of waking up in a foreign bed, but never in quite this configuration, I begin slowly, tentatively, to take as much stock of my environment as is possible without moving my head. My skull pounds in sickening asynchrony in two distinct locations.

The first thing I conclude is that I have no idea where I am. Judging from the sound of traffic and voices in the hall I am still in Manhattan, which gives me slight reassurance that I am not in my little pal Mike's Hoboken walk-up. Patting down my left side, I determine that I am still fully clothed; shifting my thighs slightly, I decide I probably haven't had sex. With that much evidence in my favor, I conclude I must have come home with Hillary, or—God forbid—Porter, and try to right myself quickly so I can get out of here before anyone confronts me. Neither option is overly favorable. Hillary's fiancé doesn't much like me and will likely not consider my hideous hangover punishment enough for talking her into last night's bender, and Porter—

I knock over the wastebasket next to the couch while groping for my shoes. It clangs on the hardwood and rolls across the floor, ushering into the room a man I've never seen before in my life.

"Well, well," he says gravely. "If it isn't Agamemnon's daughter. Made it through the sacrificial slaughter on the rocks, I see."

"Um. What?" I am really counting on this guy being Porter's roommate; try hard to remember if he ever mentioned having one. My brain is grinding slowly, painfully, to the conclusion that I did something very bad last night.

"It is Iphigenia, right? Either that or Eunice, or I believe you even tried Eustacia a couple of times. I assume your name isn't actually any of these, but since you seem to have left your ID with the bartender, I couldn't check for sure." The strange man pauses and pinches his lower lip between thumb and forefinger, considering me. "Proteus, maybe," he continues. "Yes. I was thinking about this earlier. I would have gone with Proteus."

The hangover and the fact that this guy's obviously taken a course in Greek literature at some point put me at a decided disadvantage. Did I fuck this guy? I must have fucked him. I don't even remember who Proteus is. The last thing I remember is explaining to that Jersey guy the origins of the Trojan War, and then reciting the opening lines of the *Aeneid,* because I don't know Greek and never learned the Latin translation for the *Odyssey. Arma virumque cano, Troiae qui primus ab oris* . . . I think he was that guy who changed shapes when Ulysses caught him, maybe, Proteus. My whole body hurts—my arms, my head. It feels like I pulled every muscle in my abdomen. I rock forward slightly and groan.

"Yeah, okay. You're terribly clever, and I'm really flattered that you've put that much thought into things, gone to the trouble of digging up your *Bulfinch's Mythology* and all, but I'm afraid I'm not finding this terribly amusing right now. I don't know where I am, I don't know who you are, and I don't have clue one about how those pieces fit together. So if you would be so kind as to tell me where I am and how I got here, I would be more than happy to correct the situation by getting out of it."

I raise my head enough to look at the guy again, now leaning against the breakfast bar. Vaguely familiar, but I can't place from where. He's wearing tube socks much like the one I woke up holding, blue Umbro shorts, a vintage Johns Hopkins University sweatshirt. Messy, wavy brown hair and startling Atlantic blue eyes. Not particularly handsome, boyish, and skinny enough that his ears, somewhat in evidence through the mess of his curls, look like they could spell trouble in a stiff wind. From here he looks tall, well over six feet. His lower lip continues to undulate between his thumb and forefinger like a Vienna sausage as he watches me. He raises one eyebrow.

"Hmm. You don't remember? Well, this will be fun."

"Yeah, yeah. Glad I could make your morning—or afternoon, or whatever it is. Always thrilled to be someone else's entertainment."

"I'm Robert Gilbertson."

"Darien Gorse."

"Really?"

"Really."

"Pleased to meet you. Though we met last night, of course." A pause. "At the Bear Bar."

We did? I freeze for a minute, holding my breath, willing my subconscious to deliver it to me. Happily, it does. Not the Pepsodent guy, but his dopey-looking friend, the one who made the crack about bachelor parties. Typical, a hypocrite, and I didn't even get the cute one. "Riiiight," I say. "Right. You were with your friend, umm, Marlon?" I venture a guess.

"Parlin." His voice has reverted to its earlier brusqueness. "Rick Parlin." *Parlin,* I think, as if it is of some consequence, *so that's what he was saying,* and at once the entire scene in the bar becomes vivid. I bury my head back in my hands.

"Oh, God. Did I throw up on you, too? I only meant to get that—that—that other guy. That Jersey boy. Mike, whatshisname. Shit. Sorry. Is there anything you need dry-cleaned? Here, just give me whatever it is I ruined and I'll clean it or replace it or whatever. Just—uh. Ugh. I've really got to go. Sorry." I lurch to my feet, shoeless, and pinwheel in the direction of the door. Small explosions touch off in my head, one through the top of my skull, the other in my left cheek. Robert moves between me and the door and puts his fingertips against my shoulder.

"I'd appreciate it if you'd stay for a few minutes, actually. For starters, I damaged my reputation with my neighbors enough bringing you in here looking like that last night, and I'd rather not make things worse by letting you out the same way. And more important, I'd like to tell you exactly what happened and what you did. I don't have any idea what goes on in that head of yours, but I don't want you leaving here thinking anything funny happened or I took advantage of you drunk. I didn't. But what you did is pretty messed up, and you should know about it. I've never seen anyone act like that before and it's something you"—he pauses, rakes both hands through his hair and stares straight in front of him—"at least you should know about it. So please, hang on a second. Can I get you something? A cup of coffee? Maybe some juice?"

I keep my head down and listen to my heart break.

"No, thank you," I say. I sink back on the couch. What I really need is about a dozen aspirin, but I don't trust myself to ask.

"So. Anyway. After you threw up on that guy—Mike, I guess, you said—he backhanded you pretty hard. You fell and hit your head on the bar, somewhere over on the left side, I think."

I reach up to touch my head as Robert talks, fingers patting uncertainly through sticky clots of hair to a swelling like a golf ball not far from my left ear. I look up at Robert. He is staring at the parquet, hands tucked beneath his arms.

"You didn't seem overly concerned about it at the time, kind of sitting on the floor and laughing, and—" Robert stops and squints at me uncertainly. He gives me a queasy smile and goes on. "I don't really remember, it was all kind of strange, but this Mike guy was lunging at you, and you were laughing at him and daring him to hit you again. You actually cracked your head yourself on the foot rail, which I think is what that is."

He points to the area I've just been touching. I put my palm flat against my cheek and marshal enough vanity to feel horror as I discover that most of my hair is glued to the side of my face.

"Anyway, I pulled the guy off you and passed him off to a bouncer. The bartender was calling the police. He wanted to have both of you arrested, and somewhere in there you started going after another one of the bouncers, who seemed to be trying to help you up, so I cut a deal with the bartender. Promised I'd get you out of his bar and never come back if he didn't call the cops on you. You kept saying something about your friends, your friends and your tote bag, but I couldn't find either, and you wouldn't give me a straight answer on your name or where you lived. So, rather than wander around the Upper West Side all night, I brought you here. I thought you might get sick again, so I propped you up with Walter's bed. But I promise you, nothing else happened. I tried to put an icepack on your head where you hit yourself, but you wouldn't let me get that near you."

This is a little much to process all at once. Mortification, incredulity, cynicism, and self-abhorrence vie for the top spot in my brain. *Not again, not again, not again.* College, horror and shame open up in me anew. Finally, distantly, I say, "No, no. It's a highly developed gag reflex. I threw up on him on purpose." And then, "Who's Walter?" I want to ask where Parlin went in all of this but don't dare.

"My dog. He's sulking in the other room."

"What is he?"

Robert scowls at me, puzzled.

"Walter. What kind of dog is he?"

"A, uh, golden. He's a golden retriever. Look, are you all right?"

I allow myself a little snort of disgust. "Dandy, thanks. Couldn't be better. It's really very moving, that story; all the right elements of honor and chivalry and damsels in distress. You can start calling all your friends now, let 'em know you're a real A-number-one hero." I pause to admire my response and make the mistake of looking at Robert to gauge the effect. Usually, this kind of stuff gets them cowering, but he just stands there, his arms folded. I swallow a nervous laugh and my voice comes out annoyingly high. "Might I ask how you managed to get me out of the bar where Mike and the bouncer had failed?"

Robert smiles wryly. "I'm still not real clear on that myself. You seemed to like my tie. Said it would go well with your shoes."

Oh, right. The tie. I seem to remember something about that. I glance briefly at my own bare, dirty feet as if for a clue, but there's only one thing it could be. I have a single pair of shoes that matters; I'm inordinately proud of my ownership. "Ferragamo?" I ask.

"Yeah."

"Huh. Interesting. And, uh, I'm sorry. I need to ask this bluntly. When you say that nothing else happened, you mean we didn't have sex?" I force myself to make eye contact. I've done this before, this confrontation, I can do it now. I've survived it dozens of times.

"No," Robert says. "Absolutely not." Despite my better judgment, I begin to relax. He looks troubled now, eyebrows pulled together and mouth turned down. I realize that despite the frat-boy jock getup, he's a lot older than me, deep laugh lines around his eyes and a few gray hairs mixed in with the brown. My stomach churns with shame. "Though you certainly seemed to be under the impression we were going to. Did a lot of yelling and screaming about how I could skip the wine and roses act and just do you where we were. Kept pointing at things and yelling about how I could do you in this alleyway or on the hood of that car."

"Aah. I see. Charming." My smile is not of the amused variety. "That must have been quite pleasant for you."

"Far from it, actually."

"Right. Now, explain to me again why you felt compelled to pick me up off the floor in the first place."

A handful of fleeting, unnamable emotions pass over Robert's face before he answers, and when he does, his words sound vulnerable in spite of or maybe because of their logic and formality. "Because there was a very non-zero chance that you were going to be arrested and I thought my couch might be slightly preferable to a cell in the Twelfth Precinct. While public drunkenness and disorderly conduct aren't terrible things to have on your record, assaulting a police officer is, particularly as it could conceivably get you jail time, and at the time, that didn't seem out of the realm of possibility. I took a wild guess and figured you weren't the type to have a record, much as you might want to."

"Good grief—what are you, a social worker? Somebody's mother? Jesus Christ."

"I am not Jesus Christ," he assures me soberly. He fixes me in a deep blue gaze, very serious, and a lazy wave of something akin to nausea, a cousin of my earlier shame, rolls across the base of my stomach. He is standing close enough that I can reach his hand, and without thinking about it, I do, turning it palm-up to check for stigmata. It is a surprising hand, large and warm, with long, elegant fingers, a hand made to play the piano or basketball. I hold on to it longer than necessary, suddenly sleepy, as if letting go would require unsummonable energy. Robert's fingers curve up toward me as my fingertips unthinkingly trace his palm. A slow shiver wends its way from my stomach to my spine. I practically throw Robert's hand back at him.

"I see that," I say, aiming for a cool, wry tone to belie the ludicrous pounding of my heart. And then, as if it actually requires further clarification, "No stigmata."

He smiles for the first time then, bright white teeth that overlap ever so slightly, deep dimples like parentheses that hold up his cheeks. He laughs as if I have said something tremendously funny. "I'm a lawyer, actually," he says finally, and then it is my turn to laugh, and that is how it begins.

Chapter 6

Here's something I'd forgotten about breaking a hand: it must be managed with care. In the weeks that have passed since my little lapse in judgment, life has taken on a new routine. Where once it was work, eat, sleep, go up to our underused weekend house in Eastman, Connecticut, or not, always skim along the surface; now it is work, eat, sleep, see Dr. Lindholm, plunge into the water, struggle back to the surface, pretend you never left. Eastman, no Eastman. Fumble slowly, ask for help, wear only slip-on shoes. Take twice as long as usual to do even the simplest of tasks.

I try a selectively crippled routine out on Robert, and he buys it selectively. He takes on all the cooking and laundry without critical commentary and gives Walter his weekly bath by himself, but fails to see why a cast could compromise my ability to pick up dry cleaning or operate a pooper-scoop. One Eastman weekend, he dispatches me to Home Depot to buy paint, and when I return to the house he carries the cans, but there is no discussion about letting me out of the project for which they are intended. It is a foregone conclusion that we will spend Saturday repainting the farmer's porch that runs across the front of the house, and while I have been busy debating the merits of satin finish versus semigloss, Robert has scraped down and sanded the porch and draped the scraggly evergreens beneath it with tarps. I know better than to complain. Painting the porch was a project originally slated for the last weekend in August, in preparation for a Labor Day visit from Robert's brother and his very pregnant wife. Both events were precluded by my little tangle with the bathroom wall, and now, a month later, I am sensible enough to be grateful that Robert has not chosen to position the task as punishment. But still, it is a fantastic Indian summer day. It seems a shame to waste it getting high on Glidden fumes.

"Have at it," he says. We both stand on the porch, and I do my best to look pathetic, utterly incapable of painting. Oblivious to my helplessness, Robert hands me a new paintbrush, one I purchased myself only an hour earlier, now unsheathed from its blue protective wrap.

I dip the clean bristles into the paint and watch it drizzle off, like melted white chocolate. I loop my brush around and draw a jerky "R" in the glossy surface of the paint can with the drizzle. It subsides immediately.

"Are you sure this is such a good idea?" I appeal, appealingly, to Robert. His hair and face are frosted with paint dust and a negative streak of clean skin slashes across his cheek. Against the white, his eyes are vividly blue. He is wearing old, torn jeans, and a ratty Wisconsin track T-shirt of his brother's. A triangle of shoulder shows through a hole in the shirt and I think of running my tongue over the smooth skin, following the hard line of Robert's shoulder blade in toward his Adam's apple.

"What do you mean?" He wipes another clean spot onto his face.

I shrug and twirl my brush at him, lacing small droplets across the porch. "I mean, with this hand and all." I use my brush-holding left to point at my cast-wearing right. "I can't guarantee that I'll do a good job."

Robert regards me blankly for a moment. "What are you talking about?"

I try again, gesturing unsteadily with the brush to suggest the unpredictable manner in which I might manage it in the course of the job. "You know. If clean, straight strokes are important to you, or whatever. I might not do such a good job. Maybe we should wait until I'm out of the cast."

His expression shifts, indecipherable. "I'm afraid I still don't understand."

I feel heat rise to my face. "Well, you know," I stammer. I make a few more wild circuits with the brush.

Blank turns to a slow smile. "Yes, I do know, Darien. You're left-handed." Robert starts to laugh. "Did you think I didn't know that?"

"Well, no, as a matter of fact. I never know with you." My face and neck sting with embarrassment. "It seemed worth a try, at least. Besides, I'm ambidextrous. Maybe you didn't know that. It just so happens I paint with my right hand." It's true, the part about being ambidextrous; it would have been hard for me to break my right hand, otherwise.

He laughs for another minute, shaking his head, and then, sobering, points at the railing behind my back. "Paint," he commands. "And not another word out of you. I promise we'll be done before dinner. You do a good job and I'll even cook."

"Oh, yeah?" I reply. "Your famous turducken?" One of the rare times Robert had been inspired to cook, he'd found this Paul Prudhomme recipe he'd insisted on making: a turkey stuffed with a duck stuffed with a chicken, roasted. All three birds had to be boned; Robert had to buy special knives; the process took all day. When Robert finally put his masterpiece on the table, the turkey was dry and the chicken raw. The duck, however, was heavenly. "I'm not so sure that's actually an incentive."

My face still sizzles with humiliation, but I bend over to reload my paintbrush and turn obediently toward the porch rail. A dozen strokes later, I am rewarded for my compliance with a heavy, wet wallop, full across the butt. Tiny ropes of wet paint wing out to either side of me and dribble down my bare legs and I feel the sucking print of the paintbrush, clinging damply to my backside. I stare for a minute, open-mouthed, at the white rivers running down my legs. I turn to look at Robert, who stands crouched, depleted brush held forward like a foil. Above the paint dust his eyes dance, merry, crazed.

"Uh! Weenie-boy!" I say. I start laughing. "Oh, are you ever gonna get your butt kicked."

"Try me," he urges. He dances, light on his feet, like a boxer. His brush performs figure-eights in the air between us. Walter, dozing in the sun at the barricaded foot of the porch stairs, opens one eye at the proceedings and then lifts his head.

I try to look disinterested as I watch my leaping, bobbing husband, a synchronized swimmer less his pool. "You wish," I say. "I'm not going to do it now, when you're ready. I'm going to wait until I can get you off guard."

We spend the next two hours whirling on each other, defensive, offensive, brushes loaded. As soon as I get a good shot in on him, though, Robert begins to wield his brush two-handed. I cry, "Not fair! You know I can't do that. You're taking advantage of my handicap!" I have spent the afternoon on the losing end of the game as it is, and my appearance bears testament. My clothes, my face, my hair, and even my cast are stringed with ribbons of paint. Robert acknowledges the foul, sets down the offending brush, and plucks mine from my hand.

"You're right, my bad," he says cheerfully. "Not nice to pick on the manually disadvantaged." He looks at me and then around him. There's a black sneaker print smeared the width of three floorboards, and half a dozen leaves have settled on the wet paint. On the dining-room window behind him, a lemon-sized teardrop of white slides down the glass. "I'll finish this up by myself."

I devote the next hour to a steaming bath and then watch from the bathroom window as Robert finishes the job. He covers more ground in the hour by himself than we did together all afternoon, moving from the broad floorboards to the balusters to the railing with self-satisfied efficiency. He keeps up a steady stream of chatter to Walter, who remains on guard at the bottom of the steps, tapping just the end of his tail against the grass. When he's finished, Robert lifts both arms in the air and announces, *Ta-da!* to no one in particular.

The weekly trips to Dr. Lindholm, like the broken hand, are a nuisance I learn to work around. Straight off, I make up a story to account for my regular Wednesday night early departures from Boylan and make sure everyone hears the tale. The second Wednesday I leave early, I drag Carl and Hillary out for coffee in the middle of the afternoon and commence to making a fuss about leaving early. I know they will start the rumor-mill and the word will reach Duncan before quitting time.

"God, what a pain in the *ass*." I make a show of looking at my watch, clicking a cast-bound fingernail against it dismissively. It's almost four-thirty, less than an hour until I'll have to leave.

"What?" Hillary asks.

Carl blows a smoke ring at me. "What's wrong with your ass now, Missy G?"

"That's Mrs. G to you, thank you very much. It's my mother-in-law."

"Ah." Hillary nods. "Speaking of Mrs. G."

Carl cocks an eyebrow and points his cigarette at me. "Your mother-in-law hurt your ass? This woman I've got to meet. Anyone who can produce spawn as lovely as Big Bob and hurt your skinny white ass just can't be all that bad."

Hillary rolls her eyes in sympathy and I say, "Yeah, well, I'd be happy to pass her along. In fact, I'll throw in her latest birthday present as a bonus." The segue's a little hamhanded, but I need to keep things on track. With Carl, a conversation can spiral out of control in an instant.

"Butt plug?" he asks hopefully.

"Better," I say. "Ballet. She gave me, totally unawares, a year's subscription to the Met, apparently my punishment for turning twenty-eight. Every Wednesday night, for a whole freaking year! I don't even *like* the ballet, and still I've got to crawl by Duncan to get out and do it. Robert's none too happy about it, either, but you better believe I'm dragging him along if I have to go. I told him he was going to find divorce papers tacked to the refrigerator if he found more than one week's reason for blowing me off."

Hillary looks puzzled. "Doesn't the Met start at like eight? Why would you have to leave at five?"

Why, indeed? I take a long draw on my latte. "Oh, it gets better. There's cocktails and a lecture before the show. It's some sort of package deal. You can't get into the dance if you don't do your homework first."

"So don't go," Carl shrugs. Apparently, in his book, butt plugs and the ballet don't even compare. "What's the big deal? It's not like she'd know the difference."

"I'll go," Hillary adds. "What's the performance tonight?"

"I don't know." I try to sound irritated, imposed upon. "Some Jerome Robbins modern dance thing." I went to the trouble of stopping by Lincoln Center for the fall schedule; I even picked up subscription rates. It makes me feel slightly less guilty savaging my mother-in-law resting assured that I have at least fabricated a considerably generous gift.

"Well, you know what I always say, Darien." Carl blows another smoke ring at me. "It sucks to be you. The ballet. God help us! The next thing you know, you'll be moving out to Bronxville."

. . .

Inside Dr. Lindholm's office, I dispense with matters just as tidily.

Session three, I address the Paxil question, straight off: No Paxil now, no Paxil ever, no capitulation on my position that I can foresee. Dr. Lindholm receives my verdict most unhappily, and I try to make like it's something I've puzzled long and hard over, and not a decision I'd made before even closing the door the previous week. As a gesture of consolation, I tell her she can give me the prescription if it will make her feel better, and that I can even fill it and carry around the bottle if that will really help, but that I won't promise to take even one pill. She says that to accept my decision she needs to understand my reasoning, and so I give her my cancer analogy.

"Look, Dr. Lindholm," I tell her, "did you know that something like a quarter of all people diagnosed with cancer refuse treatment? Either they're more afraid of the side effects than they are of the disease— nausea, hair loss, poisoning—or they just plain don't believe it's going to work and they don't want to compromise their quality of life for the time they have left. I think if they have the right to refuse treatment, then certainly I do, too."

She frowns severely and says, "I don't see the comparison."

I shrug and say, "Well, I do."

"Well, then, I have to say that I consider that a very dangerous thought process. I don't like the sounds of it at all. I'm not in the business of running an emotional hospice here. Your life isn't ending. You don't suffer from anything terminal."

I don't bother to correct her. Still frowning, she asks me to make a pact with her not to hurt myself, a promise to call her first or to go to a hospital if I become tempted to hurt myself again. At first I don't promise. A pact? It sounds corny, not to mention unrealistic. I negotiate. Finally, Dr. Lindholm says, "I don't negotiate, Darien. Patients I can't make pacts with go on medication or I hospitalize them."

I promise.

Session four, I report that I am honoring our pact, and I volunteer what I'm inspired to about my family, which is little. I tell Dr. Lindholm I haven't seen or spoken to my mother since college; haven't seen my two older brothers in longer than that. Although I can tell she is curious, she doesn't push, and I promise I'll tell her more when I'm ready, though in fact I'm sure I never will be. Session five, Dr. Lindholm asks me to talk about Robert, about our marriage, about our sex life. At one point, well into the conversation, she asks me if I love him.

I come back immediately. The question requires no reflection, no feigned deep thinking. "Of course I love him. I'm married to him, aren't I?"

She shrugs indifferently, as if, for her, the question has no moral resonance. "You're married to him, yes. But that's not tautological. People stay married to people they don't love all the time."

I laugh, ahead of her on this one. "Not in my family, they don't."

She looks confused for a second, unsure, and then she looks down at the notepad in her lap. She flips back a few pages until she arrives, apparently, at last week's session, where there must be written something to the effect of *three brothers, four fathers, five marriages*. She looks up at me in surprise and titters like a little girl. "Oh, Darien, I apologize," she says.

I spread my hands wide, generous, forgiving, in control. I say, in reply, "Not at all."

Chapter 7

As the weeks pass, a question builds in my brain, its voice increasingly insistent: What if there's nothing wrong with me? At my sixth session, I decide to raise the issue with Dr. Lindholm. I sit down, we exchange our pleasantries, and noodle around the family Gilbertson for half an hour. I complain about my mother-in-law, describe the emotional stranglehold I fear she has on Robert and its implications for why he chose me. When I know we're aimed at the home stretch, no time to get into anything too deeply, I throw the question out there. What if nothing's wrong with me? Dr. Lindholm blinks flatly in response.

"How do you mean?" she says.

"I mean, what if there's nothing-*wrong*-with-me wrong with me? Nothing fixable about the things that make me act the way I act and be the way I am? I mean, what if I'm just like this? What if this is the way I'm supposed to be, no big drama or trauma that needs to be undone or relived?"

Dr. Lindholm frowns at me for a second, but it is the interested frown of someone mulling over an intellectually new idea, not a scowl of anger or threat. I feel just the slightest twinge of disappointment, a thrill of fear at her equanimity. Any of my previous therapists would have been running for the door if I had lobbed that question at them.

"How do you feel about that possibility?" she asks.

"What do you mean?" I respond, feeling vaguely stupid. It's not the question I'd expected.

"I mean, what's scary to you in that?"

I frown. There's nothing scary.

"Or conversely, what's appealing?"

I shake my head. "I don't know that it's either. Does it have to be?" This isn't at all the trajectory I'd charted out.

"I think so. Otherwise, I wonder why you raised the question."

"Well, okay. Fair enough, I guess. I didn't bring it up to be glib, like that Munchausen's thing, if that's what you're asking."

Dr. Lindholm shakes her head and says, "No, I know you meant it seriously. It's an interesting question. But I'm more interested in what interest you have in it, if you see what I'm saying."

"Well, I guess it's just that I feel like I sit here, week after week, with you pushing me to uncover this big something that will be a reason to explain who I am and why I keep doing all this wacky, repulsive stuff to myself, and so far I'm coming up with nothing. It's all self-indulgent small stuff. It's navel-gazing."

"It's early days yet, Darien," Dr. Lindholm interjects. In her eyes there is sympathy, kindness.

"I mean, I'm just not one of those people who likes to run around pinning my problems on others. Assessing blame—"

"—No," Dr. Lindholm agrees, "you like to pin it right on yourself."

I ignore this. "I figure everything that's wrong with me is my own fault, my own doing, if there is a fault, and maybe it's just not that interesting. Maybe I was just born to be this way. Maybe all that stuff is just part of my program, part of who I'm meant to be. Maybe it's hard-wired into my personality."

"Drinking?" Dr. Lindholm raises an eyebrow. "Slamming your fists into walls? Vomiting? Cutting? Having punishing sex with strangers?"

I grin; I can't help myself. She looks so concerned, that one Chaplinesque eyebrow quirking higher with each item on the inventory. "I didn't say it was pretty. And besides, I'm not doing that last thing anymore, the nymphomania." She's been kind enough not to label it that. "I only have punishing sex with my husband." A pause. "That's a joke, by the way."

"So that's not a part of your program?" she says.

"Hmm," I say. *Good point,* I think. "I suppose it could be, if it would help support my argument."

"Let me ask you another question, then," she continues. "Where's the bottom?"

My stomach closes, but I breathe. "What do you mean?"

"I mean, what's at the bottom of that list? What's the worst thing you'll do to yourself?" She looks at me hard. Her eyes are deadly serious.

I recross my legs and grin at my shoes. There is a strip of leather peeling loose at one heel and a big scuffmark where I got caught by the escalator at work. "You mean, am I going to kill myself?" I drag hard on the word—*k-ILL* myself—and waggle my hands next to my head like a Baptist preacher warming up.

"Yeah," she says. "You know I do. I mean, are you going to kill yourself?"

I yank on the leather strip and a whole ring of heel peels free. *Goddammit,* I think, and rub at the scar with my thumb as if to blend it in with the rest of the heel. I practice it a few times in my head, practice the face before I lift my eyes. I'm confident I've got it down. "Of course not."

The couch squeaks as Dr. Lindholm and I stare at each other.

A little later, she says, "Let me throw something else at you. Scientists have spent decades trying to prove the existence of personality, and so far no one's been successful. So you're not going to persuade me by pinning your argument on personality. Especially not on personality. I'm one of the original unbelievers. I barely passed that course in college."

"Well, you did go to Wellesley," I say, before I can stop myself.

She pulls a confused face. "I don't see the connection."

"That's okay, then." I wave my cast at her. "Never mind." She continues to look at me. "I went to Swarthmore, so I'm biased. I just figured there probably wasn't much excess of personality floating around at Wellesley."

Dr. Lindholm considers a moment, as if this is a statement to duly ponder, and then she laughs—a heartier, naughtier chortle than I had expected. "That's great," she says. "I love it! Do you mind if I share that with a colleague in Boston? She's a sister alumna, and half her outpatient practice comes from the Wellesley student body."

I tell her to knock herself out, and then I test her a minute. Will the conversation come back to my question or are we done with it? She smiles at me expectantly, and then shifts in her seat. "So let's agree we keep personality out of this argument," she says. "What else does that leave?"

"Well, for starters, I was born with a twin who didn't survive. That seems pretty scientific. I made it and she didn't. My identical twin sister. Maybe I just wasn't meant to be born."

Dr. Lindholm's face softens. "You've mentioned your stillborn sister before, Darien, I know. What is it that that continues to mean to you?"

"It means, well, you know Darwin, right? *The Origin of Species*?" Dr. Lindholm nods her head. "Well, my sister didn't survive. We were genetically identical and she died at birth. Wouldn't Darwin say that I was meant to die, too? Biologically, I mean. We were exactly the same."

Dr. Lindholm shakes her head at me. She looks surprised, puzzled. She opens and closes her mouth a few times before she says, "Darwin

[77]

would say just the opposite. Darwin would say those who survive are meant to, and those who don't, aren't. Darwin—if he were talking about individuals, which he wasn't—would say that you were fitter than your sister, or that her death was an accident. He would say, if anything, that you were meant to survive." She pauses.

"But that seems like an unfairly cold and clinical way to talk about your sister. It sounds to me like what you're grappling with is a pretty hefty dose of guilt for being the one who lived."

"No—" My voice comes out sharper than I intended it, and for a second my head feels strange, but I want to cut her off before she wanders too far astray. I suddenly realize that she would make a masterful debate team captain. She's going to drag this thing back around to trauma if it kills her. "Not guilt. Proof. I think there's just something in my genetic makeup that makes me nonviable. It was in my sister, too, and she died when she was born, and I think that was what was supposed to happen to me. Only I screwed up, and I lived—"

"—But why was that screwing up?" Dr. Lindholm interrupts me. "Why, to use your Darwin argument on you, wasn't that just proof that you were meant to survive?"

"Because of exactly the things we've been sitting here talking about: because I do all these heinous things to myself for no reason. Because there is no other explanation. It's like—well, you're going to think I'm being flip saying this, but I'm serious. It's the best explanation I can come up with. It's like I'm the Terminator, or RoboCop—or Hal, from 2001. It's like I'm animatronic, and I have faulty wiring, holes in my DNA or something. Short circuits in my program that make me do really screwy things, like—well, like all the things I've been talking to you about for the past six weeks. I mean, that's part of the problem, isn't it? I sort of like some of it. Like hurting myself. Like drinking. And even puking wasn't so bad. Puking was the easiest thing of all."

With effort, I rein myself in. I'd been enjoying my moment on center stage, perhaps for the potential it held to shock Dr. Lindholm, but when she looks at me, her gaze is steady. She says, "I appreciate you telling me all of that. I think it's important. But I wonder where you think that leaves us."

"You mean this." I wave my hand around the room, the couch, the printwainscoting, the tissue boxes.

She nods gravely. "I mean this."

"I don't know. I'm not sure. I do know that I didn't offer it as a way to exempt myself from this or just to rationalize my lousy behavior. It's not just a defense, if that's what you're thinking." Her expression tells me nothing. "I think it means maybe I'd just like you to consider it as a possibility."

"Does it also mean that you think I'm pushing you too hard to take on things you're not ready to handle?"

The question seems tricky in a way I don't quite fathom, like the what-about-this-scares-you/appeals-to-you counter that led off the discussion. "No," I say. "At least I don't think so."

"No?" Dr. Lindholm repeats. "You're pretty sure of that?"

I repeat my qualified assertion.

"Well, then, I have a proposition for you. And if you're pretty sure, as you say you are, then you should be willing to accept my challenge. I'm willing to bet you that there's a whole bunch of stuff you've got locked down there that's all pretty painful to you, and that, rather than feeling, you've put outside yourself in these self-punishing acts, and that that's part of what you like about them so much. They let you feel physically without having to feel emotionally. If you're pretty sure that's not the case, then you shouldn't mind giving my theory a try for a couple of weeks, and talking about some of that stuff you keep saying isn't any big deal. I think what we'll find is that if we can identify and give outlet to the emotional hurt, then there won't need to be a physical hurt and you'll find those things aren't so much of your program, after all. I agree with you. It doesn't have to be one big trauma or drama; it might be a whole bunch of little hurts. But that wouldn't make them any less valid. What do you say?"

"What do I say to what?" I am not trying to be difficult; not really. Dr. Lindholm has a habit, which I assume must be intentional, of offering ideas or questions in ways that require verification, restatement, clarity. Now, I detect the real possibility of committing myself to some zany idea I don't quite understand, like Paxil redux or hypnotherapy. She's argued me better than I expected tonight. I don't want to get caught anywhere else.

"What do you say we give my approach a try for a couple of weeks?"

Still a little vague. "Let you pick at my scabs? I guess so."

"We won't be picking at scabs, Darien," Dr. Lindholm says. "I guarantee that. We won't be merely *picking* at anything. Think before you agree to this. It's harder work than you think."

I try to look chastened. It occurs to me that there is a reason Dr. Lindholm is an unbeliever in personality.

"I think there's a great deal of hurt to uncover." She points at my hand. "I think we're going to find a whole lot of broken stuff."

"Sounds like fun," I say, confident. There is nothing.

Dr. Lindholm frowns. "Not at all."

Gradually, but inexorably, the world resumes its previous shape. Bruise and swelling relinquish the last of their claim on my hand, and the pain no longer wakes me up at night. Dr. Bruce puts me in a new cast, and then another, each one bringing my hand a little closer to normal shape. Robert stops asking me daily if I'm okay, holding my shoulders or cupping my face, staring into my eyes; we begin to make love again without him having to ask every time if we should. At work, my ballet subscription becomes a running joke. I jeté into the office on Thursdays, the *Times* review fresh in my head. I grab coffee and Manhattan sunshine with Carl, sneak out at lunchtime to shop with Hillary.

One day, I discover by accident that Dr. Lindholm buys all of her shoes at Bergdorf Goodman. I'm out with Hillary, who is shopping for heels for a wedding, when I find myself facing a display of loafers that unsettle me. The shoes examine me from different perspectives: crocodile at a jaunty angle; navy pensive, the heel of one on the toe of another; black straight on like an accusation, and I back away for a better look. I pick up a pair, turn them over to see the price, and when the *vero cuoio* stamp stares back at me, I get it. They are Dr. Lindholm's shoes. I have looked at their soles now for weeks on end. Without thinking too much about it, I buy all three pairs. The following Wednesday, I heel myself eagerly into the black ones, point my feet at Dr. Lindholm all hour. I take note of the shoes she is wearing, brown slip-ons with a heavy lug sole, and I seek them out shortly after at Bergdorf's. I slip my doppelgangers on the following week. The blue loafers come out one week; two Wednesdays later, the crocodile. I march in, week after week, wearing Dr. Lindholm's shoes from the previous session, giggling inside, nearly bursting out loud the week she repeats and our shoes match. *Notice, notice!* I wait for her eyes to fall to my feet, the vague, building puzzlement. I wait for her to put the pattern together.

Another day, Duncan asks if he can see me in his office. He smiles savagely as he tells me Pharmax has another project for us and I've been requested to work on it, specifically. "They're planning to introduce several human products for animal use and the publicity needs to go just right," he says. "For some reason, your name seemed to make them feel good." His lips work into a sneer as he speculates aloud about what special attributes I may have to offer that would have the boys at Pharmax asking for me by name.

"Stand up," he says.

I do. "Why?"

"Just wanted to check on the length of your skirt."

"Yeah? Did you want to borrow it? I think you'd find it a bit snug, no matter how hard you've been working on that V-physique." I gather my things and give him a wink as I leave.

Some days I'm so light I could almost fly, like someone came in and replaced my brain with helium during the night. And flying around, I continue to wonder: What if there's nothing wrong with me?

Chapter 8

I can't sleep. I can't sleep. It's 2:07 A.M. and Robert isn't home yet, a fact I know well because my eyes won't stay shut. Despite my most strenuous efforts, they keep snapping open and staring into the green LCD readout that glares at me from his side of the bed. On my side there's a little crystal clock, an engagement gift from one of Robert's relatives, who actually believes in such things, and if I could only train myself to turn my head toward that, I would be okay. But I can't sleep when Robert isn't home, and I've grown accustomed to facing his pillow, either as reassurance that he is there or reminder that he is not.

I have spent most of the last two hours thinking, but about what, or about who, I couldn't say. Not about tonight's session with Dr. Lindholm, and not about what tomorrow's workday holds in store for me, but just—things. Suits at Barney's. Children's television shows, *Barney* and *Sesame Street, The Electric Company*. How beavers build their dams. The Latin name for platypus, *Ornithorhynchus anatinus*. Anna, anna, a-na. The name of Duncan's girlfriend, a party promoter with a face like a dried-apple doll. The mysteries of childbirth. What it would feel like to get shot, if the stomach or the knee would hurt worse. What the inside of my grandmother's house looked like.

I can't sleep.

Two-oh-seven becomes 2:08, 2:09, 2:10. Two-ten is twenty, two times five; a ratio of one to five. Two-ten is an impossibly fast mile, an abysmally out-of-the-money Kentucky Derby finish. I try counting sheep, but they won't behave. They leap trains instead of fences, turn into Tater Tots and leave fat greasemarks on my pillow. They float off in the air like balloons and I have to send out armed guards to pull them back.

When Robert and I were first together, he made the mistake of asking what I found attractive in him, and I made the mistake of telling, and the answer was this: he made me sleepy. We were friends for almost four months before we started dating, and in that time I'd had ample opportunity to get over my earlier misimpression that Robert was anything but handsome. I was a sucker for his blue eyes and his cleft chin and the oddly sensual habit he had of tracing his index finger across his bottom lip when he talked, but my attraction to him wasn't anything as superficial as that. He made me want to go to sleep, which wasn't something anyone else had ever done. It was about the highest compliment I could give.

"Sleepy?" he had said incredulously when I told him. We were lying naked, chest to chest, after we had made love for the fourth time ever and back when I was still keeping count. Already I felt drugged by the heavy thud of his heart. "I make you sleepy? You don't say. Gee whiz, don't I feel like a stud."

I kissed his chest and licked the hollow just below his sternum, still salty with sweat. "Yeah, sleepy." I spoke into his skin. "It's a compliment." And it was. In all the years, with all the guys I'd slept with, I'd never once stayed over or let any one of them sleep in my bed. If I was at a guy's place, I'd wait for him to pass out and then wriggle out from under him, maybe leaving a note if I knew his name, but more commonly just taking off. At my apartment I'd have him out the door practically before he was out of me, leaving no room for interpretation as to whether I had extended an invitation to stay. There was just something stomach-wrenching about the false intimacy of stale breath and second-day underwear. It made me too crazy to breathe, never mind going to sleep.

"Well, you could have fooled me. To me, sleepy sounds like a code word for, oh, I don't know, *bored,* maybe."

If anything, it was a code word for *safe.*

Robert had hemphed and hawed, trying to get something better out of me, but I had only giggled and shut my eyes, wiggling up to tuck my head under his collarbone. "Yeah, sleepy, you know. Just like this." Because as far as I knew he wasn't serious; as far as I knew, I was the one who had fallen in love first.

The beginning was less than auspicious. That first morning I woke up in Robert's apartment, after checking his hands for stigmata, I made a second graceless attempt to leave. I was humiliated by my girlish blushing and the tremor he was nice enough to ignore in my voice. He persuaded me to shower first, offering me both a chair to shove under the doorknob and a clean shirt to replace my blood-, beer-, and puke-splattered one. While I was showering, he ran to his corner store and returned with saltines, tomato juice, and Alka-Seltzer.

"Old college trick," he'd assured me with a grin, balancing the offering on a cutting board on the edge of the bathroom sink.

"Really?" I helped myself to a slug of the tomato juice and grimaced at my pale, puffy reflection in the bathroom mirror. "What about the hair of the dog that bit you?"

He shook his head negatively, not following.

"Beer. Vodka. I always just kept drinking."

I forced down Alka-Seltzer and a couple of saltines, and once we both were sure my resultant hiccups weren't going to lead to full-scale vomiting, he called a car. He led me down to the street, opened the cab door for me, closed it between us, then changed his mind. He pulled it back open and slid in next to me, banging his head on the top of the frame.

"Ouch," I said. "Oh."

"Where to?" the cabbie asked.

I gave my address, West 17th Street.

"You wanna take Fifth or the West Side?"

"Uh, I don't know." I turned to Robert. "Where are we, anyway?"

"West Side," Robert said softly, to his hands.

At my apartment, after I had talked a spare key out of my superintendent, Robert stood in the doorway for a few minutes, looking around as if to assure himself that it was a perfectly normal Chelsea walk-up in which a perfectly normal person might live. I didn't point out that a crack dealer lived down the hall or that I was only doors away from several hourly-rate hotels. When he left, he handed me a card, explaining that it was his business card, his head ducking modestly. He said he had hundreds of them that he didn't know what to do with, but he had written his home number at the bottom and if I ever felt like calling him, just to grab lunch or dinner, or even the next time I was in a bar and couldn't find my tote bag, he hoped I would use it.

He laughed uneasily as he said it. I laughed right along with him and then dead-bolted the door and made a straight line to the kitchen cabinet where I kept the booze. I sat on the floor, skirt hiked to the tops of my thighs, clutching a new bottle of tequila with my bare feet like some alcoholic primate. I drank straight from the bottle, glaring at Robert's card, chugging hard, and, once the level of alcohol in the bottle was visible beneath the label, crying. "Fuck you, Robert J. Gilbertson, ESquire!" Between heaves, I yelled it to the cabinets at eye level. "Fuck you, you sanctimonious, patronizing, condescending piece of shit!" I screamed it to the roach traps and balls of dust beneath the sink.

When I was finished, I threw the empty bottle across the room, badly missing the lamp I was targeting, and stumbled to the bathroom to throw up. Later, I woke up, my good cheek pressed against the edge of the open toilet bowl, my hair spread out on the vomity water. "Zhesis chrise," I mumbled, flushing the toilet over and over. I watched dumbly as my hair swirled on the surface like some giant, thousand-legged water spider and then stumbled off to bed and a spinning sleep.

That Monday, Robert called me at the office. Without even identifying himself, he said, "So I see you're an advertising hotshot. This is all finally starting to make sense."

"I'm not in advertising," I fired back. "I'm in public relations. There's a difference. Who is this?"

"It's Robert Gilbertson." He sounded hurt. Oh, Jesus. My heart flared, ridiculously. "You know, the guy from the Bear Bar? You crashed at my apartment, I bought you saltines? Beginning to ring a bell?"

"Robert, hi, oh. Sorry, sorry. It's not like I was expecting to hear from you, you know. Sorry. Shit, I'm sorry. How did you get my number?"

"I stopped by the bar after I dropped you off. I didn't find your missing friends, but someone had found your tote bag. It was in the ladies' room." *The ladies' room?* "Your name and address and all that were in your Filofax. I hope you don't mind. I tried to call you at home over the weekend to see if you wanted me to bring it by, but there was no answer, so"—Robert's voice trailed off on the implied question of my whereabouts—"I figured it was a safe bet to try you at work."

A range of responses seemed possible. First off, what was this guy, some kind of weirdo? Some anomalous New York, Clark Kent do-gooder with no better use for his time than the rescue of people and their personal effects? He must be some kind of freak, a pervert maybe, or the mastermind of a cell-phone black market scam hoping to find a fully charged Motorola in my bag. Also, it seemed a bit presumptuous, claiming my stuff like he owned it or me. What's to say I wouldn't have decided to swing by the bar to pick my bag up, and then panicked to find it gone? And rifling through my belongings— but my stomach was melting. It was perfectly absurd. I remembered the unused Tampax, its wrapper shredded and filthy, still rattling around the bottom of my bag. My ear against the receiver felt like it was on fire.

"You didn't find two balloons of cocaine while you were poking through there, did you?"

"Not that I found, no. I didn't exactly go rooting through." His reply came stiffly.

"Damn." A pointed silence. "I was just kidding. Robert? You still there?"

"Yeah. Yeah. Christ, you scared me. I was getting ready to throw the whole thing out the window. Not exactly the best thing for my legal career, you know, holding a couple of grams of coke."

"I'm sorry," I said. "It was only a joke. Besides, two balloons would be much more than a couple of grams." I saw a moving flash of orange out the corner of my eye. I looked up and there was Hillary, hands on her chin, eyebrows raised, leaning over the edge of my cube. She was eavesdropping, perhaps lured by the mention of the fictional coke. I scowled and waved her away. She just grinned.

"So, anyway," Robert said, "I was thinking maybe I could take you to dinner, give you your tote bag back then."

An enormous silence followed, in which my brain served up a range of adamant responses: *Yes! Thank you! I'd love to!*—*It's okay, no trouble, you don't need to bother*—*You can take me, all right, but it ain't to no dinner.* And, alarmingly, rather improbably, *My God, but I love you.* My voice got there first, however: "No."

I heard him swallow. "No? Just no?"

My eyes filled and I closed them quickly, rubbing an imaginary spot on my forehead. "No, thank you. I don't think so." There was no point, no reason. Why make it harder?

"Why not?" he said, his voice a little indulgent now, recovered from the initial no. "You don't eat?"

"Nope. Sorry. Hunger strike."

"Oh. Well." The confidence was gone again. I could hear him breathing into the phone. My eyes were starting to leak. *Go away, please, just go away*. He sputtered for another minute and then suggested that he could have his courier service messenger the bag over. I said that would be great. He apologized for bothering me. I nodded mutely and hung up.

When I opened my eyes again, Hillary was still standing over me. She held out a tissue. "Who was that, Dee?" she asked, barely contained. "What was that all about?"

I continued to massage the spot between my eyes. "Nothing, Hil, forget about it," I mumbled. "It was nothing."

Over the next few weeks, Robert called a couple more times, on the flimsiest of pretenses. One of his banker buddies had just announced a merger deal on two big biotechs and he thought I might appreciate the heads-up. A friend of his mother's was participating in a pilot study for Orlistat and was looking for more information. Our calls always would end something like this:

"So, how's the hunger strike going?"

"Oh, just fine." I'd laugh feebly. "Freed about a dozen political prisoners in Peru last week. It seems to be worth it."

"Yeah? I know a great place that serves stale bread and gruel. My treat. I hear they donate all their profits to Amnesty International."

"Amnesty International's corrupt, don't you know that? They're almost as bad as the United Way."

That's usually about the point when my eyes would overflow and I would go from bewildered to furious at myself. I had no idea what was wrong with me, why the very sound of this man's voice made me cry. I wasn't a crier; I never had been. *It's no use,* the voice in my brain would say, loud and clear. *Get out, getoutgetout NOW.* "Anyway, I gotta go. Things are real crazy here today."

"Well, okay. But I figure you have to eat someday. Maybe next week?"

"Maybe."

I would stay mad for hours for coming so unglued and for not just telling the guy to leave me alone. I reasoned it was a chemical thing, some sort of weird hormonal imbalance. I wondered if pheromones could be transmitted by fiberoptic line.

Finally, one day, Robert asked the right question:

"Tell me something, Darien. I guess I'm a little slow. Should I just stop calling?"

"Yeah, thanks," I said quickly, before the other voices in my head had a chance to catch up. "I'm sorry. Yeah, you probably should."

And that was that.

I hung up, grabbed my bag and Hillary, and headed for the nearest bar. I drank for pretty much the next three weeks straight, through lunches, dinners, and entire weekends, through friends, paychecks, and an endless series of bars, until finally, on a Friday, I found myself quite by chance back at the Bear Bar with Hillary. We were beyond drunk and out of money, nodding around a table for four and trying to make eye contact with someone who might buy us a pitcher. I was scrounging through my bag for enough change to buy a pack of cigarettes and muttering to myself about proprioperception and the neurochemistry of bed spins when my fingers hit on a small rectangle of cardboard. I pulled it out. Robert's card, heavy, engraved letters on white linen, going gray from the filth in my bag. "Lookathis," I said. I pushed the card across the table to Hillary.

"Yeah? Whaddizit?" she said, holding it up to the light. "Robert J. Gilbertson, Esquire. Esquire. Ooh. Who's he?"

"Just a guy I know," I said, hiccuping. "Just somebody." Another hiccup. "Nobody." Tears smarted in my eyes.

"You should call him," Hillary said, and she seemed perfectly sober.

"Yeah? You think so?"

"Yeah. Definitely." She hiccuped. "Maybe he'll have enough money for cigarettes."

There is a payphone at the Bear Bar.

Twelve-thirty on a Friday night and Robert wasn't at his office. I left a message on his voice mail and tried the other number. Robert was at home. I snarled something about being back in our honeymoon suite, how he'd told me if I ever needed help I should just call, how Hillary and I needed cigarettes and it was an emergency because neither of us really smoked. The next thing I knew he was standing in front of me. The first words out of my mouth were addressed to his hair, which was sticking up in half a dozen places and even messier than I remembered. The first words out of his mouth were to the effect that he had been asleep.

"Asleep," I crowed. "Hah! At one on a Friday? What kind of loser are you?"

He told me, if I insisted on knowing, that he'd been on a date that had ended early because he was going to be in the office all weekend.

I was subdued only long enough to process this and come up with my next retort: "Oh yeah? How come if you're so busy and important, with this great new girlfriend and everything, what are you doing here?"

He stared at me for a minute and didn't say anything. I did my best to hold his gaze, though I knew my eyes were crossing and his face kept sliding back and forth. "I'm not really sure of that myself."

He called Hillary's fiancé and flagged down two cabs. He took me home. He watched me stumble into my apartment, cracking my shoulder on the doorframe. He set up a bucket next to my bed. On Monday, sober for a full forty-eight hours, I called and apologized. I told him, a little weakly, that I seemed to have ended my hunger strike and would like to meet him for lunch to apologize more thoroughly. I'd even pay.

His tone, when he responded, was almost fatherly. Chillingly polite. "I'm sorry, Darien," he said. "I think it's my turn to say no. I guess, I just, I—" He stopped for a minute and I felt myself rising to the challenge. "This is hard to say. I guess I didn't realize— Well, I don't seem much to be helping you. I think maybe it's just better if I didn't get in your way."

If there's anything that gets me going it's the need to be right, to prove at all times that my charade is intact. I didn't want this guy seeing through me; I sure as hell didn't want him pitying me. I was as normal as the next person. At least when I thought about it, I could be.

I laughed. "Hey, man, I'm not asking you to marry me. I'm offering to buy you lunch, just to apologize. You know, a free lunch. In this town, that's a rarity. Even you should appreciate that."

The silence from his end was agony.

"Really, no shit." I couldn't keep myself from continuing. "I went to Swarthmore, and something like seventy percent of all Swat graduates end up marrying other Swatties, so statistically speaking, you're perfectly safe. Well, imperfectly safe. I'll let you pick the place. You can bring a friend if you want. I swear my blood alcohol's point oh-oh-five or lower today."

Robert sighed. "I didn't get into Swarthmore. They were the only school I applied to that rejected me."

"Well, then, see? I'm here to atone. This could be your big chance for revenge."

He was kind enough not to point out that rejecting me in return now would be the move best resembling revenge. Over lunch, we talked about work and I drank sparkling water. He didn't ask questions. He told me about the merger he was working on, delivering contracts on the sale of a German data networking company. He asked my opinion on a couple of biotech companies whose products I'd worked on. I asked why antitrust laws were applied uniformly across industries when the synthesis of brainpower and cash burn generated when joining two major pharmaceutical firms could produce advances that would more than outweigh any fair market issues. He looked at me a long minute, grinning, and said, "I don't know, Darien. I don't have any idea." For some reason, we both started to laugh.

Soon we were meeting for lunch biweekly, and then biweekly became weekly, and then lunch became dinner, and then dinner and a movie, and then dinner and the theater. Tickets to a concert. A hockey game. The ballet. We had a standing Saturday night date in short order, where our conversation evolved from work to family and then to ourselves. I was honest with him, even as he grimaced through stories of high school exploits and college parties, and he would say, over and over, "But you're not like that, not sitting here. That's just a defense, it's not the real you, the one I'm talking to right now. You're not like that at all." I believed him, I wanted to believe him; maybe I was mistaken about who I was, after all.

Robert was the oldest of three. He had a younger brother, David, who lived in Boston, and a sister, Kate, in a graphic arts program at Berkeley. His father was a portfolio manager for a midwestern investment management company, his mother a homemaker, the immediate past president of the Winnetka Garden Club. David was the athlete. Kate was a year my junior, the artist, the family rebel; I reminded him of her, just a little. She drank too much. I raised my eyebrows when Robert told me this, stroked an imaginary Freudian beard, and said, "Ah-*hah,* Herr Gilbertson, now vee get down to it: de sup-lee-mated Narcissus komm-plex!" Robert was the good son, the dependable one.

I told him about my family, laughingly, going light on details. I told him that I was poor, that my mother got married a lot, that I had three half brothers named after airports, all dumb as stumps: Kennedy, Macarran, and Logan.

"No shit?"

"No shit. I was named after Darien, Connecticut. My mother really wanted to name me Greenwich, but she didn't like the nickname, and so—" I shrugged my shoulders. "Second best."

Robert accepted without questioning that I never spoke to any of them—not the airports, not our lunatic mother—and when he asked about my father, I just shrugged and said, "Beats me." He quizzed me about ex-boyfriends, serious boyfriends, and I swore up and down that there weren't any. There weren't any. I asked him about ex-girlfriends and he looked somewhere left of me as he talked about Allison, a Titian-haired junior associate he'd dated for a year and a half and thought he would marry. I asked him what happened to her, twisting with insecurity: "Oh, God, don't tell me. She went and died on you or something, stepped on a land mine while feeding starving children in Sudan."

"No." Robert brought his eyes back to mine with a squinted smile. "She ran off with a partner in our London office. He left his wife and three kids."

Robert never made the slightest move on me, never acted like anything other than a big brother or gentleman. He would ride with me or walk me home every night, holding doors and elevators, never trying so much as to take my hand. I figured he thought me freakish, or too much of a child, or that I bore more of a physical resemblance to Kate than he was willing to admit. I worried—I knew—that he compared me to Allison and found me grievously lacking. After about four months of this nonsense, I blew it all up.

He was dropping me off after seeing *Miss Saigon,* and we'd been standing in my open doorway for at least half an hour, talking, pissing off my neighbors, no doubt. We'd said goodnight four or five times and Robert was still standing there. The hall light was off. He said, "Well, then, I guess I really should be going." His fingertips traced the doorjamb, just to the left of my cheek, and I watched him watch them, drifting lightly over the peeling paint. He was smiling, the corners of his mouth quirked up ever so slightly. My eyes went from his hand to his mouth, lingered on the geometry of his jaw, and then moved to his throat. I swallowed hard. He smiled down at me. His blue eyes flashed in the dim light, his dimples deepened, and I couldn't think of a damn thing to say. I took a deep breath and plunged toward him, kissing him the only way I knew how: deep and hard, our teeth clacking metallically. He was the first to break away, and I held my breath against the sudden horror filling up inside me.

He reached into his mouth like someone fishing for a popcorn hull. His finger came away wet with blood. He examined it with apparent fascination, rubbing pink saliva between his fingers.

"Ow," he finally said. "What was that for?"

My heart rattled foolishly in my throat. My voice sounded childish, helium-filled, around it. "I don't know. I wanted to. I just felt like it."

He looked up from his inspection. One eyebrow arched up. There was blood on his lip. "You wanted to do that? You mean that's how you kiss someone when you *want* to kiss them? I thought it was some sort of sadomasochistic cannibalistic torture thing. You know, punishment."

My heart was beating up my rib cage now, screaming, Idiot! Idiot! "Fuck you, Robert," I quavered. "You can just go to hell." I started to turn away, reaching for the door, ready to slam it on his stupid fingers, but he caught me by the wrist. Smiling now, looking like some sort of ghoulish transvestite in his blood lipstick, he drew me toward him.

Cradling my face with both hands, he whispered, "Dee, I'm not laughing at you. I think it's time for you to learn how to kiss like you like it, that's all." And then his mouth closed over mine, softly, and I felt my heart beat heavy and slow, like I'd been drugged, and I melted into him, utterly. He moved us inside like we were one body, like I was a little girl, dancing on his shoe tops, and he closed the door behind him without looking. And he stayed. I slept for days.

Chapter 9

D arien!"

    I jump and knock my cast against the underside of my Filofax, which flips up and then reverses toward my lap. My eyes are wide open, have been wide open, but I've been caught sleeping all the same, and I'm not the only one wise to this fact. As I straighten my book in front of me, Duncan gives me a menacing smile.

"Thanks for rejoining us, Darien," he says. "Hope we weren't interrupting anything too important." A little wave of laughter rolls across the conference room. A dozen pairs of eyes crinkle at me or look politely away.

Duncan cocks his head to one side, questioning, pseudo-kindly, and says, "Carl just finished running us through the market segment analysis and George Springer raised a question about penetration. Carl doesn't have the data in front of him, but we thought you might have some ideas."

As he speaks, Duncan removes Carl's last overhead from the projector, thinking he's laid the perfect trap, that I have no idea what market he's talking about, or possibly, even what meeting I'm in. We're at Pharmax, of course, pitching the PR for the pet pharma line. That Duncan would ask me to talk about market competition is as obvious as it's bizarre; he's caught me fucking up. He smiles, and the glare from the empty projector reflects from his forehead and glasses. I swap a glance with Carl, who thrusts his tongue against the inside of his cheek and then lifts his shoulders in an innocent, beats-me shrug.

I had zoned out thinking about last night's appointment with Dr. Lindholm, whom I'd told about losing my virginity to a Cleveland lifeguard the summer I turned sixteen. The story had come out in response to a question she'd asked about the first time I hurt myself, and I spoke in brutal detail, describing minutely the raw scrapings of my insides and outsides, the smell of sour towels, the taste of cheap beer. Dr. Lindholm had listened carefully. At the time Duncan interrupted me, I'd been replaying our conversation and realizing I'd omitted an interesting detail. I'd forgotten to tell her how I'd slipped on the wet floor after all was said and done and hit my head on a bench. I'd had a lump the size of an egg for weeks, and for some reason, I think I might have spent a couple of days in the hospital.

Too bad for Duncan that I caught a glimpse of Carl's overhead as he was sliding it off, and even worse, that I'd gone through a bunch of competitor annual reports on the ride to Eastman last Friday, when I was particularly bored. It may be far from my purview, but I'm all over this penetration stuff.

"No, you're right to ask, George," I say, turning to face the client. "Penetration is a key issue, of course, and pet pharma is the fastest-growing segment of the animal health market. The Animal Health Institute in Washington estimated the market at three billion in revenues last year alone. That's small potatoes compared to human drug revenues, of course, but the growth rate is remarkable at roughly twenty percent per year."

Out of the corner of my eye, I see Duncan frown. George smiles. Duncan clears his throat and makes a show of looking at his watch, then returns, abruptly, to his feet. "If I can make a suggestion, I'd like to move that we take this conversation off line, in the interest of time.

I've put together a media list and some financial projections that I know you're going to want to see, and I'd be more than happy to have my people pull together some additional information on this market stuff that we can look at next week. What say you, boys? Sounds like a good excuse for eighteen holes up in Westchester to me." Duncan smiles around the room, baring his little corn-niblet teeth.

George rubs his jaw, then waves a dismissive hand. "No, that's okay. I think we've got a couple minutes to spare on this, as long as Darien doesn't mind."

I look at Duncan, who glares at me steadily. Against the table, he pantomimes a cutting motion. I give him my sweetest smile. "Not at all, George. I certainly don't mind."

I take my few minutes, holding forth on competitor products and manufacturing locations, the barnwide hole in the market for generics. When Duncan's *ahems* escalate to full-scale coughing, I begin my wrap-up. I explain to George that an important plus for Pharmax is that the FDA doesn't require the years of clinical testing for pet products that it does for human drugs. Once a company has the product, it can get it out fast. "You guys already *have* the market for pet anxiety meds," I assure him. "It's up to us to prove to Wall Street that it's big and growing fast."

George nods vigorously, and I hear pens skritching up and down both sides of the table. I smile sweetly at Duncan. "All set." Duncan asks if he could trouble me to lower the lights for better viewing of his presentation and three different men leap up to do it for me.

I lost my virginity a week before my sixteenth birthday—terrified of the stigma of "sweet sixteen and never been fucked," I suppose. The guy was a friend of Ken's, just looking to get laid, and I thought I was cool. His name was Jeff Kaster. He wasn't even a real lifeguard, a beach lifeguard; he and Kennedy worked at the Garfield Heights Reservoir.

We'd landed on the outskirts of Cleveland just after Memorial Day and I'd done my best to spend the summer inside, reading—out of protest, out of hatred for my mother for picking us up and moving us for the second time in as many years. She was in the process of divorcing husband number four. At least twice a week, though, I ended up at the reservoir, making the scowling trip over to check on Kennedy on my mother's Bourbon-fueled exhortations. Ken was a pot-head, smoking so much dope that Mom had stopped buying oregano, and I always figured she sent me out of some twisted sense of civic duty that her son not be allowed to let anyone drown.

When I went, I would sit as far away from Ken's station as possible, and that meant Jeff's end of the beach. Jeff would talk to me, whether I wanted him to or not. Most days he invited me to the parties the lifeguards threw after the reservoir closed for the night, and for months I'd put him off with an expansive menu of demurs. I had gas. I had to bleach my mustache. My stepfather had already asked me out. One night, though, I thought, *What the hell.* I knew my mother had a date and Ken would be getting wrecked. By the time I returned to the reservoir, leaned my bicycle against the cyclone fence, and wriggled back into the right places in my bandanna top and cutoffs, Michael Jackson was screaming from a boom box and Ken was already gone—sitting around another bonfire, no doubt, in search of the perfect stone.

The air smelled of musty wood and vegetable water trapped under a heavy hood of humidity. From the edge of the parking lot, the bonfire looked hazy, as if set upon a screen. At the edge of the beach I slipped my shoes off and curled my toes in the pebbly, still warm sand. Jeff was near the fire, bent over a cooler, wearing his lifeguard shorts. His voice was loud and thick and he missed badly alley-ooping a beer to another lifeguard.

"Anybuddy gotta pen?" he shouted. "Dude, you gotta pen? I'm shot-gunning this one. Or a funnel. At school last year I funneled three beers at once."

Nobody turned to greet me as I edged toward the fire. I opened the cooler and took two beers in each fist. The heat of the fire pressed against my bare stomach and cheeks. I backed away from the orange flames and shadows and opened my first beer in the purple dark, feeling anonymous and adult as the tinny slide of Pabst Blue Ribbon hit the back of my throat. I watched Jeff stagger from one knot of girls to another, holding out beers, grabbing at shorts and tanned, exposed skin.

I drank three beers fast, burping, burying the pop-tops in the sand. My head felt pleasantly large, vague. I was halfway through my fourth when Jeff finally saw me. "Hey, Dayton," he said. "Hey, babe. I been looking for you."

The ground lurched out from under me as I stood to meet him, and I reached for his bare chest for balance. Immediately, his hand was on my left breast, squeezing it like a small, overripe piece of fruit. I squeezed his pec right back. For a minute we stood, not talking, gripping one another's chests as if someone had Krazy Glued us in some approximation of a joke. Jeff's thumb snuck over and flicked my nipple through the thin material of my bandanna top. He asked, "You wanna go up to the guardhouse?"

I shrugged and let go of his chest. His twanging fingers rolled my nipple and I said, "Sure."

I knew perfectly well why Jeff and I were heading up to the guardhouse, of course; I knew it as clearly as if we had negotiated the details in advance. When I told Dr. Lindholm this, she had pushed for the why, of course. *But why, Darien? Why did you do it? What were you feeling that made you decide to have sex then?* I will stick to the day I die with the story that I just plain wanted to, was curious what it was all about, and that a night I was drunk in August seemed as good as any else.

The roar of the fire, the music, sounded a long way off from inside the guardhouse. Jeff pressed me to my knees, his tongue urgent and slimy in my mouth. He pushed my top up and his shorts down and I wriggled out of my underpants and a few blunt shoves later he was in. It was an event markedly short on technique: penis against vagina with a *stub-stub-stub,* some manual fiddling I didn't quite follow, and then one big, burning push. Jeff groaned as he sawed back and forth, "Oh, baby, oh, *baby!*" and when I laughed, he put his hand on my mouth. But I kept giggling until tears came behind the gritty weight of his hand; I couldn't help it. He sounded ridiculous, just like I'd read in *Forever,* and from outside I could hear voices, talking and laughing as if something so ludicrous couldn't possibly be taking place.

When I got to the end of the story, Dr. Lindholm had looked at me like she was going to cry. "That's a very sad story, Darien," she said.

I knew better than to disagree with her. Five years ago, Robert had had pretty much the same reaction, though he'd gone a little further with it, pulling a hamstring in Central Park and dreaming for three nights of beating Jeff silly. I myself didn't see what was so sad. I thought it was pretty darn funny, truth be told, and remained proud of myself for handling the situation with such aplomb. Nobody had told me sex was going to be so undignified or so messy, with so much grabbing and groaning and exposing of unsightly body parts. Jeff had passed out when he had finished, as if all that heaving and whimpering had taken his utmost effort, and I lay there with him on top of me, studying the ceiling and spiderwebs. When I rolled him off me, I watched the way his penis inched back into itself like a frightened mouse. Now I told Dr. Lindholm, "Yeah, so I hear."

She said, "And what happened next?"

I put on my best thoughtful scowl. Hmm. Let's work on this to-gether. "I don't know," I told her. "I don't remember."

When Carl and I get back to the office, Duncan is, suspiciously, already there. He'd excused himself from the lunch portion of the pitch with profuse apologies to George Springer and claims of a conflicting appointment. Judging from the flush on his cheeks and the damp on the fringe of hair that curls toward his collar, his appointment was with the gym. Hillary told me recently she overheard him telling the Hospitals and HMO's manager, Marsha Moore, that he'd hired a personal trainer at Crunch who had him doing step aerobics. He'd lifted his suit pants to the knee and pointed his foot, showing off the hard ostrich egg of his calf.

He's lying in wait, leaning half across Carl's cubicle, fiddling with Carl's boxing nun doll with deceptive contentment, and we don't have a chance to take off our coats or drop our bags before he ushers us into his office for the tongue-lashing we both know to expect. On the ride downtown, Carl and I had taken bets: which one of us would Duncan go after first? I feel myself grow fifty dollars richer as Duncan starts in on Carl, not even bothering to close the door. For about ten minutes he struts and scolds, describing the sanctity of PR work, railing away about how bad we look as a whole when one of us doesn't know the easy answers. Dark Rorschachs of sweat grow beneath his armpits, and I wonder what he's going to have left for me. Carl crosses and recrosses his legs, hostility coming like radiation off his skin. I nudge him with my elbow. *We just need candles here,* I mouth. A few rounds of *Give Peace a Chance.*

Abruptly Carl and I are both dismissed. Carl turns to me, incredulous. I rise from my seat, palms lifted to indicate my own bafflement, and Duncan snaps himself a quarter turn in my direction. "Darien!" he says. "Listen sharp. I'm forwarding a message from George Springer to your voice mail. He'd like you to run the campaign." He turns his back to us and begins jabbing numbers on his telephone keypad. "Shut the door behind you, please."

Outside, Carl grabs my arm.

"Coffee," I say. "Atrium. Now."

"What the fuck was that? I just got fired, and you got promoted for talking back in front of clients. Your shit just doesn't stink."

I laugh, the safest reaction I can think of. "Carl," I say, "you didn't get fired. You just need a cigarette. C'mon. I'll buy. I'll even throw in a cup of coffee for free."

For a second, Carl flashes into business mode. His face settles into contemptuous lines. "A whole cup of coffee? You don't say. Mighty white of you, Darien."

Cut the shit, I want to say. *That wasn't my fault and you damn well know it.* "Don't you mean yellow?"

Carl holds my glare coldly and then starts walking. "If the shoe fits."

We end up not in the Atrium but a place down the street, hunched over a table with the oak veneer peeling up. Although it isn't even three o'clock, the place is packed and the air hangs blue with smoke. It makes me think of those elementary school safety videos about fire, *Stop-drop-and-roll*; it makes me think of those Tot-Finder stickers we got to put on our bedroom windows, those neat reflective hot-dots you could put on your shoes. I see them, strips of spongy red circles on white paper, like button candy, my thoughts moving with liquid ease. *Hot-dots, hot-tots, I guess that's what you'd call a kid on fire.* I think about sharing this insight with Carl, but he, across the table, still looks in need of a snuffing himself. He's practically chewing on his cigarette and I can't be certain the smoke around his head isn't coming from his ears.

"No offense, Darien, but I just can't fucking believe it," he says. "I mean, you're the one who made Duncan look like shit, am I right? All I did was space some information he never asked me for. I really should quit. I really should just fucking up and quit. I mean, I'd have taken that job at Harvard if I wanted to spend my life sucking up to assholes."

"Oh, Carr-*ulh*," I say. "Come on. You know you can't take Duncan seriously. He's just got his panties in a wad and he's looking for somebody to step on." I reach for my mug and take a swallow.

"In fact, he's probably back at the gym right now, imagining your face on his little aerobics step." I laugh. "He's probably sweating his little heart out in his little class, picturing someone else he needs to climb over to claw his way to the top with each step." I put on my best Duncan voice; affect only the hint of a lisp: "There's Carl! Eh! Right on his face! There's Darien! Eh! Stupid bitch! Hillary! Eh! Marsha, in Hospitals! Ned, in Biotech! Dr. Weller! Chip Pederson! Dr. Witherspoon! Eh!—Eh!—Eh!"

With each name I make a little grunt and raise a casted fist in the air the way I see women in the step classes doing at my gym. I describe Duncan in a spandex thong and leg warmers; a matching headband parked like a honey-glazed doughnut between his glasses and shiny crown. We're at a place not unpopular with other hoi polloi of Boylan, but I don't try to keep my voice down. I don't particularly care. Finally, Carl bursts out laughing. When he stops, he wipes his eyes.

"Don't take this personally, Darien, but I hate you. You're like the Teflon woman or something, everything always under control."

I give Carl a triumphant smile, but when I flex my fist in my cast, it hurts, sending a knife of pain up the length of my arm. I suppose he expects some kind of witty retort from me; I even open my mouth like I'm going to offer it, but it is only to make way for my third beer. I tip the glass back and chug, downing a four-dollar draft in half a dozen gulps, as close as I can get to taking it intravenously. The silky buzz of alcohol melts through my veins to my head and washes away all the words, gloating or otherwise.

My luck is holding when I get home. Robert isn't there, just his voice on the answering machine. I listen to the message as I brush the beer and cigarettes from my teeth and tongue: *Hey, Dee, just wanted to let you know that I'm going to be late tonight, sorry, sweetie. Ryan screwed up the proxy statement for IntraTac and we're supposed to be filing tomorrow, so I'm headed over to Sal Martin's office at Morgan to see if we can't straighten things out. Hopefully, it's not going to take too long, I'm hoping to be home by midnight, but you should definitely go ahead and eat without me. You know how it goes. I tried calling you at the office earlier, but Isabel said you left hours ago. Not sure where you went—*

I turn on both taps full blast to drown out the question rising in Robert's voice, and miss entirely the instructions on where to reach him and how. I figure he's probably asking me to pack for him; he's leaving tomorrow for a conference in Dallas and will be gone through the weekend. I'll do it anyway, I figure, to atone for the drinking, and just to be nice. I realize how badly I'm still buzzing as I throw his clothes on the bed, aiming suits for the hang pole on his garment bag, giggling as they miss and slump to the floor. I give him five ties even though the first half of the conference is casual dress, golf games and barbecues; load an armful of underwear into the bag. "You never know," I say to the empty room, not entirely sure what I mean.

I'm feeling more hyper by the minute, as if the alcohol were multiplying in my bloodstream. I'm a little bit hypoglycemic and haven't eaten anything since the Pharmax lunch. I know it's bad to be so drunk, and I'm somewhat amazed that I am. "Four beers," I complain. "It was only four beers. So bad."

Walter comes in and climbs on the bed to watch me pack, his expression glum. He knows the significance of a suitcase and his eyes are reproachful in anticipation of betrayal: another incarceration at Uptown Dog.

"Hey, no, Walt, you got it all wrong," I tell him. "It's only Robert that's going away. I'm still here. We're not going anywhere. Just you and me, pal, hanging out here."

He sighs and lays down next to Robert's bag, his chin on his paws, Eeyore-sad, unbelieving. I sling the bag to the side and jump up next to him on all fours.

"No, man, I'm telling you, you got it all wrong! I'm staying here and we're gonna have fun. You and me!"

His head pops up and I reach for his belly, scratching, tickling, rolling him from side to side. He grunts and thrashes a little, trying to stay upright. "Wally-wally," I say, pretending to bite his belly, "Wally-wally-bo-bally. That's my dog! That's my dog."

I flip him over and he barks once, in protest, then is immediately on his feet. I lunge for him and press on his backside, trying to get him to sit, planning to pull his paws out from under him and roll him over again. He wriggles away and stands at the far end of the bed, tail and ears up, alert, anxious. Pussy-dog.

"*WALLY!*" I scream and leap forward.

He shies hard and his haunches jerk underneath him, his tail pressed flat against his legs. I laugh and dig my fingernails into the comforter. "Scaredy-dog," I bellow. "You big scaredy-dog!"

His eyes roll white. He barks at me and I bark back, big Rottweiler *roof-roofs* that burn my throat. I bare my teeth. I make a tackling dive at him and he flips backward off the bed, twisting over the footboard. He hits the blanket rack and then the floor with a loud, scrambling crash and a cry. He's a flash of white gold as he races out the door.

The room seems suddenly, awfully, quiet, whirling in big, silent *click-click-clicks* around the bed. "Oh shit," I say.

When I go find Walter he is on his bed, back tucked firmly into the corner, and he won't look at me at first. "Walter," I groan, on my hands and knees. "I'm so sorry, I'm so sorry, baby-dog. I didn't mean to hurt you, puppy dog, I didn't mean to hurt you, honestly." I crawl toward him. I don't blame him for being angry. I hurt him. I hurt my dog. "Walter, honey, are you okay? Did I hurt you? I didn't hurt you, did I? I'm sorry, Mommy's so sorry. Please forgive me, honey-dog."

He does.

He turns his big eyes toward me, human pools of liquid brown, and I hold out my good hand to sniff. He licks it once, timidly, his pink tongue just testing my fingertips. His eyes hold mine and I feel the swipe of rough velvet the length of my palm, and then he noses my hand up to the top of his head.

Chapter 10

I hurt my dog. I hurt my dog.

It is morning, Robert's gone and I'm hungover, but not enough for it to be punishment. Walter is awake, happy, breathing doggy in my face as if he has forgotten, and maybe he has, but I can't let myself off so easily. He stands over me and licks my face, barking like a cheerful canine incarnation of the alarm clock I've slapped off three times already. I open one eye at him and then the other, and he digs at the covers as if he's going to unearth me. I lean against him as I pull myself into a sitting position. I drag myself out of bed and into the kitchen and turn the stove to high.

In the light of morning, it is much easier to hate myself, to recognize how badly I have gone astray. Drinking, smoking, lying, hurting Walter, a twenty-four-hour universe of the bad things I have been and done. My brain pounds against the casing of my skull and my knuckles pound against the hard walls of my cast. My tongue, huge, woolly, obtrusive, lifts dully in the dry basin of my mouth. I shift my head, drop my hand, swallow hard. Tiny flares of pain subside almost instantly. Not good enough, not nearly good enough.

Walter follows me to the kitchen, and I watch for a limp as he pads across the tile. I stoop down on all fours to examine him for cuts or swelling, any tenderness. I pat each leg down carefully, starting in the back. His right hind leg feels hot, and when I try to flex it, he gives a short bark. He holds his leg cocked for interminable seconds before lowering his paw in cautious dips to the floor.

"Oh, *Walter*," I say. He licks the side of my face apologetically. I make him sit so I can check his front legs. When I reach the left, he puts his paw out for a handshake. I take it and he smiles expectantly. "Old buddy, poor old buddy," I groan into his coat, "you trusted me. I hurt you. I hurt you and you trusted me." He shoves his nose into the side of my neck and I reach up behind me, feeling across the counter for the jar of doggie treats.

The weekend after I threw myself at him and he stayed, Robert took me to his house in Eastman. We had our first fight there. It was a big fight, by my lights, at least as first fights go. It was the first time I'd had a first fight and I'd thought it meant our relationship was over. We had fought about Walter.

We drove four hours north through Connecticut in Robert's old green Honda, jabbering nonstop above the voice of the radio. Robert held my hand in his on top of the gearshift, and occasionally we sang snatches of one song or another. After a while, as we encountered more and more songs we didn't remember, we started making up dirty nonsense lyrics like a couple of twelve-year-olds. A Flock of Seagulls, Bryan Adams, the J. Geils Band rolled out of the speakers. We howled at each other, showing off.

"*Tempted by the boobs of another*," I sang to Squeeze, a song that reminded me dimly of a guy I'd slept with in college. "Tempted—" I beat the rhythm out on the dashboard.

Robert chimed in with the next few lines, his speaking baritone rolling up to a strained, toneless tenor. Something about his mother, the length of his penis, no butter.

Butter ended on an enthusiastic, warbling tremolo and I burst out laughing. Robert smiled modestly, under the apparent misapprehension that his lyric had been particularly good.

"Oh my God," I said. "You're awful. You can't sing a note!"

He frowned. "I can so. What do you think I've been doing for the past two hours?"

"I'm asking myself that very question."

"My mother always said I had a beautiful voice. I even sang in the cherub choir at church in third grade."

"Did they let you back for fourth?"

Robert's frown devolved to a scowl. "I was playing soccer then. I made the traveling team and the schedule conflicted."

"Uh-huh. But did they ask you back? Did they request your presence? Did you have to turn them down, with great regret?" I couldn't stop laughing.

Robert was silent a minute, grimacing at the pale asphalt. On either side, trees pushed by us, tall pines and brilliant maples with rusty leaves already collecting around their bases. Bon Jovi now sang above the hum of the tires and the old car's radiator, and, despite the thermos of coffee raging through my bloodstream and the early morning sunlight streaming through the windshield, I felt myself growing sleepy.

"I don't remember," Robert said finally. "I'll have to ask my mother."

"Yeah, you do that," I mumbled, leaning over to rest my head against his shoulder. "In the meantime, I think I'll pass on the lullabies." He jerked his shoulder—*Hey*—and I smiled myself to sleep.

I woke up to the lumbering gait of the car on an unpaved road. Robert was pulling into his driveway. I rubbed my eyes, and a foreign world squinted open in front of me.

"My God, Robert," was all I could manage. "It's beautiful. It's beautiful."

And it was. As we'd left Manhattan, before the song contest took over, Robert had offered all sorts of precautionary disclaimers about his weekend house: it was old, it was an unfixed fixer-upper, his lawn guy had quit in August. He'd bought it as a tax shelter, ex-girlfriend Allison had wanted it; his dad had thought it was a good investment. En route, he'd mentioned mice and a barn and I'd imagined something straight from a Wyeth painting. He'd undersold it, of course. The house was three times the size of anything I'd ever lived in, a white center-hall Colonial with two chimneys and an attached barn. A couple of shingles were broken or missing, and one shutter hung slackjawed on its hinge. Curtains flickered through an empty window on the second floor and mildew grayed the Cape Cod shakes under the windowsills, but it was perfect, paradise, the most beautiful thing I'd ever seen.

The house was surrounded by fields and a small orchard that bled into woods; rotting, ravaged apples dotted the yard and popped under the tires. I cranked down the car window as we approached and craned out for a better view. Walter, in the seat behind me, poked his nose out next to my ear. Flaming mountains, low hung with clouds and dusted with an early snow, rolled out on all sides, the Berkshires. As far as I could tell, the house was alone, only faint curls of smoke in the blue air giving evidence of neighbors somewhere beyond the trees.

"Yeah? You like it?" Robert guided the car down the rutted driveway and I studied his face. The question was deliberately casual. I could see full pride restored to the set of his shoulders, a hard spark of colonialism in his eyes. I felt like crying.

"Of course I like it. It—it's beautiful." I swallowed hard. "It's a real chick magnet. You must bring the ladies here when you really want to woo them."

His lips compressed in a quick pleat. "Just the ones I really like." He shook his head, then laughed. "You may want to reserve judgment on the chick-magnet factor until you have a look inside."

We pulled up in front of the barn, where the driveway widened into a turnaround. An uneven walkway of mossy bricks wandered through the tall grass to the front door of the house. I unbuckled my seatbelt and stepped out.

"Hey, this is funky," I said. The air smelled cold and clean, crisp with old hay and older apples. The barn doors gapped open about six inches and I hauled one all the way back, revealing rows of shelves, old bushel baskets, a small work table. "Cool!" I exulted. "Very cool. I bet someone used to use this as a farm stand to sell stuff from the garden. This was probably an operating orchard at one time."

Robert walked up behind me, carrying my coat and a dog collar. "It was. It's what, or I should say, it's one of, the things I liked about the place. There used to be an old cider press in there"—he motioned to a door to the right. "The guy who came to take it away said it still worked, one of those big, old-fashioned, manual-crank things, hand-lathed maple, probably worth a lot of money. I couldn't really see spending my weekends making cider, though, and it turns out that apple trees require a fair amount of maintenance in terms of spraying, pruning, pollination. Nobody had touched these in twenty years or so, so I wouldn't be expecting Gilbertson's Best out of them any time soon."

"Moonshine, maybe. Can I get in this way?" I turned to mount a short staircase that led from the barn to the house.

Robert fished around in his coat pocket and lobbed his keys in a soft underhand up to me. "It's the square key, the silver one. If you wait a second, I'll give you the guided tour. Reach up and throw the power main, will you?" The big silver circuit panel was next to my head, new, the negative of the old fuse box outlined in raw wood on the bare wall. I pushed the double bar marked MAIN to the *on* position as Robert crouched forward and whistled for Walter, the collar slung over one arm. "Here, Walt," he said. "Walt, here. You know better than that."

The collar in Robert's hands looked like the one Walter was already wearing, but with a small, plastic box, the size of a deck of cards, clipped to the side. Walter, circling the barn with his nose held high, came over reluctantly. Robert slipped his old collar off and buckled the new one on.

"What's that?" I said.

He rubbed Walter's head and sent him off. Walter moved toward the lawn, plowing through the high grass, lifting his leg against one of the closer apple trees. Robert climbed the stair behind me, took the keys from my hand, and shook the square one loose. He unlocked the door and swung me up, like a bridegroom crossing a threshold. He set me down with a grunt.

"Jesus, I'm getting old," he said. "I know you're not that heavy."

"Thanks, I think," I said.

Robert smiled down at me. "One of the first things I did get done, and when you take a look around, I know it won't look like much, is install an electric fence. That's the collar. The sensor costs a small fortune and he's always trying to scratch it off. He only wears it while we're up here."

The room was behind me, a tongue-in-groove-paneled study with worn leather furniture, built-in bookcases, and the first of the fire-places, but I barely saw it. I moved back toward the open door. "An electric fence? That's the collar?"

"Yeah," he said. "You've never seen one of these? There's tons of deer in the woods, and they like the apple trees. Rather than fixing the place, I've been buying acreage. I've got almost fifteen acres now."

I looked at Robert without saying anything.

"It keeps Walter from taking off after them. The first time I brought him up here, he was off like a shot—blam!" Robert smacked one hand on top of the other. "I wasn't sure I was going to see him again. He was just a puppy then, little Wally, off chasing ten-point bucks. Never had any luck, as far as I know. I called one of those invisible fence companies the same weekend, got the electric upgraded and the fence put in."

"I see," I said. I wasn't sure if I wanted Robert to shut up or step deeper into it. He paused a second and then made the choice for me.

"It's pretty sophisticated technology, actually. There's a transmitter in the barn that sends a signal to a receiver in the collar, and they both communicate with a wire at the edge of the lawn. If Walter gets too close, the receiver warns him off with a little jolt. It's like a computer, almost. It's really impressive. I bet the guy who invented it just looks at himself in the mirror every morning and smiles." Robert smiled himself.

"Really impressive?" I asked. "A little jolt? What—so—that's like a little shock box, or something? Electrocution behavior modification therapy?"

Robert's smile shaded just a little. "It doesn't hurt him, Darien. It's just a little thump, like static. It doesn't apply any real voltage unless you actually cross over the wire, and Walter's been trained not to do that. And besides, even that can't hurt too much. Every now and then, if there's something he really wants in the woods, he'll bust through. He wouldn't do that if it hurt." He laughed. "It's really kind of funny."

"Oh, and like you know this? I suppose you put on the collar yourself, gave it a try? I suppose you got down and explained it all to Walter in dog-ese, why he was being punished, why he gets to come up here and get the crap knocked out of him for no reason at all?"

Robert walked over toward me. His arms reached out for a big, paternal hug. His face was soft. "Darien, hey, it's okay. It's for his own protection."

I put up both arms. "For his own protection? A nice seventy-thousand-volt blast for his own protection? Why didn't you just put up a wooden fence, for chrissakes, like a normal person?" I backed away from him and ran through the doorway. The circuit box was still open and I flipped the main back off as I stumbled down the stairs and into the yard. Walter was sniffing the walkway, nibbling the grass that sprouted between the bricks. "Go, Walt," I yelled, rushing him and waving my arms. "Go, boy. It's okay. Run! The fence is off!"

Walter's eyes went wide, and he raced from side to side, barking. I ran, tripping over fallen apples, the long grass like fingers against my jeans. Where the lawn darkened to woods, I stopped. I doubled over and beat my fists on my thighs. *"Come on, Walter, it's okay!"* I screamed. "It's not on!"

Walter whined and turned to Robert. I ran back toward the house, closing in on the dog just as Robert did. I latched my fingers around the collar and dragged Walter toward the treeline. I'd show him. It was okay. He yelped, and Robert grabbed my upper arms from behind, pulling me backward toward him.

"Darien, stop, please stop," he said quietly. "He's trained now. It doesn't even matter if the power's on, he knows he can't go off the lawn when he's wearing that collar. All you're doing is scaring him."

I refused to come inside for hours. I sat on the broken stone steps and watched my breath unfurl in front of me. I dug my frozen fingers under my buttocks and rocked on them, my bladder full to bursting. When it got so cold that my feet no longer ached and my teeth stopped chattering, I took off my coat. Walter nosed the edge of the lawn, loping cheerfully after the few squirrels who didn't understand that they had crossed over into his kingdom.

"I'm sorry, Walter," I said, every so often. He raised his head and wagged his tail.

The sun set. Robert clattered and banged inside the house. The earthy scent of wood fire and roasting meat drifted out. I was starving. The door opened and Walter bounded by me. Robert stepped outside and sat down on the steps. He stroked my hair and kissed my forehead. He spoke into my skin, "Will you please come inside now?" His lips felt nice on my face. I did.

In bed that night, after we made love, Robert apologized. He said he finally got it. "I'm sorry, Darien, I'm slow on these things. God, I'm such an idiot! I just didn't realize." He pulled his arms around my abdomen so tight I felt air in my intestines shift.

"Didn't realize what?" I asked.

He said it slowly, as if he needed to introduce the idea carefully. "You. When you were younger, all that therapy you told me about. I couldn't figure out what had you so upset about Walter and that stupid fence, why it would matter. I wasn't thinking, or maybe I didn't want to."

I held my breath and kept completely still. When I didn't say anything, Robert rolled me onto my back, cradling my face between his elbows. There were no shades on the windows and the room was bright with moonlight, shadows from the moving trees throwing patterns on his face—handsome, marble, grave. I could smell the slight mustiness of the sheets, the dry dust of the old heating system. His fingertips touched my face and traced my hairline, seeking out my temples. He whispered, "You had electroshock therapy, didn't you?"

I laughed so hard I had to get out of bed. I laughed and laughed, cross-legged on the floor, flat on my back, kicking my feet in the air. I laughed until I couldn't breathe, until the tears collected behind my ears and glued my hair to the floor. "E-LEC-troshock therapy," I gasped. "Jesus, that's a good one. That's a great one!"

I turned, fetal-style, away from the bed. "I say, Dr. Freud, why don't we hook her up? It would be so much easier, don't you think, if we crafted a little collar with a box that she could wear? We could market it as a fashion statement, the *de rigueur* accouterment of the nineties."

Robert knelt beside me on the floor. "Darien, don't think I don't understand your defenses. The very fact that you're reacting like this tells me it's true."

"Oh, yeah," I snorted between gasps. "You really know me. You read me like a Dick and Jane primer. Darien Gorse response number four-seventy-two: when confronted with the painful truth, laugh hysterically." My laugh was turning to a wheeze.

Robert tried to pull me up in his lap. "It's okay, Darien, really. You can trust me. It's okay."

An awful, warm spasm gripped me, and for a second I couldn't breathe. It had nothing to do with electroshock therapy; it wasn't true. ECT had never even been suggested, and I might not have been averse to it if it had. *You can trust me.* For a second I was small, seven years old or maybe eight. I put my hands over my eyes. I said, "Robert, check your facts. ECT went out of vogue in the sixties. Hardly anybody does it anymore. Except, of course, a select handful of sadistic dog owners, who have, like, fifteen acres to protect."

I cracked up again and he left me on the floor, climbing back into bed. He muttered, "Jesus Christ. Forgive me for trying to care."

I lay there for a while, shifting my spine against the hard wood and listening to the indignant creaks of the bed from overhead. I was just beginning to drift off when Robert's voice came again. "I hope we don't have to go through this routine again the first time you see Walter go AWOL."

And of course, five weeks later, when he did—sniffing the air for the scent of a particularly enticing deer, looking back at us in our robes on the porch like a naughty child, head ducked in something like shame as Robert called to him threateningly, *Walter, no,* gathering himself up at the edge of the lawn and racing through the unseen enemy line, stopping stiff-legged midair, falling with a shaking thud and an inhuman cry, gathering himself slowly, dazed, tacking raggedly through the underbrush and fallen trees for the leaping deer he would never catch, not even without the 5,000-volt handicap—we did.

I conclude with more hope than conviction that nothing of Walter's is seriously injured. No longer willing to stand patient for my inspection, he begins backing against me, trying to maneuver his butt under my casted palm. He grunts a few times, as if giving instructions, as if I don't know he'd trade anything in the world for a good rub at the base of his tail. I shift my position to a squat and scrub him briskly with the rough fiberglass. His haunches drop out from under him, weak-kneed with pleasure, but I notice that he continues to hold his right leg above the floor. His nails slide across the tile and he pulls himself back up; every time his right paw touches the floor, he pulls it away. After about five minutes of this, *slide-touch, slide-touch,* I stop. My legs are starting to cramp. "Okay, buddy," I tell him. "That's it. This doesn't seem particularly good for either of us."

I reach up with my left hand for the counter, to pull myself up. My fingertips touch heat and jerk away. A bright yellow flash of pain races up my arm. I jump to my feet and address myself directly to the stove.

"I meant to make tea. Honestly!"

The livid orange burner glares at me, an empty, accusing eye. Heat rises off it in small waves, forming vague bends in the air over the clock. The teakettle sits on the burner opposite and I put my hand to it, as if touch is needed to confirm that it is cold, the gray coils under it off, and as my fingertips meet the heavy skin of the pot, I know they are burned. Just a little. The iron surface of the kettle is soothing, pebbly cool. Just a very little bit.

The fat orange coils give off a carnival glow, unreal and enticing, like Popsicles or Jell-O. The color is brash, alive, a challenge. The burner taunts me. I pass my hand over the plate, just casually, just testing. A fat cushion of air holds me up.

It wouldn't hurt at all, not at first, and when it did it would be a big, throbbing, restless ache, a delicate pulsing just at the surface, the kind of hurt clamped at night between thighs. Blisters would form like chrysalises, taut with serum, that when slit would run clear and fill again. Scar would form in thick, shiny strips, obliterating line and whorl. I imagine the tight, quick sear, the devotion of flesh to metal. I bring my hand closer, three inches, heat intense enough to bubble my fingertips. Already, throb balloons.

[118]

It wouldn't hurt at all, not at first. It would hurt good.

The world wavers and dances, the coils swim in the tears that come to my eyes. I look inside. I see Robert's sad face, I see Dr. Lindholm. I remember my promise. I imagine myself doing it, thrusting my hand downward through all that thick, red air, mashing my fingers into the screaming metal, skin boiling down to bone. I imagine sitting in Dr. Lindholm's office, trying to explain to her what I had done. I say, out loud, "You don't get another chance, Darien."

Walter pushes himself between me and the stove. I feel the heat of his body as he presses against my legs, leaning, hear him whine anxiety as the tight space fails to give. Without taking my eyes off the burner, I fumble with my right hand for the knob that turns the plate to *off*. Reach down, step back, find Walter's head. Though the coils are blurred beyond discernment, I keep on staring until ember drains to coal and steam no longer rises from the wet, fat drops that fall.

Chapter 11

W hat happened to your hand?"

"I got a new cast. It's blue." I thrust Dr. Bruce's latest hand-iwork forward and turn it side to side. "See?"

Dr. Lindholm doesn't even smile.

She is wearing an outfit I have seen before, black suede boots and black crepe wool pants, a cropped bouclé cardigan in mauve. Last time, she wore it with an Hermes scarf and tiny, discreet gold hoop earrings. Today she wears an elaborate, multicolored necklace of glass beads and earrings to match. Her husband, I have learned, is a jewelry dealer who does most of his work with estate sales for Sotheby's, which accounts for the pile of platinum and diamond on her left hand. She has had her hair cut since our last meeting and her bob now feathers girlishly around her ears. There are two new books in the case behind her left shoulder and her *DSM-IV* has been moved.

"I burned my fingers. It was an accident. Really, this time. They're hardly burned. I was sitting on the floor with my dog, in the kitchen, scratching him, and I reached up to pull myself up. I put water on for tea, but I put the kettle on the wrong burner." Though I hardly need them, I'm still wearing Band-Aids on my fingers. I pick at them instead of the deflating blisters on my fingertips.

"Uh-huh," Dr. Lindholm says.

"Look, I know what you're thinking, but I didn't do it on purpose. God, I'm not that stupid. We were just talking about this stuff a couple of weeks ago."

"I know we were." She nods her head at me.

I raise my fingertips at her and say, "I don't even really need these, the Band-Aids. I did it almost a week ago. They're more my scarlet letter, and I figured you'd notice them." I think, a little irritatedly, about how easily I could have gotten away with not bringing this whole business to her attention.

"Were you going to tell me about them, or wait and see if I noticed?"

"I don't know." I shrug. I can hear how annoyed my voice sounds. "Probably wait and see, I guess. I didn't figure it would take you long. It's not a big deal. I'm telling you honestly. It really was an accident. The important thing, I think, is that I didn't make it worse, which is my usual temptation, I told you that. Start with something little and make it worse. And I actually struggled with that. I looked at the burner for a minute, imagining how it would feel to do it, and I wanted to. But I didn't. I stopped. I remembered our pact and I stopped myself. Good Darien." I feel like Walter, wiggling expectantly, waiting for pats.

Dr. Lindholm studies me. "Good Darien," she says. She extends her hand to take mine. "Let me see." Her fingers are gentle, clinically expert, as she peels away the three Band-Aids. My fingertips look like tiny white brains. Sagging blisters blossom in the middle of each tip like tumors, marshmallow soft. I feel a stab of disappointment at how small and innocuous the burns look, embarrassment that Dr. Lindholm cannot possibly be impressed.

"That looks like it hurt," she says.

I pull my hand back. "Not really."

"What did Robert say?"

"Nothing." I press my naked fingers into my palm.

"Nothing? He didn't ask about the Band-Aids?"

"He hasn't seen them. He's been away since Friday morning, at a conference, in Dallas. He gets back tonight." I look at the clock. "He's probably already back. At the office."

Dr. Lindholm nods. "Are you going to tell him?"

The Band-Aids lie on the coffee table between us, folded up in little rectangles. I lean forward and drop them in the trash on top of a tight wad of tissues. I count the tissues—five—and see Dr. Lindholm extracting misery from another of her patients, delightedly, like a surgeon draining a cyst with a knife. Hold the bucket beneath, *drip-drip*, count it up, weigh it out. "Probably not," I say. "It's over with. I've told you."

"Well, thank you for that. Thank you for telling me."

"My pleasure."

Then she says, "Well, since you remember our deal, I'd like to keep going. What were you feeling when you wanted to burn yourself more?"

I think about it a minute and feel again the tug of temptation, desire, at the pit of my stomach. "I don't know. Excitement, I guess. Desire?" It seems like a strange word, and I wait for Dr. Lindholm's opinion. She shakes her head.

"No, I mean what were you *feeling*. Not here"—she points to her head—"but here." She points to her heart.

"Oh." My mind goes blank. I understand what she's looking for but I can't come up with anything. What was I feeling? Trying to comprehend my feelings is like trying to comprehend eternity, that clench-stomached, unconfinable impossibility you feel when you look up at a cloudless sky. *But there has to be an edge, a rim, a bowl to hold it. A solid wall that circles back on itself.* I try to think for a minute. I focus on her necklace, three interwoven strands of beads of varying shapes, sizes, and colors, perhaps none of them mauve. It's incredible. I'm not one for jewelry, particularly necklaces, which unfailingly exacerbate my tendency toward hives, but suddenly, I wish this necklace was mine.

"Darien?"

"I like your necklace," I say.

Dr. Lindholm hooks her thumb behind the necklace, lifting it up toward her chin to show to herself. She frowns down at it as if at something she does not recognize, a lobster bib someone has snuck up behind her and fastened unawares.

"Thank you," she says, dropping it back against her sternum. "It's Venetian glass. My husband bought it for me on a trip several years back."

Robert sometimes brings me little guest bottles of shampoo and soap from the Dulles Hilton or the Mandarin Oriental in San Francisco. Once, he pinched a can of macadamia nuts from the minibar. "Wow," I say. "Nice guy."

Dr. Lindholm smiles. "Yes." She waits. She tilts her head, like an Airedale. "But that doesn't have much to do with what you were feeling when you wanted to burn yourself, does it?"

"I suppose not. Unless I was feeling envious of you at the time."

"Were you?"

"I guess I was feeling mad at myself. I wanted to punish myself."

"Why?"

"Because I hurt my dog."

"You did?"

"Yeah. The night before. We were playing on the bed, and I flipped him and he fell off. He was scared." That's enough detail for this exercise.

"And you felt sad, too."

"Did I? I don't know."

"Your face just got sad."

"When? It did? It doesn't feel sad." I reach up and touch my face with both hands.

"Just then, when you talked about your dog."

"Well, I guess so. That's not exactly surprising, is it? I hurt my dog. That made me sad."

"What made you sad about it?"

I twist in my seat. "What wouldn't? I don't think I understand the question. I hurt my dog, who never did anything wrong to me, and that made me sad."

"Okay," she says. "Good. We're onto something, now."

"For him," I add. "Sad for him. Not for me."

"No?" Dr. Lindholm pulls her surprised-eyebrow routine. "Why did you want to tell me that? Why is that distinction important?"

"Because I do remember the stuff we talked about last week, whenever it was, and I know you're going to try to make this be about something it isn't, like all the times my mommy hurt me when I was younger and I didn't deserve it, and it isn't true. It's a total red herring. Nothing like that ever happened."

"Okay, then," she says. "So what did happen?"

"You mean, how did I hurt myself? What did I do? Or do you mean, how did I *feel* about it when I did?" I draw the word out sarcastically. The thing that nobody ever tells you about therapy—the thing, in fact, that they sometimes expressly don't tell you—is that there is a right answer to just about every question, and shame on you if you don't figure out what it is.

"I mean, how did your mother react, what did she say?"

Oh. For a change, it's the easy question, the one I can answer no problem. "Nothing, really. She wouldn't much comment on it."

"Nothing?" Dr. Lindholm looks skeptical; no, just surprised. "She wouldn't say anything? Forgive me, Darien, but I have a hard time believing that's true."

"Well, okay. Maybe not nothing, but definitely not much. Maybe something on the order of, 'Jeepers cripes,' or, 'Gosh darn it.' "

Dr. Lindholm's eyebrows come right over the tops of her glasses.

"You'd come home with a knee all blown up and bloody or your fingers dangling from the sockets and she'd say, 'Jeepers cripes'?"

"She didn't swear. It was her one great virtue. Honestly, I never heard her swear. I think it was a Midwest thing. She grew up in Iowa and always had the funniest names for things, davenport for sofa, chifforobe for dresser." A pause. "I don't know, I guess she'd usually tell me that was great, just great, what had I done this time, thanks a lot, Darien."

"How did that make you feel?" Dr. Lindholm's voice swoons low, now, soft and maternal. I squeeze my blistered fingertips into my palm.

"Well, I don't know. I mean, I expected it. She was right. I knew we didn't have insurance, or the money to pay for trips to the emergency room, for that matter, and that doing it was a real pain in the ass. Applying for free care, or whatever, getting the dirty looks and answering the awkward questions when she brought me in. I'm sure it was humiliating, and a little tedious, too. It happened all the time.

"And it's not like I was ever honest with her, ever told the truth about what happened. It's not like I came home and said, 'Guess what, Ma, I filched a petri dish out of Advanced Bio today and during study hall I broke it and carved little hearts and puppies on my arms. Wanna see?' I made stuff up, airtight stories, things she would never question. She wouldn't have had any other information to be working from. Why wouldn't she be mad?" I can tell my voice is rising and the look on my face is probably all wrong, but I just keep going and going, because maybe if I keep talking, Dr. Lindholm won't get a chance to ask the question I know she is really asking, *How did it feel to have a mother who didn't care what happened to you?*

I can talk for days about my mother, really, when I'm pushed to it. Just don't ask me to talk about how I feel about her. I just can't. You might as well ask me to talk about how I felt the day Pearl Harbor was bombed.

• • •

"Hey, Mom?" I enter my mother's room cautiously, hands cradled behind my back. "You busy?" She's lying on top of her bed, ankles crossed, head propped up with pillows. The shades are down and she is still wearing work clothes. An olive pantsuit showing a sheen of age where it stretches across her angled thighs. A nubby cream sweater, its bandeau collar slumped so promiscuously far down one arm I can see the fold at the side of her breast. Bronze pumps, tumbled off at the end of the bed. My mother is feeding herself continuously from a bowl of popcorn, smelling of butter and scorch even from the far side of the room. A burning cigarette sends up a curl of smoke just to the left of her elbow. Her head tips to the side as her hand crosses her face. She answers me without breaking the television's gaze.

"Mmm. In a second, Dee. This is the big scene."

It's ten to four and *General Hospital* is just winding up for the day. On the screen, Lila Quartermaine is confronting Alan about Jason, his illegitimate son. Monica, Alan's wife, lurks behind a banister, listening. Here at home, my mother's career as a furniture saleswoman is about to meet its own conclusion because she refuses to accept shifts that run past two-thirty in the afternoon. She is sleeping with the manager of the Pool and Patio Department, which both of us foolishly believe provides her something like job security.

I lower myself onto the edge of the bed and shift my hands to my lap. My knuckles pound with the movement and the weight of my legs. I straighten my index finger, feel the metacarpal roll, and a wave of lunch—yogurt, tannic and watery—rushes my throat.

My mother absently pats a spot next to the burning cigarette. "Sit here," she says, addressing herself to Alan Quartermaine. "Share-sies." She thrusts her bowl of popcorn at me.

"No thank you," I say. Silent tears runnel my makeup. The pain is delicious, enormous, agonizing. I fantasize about taking the offered popcorn, stuffing my face with it, and throwing up all over the bed. "Mom?" I let a note of pleading, of childishness, enter my voice. I snuffle a few times, loudly. My nose is leaking and I can taste the salty snot where it seeps between my lips, but I'm afraid to move my hand to wipe it off.

"Hon-e-ey," she protests. Monica has burst into the room and is weighing an heirloom vase to launch at Alan. Her eyes flash with fury. Alan smirks. Lila holds both hands to her cheeks in dismay. I lower my face to my arm and wipe my nose up the length of my sleeve. I jerk my head up and will myself to pass out. The school bus ride home was hard, much harder than I had expected. I sat in the back, rocking and slamming over every pothole and each sudden stop, the speed bumps at the entrance to the Lord Chesterton Estates. Finally, the *General Hospital* theme song blares on and the credits roll up. Mom sets the bowl of popcorn between us, picks up her cigarette, and clambers to the end of the bed to switch the television off. She snaps a floor lamp on.

"Hang it all! Now I have to wait until Friday to find out if Monica does it. I hate the way they switch the story lines around. Why do they always make you wait two days to find out what happens? I don't really think she'll leave him, though, do you?" She traces the faint lines in her forehead with her thumbnail, delicately, the burning cigarette still perched between her fingers. "The money's all his, they're in that great big mansion, and for a doctor she sure doesn't ever seem to work. And Alan Junior's only a baby." My mother's eyes take on a hard gleam. She freezes in her pose, kneeling, fingers on forehead. Her thumb etches frown lines like a toddler fingering a blanket, endlessly.

I let out a genuine sob. "Mo-om," I say.

"What, Dee?" she replies. There is vague irritation in her voice.

Supporting my wrist with my left hand, I hold my right hand out and the room spins. "I hurt my hand, at school." Sniveling. "I was at

[127]

the lockers, talking to this girl from my Latin class. The locker next to mine was open and I had my hand in it, not really thinking, I guess. The guy whose locker it is didn't see my hand and he slammed it shut, really hard."

It is not completely a lie. After I broke it, after the last swing against the bathroom tile, I had slammed my hand in my locker to lend my story authenticity. A depressed purple line runs diagonally from the heel of my thumb up toward my pinkie like a string through a thick piece of meat. My hand is swollen to double its size again and the line divides it in two, a faint dimpling of knuckles marking one side, a crest of broken bone the other. There is no blood this time, just the long, purple line and an angry mottling. Other than the color, mine could be the hand of a very fat person, sausage fingers, creased at the wrist.

"The school nurse said she thinks it's broken. She said we should go get some X rays done."

My mother looks at my hand without touching it. Her own hand comes down from her forehead and she takes a long draw on her cigarette. She exhales evenly, fixes me with a stare that is neither angry or empathetic, anxious or curious. Her face is unreadably, deliberately blank. It is as if with the exhalation she has emptied herself of emotion entirely; drained away her concern for Monica and her anger at Alan so there is nothing adamant, compassionate, or conspiratorial in her tone or her eyes when she puts down the cigarette and says, "I'll go get some ice. You stay put. I don't think it looks broken, do you?"

"Look," I say to Dr. Lindholm, "I took developmental psych. I read Harlow. I know where you're going with this and you're wrong."

"Harlow?" She asks as if she doesn't know.

"Yeah, you know, the rhesus monkey studies on comfort and attachment."

She continues to play along, looking puzzled, and, now, interested. "Say more about that. I'm not sure I follow."

I try to screen the irritation from my voice. "It was Harlow, wasn't it? He took a group of baby monkeys and gave half of them surrogate mothers made out of cloth and they all turned out normal, formed attachments and were able to comfort themselves, blah-blah-blah, and then he gave the other half mothers made out of wire and they were all screwed up. The hypothesis was that the monkeys with the cloth mothers were okay because they received comfort from their mothers and the other ones were messed up because their mothers were made of wire. Isn't that pretty much what you're driving at? Your big theory of my pathogenesis? That my mother didn't pay enough attention to me, so I did a bunch of totally insane stuff just to get her to prove that she cared about me, and then when she didn't, I did things that were even worse?"

Dr. Lindholm frowns for a minute, but when she opens her mouth to speak, I cut her off. I can't not. "And anyway, even if that were the case, so what? I mean, you gotta be kidding me, right? My mommy didn't love me? My mommy didn't pay attention to me? Well, boo-hoo. How pedestrian! How pitiful! Nobody's mother ever loved them enough. Talk about your garden-variety angst. We're not talking about being Satanically abused or starved or—or—sent to the gas chamber, we're talking about being *ignored*. Ignored. Big deal! Get over it! I mean, how self-serving and small can you get?"

"Right." Dr. Lindholm nods her head at me. "The old starving-children-in-China defense."

I snort and shake my head back at her. I can't believe this shit. "That's right," I say. "You got it. A cliché's only a cliché because it's true."

"You're right," she says, "it is. So let's go back to Harlow for a minute. Of course you're not a rhesus monkey, but I do think some interesting arguments come out of Harlow that maybe can help us answer some of the questions you raise. In fact, I see some rather striking parallels. Don't you?"

For a second, I am able to feel—and name—my emotion: I am abruptly, irrationally furious. "Yeah, of course I do," I say. "I brought it up."

"Okay," Dr. Lindholm nods. "Good. Tell me."

"Well, for one thing, I really like bananas." I lift my cast. "And I'm familiar with the problem of manipulating objects without the use of opposable thumbs."

Dr. Lindholm doesn't flinch. "You brought it up."

"Yeah, and I'm dropping it, too."

"Do you want to stop? You have to tell me."

I snort. "I should think that that's perfectly obvious." I drop my cast hard against my leg, and it clips nicely against my kneecap.

Dr. Lindholm shakes her head negatively. "Perfectly obvious doesn't do it. You have to articulate it for me. That's everything we're talking about, here; that's the crux of it. Putting your feelings into words."

I mutter to myself, *Jesus Christ*. I'm a fucking four-year-old.

Dr. Lindholm jerks her chin at me. "What are you feeling now?"

"I'm feeling annoyed. I'm irritated."

"Annoyed? Irritated? That's all? Just those two little wishy-washy words?"

Her chin juts forward, challenging. I lock onto her icy eyeballs and think, *No, bitch. I'm feeling like hooking my fingernails into the underrims of your eyes and ripping that smug little expression right off your face. And I could do it. So help me, I could.* "This is bullshit," I say.

Dr. Lindholm holds up her hands. "Hey," she says. "This is the agreement. This is the stuff we talked about, the stuff you said was no big deal. You don't want to talk about it, we won't, but you've got to tell me so. We don't have to talk about anything, but you've got to make the choice. Pull the plug, hit the accelerator, the decision is yours. So what's it going to be, Darien?"

I look at the clock, impassively ticking. I burp to myself and taste bitterness. I look back at Dr. Lindholm, still waiting for me. I say, "You're really enjoying this, aren't you?"

"I'm not," she says. "I'm not at all. I know how hard this is for you, how hard it is for you to show yourself. I know that in some ways it's easier for you to be tough and self-reliant and muscle through to get what you want, and I suspect that that's a behavior you learned early on. But I promise you, there are kinder and more effective ways to come by it. It's risky, and I understand that, because those ways involve revealing yourself, and risking getting hurt, and I know you think it's safer to hurt yourself and stay hidden inside. Safer to swing a pan at your knee than tell your mother you need her, safer to punch a wall than tell Robert you miss him."

"Good God," I say. "Do you have an audition tomorrow for *Barney*, or something?"

Dr. Lindholm looks steadily at me. "The tricky thing is, those ways of asking for what you want, in a backwards way, almost work. Your mother gets angry and that's better than no attention. Robert gets scared and brings you here. But they only almost work. You smash your fist into a wall to say, 'I'm hurting,' and what you get in response is, 'Gosh, what a stupid thing to do.' And that's an awfully hard way to get just the tiniest piece of what you need. I'm trying to help you learn to say, 'I'm hurting,' or, 'I need this,' in a place it's safe to practice. I promise you, Darien, if you really do this with me, you'll see the good that comes out of it." Dr. Lindholm pushes both hands through her hair. "Aren't you tired of just hoping to get what you want? Aren't you ready to—to—*connect* with your own life? This is where it can start. I'm not trying to be difficult, and I'm certainly not enjoying it. I'm sorry that it has to be so hard for you."

I squeeze my blisters, squeeze my cast. I glare at the floor and picture Dr. Lindholm, the necklace, the sweater, the perfect family captured in photos that face away from me on her desk. She is chicly thin, model-tall in her chair. She drives a Volvo, she has a house in the Hamptons, her kids take violin and horseback lessons. *God, I think, what I wouldn't give to be you.* I cannot imagine how we got here; cannot imagine how I let this go on for so long. What's the big deal? It isn't; it is. I think of the tissues in the wastebasket, soggy little lumps of someone else's weakness. I see Dr. Lindholm, Frau Schadenfreude, murmuring condescending sympathies from the height of her throne.

I look up, ready to beat her at this game of bullshit, *My mother held both of my hands to the stove every Tuesday while she raped me up the ass with a knife. Happy?* but then I see the look on her face. She looks worried. She looks tired. She looks entirely unsure of herself. She bites her lip and for a second she looks the way Robert often does.

"Okay," I say. *You'll do this for her sake,* I tell myself. "Okay, Dr. Lindholm." My voice shakes and my mother's indifferent face floats in front of me. I swallow hard and then the words come out strong. "You're right. I want to stop."

Chapter 12

For the next few weeks, Dr. Lindholm doesn't push. She lets me choose what we talk about, starts each hour with a smile and a, "So what's on your mind this week? The World Series? The post-verdict fallout from the O.J. Simpson trial?" It's somewhat like going shopping. One week I put work in my basket, complain about Duncan, brag as obtusely as I can about what I do and how well I do it. The next week I talk about college, the sheer quantity of men I screwed, the insane aggression that emerged any time I had too much to drink. I throw my mother in the basket occasionally, or my brothers, how weird it was to discover when I was little that everybody else had a father when I did not. I talk about it just a little bit. I know Dr. Lindholm will find it suspicious if I don't mention it at all.

When I change topics, or stop myself mid-story, Dr. Lindholm lets me. She might ask me if I can tell her why I needed to change the subject—did it hurt? Was it too hard? Scary? What did I think would happen if I told her the rest of the story?—but if I don't, or can't, she drops it. She queries me on my expressions, sometimes, and I'm amazed to discover slowly that she's usually right. She points out emotions I don't realize I've been having: I do feel happy, or fearful, or sad, in fleeting, microscopic moments. But I'm still not able to tell her what I'm happy, fearful, and sad about, because I have no idea myself.

The hours pass, and I begin to look forward to our visits. I stop watching the clock so much. I discover that I like to talk. One week, I babble on for fifteen minutes about my childhood obsession with Hostess products, describing how I used to stand in the store and break the fruit pies, push my thumbs in the Ring-Dings, crush the Yodels in their packages, reasoning if I couldn't have them then nobody else should enjoy them either. I wonder aloud if this act marked the origins of my eating disorder. Dr. Lindholm smiles and says, "It's an interesting idea, isn't it?" She asks me to tell her about the happiest moment of my childhood.

"Happiest moment?"

I have to think about this for a minute, but I really do think. My mind, however, is a solid wall. I realize suddenly that not only do I not have a happiest childhood memory, I don't have any clear childhood memory. It's all just a prismatic collection of smells and sights and sounds anchored by a couple of facts—we were poor; we moved a lot; I had two brothers, two and three years my senior, and then, when I was eleven, another. That doesn't seem okay to tell Dr. Lindholm, though, for whatever reason, and so I latch onto the first sliver that presents itself to me and hope the rest will come along. "I don't know," I say. I'm aware that I've taken too long to answer her. "This is going to sound weird. Probably I'll think of something else, but for now I guess I'd say what stands out is the first time we ran away, the whole family. I was probably five. It was like a big adventure or something."

"Tell me more about it," she says.

I tell Dr. Lindholm about my mother waking me up in the middle of the night already dressed, with her coat and boots on, holding my favorite sweatshirt in her hands. I describe my sleepy, grumpy brothers, the four child-sized suitcases that huddled by the doorway, the painful, rubber-cement cold of January air in my nose. I see our car on the empty highway, a station wagon, low and wide and headed south. Someplace warm, my mother had said we were going, I think; yes.

We stop at a roadside diner, pull the car up to the plate-glass window so my mother can see Mac and Ken, still asleep in the car. I order pancakes with whipped cream and pour the syrup right on top. My mother drinks coffee and smokes and doesn't get mad when I eat only the mapley whipped cream and a small pancake smile. A baggy-eyed old man forks eggs continuously into his mouth and a lady holds a magazine she doesn't read. While we eat, it starts to snow, fine flakes that sizzle and vanish beneath the heavy scrape of the windshield wipers once we're back on the road. The heater blows hard, a steady roar beneath the wipers and the thump of the pavement and my mother's voice, singing softly to herself about green Russian toes. She catches my eye in the rearview mirror, then looks to either side of me. On my right, Mac snores away. "Just us girls, huh?" she says.

I look around me, too. "Just us girls." My voice, an echo, comes back.

"Where did you end up?" Dr. Lindholm asks.

"I think that was Atlanta," I say. "I don't remember for sure."

"What do you think your mother was running from?"

"Take your pick." I shrug. "An abusive boyfriend, someone she owed money to, somebody's angry wife. I never asked. I don't think she ever did anything illegal, though, at least not unambiguously so. I wouldn't be surprised if she skimmed some money or something here and there, but it wasn't like she held up a bank or something and then had to skip town." A new thought occurs to me: maybe my mother was actually an escort; but my eyes travel to the clock even as I muse upon the idea and I see Dr. Lindholm do the same. She assured me, several weeks ago, that she could count off fifty minutes

[135]

anywhere, without a clock, in her gut, and I volunteered that I could too. Our eyes meet and we smile at each other, like sisters or old friends, in perfect synch. "Time's up," we both say.

Things with Robert, too, get better and better. The stock market burps and his workload lightens; we spend evenings in Manhattan watching television and reading, and weekends on home improvement in Eastman. Robert suggests that we start in on a long-overdue project: remodeling our master bath. "You should figure out what you want to do in that bathroom, tile or beadboard, whatever," he says to me one evening over *Seinfeld*. "We should get bids from a couple of contractors."

It's something I've been hassling him about for as long as I've known him: the bathroom is ancient, pre-shower; a wrench is required to turn the hot spigot on in the tub. Over the last couple of months, it's been a particular challenge, bathing one-handed. "Oh, sure," I reply. "Great! Just in time for me not to need it." With my right hand, I dig teasing fingers into his ribs. Robert catches my hand and kisses my cast.

I report to Dr. Bruce and get downgraded to a half-cast, a bony hood of plaster over my knuckles held in place with an Ace bandage. When I get home, I model this new contraption for Robert and caution him not to get too fond of it since it's likely coming off—finally, completely—in two weeks. His face lights up and he high-fives me as if this news marks exemplary progress I am responsible for putting into effect. He sweeps me in a hug and kisses my hair, over and over, issuing a muffled "I'm so proud of you, I'm so proud of you" into my part. He begins to beam at me, regularly, like a proud father. He suggests, casually, that perhaps I'll be quite finished with doctors soon.

The first weekend in November, contractors start in on the bathroom, and so we decide to stay in Manhattan. On Saturday, we sleep late and head down to the West Village for our favorite brunch spot, a tiny, overcrowded café where the line regularly snakes out into the street. It is a perfect late fall day, made for turtlenecks and football games, and I don't mind waiting, particularly once Robert buys me a cup of coffee to hold. I jump up and down in place, breathing into my scarf. I'm a nineteen-year-old girl cheering her quarterback boyfriend from the stands, her shiny blond hair streaming in the crisp autumn wind.

Inside, we order cafés au lait that come in giant bowls and hunch over the table toward one another. We linger over plates marooned in maple syrup and egg yolk, twining our legs beneath the table. We talk about work, dishing on clients and coworkers. I tell Robert a story about Duncan, Hillary, and a wayward snot that makes him laugh until he cries.

After brunch, we wander SoHo, then walk all the way up to Times Square, where we are rewarded for our hard work with same-day tickets to *Les Misérables*. We hurry home to change, and after some consideration, I pull a navy blue dress from my closet: flowy and seed-pearled; the kind of thing I'd never be caught dead wearing at work. I'd bought it for an early Gilbertson gig, Robert's cousin Chip's wedding to a Lake Forest debutante, selected it at an Eastman boutique that specialized in chintzes and straw boaters. When I'd put it on for the wedding, I'd been repulsed by the sight of myself: tidy hair, tidy bag, Jackie O pearls; who the hell did I think I was kidding? I'd stripped off my underwear from beneath it all and felt a thousand percent better. When Robert had come to collect me, he told me I looked like an angel, and I'd flashed him to wipe the soft, stupid look of want off his face. His expression hardened in instant, predatory lines. "Robert? Darien?" his mother had called from downstairs, jangling keys impatiently, "Are you coming?" "Apparently not," Robert had muttered darkly. "Shit." *Later,* I'd promised, running my fingers across his lips.

Later, we sit across a dinner table, drunk with music and candles and a bottle of wine. Eponine and Marius climb the barricades inside my mind. Between bites of cajun steak, Robert asks me if I remember the first show we ever saw.

"Ugh, yes, *Tommy*. Who could forget? I try to remind myself you had no idea I hated The Who."

"I seem to recall that you let me know that pretty clearly."

"But not right then," I say. "Not right away. I sat through the whole, entire show."

"Oh, no." Robert raises both hands in a mock protest, *perish the thought,* but his smile is happy, teasing. "You waited until we were at a party with half of Adelstein and then turned to me and said, 'And by the way, *Robert,* I fucking hate The Who!' I thought Neal Bicks was going to just about split his pants." Robert starts to laugh.

"They were playing 'Pinball Wizard' on the—you know, CD, radio, or something," I offer lamely.

"Oh, yes, 'Pinball Wizard,' " he says, laughing harder.

"But I *never* liked The Who," I say. "One of my brothers had the *Tommy* album, and it freaked me out as a kid. All that *you didn't see this, this didn't happen* stuff."

Robert looks down at his plate, still chuckling, and as he raises his head to look at me the laughter fades to a smile, happiness tucked up into the dimple in his left cheek. The candlelight makes shadows on the rugged geometry of his face, accentuating the laugh lines around his eyes. My throat constricts to discover all over again how handsome my husband is. His smile melts as he takes my hand across the table and says, "I love you, Darien. I've never known anyone, or anything, like you. My life would be so empty without you."

A little drunk, I squeeze his hand hard, tears starting in my eyes. "I know, sweetie, I love you, too. Thanks for sticking by me. I know you must ask yourself why you do it, at times."

"I don't." He shakes his head at me, his face very serious. "I never do, Dee. You're always—No." He shakes his head more adamantly.

"You're my best thing." He squeezes my hand back. And then, with a sigh, he says, "God, I want to make love to you."

I slide forward on the bench seat and put pressure on the insides of his knees with both of mine. He unclasps my hand and slides his fingers up inside the sleeve of my dress, stroking the underside of my wrist. His smile is roguish as our eyes meet. "Have I ever told you," he says, "you look like an angel in that dress?"

Chapter 13

We finish the wine and head home, Robert already so excited he has to hold his *Les Mis* program in front of him as he flags down a cab, and before we're even in the apartment we're on top of one another. I tease him, nibbling him through his wool pants, murmuring encouragement. He fumbles for his zipper with one hand, the tiny buttons on my dress with the other. I tell him he needs to take Walter out to the dog run before we go any further.

"Walter can wait," he says raggedly, caressing the back of my head. We stagger toward the bedroom, and Walter runs between us and the front door, his soft barks taking on increasing urgency.

I sit back on my heels and look up. Robert's eyes are half-closed and he bites his lip. I run my hands up his pants front. "Mmm, I don't think so. He's distracting me."

Robert groans, frees his hands from my hair, and hobbles stiffly for the door. He snaps for Walter. "Okay, boy, this is gonna be *quick*." He shoots me a look, half-drugged, desperate. "I can't believe you're doing this to me. When I get back you better be naked."

I am.

· · ·

When everything's over and we are lying on top of the evening's earlier outfits, he wants to talk. He brings up the subject of starting a family, a conversation we have on a fairly regular basis but one I thought breaking my hand would spare me from for at least several more months. We lay in our customary postcoital positions, Robert on his back with one arm behind his head, me on my side with my cheek on his chest, listening to the heavy drum of his heart. I feel something—his sweater, maybe—tickle the small of my back as he plays with my hair.

"Did I tell you Doug and Tish are having a baby?" he says. He curls a section of hair around his finger and then drops it against my cheek. Doug is Doug Vernon, another one of the junior partners at Adelstein; Tish his preciously nicknamed wife, Patricia. We go out with the Vernons socially on occasion, the type of arrangement where at the end of the evening we all heartily agree that it was great fun and we must do it more often, and then privately promise ourselves we'll come up with a better excuse for canceling next time.

"Mmm, yeah, you did. Twice, in fact."

"I did? When?"

For a second, I stop to wonder if all of this is a ploy on Robert's part to rehash the conversation we'd had yesterday, in which the Vernons' miraculous news had come up. He'd called me at work, interrupting a particularly good game of Tetris, to relay what Hoyt Waldron, his boss, had had to say about his work on a current case, how savvy his mediation in the morning's meeting had been, blah-blah-blah. "He actually *saluted* me, Darien!" Robert had said, fairly bursting with pride. "The managing partner!"

I sigh impatiently.

"First yesterday, when you called to tell me about IntraTac, and then again at dinner tonight. I was breathing fire from my catfish and praying for the waiter to come by with the water and you said something about how Doug Vernon said Tish is having so much trouble with spicy foods and morning sickness because she's pregnant. Remember?"

"Right. Sorry."

A silence between us takes hold and expands, and I cast about for some neutral comment to offer.

"That fish was pretty spicy. I'll be blowing my nose for a week."

Silence.

"I hope you didn't overtip that guy. He really didn't come around often enough with the water."

Still nothing. I sigh again. "Do they know what they're having yet?"

"No. Doug's secretary is organizing a pool." Robert pauses casually, holding a hank of my hair suspended over my head, but I hear his heartbeat quicken beneath my cheek. "One of two pools running right now, actually. The other is when we'll announce ours."

"Ours? Ours what?" I feel my face stiffen.

"Ours what?" he echoes in a high, pinched voice that's supposed to be an imitation of me, and I know he is only half-teasing. "Our new pet kangaroo. Knock it off, Darien. You know I want kids. And things are good now. Don't you think it's about time? I'm thirty-five already. I don't want to be eighty by the time our kids get out of school."

Now it's my turn to offer silence.

"I don't want to be that old guy you see at every graduation pushing his walker up the aisle, wearing a tweed cap and a giant picture-button that says, 'Proud father of Jimmy, class of 2020.' "

The last of this seems a bit dramatic, coming from Robert, and a number of possible responses offer themselves, including an argument about whether there's really an old guy with a tweed cap and a walker at every college graduation. I wait a few seconds to see if Robert is going to push it any further. He doesn't. The silence grows hostile.

"Those would have to be some pretty dumb kids," I finally say.

"What?" Robert's tone is quick, irritated.

"Nothing. Never mind. I was just figuring that our kids would have to be like forty-five years old for you to be eighty when they graduated from college, and that would make them pretty stupid."

I feel his eyes search my face, but I don't look back at him, stare at the ceiling instead. I am suddenly angry in a way I can't explain, small tidal licks of irritation building under my skin. I think to thank Dr. Lindholm; right now, knowing I'm angry doesn't seem so useful. I fight to keep the waves small. *Why do you have to ruin it?* I hear my brain ask. *Why do you always have to push it?* Robert speaks softly. "It isn't a joke, Dee, not to me."

I don't say anything, willing him to drop it. This conversation could go anywhere, or almost anywhere, else, and that would be fine by me.

"Is it that you're scared, Darien? Are you scared to have a family? I know your family life was messed up, but ours doesn't have to be."

There is a spider on the ceiling, a pale, almost translucent gray spider, and I watch his progress as he moves toward the light fixture with admirable speed. I realize I've never before thought about it, how difficult it must be to coordinate eight legs into a single motion, and now I try to see if all eight move at once, in careful synchronization, or if there is a pattern, two on one side, two on the other. Or perhaps four and four at once, forward and backward in a single unit like a human walking or one of those buggy-pulling horses that race that way. Trotters, maybe. No. Pacers.

The truth is, the concept of motherhood leaves me cold, which is kind of a shame, because I'd love to know what the pain of childbirth feels like. I bet it's good, not to mention entirely socially sanctified. But children? No way. I can't imagine being that responsible for someone, having someone depend on you for their very life. I'm terrified by the very thought of that depth of responsibility: creating someone who you couldn't then someday just get up in the middle of a conversation with and walk away from without ever turning back.

"I wish we could actually have a conversation about this, for once, without you clamming up or changing the subject," Robert continues. "Because I'll tell you how it feels to me. It feels like you're hedging your bets, like you haven't really decided if you're going to stick around with me forever and you don't want a kid to complicate things. I'm sitting here trying not to feel hurt and rejected and silly about all of this, but that's really what it feels like. Like you're rejecting me, like you don't want to have a baby with me." He waits a minute. "I feel like a woman, or something."

This last is meant to provoke me, undoubtedly, and for a second I fight with a flash of rage, the unexpected words that leap to my brain: *Yeah, you know all about what it feels like to be a woman. I bet you were really feeling womanly a minute ago when you had your dick down my throat.* For a minute, I am so angry that it is hard to keep still, angry that he insists on pushing it, that he just doesn't get it, that I have to work so hard to manage the line between sick and healthy. Did I ever tell him we'd have kids? A long time ago, maybe, yes, stupid bitch. I lock it down, lock it down, feel the grind of angry consonants against the walls of my stomach, but the words break through anyway.

"Yeah, that's it. You guessed it. I don't want to have a baby with you because really I think you're just a big, hairy-assed faggot. Maybe I'll start calling you Roberta."

"That's not what I was saying and you know it." Robert's voice is even and calm, which only adds to my frustration. I am letting myself be drawn out, taking cheap shots, acting like an idiot. There's nothing I hate more than losing my control while Robert exercises his, a four-year-old lectured to by a parent. Once it starts, though, I'm powerless to stop.

"Shit, Robert, are you so clueless about what's going on with me that you honestly think having kids at this point would be a good idea?"

"Well, I don't know, Dee. That suddenly seems like a good question. Am I?" I feel muscles tremble as he lifts his head off the pillow to look down at me. I glare at the ceiling, crushing my molars against each other so hard I expect them to stick.

"Well? Am I? Because if I am—and it seems I might be—that's something we better get straight right now. I was under the impression that this wasn't any big deal, that things were going well with Dr. Lindholm and that you were doing better. That *is* what you tell me. That's *all* you tell me. Every time I ask how things are going with Dr. Lindholm, you say fine and change the subject. Am I supposed to be guessing? Am I supposed to be pushing further?" He shifts out from under me and rolls onto his side so he can stare down at me.

"Dee? Don't do this to me, please. Don't shut yourself down in there. I try so hard not to worry about you—if you're drinking, if you're hurting yourself, all those other things—because I thought you'd hate me if you felt like I was checking up on you, but it's hard for me to just sit by and say nothing, and if you tell me you're okay, then God, I want to be able to believe you. I've tried not to pester. I've tried to give you your space on this, but I keep waiting for you to start talking, and since you don't, I think maybe there just isn't anything to talk about. But if there is, sweetie—"

Robert lurches to a finish and pets my hair awkwardly and I realize the mistake I have made is enormous. It is the most he's said on the subject since the first night at Dr. Lindholm's office, and I know he's right. I know it's my fault. I should be telling him more, but I can't; just physically *can't*. Everything true, everything real, is locked down so hard inside of me it feels like there's a metal plate running across the base of my throat, and every time I open my mouth to try to say something to him, the words run up against the plate and stop.

Sometimes, I want to be able to tell him that I am scared and angry, that he is the only good thing in my life. I wish I could rip open my abdomen with my fingernails and show it to him, let him see the stink and the hurt and the rot, *see? see?*, wish he could see it and understand and not be driven away. Other times the only thing I want is to hide the truth from him, to protect him from it and from me, the real me that seeps out when I'm not looking. I get mad at him for pushing. *You don't know what you're asking for. You have no idea how awful it really is.* And then I run like hell to get in front of him, to block him with my body, because I'm not only the bullet aimed straight at his heart, I'm the one who fired it at him.

I drag my eyes away from the spider and find Robert's face with effort. "No," I say, "you're right. All of those things are right. And I'm fine. I'm *good.*" I swallow.

He looks at me, his face filled with confusion. Grief-stricken. *I don't believe you,* it tells me, *I can't believe you.* "Well, then, why not?" he says.

"Why not what?"

"Why don't you want to get pregnant?"

I beg with him. "I do, Robert, please. Just not this instant. I just need a little more time."

"How much time? And time for what? Dee, sweetie, please. Talk to me. If you won't talk to me, how am I supposed to help you get better?"

"You're not *supposed* to help me get better, Robert. You're *supposed* to give me some room so I can get better by myself."

Hope sinks from his eyes. "Why are you so pissed at me?"

"I'm not pissed. I'm frustrated. I don't want to have this conversation again."

"No; you're mad at me. Give me credit for understanding that much, at least. What am I doing that's so wrong?"

"You're smothering me is what you're doing—hovering around like some goddamn emotional waiter waiting for me to spill that first drop of blood so you can come rushing over to clean it up!" *Blood,* I think, *shit.* I'm getting rattled now, selecting words carelessly.

"Well, pardon me for giving a shit," he says quietly. "You happen to be my wife, and I happen to love you. I'm not very good at this standing by and waiting stuff. I want to help you, if you'll let me help you. I'll do anything it takes."

Jesus Christ, here it comes, now, the white knight act, complete with gallant steed. Robert doesn't appear to understand that it's his goal in life to rescue me because it makes him feel better about himself. His sister, his mother; I get his grief over his old girlfriend. He may be a junior partner, not as good as the guy in the corner office, and he may be a working-class stiff, but at least he's got a little woman to rescue, somebody out there guaranteed to be smaller than him.

I can't stay still any longer. I sit up and my naked skin feels wet, shocked-cold, where our bodies no longer connect. I scan the bed for something to pull on. An arm of Robert's sweater clings to the side of the bed. I reach for it and pull it over my head before continuing. I catch a powerful scent of Robert, of Speed Stick, as I drag the fabric over my head. My static hair snaps in my ears.

"God, Robert. You're blowing this thing way out of whack. There's nothing for you to do, no burning buildings that need to be put out. I just— Look. It's only been a couple of months since I broke my hand, you know? I'm working through some stuff with Dr. Lindholm. Getting pregnant right now wouldn't even seem responsible. I mean, what would you do if I screwed up and hurt myself while I was pregnant and accidentally hurt the baby? You'd hate me. So the only thing I need from you right now is to lay off the pressure. I'm just not ready. Please, Robert. Don't push me."

Robert scowls. His voice is petulant. "It seems to me you used to need a lot more from me. I wasn't ready for that to change."

My God! my brain screams. *Are you even listening to me? Did you even hear what I just said?* "No, I'm sure you weren't," I snarl. "Always nice to have someone who *needs* you; wouldn't that be nice for a change! I'd imagine it's downright great to wake up every morning knowing that someone else's world would stop revolving if it weren't for you."

"That's *bullshit,* Darien. You know goddamn well it's not like that. You don't know how horrible it is, how helpless I feel, not being able to do anything, not being *allowed* to do anything but stand by and watch you. You don't know how many times a day I pick up the phone, how awful it is when I'm traveling. Every night, practically, still, I stop outside that door and hold my breath when I think of—that night—when you hurt yourself. When I think about what else I might come home to."

Guilt invades me now, and defensiveness. I know he is right. "Yeah, right." I laugh, bitterly. "Like you're thinking about anything but briefs and contracts when you walk through that door. Like you're sitting in your hotel room saying the rosary over me while everyone else is out at the strip clubs."

"Say the word right now, and it all stops, Darien. I'll walk in and resign on Monday."

"Yeah, right," I say again, moronically. "And then what? Get a job at McDonald's? Don't be ridiculous."

"It's not ridiculous at all, not if the alternative is losing you. I'll do it right now. Hand me the phone and I'll leave Hoyt a voice mail."

My heart starts to pound with an emotion somewhere between terror and anger.

"I need you, Darien." Robert sits up suddenly, locking his arms around me. "I need you more than anything."

Another truce in our marriage, as close as we will come to one tonight, and I am not fool enough to reject it. "I need you too, Robert," I say. I hug him back, as hard as I can, feel the bony ridge of his spine against my arm. His grip on me tightens. We are twisted toward each other, Robert's legs still beneath me, mine pointed away from him, a strained serpentine. My neck is thrust back awkwardly, Robert's shoulder blade applying steady pressure to my windpipe so I can barely speak or breathe. He is breathing in heaving gusts, every inspiration driving his shoulder a little harder against my throat, and smarting tears come to my eyes. "Time, Robert," I say, my voice flattened to a whisper. "Just give me a little time. Everything's going to get back to normal."

The clock on his side of the bed counts off three minutes as we stay that way. Slowly, we untangle ourselves and the conversation retreats. Robert brings up Thanksgiving, which is fast approaching. His mother has invited us to spend the holiday in Winnetka, repeatedly. He reminds me that we owe her an answer, that she'll have to make other arrangements if we don't come out, that it isn't fair of us to string her along. Because he doesn't ask me if I think I can handle it, because of his unexpected surrender, I tell him it's fine by me if he wants to go. It doesn't seem like too much to ask. "Thanks," he says. "I'll tell her tomorrow we're coming." He absently strokes circles onto my hip. "I know you don't like to go."

There is a pause, and I can tell there is something else. The circles on my hip wobble in anxious orbits and then stop as he says, "Listen, I'll promise this is the last time I'll bring up the whole baby thing until you say so, but I just want to make sure that you're not uncomfortable with the idea of other people having babies." I tell him of course not and he says that's good. "Because Doug invited us out to the Poconos next weekend with a couple other couples from work and I already said yes, because I just thought— Well, I don't want it to be awkward between us because Tish is pregnant."

I could choose to fight—I have a case, certainly—but I don't; it is almost two-thirty in the morning. It is a cowardly move on Robert's part, a sabotage after the olive branch has been extended and accepted, and I would be well within my rights to refuse. We never make plans without consulting each other. Next weekend is Veteran's Day. We have our own house in the country. It's the Vernons.

"Dee? Did you hear me?"

"Of course I did."

"Well?"

I sweat it out of him.

"I know I should have asked you first, but Steve O'Brien was standing right there and he accepted, and I thought it would look really weak if I equivocated and said I would have to check with my wife first, and besides, you know we still aren't going to be able to go up to the house. Those guys aren't going to be done with the bathroom. They have to put all new pipes in, and since we're putting down tile . . ." Still nothing. "It's good for my career. Steve's a partner. He's pretty well connected."

"Sure, Robert, whatever you say. I get it. I'm sure it will be a real hoot, hanging out with Tish Vernon in the shuffleboard capital of North America. Maybe we'll do some couple-swapping. Some dirty dancing."

"That's the Catskills."

Whatever.

After a while, he turns off the light. We lay in the darkness, not speaking, and after an interval I pretend to fall asleep, scaling my breathing down in long, rolling waves, turning lazily onto my side, away from Robert. He is not sleeping. He lies with his fingers laced under his head, against the pillow, and I know that if I look at him he will be staring at the ceiling, unblinking, like someone on a hillside watching a sky full of stars. He clears his throat occasionally, gives a curt sniff. He coughs, experimentally, and I murmur and shift under the blankets in sleep-reply. His voice, when it comes, is soft, meant neither to startle or awaken me, but sodden with self-pity. He is talking to himself.

"You don't love me," he says to the ceiling. "Not the way I love you."

The room goes silent again. I don't answer him because I am sleeping, and because he is right.

Chapter 14

As the Pennsylvania Interstate slims to single-lane blacktop, the car raises its voice a notch and I know we are almost to the Vernons' house. Robert and I have been in the car for more than two hours, working like mad to cultivate an air of festivity, eating junk food and singing songs, but it's pretty clear at this point neither of us is convinced this trip will be fun. Walter has been left behind at Uptown Dog, a point I try not to harp on, but, as Robert would say, *prima facie* evidence that there's something about this weekend that's really wrong. Who ever heard of a country house where pets weren't allowed? It seems that someone in this weekend's party is terrified of dogs, and when we confirmed our invitation we were informed that Walter would be denied the opportunity to provide cynophobia relief.

I've been trying to take it easy on Robert—about Walter, about his singing, about the fact that he's nearly polished off a box of Dunkin' Munchkins by himself. He's had a rough week. He's put in fifteen- and eighteen-hour workdays every day, traveled twice down to D.C. on the 6:00 A.M. shuttle, fallen asleep curled away from me, his body twitching in tiny, feeble jerks. Sunday morning, after our fight, he'd resumed the conversation just long enough to say he was going to cut back on his caseload so we could spend more time together, and at the time I'd lied and said that would be great; I tried not to cheer on Monday when he called to say that two of his slow cases were ramping back up. Every night, I've been in bed when he's gotten home and still there in the morning when he's left. His shoulders sag and the gray stands out in his hair. His eyes look like bruises, thumbed heavily in black.

Despite his exhaustion, Robert has insisted on driving, leaving me in charge of navigation, an honor post I execute with only marginal efficacy. Shuffling now through two maps and Doug's directions, I point to a turn looming up on the right and calculate we'll be at the Vernons' within fifteen minutes. As we draw nearer, we speak to each other more politely, almost formally, like coworkers just learning how to share office space. Anxiety twists my stomach tight. Robert puts on the right blinker a full mile in advance of the exit. He yawns and groans to himself and I feel a flash of guilt. Whatever is wrong, everything that is wrong, has to be my fault. I run my eyes over the dashboard blankly, searching for something to say, the radio knobs, the cigarette lighter, Robert's hands on the steering wheel. There's the clock, a cheap, digital piece, Velcroed to the dash; Robert did a song about it once. *O, Velcro, sticky and slim—* Nothing. My eyes see nothing. The blinker is tauntingly loud.

"So," I finally say. I clear my throat. "How did that meeting go, the other day, down in D.C.? Was that IntraTac?"

"Data Mast," Robert says. "Not so well. It looks like there are going to be hearings." He lapses back into a discouraged silence.

"Hearings?"

"Yeah, the Justice Department. The SEC's been ringing the bell on the merger and so we were meeting with the Anti-Trust Commission to try to work things out, but it looks like it's going to be handed up to Justice, so that's not good news for the merger. Aaach." He stretches against the steering wheel.

"But that's good news for you, right? I mean, wouldn't that be pretty cool stuff, working down in D.C., doing, doing"—I flap my arms

[153]

around the car helplessly; my mind is drawing an utter blank—"doing, I don't know, antitrust stuff?"

He gives me a kind, tired smile. "I wouldn't get to work on it, Darien. The work would get handed over to the antitrust group, if it stayed inside the firm at all." He grimaces. "Jared Hirth might get it." The fourth lawyer we are on our way to meet right now. "Lots of times, companies like to keep this type of business separate, though. It might go to another firm entirely."

"Oh." I slump back against my seat. "That sucks."

We exit the interstate. The blinker continues to ping in rhythm as we turn on to local roads and I reach across Robert to turn it off. "Well, at least I don't have to worry about you sleeping with Janet Reno to get the deal done this way."

Robert smiles again, out of politeness more than anything; even I know it is a truly lame joke. I needle him in the ribs with my good hand: "Aren't I funny? Aren't I funny?"

He catches my fingers and says, "Yes, Dee. Yes, you are." He turns and smiles at me, wistfully, I think. His hand reaches for my hair, then retreats.

Please, I think. I want it back.

"So how about this Hertz guy, then? Mister Jared Hertz? Is he the kind of guy who'd be Janet Reno's type?"

Unexpectedly, then, Robert laughs for real. "Jared and Janet Reno," he says, "oh, Jesus! Just wait till you meet him. Do me a favor and be sure to bring that up." Robert reaches across the gearshift and takes my hand.

For a few minutes, the world is all good. We both snicker as we make our final descent down a winding dirt road, marked with a cheery, ridiculous sign: *Welcome first annual Adelstein weekend conference participants!!!* The bubble-writing and emphatic exclamation points surely seem Tish's touch. Our Honda looks more than usually shabby as we park behind a Land Rover, a BMW roadster, and a late-model Saab sporting the license plate POKNOZE. The sight of the last of these alone is enough to motivate me to throw myself on Robert's mercy. I grab his arm as he yanks up the parking brake.

"Robert, come on, please. Let's blow this off." I point to the clock; it is barely lunchtime. "We can be back in Manhattan by two-thirty and in the country in time for dinner. We'll call from the road and say we had car trouble. Or, or—or that I was sick, or something. Please, don't make me spend an entire weekend with Doug and Tish Vernon!"

Robert smiles as if my last-ditch plea for deliverance is humor on par with sex between Jared Hirth and Janet Reno and hands me the wine we brought for our hosts. I peer into the bag. Proving that my husband is not above vanity, he has purchased two bottles of expensive cabernet, a '91 private reserve Mondavi and a Dominus that cost more than an entire night of debauchery with Hillary, if its price tag is to be believed.

"Oh, no," I tell him. "I'm very sorry. This won't be nearly enough."

Bearing our bags and the wine, we make our way into the house for introductions. There are the Vernons, of course, and when Tish sees us, she throws her arms wide and announces, "Welcome to Shi-hola!" which I take to be the name of the house. There are also Jennifer and Steve O'Brien, whom I've met once before, and the infamous Jared Hirth. He bares giant, white teeth at me as we are introduced and I begin to see the joke. The young woman who presses herself against him looks nothing like Janet Reno—not even on the attorney general's best day at age twenty-two.

The O'Briens are slightly older, late thirties most likely. Steve is a full partner and if I recall right they have two daughters, somewhere around eleven and eight. The woman with Jared is Hannah, a perfume girl at Saks who looks to be about my age and apparently took her cue on country weekend wear from watching reruns of *National Velvet*. She has on jodhpur pants and a thin, tight sweater that emphasizes preternaturally large breasts; it seems that she is cold. During introductions, she caresses Jared's hamstring, looking as defensive to be here with all of these married couples as I feel among so many prolific ovaries. When I give my name, she asks me if I'm one of the dog people, and I conclude I have found the judge behind Walter's Gulag sentence.

"And you're Hannah," I reply, avoiding the dog question. "Is that Hannah with an 'h,' or without?" Hannah's eyes narrow suspiciously, and dart to Jared as she says, "Hannah. With an 'h,' like *hand*. Not Anna."

"No, no, I mean, do you spell it with an 'h' at the end, Hanna-*h*?" Robert, across the room, gives me a quizzical look. I smile and send him a little wave.

"With an 'h,' of course, how else would you spell it?"

"Ah! So you're a palindrome. Oh, can a leper repel a nacho. How interesting." I nod enthusiastically and turn to bestow similar pearls of cocktail-party banter upon Steve O'Brien, watching as Hannah's face shutters from bewildered to blank.

One thing that becomes clear early on is that this is to be a chest-beating weekend, with the men lighting out to forge homoerotic bonds over such rituals as putting boats in winter drydock and foraging for firewood—Jared looks likely to burst into a round of "Men, men, men, men" any minute—while the women make beds and worry about what to serve for supper. Indeed, the lawyers take off as soon as introductions are accomplished, slapping each other on the back and shoving cigars into front pockets of one another's flannel shirts in absurdly earnest parody of a *Men's Outdoor Living* ad. *This is good for Robert,* I remind myself, as I watch him leave without so much as a glance back at the house. He needs a break from worrying about me; he needs friends of his own—nice boys he can play with. It's good for him to be rubbing elbows with Doug and Steve.

The afternoon hours are an eternity. Tish assigns beds and hands out linens, then holds court about the wonder that is her pregnancy. The men return in time for dinner, bearing not hand-hewn logs and a brace of pheasants but two shrink-wrapped bundles of firewood and a handful of grocery bags that appear to have been caught at Mel's Country Store. Hannah spearheads a teasing protest, and Steve O'Brien points out, "Hey, ladies, cut us some slack. We're M&A lawyers. We specialize in *acquiring*. How much can you expect of us?" Doug, Jared, and Robert roar their approval and give each other high-fives. Jennifer rolls her eyes at all four of them.

Robert sidles over and puts his arms around me. "Are you having a good time?"

I'm this close to telling him that I'm climbing clean out of my skin and if I have to hear one more reference to Tish's pregnancy I'm going to pull my own head off my shoulders, but then I see the hope and laughter in his eyes. He looks five years younger than he did when we left Manhattan. It's not fair of me to deny him. I can give this much to him.

I conjure up the funniest thing I can think of—an image of Carl trying to weasel samples of Rohypnol, the date rape drug, out of a client in support of his already considerable luck at bars—and summon up a genuine smile. "Of course I am, sweetie. It's beautiful up here," I say.

Briefly, he looks puzzled. "Really?" he asks.

Carl, Rohypnol. Carl, Rohypnol. "Really."

The relief and gratitude that wash over Robert's face are more than reward enough.

Seven of us split three bottles of wine over dinner: the two Robert and I brought plus a dusty Lafite-Rothschild from Jared that makes Doug whistle when he checks the label out. "Good wines, good times," Jared says modestly. "Hannah knows the sommelier at Gotham." We eat steaks, potatoes, and corn on the cob, all grilled in the charcoal fire, and the men talk work and stock market as if denied the opportunity to do so earlier. "What do you think of the techs right now? How much are you into emerging markets?" The women mostly stay quiet. Index funds become the hot topic; the merits of U.S. versus international are debated.

"Personally, I really like the looks of Janus," Jared divulges.

Hannah socks Jared's shoulder. "Janice?" she says.

I chip in to help her out: "I think he means Janet."

Robert frowns slightly and waves me off. He's hardly touching his wine, so every so often when he isn't paying attention, I help myself to a little slug. It isn't long before I'm starting to buzz.

After dinner, the women clear the dishes and then join the men in the Great Room, where Tish asks each of the couples to talk about how they met. We follow the Vernons, who share a predictably dull story about meeting in college, at the Intervarsity Collegiate Sailing Regatta, and Robert only shrugs and says, "We met at a bar, the night we took Rick Parlin out." Doug and Steve both nod at this; the name obviously means something to them. "She was beautiful. I picked her up."

He does not mention that he means this literally. I exhale, discreetly, just now aware that I've been holding my breath, that I have not trusted Robert to be careful how he describes our first meeting. The voice in my head scolds me for my cynicism. Against the sofa cushions, I give his hand a small, grateful press.

"That's it?" Jared says. "You met in a bar? No scandal, no extraneous boyfriends or girlfriends to do away with, just, 'Hey, baby, let me buy you a drink'?"

Robert turns to look at me and there is a wicked light in his eyes I don't recognize. In an instant, I understand he is going to do it, blow my cover, and my heart kicks into panicked overdrive, punching my sternum so hard my sweater shakes. *Fuck you, Robert,* I think. *Don't you dare.*

He grins at me, his left dimple like a knife wound. "Uh-huh," he says. He winks.

I suddenly feel completely exposed, as if I am sitting naked at a birthday dinner, some grotesque old woman resting her ropy, blue breasts like a pair of skinned rabbits on the table. I scan the faces for hints of ridicule or at least recognition. Nothing. Jennifer O'Brien smiles politely and then leans over and says something to Steve that appears to be about checking in with their nanny. Hannah has resumed her vigorous massage of Jared's thigh, and Tish is turning her full attentions to dessert. She lifts a piece of strudel to her face with both hands and murmurs blissfully to herself. Doug is stealing glances at Hannah's underclad breasts, which once again leave little to debate about whether it is chilly in the room. Jared catches Doug's micro-leer and raises an eyebrow in a gesture that seems to connote less possessiveness than pride. The two men share a smile. Tish licks crumbs off her fingers. Robert's hand strokes my hair. Poor Robert. What humiliation did he suffer, marrying me?

"It *is* getting cold in here, isn't it?" I say, looking directly at Doug. I stifle a giggle when he jumps.

"Wha'sat?" he replies. His smile at me is a blend of ingratiation and menace.

I slide my eyes past him to Hannah and back again, flicker briefly on the oblivious Tish. I menace-smile back at him and say, loudly, "I was agreeing with you, Douglas. It's rather nippy in here."

Doug looks at his wife, hangdog now, an appealing, irresistible admission of guilt. But she has spent the entire exchange engrossed in the business of making love to her dessert and she just huffs at him, mock-exasperated, and cuffs the back of his head. "You heard Darien, get the fire going. You know I can't tell if it's cold in here. I'm heated up like a furnace these days."

Doug kneads her shoulder, a conciliatory gesture, and gives me a quick, assessing glance before he heads toward the fireplace.

"No, Doug, don't bother," I say as he rises. "I was just making conversation. Really, I'm fine. Hannah, you fine?"

Hannah's head snaps back. She draws herself up, eyebrows down, scowling slightly. "Yesh," she begins—stops, an expression of alarm, turns her head away and reaches into her mouth. "Yes," she starts again, "I'm fine."

"Sorry," I say, both hands up. "Just checking." Robert's arm around my waist tightens significantly. "What?"

"Hannah has retainers," Jared volunteers. "She did the braces-as-an-adult thing. They make her lisp a little sometimes, but she's fine when she doesn't wear them."

Hannah pulls away from him and glares, her fists at her waist. "Jared, thanks a lot." He makes some helpless, defensive sounds. "Well, maybe people wouldn't notice that I have a lisp if you didn't point it out." She locks her arms across her chest and drops back against the couch. Jared looks bewildered, and Steve generously pitches in, revealing that he had a mild stutter as a child and felt self-conscious about it for years.

"Well, you'd never know it to hear you now," Robert offers. It is possibly the most suck-up thing I've ever heard him say to anyone other than his mother. Jared goes into overdrive, kissing Hannah's neck and calling her *honey, sweetie, sugar pie*; all variety of calorie-laden names, but none of it sticks. Finally, Robert stands up, excusing himself to the bathroom. "Behave yourself," he mutters close to my ear.

For a minute, the room is awkwardly silent. The fire roars to new heat-giving heights and Hannah flicks defiantly through a back issue of *National Geographic*. Jennifer O'Brien murmurs something to Steve about maybe trying the nanny for real now and Steve pats his pockets in an exaggerated and fruitless search for his cell phone. Jared offers his, and then Doug offers the landline, and the three men are about to leave the room in pursuit of fiber optics when Tish fairly leaps from her seat with an abrupt, manufactured, "Oh!"

"You okay, honey?" Doug stops in the middle of the room, all solicitousness.

"Baby's kicking." Tish sinks back against her chair. She rubs her abdomen like a bowler rewarding her favorite ball for a furnished strike.

"You aren't going to have that baby right now on us or anything, are you?" Jared asks.

"Heavens, no. I'm not due until March 1. Well through that first trimester though, thank God. We knew two poor souls who were due about the same time as me who lost their pregnancies, just the saddest thing. They say one in five do." Tish looks around the room at all our faces, and I see that hers is strangely smug, as if the phenomenon she is describing were competitive, something like roller derby; you get to keep your pregnancy by bumping someone else's off. She'd bumped off two, no doubt evidence of her procreative superiority. "You really can't relax as a parent until you're through that first trimester." She nods at Jared and then Steve. "There are so many things that can go wrong."

"Mmm." Jennifer O'Brien concurs, but noncommittally. Hannah continues to crack through her magazine. From the bathroom, the toilet issues a throttling, choking flush. I feel my head begin to rise from my shoulders, and I know what I say next will be unnecessary; worse. "Actually," I say, "there are plenty of things that can go wrong late in pregnancy. Abruptio placenta, for example. The placenta rips away from the uterus and the baby basically suffocates. Or Group-B strep, which the mother can carry without any symptoms at all, but if the baby picks it up in delivery it can die."

I pause a moment. Tish's expression of bovine maternal complacency has vanished, and briefly, she looks uncertain, frightened even. "Then there's incompetent cervix," I say. "A woman I worked with had that."

"Incompetent cervix?"

"Yeah. It's when the cervix isn't strong enough to support the baby's weight, and it just basically falls out before it's old enough to survive. She was like twenty weeks, this woman, out shopping for cribs."

Jennifer gives me a strange look, half-horrified, half-admiring. "I think, Darien," she says, "you should explain that all those conditions are very rare. And fixable, too, if I remember correctly."

"Oh, absolutely, absolutely." I wave my hands. "So long as they catch them soon enough. Though of course there are things that aren't, like preeclampsia. Baby's life or yours, you choose." I turn to Tish, reassuring. "But with incompetent cervix, say, it's *completely* fixable. Next time, they just sew your uterus shut."

Jared leaps to his feet. "Oh-kay!" he cries. "Bedtime!" All at once the room is in motion, stretching, yawning, coughing in hands. Tish rises from her throne heavily, moves with cautious steps across a suddenly land-mined floor.

In the bathroom, as Robert and I are getting ready for bed, I'm still buzzing from the wine. We're the last ones, and I'm thinking of the other couples, already snoring away swaddled in flannel or making silent and surreptitious love. Robert is quiet. He takes on the task of flossing his teeth with utter gravity, squared off against the mirror as if anticipating some sort of confrontation with the person there. When he turns away for his towel, I reach into his travel bag and load my hand with shaving cream, smear it all over my face. I perch myself on the edge of the sink and, when he turns back, wrap my legs around his waist. "Shave me, Robert, shave me," I breathe, trying for Hannah-husky, and it is a test. Will he get it, or won't he? A stay of execution; he does.

"That's not funny, Dee," he says. He wipes me off with someone's used washcloth, holding my chin with his hand. His eyes follow the cloth across my face. When he finishes, he kisses me. "I love you, Darien, you know."

His gesture is tender. He pushes the hair away from my face, traces my cheek and jaw with his thumb. His gaze into my eyes is serious, patient, sad. I look right back at him. I breathe deep, smell fresh-split wood and autumn frost. Something crawls down my neck, warm and wet, and I put my fingers to it. Robert hasn't done a good job of wiping me off. I poke a wet finger against the tip of his nose and the shaving cream hangs there, like a dollop of frosting. On our wedding day, Robert and I had made a deal: no smashing wedding cake into one another's faces. Instead, we'd tap each other on the end of the nose and then lick the frosting off. I almost missed Robert with my piece, though, I was laughing so hard: he'd watched the cake descend toward his face in a state of readiness and terror, sure I was going to blow the deal and mash it all over him at the last second, after all.

"I love you too, Robert," I say.

Robert sighs and bites his lip. Then he tweaks the end of my nose and I smell the cologney scent of Noxema. Against the countertop he slides his fingers between mine. He inches his body in closer and I lock my legs harder around his middle. His lips tug up in a half-reluctant grin.

Chapter 15

I never fill Robert in on the conversation he missed by going to the bathroom at the Vernons' house, and likewise, on Wednesday, though I describe to Dr. Lindholm Tish's irritating smugness, I neglect to go into my own behavior in response.

"Sounds like your weekend away was a lot of fun." Dr. Lindholm rolls her eyes.

"Well, yeah," I reply. "I mean, no. Sort of, I guess."

"Which is it? 'Well, yeah,' or 'no'?"

I consider the options. *Well, yeah,* is safer, but *no* is more honest. I'm trying to be honest, but I'm not sure I'm up for it tonight. "Can it be both?"

Dr. Lindholm smirks and runs a hand through her hair, pushing her ever-shortening bob behind her ears. "That would be 'Sort of, I guess.'"

"Damn!" I snap my fingers in mock disappointment. "I missed that. 'Sort of, I guess,' it is."

The smirk spreads into a smile. "Now that we've resolved that. What do you suppose it means?"

Aah, of course, what it means. The all-important question, the question Dr. Lindholm attaches to every story. It's an interesting story,

Darien, but what does it mean? I sometimes imagine she fancies herself a Zen master, a Buddhist priest serving up sound bites of inscrutable wisdom. What is the *meaning*, Darien, what is the meaning of the world? What is the sound of catharsis at $200 an hour? So far, I am getting good only at telling the stories. I still have a ways to go before I am good at saying what they mean.

"What what means?"

"What it means that you hated spending the weekend with a pregnant woman who couldn't stop talking about her baby."

"Oh, that." I shift. "I never said hated. I don't know. I find that much socializing—behaving—exhausting. All that hanging around other women. God"—I feel my face register revulsion—"that's like torture to me."

Dr. Lindholm's face returns nothing. "Really." She pulls her right foot under her body with her left hand. Her chair rocks precariously, back and right; she seems not to notice. "Do you not have many women friends?"

I pause to take inventory, and to consider this question's relevance. About the only thing I can determine is that it does, in fact, have some. The blankness on Dr. Lindholm's face is a dead giveaway, the one sign of weakness she betrays. If something is of topical or polite interest to her, her face will show it, eyebrows lifting in surprise, mouth quirking down in concern. But if something is of clinical interest, her face becomes careful, unreadable. It is a response I recognize because it's my own. I can't find the harm, though, the malignance in the question. "No. I don't have any," I say.

I think briefly of Hillary, our early camaraderie; she was about as close as it came. We'd started at Boylan at the same time, both less than two months out of college, and we'd hated each other at first. We were too much alike. Like me, Hillary had gone to an elite liberal arts college and was well versed in defending such against the Ivy League; like me, she was used to being a star; and like me, she was a loud, aggressive party girl. We'd competed for assignments and maintained a tacit enmity until one Thursday night about three months along, when our manager took the entire health care group out for drinks. Hillary and I both got conspicuously drunk and decided to stay that way after everyone else went home. We did shots and smoked cigarettes and traded college stories, and I got the cabbie to stop in Hell's Kitchen so Hillary could puke on the sidewalk. The next day, we'd bonded over ginger ale and potato chips—*Oh, my God! I can't believe we drank all that vodka! Do you remember bullshitting the cabbie? Um, pardon me, sir, but if you could be so kind as to decelerate your vehicle toward that sidewalk, if we could debark for just one moment . . . huuuYUUUH.* We'd taken turns reenacting the audio portion of our evening between giggles. Until Robert and I started dating, Hil and I had been as thick as thieves.

"Why is that, do you suppose?" Dr. Lindholm asks.

"Why is what?"

"Why don't you have any female friends?"

I shrug. "Because I'm a bitch and no one likes me?"

"Really."

"I don't know. Why does it matter?"

"It might not. But I'm curious about your intimate relationships. I'm struck that there's a level of distance you insist upon between yourself and Robert, and it makes me wonder whom you trust and confide in, if there's anyone. I know it's not your mother. Most women have a girlfriend, girlfriends, someone, if it's not their spouse. I'm wondering if it means anything particular for you."

I don't have much to offer by way of response. *I hate chicks,* I almost tell her. *They're whiny, weak, manipulative.* I shrug again.

"Not compelling? Let me ask another question. When do you remember learning about your sister?"

In an instant, everything inside me freezes—muscles, blood, internal organs. My breathing stops, lungs instantly jerked and hooked behind my frozen stomach. Frozen brain shrinks away from the heavy case of my skull. I hold myself still and feel a sheet of something separate from the wall of my stomach, rise to perpendicular, and set itself free. An ice floe. It drifts from one side to the other, feeling its way along the layers, rises, sinks toward my leg. Ripples of nausea surge around it like air bubbles.

"Darien?"

Shake my head, brain rattles, *shake it off*. Force air in, words out. "How do you mean?" I say. My voice sounds helium-thin.

"If your sister was stillborn, I presume you didn't learn about her until you were older. I was just curious about who told you, or how you found out, what you remember about that."

Melting quickly past solid, watery relief. I am close to wetting my pants, can't keep from laughing hysterically. My heart bangs. "Oh, that. I didn't know how you meant that, what you meant. I thought I was losing my mind for a second, and I was like, I beg your pardon? Did I tell you *what*? I thought maybe you had me confused with another patient, or something, or that I was talking in my sleep one week or having a *grand mal* seizure. It's like, *Hel-lo-oo*." I thump the heel of my hand against the side of my head for emphasis and then, very quickly, before I can think about it or stop myself, put my hand in my mouth like a gag and bite down. Hard. I hear the soft crackle of fat between my teeth and a startle of pain leaps from the fleshy outside, near my wrist.

Dr. Lindholm nearly bolts from her chair. "Did you just bite yourself?" It is not so much question as demand. The room is moving much too quickly.

"No. No, of course not." I laugh.

"You did. Let me see."

The pain is starting to take effect, to soothe me. My heart beat slows. "No, I didn't." I pull my sleeve forward over my hand and wipe saliva against the inside. I anchor the sleeve in place with my fingers so that my palm is completely hidden. Bones, blood, organs begin to rejell. There's only a dim, fuzzy whining left in my brain, a heavy, erotic tingling in my hand. The ice floe sinks.

Dr. Lindholm kneels in front of me and grips my ill-behaved hand in both of hers. She peels my fingers back and slides my sleeve up past my wrist. She turns my hand over, examining back side and palm. An unmistakable horseshoe of toothmarks on either side betrays me, perfectly neat. *Damn Dr. Goldfarb,* I think; my orthodontist. Dr. Lindholm looks at me very, very seriously. I hear the dry hiss of her breathing, the tiny metal snicks of the clock on the wall. My head lifts off my shoulders. I travel up and over, hide behind my numeric Swiss friend. I travel to Switzerland, eat a pot of fondue, *I find your fondness for fondue phenomenal.* I ski the Matterhorn in lederhosen and clogs.

I look back down and over at Dr. Lindholm, and for a second, I don't get it. She is kneeling on the floor in front of me, holding one of my hands in both of hers. She looks so grave I have to giggle. For a second I wonder if she is about to propose to me.

"Darien," I hear her say, "what just happened?"

She speaks quietly, and I have to pull myself back onto the couch to answer her. My head is Styrofoam.

"What just happened?" I feel the laughter building, the crazy smile. "You're asking me? I don't know."

"You don't know?"

I shrug. I titter a little, sloppy-like. "No, I don't know. I mean, shouldn't you tell me? You're the one on your knees on the floor. Holding hands with me."

I feel Dr. Lindholm's eyes search my face, but I have to look away. From this distance, it is too strange, too intimate. "I'm here because you bit your hand, Darien. Isn't that right?"

Well, strike that. I *do* have to look at her. I look at her like she's crazy. "No I didn't."

She makes a sneering sort of face and lifts up the hand she's holding so it's between us. "You didn't?"

"No."

She lifts my hand a little higher, showing it to my face. "So what's this, then?" A little red ring of toothmarks on my palm smiles up at me. Frowns, actually; they're upside down, on the heel of my thumb, sort of sideways.

I have to admit it: for a moment I am stumped, and it's on the tip of my tongue to say that I don't know. It's like crop circles or spontaneous combustion; things that happen without scientific reason. It's a birthmark, maybe; a trick. But then I see Dr. Lindholm's face. It is cautious, almost frightened, and I know that she is begging me to be smart, to be a good patient. She wants me to give her the right answer—she has already given me the right answer—and I want to help her, too, so I say, "I guess you're right. I guess I bit myself."

At first, I can't tell if it's good enough. She nods her head and lets go of my hand, laying it across my lap. The toothmarks stare dumbly up at me. "You guess you bit yourself?" she asks.

"No," I say. I say it loudly, firmly. I get this one. "I *did* bite myself. I remember doing it, just now."

"You do."

I nod, yes, indeedy, as emphatic as possible.

"Do you remember why you did it?" Dr. Lindholm crab-walks backwards to her seat.

This one is harder, a trap. I feel a flash of irritation. I cast my mind back for a reason, for anything, but my brain is hollow. Everything is slippery; there are no edges. Why I did it. Wye eye diddut. Why I did what? I look to the bookshelf for answers and find new volumes, *Starving for Attention*, *The Magic Years*, *Metabolic Processes in Inherited Disease*. Something that says *Jung* and I squint one eye at it; I need glasses. *Carl G. Jung*. Interesting. I wonder what the "G" stands for.

Gustavus, probably, or maybe Godfried. German. I like the thought of that.

"Darien?" Dr. Lindholm says. Her head is tilted to the side, her tone expectant.

"Sorry," I say quickly.

"Where did you go just now?"

"Go? I didn't go anywhere. I'm right here." I point to the couch for emphasis.

"I mean mentally. It looked like you went away for a minute."

"Oh." I squirm. The observation makes me unaccountably uncomfortable. *Deny, lie, admit.* "I was just looking at your books, wondering what Carl Jung's middle name was."

Silence.

"Do you know?" I ask.

"Do I know what?"

"What Jung's middle name was."

"Gustav," she says.

"Oh!" I cry, "I was close. I thought Gustavus. Was he German?"

She shakes her head negatively. "He was Swiss."

Swiss. There is a sudden spark of connection, disappointment, triumph. A question from Dr. Lindholm, *wye eye diddut*. It should matter. It is supposed to matter. I close my fingers over my palm and wring out what little pain remains in it; a thin ache near the base of my thumb. "I suppose I was maybe—" I start, but Dr. Lindholm's eyes dart to my squeezing hand and she puts up one of her own to cut me off.

"Darien, wait, please," she says quickly, and I am more than happy to stop, because *I suppose I was maybe* was just about as far as I got.

"What are you afraid of?"

This comes as a surprise, and my face must show it.

"Just now," she says again. "What is it you're afraid of? What do you think is going to happen if you tell me?"

I'm not afraid; in fact, I'm quite empty. Pleasantly devoid of all feeling, a fired ceramic jug. *Afraid*, I think. Okay. I can do that. "I don't know," I say. "I'm not really sure."

"No?" she says.

I shake my head no. "I don't know. I guess I'm afraid of disappointing you."

"Disappointing me? How?"

"Well"—I squirm—"because I bit my hand, and that's bad, and I was wrong to do it, and you're going to be disappointed in me—"

"Leave good and bad out of this, disappointing or not disappointing me. Those aren't words that mean anything to me." She waves her hand again, dismissing the notion. "Now what is it you're afraid of?"

She has pulled my feet out from under me and she knows it. She looks at me challengingly. Impudently. Good and bad, disappointment; what's left? And it's not true; it isn't. Whatever I say next will be bad, and wrong. And I'm right, it is. I say, "I don't know," and Dr. Lindholm frowns and snaps her leather folio shut. "Then I want us to stop here for tonight," she declares, and though I haven't chosen it and don't want it, don't want at all to leave myself in such a terrible position, we do.

On Friday, Dr. Bruce wants to look at my hand, too, and unlike Dr. Lindholm, he finds no cause for concern. A few snips of the scissors, and my badge of dishonor falls away. "Let's have a look-see," he says. My hand is small and yellow, desiccated-looking, and Dr. Bruce turns it from side to side. He pronounces it perfect. "Good as new," he says. "Congratulations. You're an excellent healer."

"An excellent healer," I echo, "why, thank you!" Dr. Bruce smiles, and the door shuts between us. Case closed.

Robert is traveling, and I don't mention my orthopedic appointment. After the hospital, I pick up Walter, then head toward New Haven to meet Robert at Tweed Airport. With Friday night traffic I am late, and he is already outside the terminal and on the sidewalk, spotlit against the late autumn darkness, as I pull up. He hoists his bag in the backseat and climbs in the car, his kiss just grazing my cheek. "Hey, hon," he says, "let's make tracks." His greeting to Walter is tangibly more enthusiastic. "Wal-*Mart!*" he cries, tugging at both of Walter's ears. "How ya been, buddy?" Walter shakes his big, boxy head.

I drive the rest of the way to Eastman, waiting to see if Robert will notice. He spends the first leg of the trip on his cell phone, the map light on, a brief spread across his lap, giving changes to one of the new associates. He is patient and slow as he walks her through the document, absolutely certain once he's done he won't have to work this weekend at all. "Okay, next," he says. "It's my page twenty-seven, paragraph four, about halfway in. Second or third line. Do you see the line that begins, 'Insofar as both parties tender unrestricted equity holdings in amounts proportional to their pro rata share of the purchase price'? No? Second or third line? Second sentence. What's the header at the top of the page? Oh, okay." He begins flipping pages. "All right. Tell me when you find the page with the header 'Dilutive transactions.' "

I sigh and drum my fingers on the steering wheel obtrusively. From the passenger's seat, my hand is almost eye-level. Walter noses forward and I bend my arm back to scratch under his chin. He surges forward, straddling the gearshift, and I hear the sharp complaint of paper as he steps on sheafed pages of Robert's brief. "Walt, c'mon, man," Robert says, pushing him back into the rear seat. "Hang on a second," he says to the phone. "My dog's waging war, here. Darien, could you leave him alone until I'm done, please?"

He doesn't get it until I hand him a soda, more than an hour into the trip. He turns the overhead light off and shuffles papers, tapping them into an orderly stack against his leg, and I pop the soda top with my newly freed index finger and hand over the can. Our fingers brush and he takes two long swallows, sighing thanks, before the realization hits.

"Hey!" He pokes the light back on. "You got your cast off! Why didn't you tell me?"

"I wanted to surprise you." It's sort of true. "I figured you'd notice immediately. Then, when you didn't, I was just kind of curious to see how long it would take."

He lifts my hand off the steering wheel and takes it between both of his. He rubs it lightly, his left palm supporting, his right hand gently buffing my knuckles, and then holds it up toward the ceiling. All evidence of bruising has retreated, and there's only a small, pinkish kiss where my Swat ring pushed back into my knuckle. In the jaundiced glow of the map light, my arm looks truly yellow, and, against Robert's large, strong hand, oddly flat.

"Wow, is that ever ugly."

"Yeah, I know. You should have seen it before they cleaned it up. It was all scaly and scungy and it smelled like gym socks. It was totally disgusting."

"Does it hurt?"

"Nope. It's a little stiff, though. Dr. Bruce gave me some exercises for it." I close and open my fist a couple of times, quickly. "He said I should get full range of motion back in a few days."

"Well, that's good. I'd kind of like it if it didn't look like that when we head out to Chicago."

Aah, of course. Chicago. Robert's mother. The ultimate audience.

I slap him heartily on the thigh, give his quadriceps a squeeze. A mellow tang of pain rises across my wrist. "Will do, chief. I'll get right on that. I'm all over that for you." I pause. "In fact, Dr. Bruce wanted to keep me in a cast for another couple weeks but I told him, oh, no; we couldn't be having that. I needed to heal faster than that. I had a mother-in-law to impress."

Robert doesn't say anything.

"I said, no, no. Send me back out broken-handed, if need be. Damn the long-term consequences! I wouldn't want to upset my mother-in-law."

"Dee," Robert says heavily, "don't start with me."

I see my face reflected in the windshield under the glare of the map light. I turn the light off and mouth the words to the image's afterglow: "You started it first."

It is almost midnight by the time we reach Eastman. A snow has fallen, the first of the season, and Robert cautions me as I turn the car down the unplowed driveway as if I have never seen snow or driven in it before. Only a few inches have fallen, light and powdery, and it rises in dry puffs behind us as I steer down the drive. Most of the trees are still in partial leaf, and they catch the snow in curled brown fists. The lawn sparkles like beach sand in the headlights. Inside, we stamp our snowy shoes in the breezeway and I hurry to turn on the heat as Robert lets Walter out and heads to the barn with the wood carrier to make a fire. He doesn't put Walter's electric collar on, and I don't say anything.

We sleep on the first floor, which heats up more quickly, and leave the door between the den and guestroom open to draw the warmth of the fire. The sheets are cold and even the pattern on the quilt, one of Robert's mother's, feels icy, as if the green and blue tumbling blocks have frozen in place. Flames throw long shadows across the foot of the bed and the bare floorboards, the fire pops and crackles to itself. In the basement, the oil burner kicks dully. Robert and I sleep back to front, his arms around my waist, his knees tucked up behind me. His body is hot. I snuggle tight into his lap and the beginnings of an erection pulse against me, once, twice, but Robert makes no other move and soon he is jerking and twitching and then he is asleep.

Chapter 16

"You got your cast off. Congratulations!"

On Monday, when I return to work, I hear this over and over. People point, pat my shoulder, wiggle their own healthy fingers at me, and I reward everyone who chooses to commemorate this grand occasion with a demonstration of his or her keen sense of the obvious with the only appropriate response, Dr. Bruce's: "Thank you. I'm an excellent healer." "An excellent healer, I am. That's me." I fling it at people like a Frisbee, *la-di-da*, like an overripe tomato at a wall.

When I try it on Carl, though, he just sniffs and looks at his watch. "Gimme a break. You broke your hand in, what? July, or something? It's the middle of November. How good a healer can you possibly be?"

"Cut me some slack, man, it wasn't July, it was August. Practically September."

"Well, whatever. I was beginning to think it was a permanent accessory."

"Yeah, well, you try to do any better." I give him a jolly elbow to the ribs.

"Frankly, I can't imagine breaking my hand like that, Darien."

"Like what? Like how? What's that supposed to mean?"

Carl looks at me for a long moment. A little warning flare goes off. "Badly," he finally says.

On Wednesday, I don't use the line on Dr. Lindholm. I don't get the chance. As soon as I enter her office, she looks at both my hands and takes a deep breath and says, "I'm so glad to see you here tonight. I've thought about you all week."

"You have?" I ask. I'm mildly flattered, unsure what I've done to merit such attention.

She nods and says, "I have. I owe you an apology."

"You do?"

"For last week," she says, and I think about what happened last week, I wore the blue shoes, my co-pay went up to thirty-five dollars, and is that it? "For letting things get so out of control that you had to bite yourself."

Oh, that. "I know," I say. "I'm sorry. I don't know what happened. I keep trying to figure out what happened, and what I think is, I just wasn't thinking. I had an itch, maybe, or something, and it's just this automatic, dumb-ass response, I stabbed myself with scissors that way one time, a mosquito bite—"

"—Darien, Darien," Dr. Lindholm interrupts me, "please."

I stop. "What?"

"Can you do this for me, can you relax?"

I wasn't aware that I wasn't relaxed, but as soon as she says it, I feel the pressure in my arms and neck. My palms are held out in front of me, pressed together at chest height like someone praying with a particularly physical fervor. My biceps tremble from the effort of pushing against one another and my right hand hurts.

"Uncross your legs. Let your arms go to your sides. Take a few deep breaths."

I breathe noisily, enjoying the slightly adenoidal rattle I make as I suck oxygen. I let the air back out in noisy huffs.

"How's that?"

I nod my head; better.

"I don't want to hear what you think you bit yourself about. We did something wrong last week and moved too quickly toward something that threatened you, and that was my fault. I'm sorry."

"It wasn't," I start, but she interrupts me again.

"Just listen, okay? This is your big chance to hear me talk." Dr. Lindholm smiles. "I know it will come as a shock to you to hear that I'm not perfect, but really, I'm just trying to figure out all these things alongside you. Last week scared me, and I think it scared you, too." She looks at me, and, knowing I'm supposed to nod, I do. "I'd like for us to figure out how to slow things down. I think we're getting close to something important for you, but we're not doing it in a way that feels safe and that's just"—Dr. Lindholm shakes her head—"it's wrong. This is supposed to be a helpful process, not another form of self-abuse."

"For Pete's sake," I say, "I only bit myself. I didn't even break the skin."

"Did you remember that you did it?"

"Of course I did."

"You did?" Dr. Lindholm looks at me a long time. I cross my legs and uncross them again, grip the arm of the sofa and then let go. She doesn't move. "Darien," she says, "if you can't trust me—"

"I trust you."

"You do?"

"Do you trust me?"

"That isn't what this is about."

I look at the Central Park print. "Trust takes a long time. I'm not going to trust you just because I pay you money."

"Okay," Dr. Lindholm says. "What if you start coming in more often?"

"So I can pay you more?"

"So we can spend more time. You're right. Trust doesn't happen overnight, and it doesn't happen if you feel rushed. I'd like you to start coming in twice a week." I give a little laugh of disbelief, but Dr. Lindholm holds me off. "I know it sounds backwards, I know it's a pain in the rump, but I'm concerned about your safety and I'm trying to be respectful of your wish to stay off medication, unless you can think of a better way to do this."

"How does coming in twice as often slow things down?" If anything, I thought she'd suggest skipping weeks, or maybe taking a break.

"You don't have to take such large bites if you get more turns at the table."

"And what if I'm not feeling particularly hungry?"

"Then you don't have to eat anything. But you do have to sit at the table. You can say whatever you want to me, or nothing at all. We can talk about the weather, or the Knicks, or—you can even go to sleep. You can help me work on my personality." Dr. Lindholm tries an awkward wink.

"I can sleep? I can sit here and not say anything?"

She nods. She agrees. "You can just sit here and not say anything."

"And how is that different from what I could do for free at home?"

Dr. Lindholm smiles. "Silence in therapy is a good thing. You'll be amazed by what you discover. Sometimes it's nice to have someone there with you when you find you have something to share. Okay?"

I say okay.

Dr. Lindholm combs at a section of her hair with her fingers and points to my uncasted hand. "And now, why don't you tell me how you feel about that?"

I put Dr. Lindholm's theory to the test that silence in therapy is a good thing. I start coming in early Friday mornings in addition to my Wednesday evenings, and for the next three sessions I don't say anything. I enter the office, I arrange myself. I smile politely, as if Dr.

Lindholm were one of my clients, and then stare at the clock or the printwainscoting. I read the book titles. Sometimes Dr. Lindholm will ask, "Do you want to talk about it?" and I shake my head no or just ignore the words. She won't say anything else unless I start to pick at myself, dig my nails into my palms, twist my fingers, clamp down on my fingertips. Then she'll say, "Darien, try not to do that to yourself, please," in a voice so quiet I'm not sure if I've heard it or just made it up.

I don't look at her, not directly, but know if I do I will see her watching me calmly, her face registering nothing. *I'm ready when you are.* I fight the temptation to cross my eyes and stick things up my nose. Part of me feels tremendously naughty, defiant, the kid playing on the jungle gym even after the teacher's called time for math class. But a greater part of me feels comforted, soothed, protected. I think about the time I put my teeth through my lip, I think about the spiny chestnuts I used to collect from a graveyard next to one of the places I used to live. For minutes at a time, I drift off. Once, I dream I am young again, lying in a hospital bed, delirious with fever. My mother settles a blanket over me.

In the silence, I admire the soundproofing of the office. I imagine I hear traffic noises, sirens and blaring horns, the insistent bleat of an unchecked alarm, but when I focus on them, the angry sounds all melt into oblivion. I learn I can hear the tiny, metal click of the hands on Dr. Lindholm's clock, marking off four dollars per minute. I count the clicks, and at the end of the third session, when I come in Wednesday noontime instead of evening, as the fifty-first minute snicks to, I break my silence. I stand up and extend my hand toward Dr. Lindholm. "Well, Doc," I say, "Happy Thanksgiving. I'm outta here."

I bounce through Dr. Lindholm's door, down two flights of stairs, and onto Park Avenue. Robert is already there, waiting for me, pacing back and forth alongside a Lincoln Town Car with a SkyCab sticker in the window, his ear pressed to his cell phone. His back is to me so I smack his butt to get his attention and shout, "Hey, babe. Let's make tracks!" He holds up a hand to warn me off, but I don't pay any notice. We've been far too polite to one another for far too long. It's Thanksgiving and I'm on my way to the airport. It's my favorite holiday. I love to fly.

Robert frowns into his phone and says, "Let me call you back." He flips the phone off and pecks me on the cheek. "Hi, sweetie," he says. "How were things with Dr. Lindholm?" He pulls the car door open and I slide into the backseat.

"Things are good," I tell him. "She said to say hi to you and Happy Thanksgiving."

Robert climbs in next to me and leans forward to tell the driver that we're going to LaGuardia Airport, American Airlines terminal, please. Our flight is at three o'clock; it is now five minutes before one. He turns back to me and smiles. "Well, I hope you said hi and Happy Thanksgiving for me right back."

I grip his hand, hard. "Absolutely. I wouldn't want her thinking you were rude."

Robert nods and reaches for his phone again. I grab it from his hand and flip it shut, then toss it into the front seat, next to the driver. "Coming through," I crow as it clears the Plexiglas. I turn to Robert. "So talk to me."

"Dee," he protests. He reaches forward and apologizes to the driver, who startled hard and nearly swung into a Volvo wagon when the phone plunked down next to him. He frowns again and shakes his head at me. "What's your deal?"

I shrug. My deal is nothing. "My deal is nothing," I say. "Tomorrow's Thanksgiving. I'm getting on an airplane. I've got *People* magazine."

I smile at my husband and make monster fingers with both hands, wriggling and closing like Frankenstein. "Lookin' pretty good, wouldn't you say?" I hold my right hand up to Robert's face to admire.

The sallowness is gone; my range of motion is expanding. My knuckles make only a couple of snicks and pops as I move my fingers rapidly. "My secret's safe with you. Phyllis wouldn't even guess that anything was ever wrong."

Robert takes hold of my hand. He looks so tired, so weighted. I'd take it all away, if I could. "What's going on, Darien?"

"Nothing," I say. I unclip my seatbelt, climb on top of him, and take his face between my hands. "Nothing. It's Thanksgiving. In two hours we'll be in the air. I'll be eating gumdrops and reading my magazine. I'm in a good mood, silly. I'm still allowed to have those, aren't I?"

Robert thinks for a minute. "Of course you are," he finally says. "Now would you please sit back in your seat?"

In two hours I am not in the air—our flight has been delayed until six o'clock—but the change of plan does little to stanch my good humor. I double down on magazines and order soft pretzels from the food court bar to pass the time. Robert works the phone, which I promise not to throw at anyone, and talks an American customer service agent into letting him hook his laptop to her printer. By the time we board the plane, it is quarter to seven and I'm nearly ricocheting off the gate walls on sugar, caffeine, and tabloid gossip. I do my best to behave as the flight attendants explain the plane's safety features to all of us. I take the middle seat, between Robert and a mothball-smelling businessman, but even that doesn't bother me.

It is not until we reach Chicago and get off the plane that my blood sugar drops, driven floorward by the sight of my mother-in-law just outside the gate. She sails toward us, gloved hands extended. "Robert!" she cries.

Robert falls into her embrace like Phidippides at last bridging the twenty-six miles between Marathon and Athens. "Mom. Mom," he replies.

Robert's mother closes her eyes, and Robert and she hold each other silently. I stand to one side, swaying, holding my rolled-up magazines. I try on a few expressions, aiming my best warm sympathy somewhere into the middle distance. I pick up Robert's briefcase, feeling much like a valet. I am suddenly very ready to go to sleep.

After three or four of our fellow fliers have knocked into her, Robert's mother asks him for his handkerchief, and as he fumbles for it she reaches for me, offering her soft, powdery cheek for a kiss. "Hello, Phyllis," I say. I pat her arm like a medium-sized animal, a hedgehog or skunk.

"Hello, Darien, so glad you could make it," she replies. She daubs at her eyes with the edge of Robert's handkerchief.

On the trip from O'Hare to the house, she asks Robert to drive and sits up next to him, nattering on about local gossip. This friend was getting a divorce, that neighbor had built a greenhouse, this miscreant painted her house a horrible, fleshy beige. I sit in the backseat and stare out at the other late-night commuters trying to force their way through the holiday traffic. A man in a late-model station wagon stares back at me, no doubt thinking that no one sitting in a Lexus has the right to look so unhappy, no doubt right. *But I'm in the backseat,* I mouth to him. *It's totally different. Two hours ago, it would have been another story.*

"You still back there, Dee?" Robert asks as we clear city limits. He shoots me a worried look in the rearview mirror. The traffic thins out and the trees start crowding in.

"Yep. You still awake up there?"

"Of course. I'm fine." The latter statement is smeared by a prodigal yawn. Robert stretches himself upward, both hands off the steering wheel, palms flat against the ceiling of the car.

"You're not too tired to drive, are you, honey?" Phyllis asks. "You know how I hate to drive late at night, especially in the city. You know I always left that up to your father."

"No, Mom," he says, turning toward her, his voice soft with pity and deference. "Of course not." His arm snakes over the back of the seat and around his mother's shoulders.

From the passenger side of the car, I hear a short, soggy sniffle. Then Phyllis Gilbertson says, "Robert, please. Keep your eyes on the road."

Robert's father died almost three years ago, of a cranial aneurysm. He went to work one March morning with a headache and collapsed in the commuter lot at the end of the day. A mother of two called 911 from her car and EMTs took him to Cook County General Hospital; he was in a coma when Robert's mother got there and brain-dead when we arrived. Despite the neurologist's kind remonstrations and several definitive EEGs, he lingered on life support for two days; another two days and he was interred in the Gilbertson family plot in Winnetka. He had just turned sixty-eight.

Robert's mother handled the entire chain of events with what I can only call a terrible majesty. She marched through the days at the hospital and made arrangements for Robert's father's funeral with precision and deliberation, debating at length with the organ donation team about the viability of Harris's heart, liver, and kidneys; finally agreeing with some satisfaction to the harvest of his cruciate ligaments and corneas. She negotiated a bargain with the funeral home director, who had made the mistake of suggesting that a man of Harris Gilbertson's stature in the community certainly *required* a copper vault. She chose the charities to which donations should be directed; she commanded the dry cleaners to rush the order on cleaning his burial clothes; she selected the memorial hymns. Not once did I see her cry.

She telegraphed to the rest of us quite clearly, though, that her calmness and rationality were born of necessity, because she was the only one in the family who had it together enough to get the group through the ordeal. Kate spent the days crying and reeking of vodka, and Robert and David stumbled around uselessly. Phyllis even arbitrated an unexpected argument between me and Robert when I found myself refusing to go to the burial at the last minute and couldn't explain to him—or myself—why. *If this is just another of your little manipulations, Dee, understand that this is neither the time nor the place for it.* In the bone-cold of the sanctuary, he'd turned on me with real fury. I'd given him my biggest, goofy-lurchingest smile and she'd pulled us apart, speaking to Robert calmly. "Robert, please. You know this can't have the same meaning to Darien as it does you and your brother and sister. She hardly knew your father and perhaps this seems unnecessarily morbid." He'd bought her version of things, however grudgingly, and sent me home with two infant second cousins and his ancient great-aunt. I knew I should have felt grateful to Phyllis for bailing me out. Instead, I found that I hated her and Robert both.

In the end, Robert's mother expected something in exchange for her bravado, and that was his undivided attention and indulgence when we're with her. She'll cry, just a little, to remind us, and she'll take the occasional dip into the mawkish, messy well of self-pity, but mostly she just expects everyone to remember to handle her with a great deal of deference, as if she is a priceless family heirloom, Limoges china or Tiffany glass. My specific role, which has been demonstrated to me time and again in action if not word, is to cede all rights to Robert for the duration of our visit. It's never been too much of a problem: Robert always turns into someone other than my husband around his mother, anyway, and on past trips I've found other ways to amuse myself. All at once, though, sugar sagging in my bloodstream, Phyllis dithering on about pachysandra and zoning ordinances, I'm not so sure I'm going to be up to the challenge this trip.

"Well, here we are." Robert steers Phyllis's car into the wraparound driveway and puts it in neutral. He walks around to open her door and she waits for him, standing just outside the pool of light on the front steps as he thumbs through his own keys for the one to the front door, twists open the brass lock, and flips on a panel of lights inside. Entryway, front hallway, front stairs emerge from the darkness. Burlap-bundled rhododendrons stand guard on either side of the door.

"All clear," he announces, kissing his mother on the forehead as she steps past him, inside.

"Thank you, dear."

I take up the rear, hauling both Robert's and my suitcases. Robert holds his briefcase. Phyllis turns to me as I step across the threshold, thump both bags down, and shake out my right hand.

"You won't be insulted if I go directly to bed instead of staying up to visit, will you? Such a busy day tomorrow, and it all goes so fast. You almost wonder why it's worth it." Her eyes fill, and almost in unison, Robert and I urge her upward. She starts up the stairs and pauses at the landing where they take a left turn and disappear to the second floor. "There are towels in Katie's bathroom, and fresh sheets on the beds. You'll make yourself at home, of course."

Her footsteps squeak across the ceiling and Robert waits, his eyes turned up, his hand on the Newell post carved with his grade-school heights: 39 inches, August 1967, 54½ inches, June 1973. When the squeaks stop, he turns to me. "Want anything?" I follow him to the kitchen. He leans into the refrigerator in the darkness and I slide my hands up his sides. "How about whipped cream? Or Crisco." I nibble on his earlobe and murmur, "Isn't that what you put on turkey? Crisco? Butter?"

Robert turns away from me and emerges from the refrigerator with a carton of milk. He reaches for a glass and shakes his head as he pours. "Dee," he sighs, "I'm really tired."

Robert says, "Dinner looks great, Mom." Thanksgiving dinner is the three of us, Robert's grandmother, Nana Gilbertson, up for the day from her assisted living center in the city, and Mary Burdick, Robert's mother's best friend. Three widows, the good son, and me. Outside, a steady rain is falling. At three o'clock in the afternoon the sky is almost black.

"Thank you, darling," Phyllis says with a gracious smile. "But I don't know why I keep buying such large birds. I'll have to call up meals-on-wheels to take the leftovers when we're through."

Mrs. Burdick flaps her napkin into her lap. "Nonsense, Phyllis. That can't be more than fourteen, fifteen pounds. Last year, if you remember, I cooked an eighteen-pound bird and it was just Rick and Molly and myself, three dozen oysters in the stuffing. Now that was too much bird for the table."

"Yes," Phyllis agrees. "Molly and Rick. How nice to have all your children with you for the holiday."

Robert stands up and tucks his tie into the front of his oxford shirt. He reaches for the carving knife and fork. "Well, I wouldn't be calling anyone from meals-on-wheels just yet. I bet the five of us can put a pretty good dent in this old bird. You ladies are going to have to keep an eye on me to make sure some of this gets onto your plates. I have a feeling I could polish the darn thing off without any help."

The three older women all titter obligingly. "Well, gaw-lee," I mutter into my wineglass.

Phyllis smiles and pats Robert's cheek. "Oh, Robert. Don't any of you listen to a word he says. He's always had impeccable table manners: always please and thank you ever since he could talk, has everyone had enough?" Phyllis beams around at all of us, as if what she has just furnished were irrefutable evidence of Robert's remarkable table skills, a chimp trained to use flatware and a glass.

"Gee, thanks, Mom." Robert hands a platter of turkey to his grandmother, then gives his mother a wink. "I do try to keep my Emily Post membership up."

We all fall to eating, brandied sweet potatoes, green beans with almonds, fruit salad in a lemon-poppy vinaigrette, Mrs. Burdick's infamous oyster dressing. Silver clinks against china and someone kicks off a chorus of "Umm—delicious-es," that survives several rounds of the table. Mrs. Burdick sniffs between forkfuls and Nana Gilbertson, eating stuffing, says *ha, ha* as she chews.

Phyllis watches her mother-in-law for a moment, her own empty fork suspended in midair, then turns back to Robert once again.

"Your brother, of course, he was a different matter entirely. Do you remember the year he brought that girl home for Thanksgiving, that tiny little thing, and he ate an entire casserole of stuffing just because he thought she'd be impressed?"

"Right"—Robert laughs, his fist across his mouth—"Lara, the gymnast. He was so sick that night. I kept saying to him, 'Buddy, you're gonna kill yourself. It's *bread*. It's going to expand in your stomach—' "

"I swear to you, I was mad enough to watch him suffer. All that stuffing! Your poor father practically had to tie me to the chair. And he was the one who I was upset for. You know how he liked his turkey sandwich the day after Thanksgiving, cranberry sauce and stuffing . . ." Phyllis's eyes go watery as they drift across the table to Nana Gilbertson, chewing blissfully away, and to Mrs. Burdick, her face clenched in an expression of fierce rectitude, before settling on a dish in the center of the table, mounded with untouched stuffing like a reproach. "Well," Phyllis says. The syllable is short and loud, shaky-brave. She sets her dinner fork back on the table, lining up the tines with her salad and dessert forks just so. "Of course, now your brother counts calories and watches his weight like everyone else. And I've eaten Cynthia's cooking, no offense. I daresay he's not spending today gobbling any casseroles of stuffing up."

Phyllis sniffles once, head high, and I think, *Okay, let's get this over with*. She's been spoiling for hysterics all day. At breakfast, she'd waxed maudlin about the way Katie always used to get up early to make the cinnamon rolls before anyone else was awake (and pound a few mimosas, too, to help her through the day, I presumed); after the turkey was in the oven there was a lament about the loose washer in the kitchen faucet, and, once that was fixed, an apparent crisis with her Keogh plan. All morning long, Robert had rushed to fix everything, wielding Pillsbury cans, monkey wrenches, and Excel spreadsheets while I ironed the tablecloth and put on my own polite plaid Illinois disguise. Now, he takes his mother's hand across the table in an attempt to set things right once again. "How's things at church, Mom? Did you find that new minister yet?"

"Oh, goodness, now." Phyllis clears her throat. "I'll live to see the day I regret joining the Diaconate. Charles Patton won't take a hard line to save his life, and the way the by-laws are written you'd think meetings were a sixth-grade grammar class . . ."

For the first time all day, I find myself thinking of Walter, alone and lonely in his carpeted Uptown Dog prison cell. I wonder if the staff are treating him well, feeding him scraps from their own turkey dinners, tempting him with his squeaky-foot toy. I imagine him staring dully ahead, sighing, chin on paws. I see him laying next to his bed, on the floor, a favorite rebuke, the contents of his dog bowl drying and untouched. *Walter!* I reach a hand out to Robert, nodding along to his mother's conversation, and Phyllis's eyes fall quickly to where our fingers meet.

"Well." She folds her own hands under her chin. "What am I prattling on about, church? You probably haven't been inside a church since you were married."

Something shifts within me, the ice floe rising again as it had at Dr. Lindholm's office several weeks earlier, traveling along the front of my stomach, pushing turkey, stuffing, out of its way. The comment is aimed at me. Robert had gone to church every Sunday growing up in Winnetka, Sunday School classes, confirmation; at Hopkins, he even did the occasional Sunday penance thing. I was the one who'd wanted to get married at City Hall, who'd showed up at St. Mark's-in-the-Bowery only on Phyllis's insistence. I'd been to a church only once in my life before, in eighth or ninth grade, it must have been, and even now I don't remember the reason for going. It must have been that one of my classmates invited me along for Easter services. It was definitely springtime.

"Now, Mom—" Robert protests.

"No, no." Phyllis puts her hands up. "I stand corrected. You're right. There was your father's funeral."

She gives a little gasp and pushes her chair back from the table. Robert unlatches his hand from mine and follows her out of the room. "Oh, Phyllis," Mrs. Burdick says distractedly. I sit still as the ice floe bangs from one side of me to the other, its edges describing all my empty inner space. It feels for the layers, delicately, precisely, like something human. I freeze for a moment and experience the strange, deliberate searching, the kid-gloved fingers of a burglar probing for the kill switch to the homeowner's alarm. My entire body goes hot.

Nana Gilbertson turns to me. "When I was a little girl, we went to church every day. We had to wear itchy wool stockings and starched dresses and Mother pulled my hair so tight I could hear the blood pound in my temples. It sounded just like someone was squeezing a wet bag of sand." One of her hands trembles across the table and covers mine. Her wrinkled skin is soft, nearly textureless, dry and cool against my hot fingers. She pats my hand firmly. "Now I'm an E-C Christian, Easter and Christmas only, and even then only when I feel like it. I say from now on, the only way you're going to find me in a church when I don't want to be is in a casket."

Nana's grip on my hand is suddenly vigorous. Her lips jerk in counterclockwise circles, as if still working over the defiance of her words. A stiff black hair sprouts from the underside of her chin and there's an orange smear of sweet potato on her cheek. I squeeze her hand back, suddenly sick with grateful affection. I've had absolutely enough of this crap. I don't tell her I'll do her one better than that. I don't say I doubt you'll find me in a church, in a casket, ever.

In a minute Robert and his mother return, Phyllis bearing a covered basket in both hands. Her eyes are rimmed with pink but she gives us all a wide, luminous smile.

"I apologize," she says. "I forgot all about the dinner rolls. Does everybody still have room?"

"Not me." Mrs. Burdick lays her hand against her stomach. "I couldn't have another bite and still fit pie."

"I'm full right up," Nana Gilbertson adds.

"Well, I have room," Robert says. He reaches over for the basket and stacks three shiny, brown biscuits on his plate.

Chapter 17

Robert never realizes that I stop speaking to him spontaneously. For the duration of the weekend, I respond to him and Phyllis only when addressed directly. It is easier to get away with than I expected. On Friday, we make a trip into downtown Chicago for Christmas shopping and to take Nana Gilbertson home. On the ride down, I lend a sympathetic ear as Nana bemoans the indignities of assisted living, and then lapse into monastic silence for the tour of Bamberger's and the retreat up Route 41. On Saturday, when we meet a couple of Robert's friends from high school for dinner, I make brilliant, cheerful conversation with everyone but him. I trade notes on suburban Philly with one woman, a graduate of Bryn Mawr, and assure another that New York's reputation for savagery is largely unearned. When one of the friends says, "So, four years, huh? You guys have been married four years?" I ignore Robert's chummy squeezing of my shoulders and say to the speaker, "Hard to believe, isn't it?"

Sunday morning, Phyllis requests private time with Robert for an important conversation, and by noon we are back at O'Hare. Robert is on his cell phone, checking voice mail, even before we reach our gate. On the flight, he works and I stare out the window, too tired for Cosmo, too early for Chee-tos and chocolate. In New York, he talks to the cabbie and we both talk to Walter, and it is not until Walter's been to the dog run and the first load of laundry's gone into the dryer that Robert says, "Hey, what's up?"

"Mmm?" I reply.

"What's up?" he says again. He crosses the room and wraps his arms around me. "You're quiet." He kisses the top of my head.

I've been quiet for days, I consider telling him; *haven't you noticed?* But the answer seems perfectly obvious.

"I'm just tired," I say.

"You didn't sleep well?" He starts rocking me, pulling my hips in closer between his legs.

"Did it seem like I slept well?"

"It looked that way to me." The room is silent except for the steady clank of something metal in the dryer and the occasional jingle of Walter's collar against the hardwood. He lies in his favorite spot, a sunny corner, hard at work on a deer hoof he refused to leave behind at Uptown Dog.

"Did I snore? Was I a bed hog?" Robert's tone is light and teasing, and I can tell by the way his voice angles down that he is watching me. I close my eyes and let him hold me. For all my anger, he still feels good, still smells good. I *haven't* slept well. I spent Friday and Saturday night counting sheep and staring at the ceiling. Here, home, with Robert and Walter, I could go to sleep in an instant. Robert pulls tighter and gradually, inevitably, he grows hard against my stomach. I suck my breath in, as if I can retract my internal organs without breaking skin contact, but I don't say anything to Robert. He begins rocking me toward the bedroom.

"Maybe you need a little nap," he murmurs. He drops his face down to mine and his lips feel along my cheekbone, making their way to my mouth. I turn my face away and press the bridge of my nose into his collarbone. I open my eyes and stare hard across the room: our gutted suitcases, a pile of the *New York Times* still in blue plastic sleeves, a big ball of Walter hair against the baseboard.

"Maybe so," I say.

Robert kisses my ear, my neck. He slides a hand over my ribs, beneath my sweater. His palm on my skin is hot, moist; his tongue is bivalval in my ear. I lean back from his embrace and pull off the sweater, he leans back, too, and unhooks my bra. His eyes and hands go to my breasts, greedily, compulsively, like a teenager, and, suddenly, I want him for that. I want to beat him with my fists, want to be crushed to death beneath his weight. I hate him. I hate him. I want him so much I could cry.

I push myself back against him, hard, his thumbs massaging my nipples, and I go for his belt. His pants, boxers, fall to the floor. His penis bangs against my hip and I pass by it tauntingly, just brushing the tip, as I unbutton my skirt and let it drop. I shove Robert backwards into the bedroom and he staggers willingly, falling down on the bed on top of me. I grab his buttocks with both hands and grind his pelvis against mine. He breathes out hard and shifts himself lower, dragging his mouth from my face to my neck to my chest. His tongue covers my breasts in avid, devotional strokes; his fingers trace expert lines from the curve of my breasts to my belly. An urgent knot builds in my stomach.

I throw one hand out and feel around for the handle on the bedside table. The drawer squeals as I jerk it out. "Not this time, Dee, please," Robert pants, "just this once."

My hand releases the slippery foil packet and there's a tiny, wet smack as the condom hits the floor. "Okay," I pant back at him, "just this once."

His fingers find me beneath my underwear, and he murmurs into me, *Oh, you like that.* From the inside, my thighs grow warm and watery. Aching warmth expands in my abdomen. I clench my eyes

[193]

and give in to the proprietary rhythm of his fingers. *You bastard. You confident bastard.* I bear down hard on Robert's hand, make a deal with myself, *This first.* I change my mind, start an argument, *please—no—please*—Robert groans, and it is with tremendous effort that I open my eyes, find the corner of the curtain rod, and say, "So what was your mother so upset about?"

"*Uhh,*" he says. He kisses my ribs and draws a wet line down to my belly button. His free hand slides my underpants down and I lift my hips to help him. "*Shhh.*" His lips tickle the blade of my hipbone. His fingers start light, feathery strokes against the inside of my thigh.

Oh, Jesus. I squeeze my hands hard as I can. I lock them in Robert's curls and pull his head away from my skin. His hands stop moving. He looks at me, drugged, confused, and for a second I won't do it; I can't. I want him, want this too much. In my mind, we make love, move in perfect, Harlequin harmony, fall asleep in one another's arms, his body curled around mine like a protective shell. I look at his beautiful face, his tired eyes, his dilated pupils. I swallow hard. "No, I'm serious," I say. "I want to know what your mother needed to talk about this morning."

Robert goes back to kissing my hip. His voice is muffled as his head drops down between my thighs. "She was upset because her son was a man of such wanton lusts, because he couldn't wait to get home and make love to his wife." He pushes my thighs apart.

I tug his head back up again. Perplexity slaps across his face. "Robert, I'm serious. Before we do this, I want to know."

Everything stops moving.

"Now?" he says. His voice is tight. "You want to talk about this now?" I feel the anger vibrate through his skull.

The knot in my stomach loosens. I go to the curtain rod again. "Yeah, Robert. I want to talk about this now." I find his face for a second. "Talk to me about your *mommy,* Robert." I smile.

[194]

He jerks away from me. I sense his glare dimly, peripherally, but I lock back on the curtain rod.

"Goddammit!" he says. He slams his fist into his pillow. The wind whooshes by my ear.

I start to laugh. *Hit me, you bastard. Come on, do it.*

"Goddammit, Darien!" He whips the pillow across the room and I hear the bright crack as it hits his dresser. A picture frame, his watch, a whole bowl of collar stays. Then he stomps out of the room and into the bathroom and stays in the shower a long, long time.

The only thing I tell Dr. Lindholm on Wednesday is that Robert doesn't get it.

"Doesn't get what?" she asks.

I shrug at the printwainscoting. "Doesn't get anything."

"Doesn't get *anything?* Well, now, that *is* a problem."

She waits for me but I don't respond. "What are we talking about, Darien? Multivariate calculus, the sociopolitical themes of *War and Peace?*"

"He just doesn't get anything about me. Like it isn't obvious. It's like he doesn't think there's anything wrong with me."

"Do you tell him otherwise? What do you want him to get that he doesn't?"

"I shouldn't have to tell him," I say. "I mean, for God's sake. I shouldn't have to sit down and explain it all to him." I scowl at the print. It doesn't change, week after week.

"He's not a mind-reader, Darien. Robert isn't Superman. He's just your husband."

"No, I know that." I look at Dr. Lindholm.

She gives me a quizzical smile. "Then why are you upset that he doesn't get things that you don't tell him? You know you're smart. You know you're good at hiding the things you don't want other people to see, even Robert. We've been over this, right?"

She tilts her head at me.

"Right? Haven't we been over this?"

I sigh at the bookshelves and tell her she's right. I don't tell her that I'm upset because Robert's the only one I rely on to verify my sanity, and if he doesn't get it—doesn't get anything—then what is there of reality that I know I can believe?

Chapter 18

"Dontake this personally, Duncan, but I'm gunna take a few steps back because—huh—Ican truly feel how happy you are for me."

It is Friday night, bonus day, December whatever, and I'm at Boylan's annual Christmas party. That's a stupid thing to say, of course, *Boylan's annual Christmas party,* because of course Boylan's Christmas party is always annual, unless Christmas comes more than once a year or gets skipped for some year for some reason. And I am drinking champagne. It seems perfectly appropriate, for a variety of reasons, but it's been hours, or no, days, maybe, since I've had anything to eat, lessen you count the raspberries at the bottom of my glass, one, two, three. One two three, onetwothree. I've lost count by now but figure I'm well on my way to a pint. I'm celebrating, see. Hooray for fucking me.

Robert is here, on the other side of the room, deep in conversation with Mr. Kleinman, head of the Health Products division, and with Carl. Everybody loves Robert. He's cute, and he has a great butt, still. He's a lawyer. I try to catch his eye, over Duncan's shoulder, but he's busy, staring as intently at Mr. Kleinman as Carl is at him, and as Duncan is at me. Like a big bunch of dominoes, or elephants, trunk to tail. *Robert,* I lip to him, *Robertrobert.* I want him to come over and save me from Duncan. If he doesn't, I'll have to consider it all his fault. I am having an awful day.

"I wish you could, Darien," Duncan says to me.

"Could what?"

"Could feel how happy I am for you."

Duncan smiles a wide yellow smile. There's a pianist playing somewhere and a fragile Asian boy in a toque rolling sushi. People laugh at jokes overloud, *har, har, har,* and all the wives wear velvet and sequins, holiday plaids, reds and greens, but purpleyellowblues, too. *The December session of the New York Junior League will now come to order*—Duncan rests his hand on my shoulder. "You are something, Darien, you really are something," he says.

His thumb is against my bare skin. I feel with alarm, revulsion, hilarity as it caresses the hollow of my collarbone like a slug in a bowl.

"You've been my favorite employee, Darien. Always. I always liked the way you'd fight me. I have to say I'm going to miss that daily struggle."

He takes another step toward me, and I take a sharp step back. *"HAH!"* I say, finally. "Well, I'm not, Duncan. I'm not one single bit!"

Duncan's turtle head swings around the room and then comes back to me. He sucks down his neck and shrinks his body and takes another step closer. "Now, Darien, don't say that. You'll hurt my feelings." More steps, then something touches my thigh, a kneecap. Duncan bends his head closer and whispers, "And besides, I don't think it's true at all."

Arms and legs go wet from the inside, tingly watering; Duncan's jugular throbs over me in a hard, aggressive line. I see his breathing, little round sniffs coming in through his nostrils. Duncan's jaw is clenched and he glares at something over the top of my head. I pull up my shoulders and arch my back, take a step closer under the sluggy thumb. I breathe in deep, deeper. I put my hand on Duncan's biceps and it is the biggest I ever felt. I try to find an eye to lock on but

[198]

there's only lips and it makes me want to throw up and so I say, "And what if you were right?"

"If I were right, I'd say, congratulations on your new office. I'd say I'll give you pointers on how to furnish it up right." A hand sibilates up my side. "I'd say I have a master key and that office has been empty since Rice left and it looks like everybody's at this party, to me."

"You know, I got promoted today."

"I know."

"Senior relationship manager for Hospitals and HMOs, working with Marsha Moore. Your equal." I stab a finger into Duncan's chest for emphasis, once, twice, three times. "I'm your equal."

"I know." I taste Duncan's onionstinky breath, overclose to my cheek. Slug slides again against collarbowl. "I have some very specific congratulations for you."

"Well, wudderwe waiting for, soldier?" I say. *Robertrobert*. Duncan's belt buckle is at eye-level; silver. I touch a finger to the shiny tongue. "Lead the way."

In the morning, this is what I knew: I had a huge headache and some small animal had died inside my mouth. I opened and shut my eyes many times over the course of many hours before I committed to trying to focus; dressers and closets swung as if the room were on a yo-yo string. I was sitting upright in bed, propped with four pillows— all of Robert's, all of mine. There was a glass of water on my night table, a bottle of aspirin, a gutted Alka-Seltzer packet. The bathroom wastebasket, empty of tissues and trash, lay across my lap. My dress was hooked over the closet door. I put my hand to my T-shirt. Underneath, I was still wearing a bra.

Eventually, I eased myself out of bed and made my way toward the door, dreading each step. I didn't remember much about last night, but what I remembered wasn't good. I remembered champagne dribbling over the bridge of my nose, raspberries rolling toward me. I remembered sending one of the interns off to fetch me another glass. Some unpleasantness with Duncan where I told him off. My right shoulder and neck were stiff and I rolled them out, like a swimmer. I didn't remember leaving the party, coming home.

Robert was in the living room on the couch, huddled over his laptop. Walter lay asleep in the corner. I rapped the doorframe lightly. "Hi."

Without looking up, Robert responded in kind.

"How come you're not working in the study?"

Robert shrugged. There were a couple of loud, hard clicks as he punched at the space bar on his keyboard. I made myself walk across the room.

"What are you working on?" I tried to sound teasing, but my voice was hoarse and grumbly. "Divorce papers?"

He gave one humorless snort and shook his head at the computer. "Expenses. Couple of memoranda."

"Did you stay up all night? You must be tired."

"I had a lot of work to do." He sounded exhausted. "I left work early last night so I could go to your party." *Party* had a spit in it; a note of contempt that I understood I deserved implicitly. I must have done something pretty bad.

I reached out and touched Robert's shoulder.

"Are you up now?" He asked the question without moving, or looking up at me. "Because if you are, I think I'll go to bed now for a little while."

I nodded and bit my lip, hugged myself. My skull pounded miserably, a squeezing whine in my ears. It really did sound like wet sandbags, as Nana Gilbertson had said. I suddenly wished myself back at Thanksgiving dinner, any place that would put me back far enough in time to undo the past twenty-four hours, which hung over me like a cloud of unknown quantity. I'd gotten a promotion at work. Mr.

Kleinman had shaken my hand and told me I was one of Boylan's biggest stars. I couldn't remember if I'd told Robert about that.

Robert stood up and maneuvered himself around me deliberately, exaggerated sideways steps marking off a clear distance between our bodies. His eyes went everywhere but to mine. He looked resigned, utterly defeated, like the way he had sounded on the telephone after our second meeting at the Bear Bar, when I'd called to apologize for making a fool of myself. Detached and adult. Then, he'd been polite but distant, washing his hands of me, and I'd spun like crazy to bring him back. It had worked, and his patience with me had been limitless, his admiration of my outrageousness palpable. I'd never thought, truly, that there could be a limit to either.

"Robert?" *An apology,* my brain told me, *for God's sake, Darien, tell him you're sorry.* I bit my lip harder and tasted blood.

He looked beyond me. "Would you mind taking out the garbage, if you're up to it? Walter went out a couple of hours ago but he'd probably go for another walk in a little while. You could do it on your way out." His eyes stayed on the kitchen. He took two steps past me toward the bedroom.

"Robert, I'm sorry. Wait. Please." I reached out and grabbed his arm and his eyes met mine for the first time. They looked paler in the morning light, deltas of blackish-blue beneath them trickling away in heavy lines, crow's-feet running exaggerated cracks to his cheeks. I put up my hand to touch his razor stubble. Thirty-five years old and he still had quarter-sized blank spots on either cheek, like a teenage boy just getting a beard.

"There's nothing to apologize for, Darien." He reached out for my face, a corresponding gesture, and for a foolish moment I felt relief, deliverance. His fingers touched my lip. "You're bleeding," he said, rubbing blood between his thumb and fingertips. His eyes shifted to the coffee table. "I'll clean all of that up later." He waved in the direction of his paperwork and kept going. He shut the bedroom door. I sat down on the couch, in the spot he'd just left, still warm from his body, and closed my eyes.

Shake it off, shake it off, she would say, my mother, in a singsong, when one of her boyfriends would spank us for running in his house or twist our arm for tracking muddy footprints from the pool. *Shake it off, shake it off,* she would murmur as we drove away from another town, another life. *Shake it off, shake it off,* she would say when the kids at school would pick on me for my triple-patched Toughskins and Speed Racer lunch box. I'd hear her singing it to herself softly as she daubed ointment on a split lip, or layered makeup over the creases growing in her forehead and feathering out at the sides of her mouth. *If you're gonna grow up tough you gotta learn to shake it off.*

I am still shaking it off when I get to work on Monday. All weekend, Robert has barely spoken to me, save suggesting that my sore shoulder and neck are no doubt related to passing out in the women's bathroom, yet another feature of the evening I don't remember. Perpetual nausea roils my guts. Sunday night, I decide I will call in sick, but morning comes and Robert yanks the covers back. I cling to my pillow. "I'm not going to work today," I tell him. "I'm staying home."

"No, Dee, you're not," he replies. "Not unless you plan to stay home forever. There's such a thing in this world as paying the piper, and you've got to go in there and take your lumps to put this past you. I'm not going to let you hide from this, not this time."

"Oh? Is that this morning's selection from life's big book of platitudes?" I push my face against my pillow, hard.

"I don't have time for this." Robert tugs the pillow. "Up."

"So fucking go, already. Jesus Christ. Who do you think you are, my dad? It's not your job to tell me what to do. You're not the one who has to go in there and face everybody."

"No, and I'm not the one who decided to get drunk at her office party, either."

I crush the pillow tighter. "Fuck *off*, Robert. Leave me alone." I yank at the covers but he continues to hold them away from me. "Maybe I will stay home forever. How about that?" I challenge him with a glare, but he only shrugs at me, a gesture that appears to take great effort. He is already wearing his coat and holding his briefcase. His face is parental, weary with contempt. He couldn't care less about me; this is duty only. "I'll go in tomorrow."

He sighs again tiredly. "No, Dee, I'm sorry. You'll go in today."

Robert's bland disdain propels me out of the apartment and off the train at Hudson Street. I see his casual disgust in the glass doors at Boylan and on the 17 button on the elevator. My heart pounds and I feel sick enough to pass out. I will stagger through the day, I vow; get myself fired for real. That will serve him right. I hate him for not supporting me, bringing me to work like kindergarten, holding my hand. I forgive him just a little as I round on my cubicle and don't spot a stack of packing boxes at the entrance. I scan my desk, phone, and computer monitor, all Post-it notes free; no message light on my voice mail. Apparently, whatever I've done, it isn't so egregious that Mr. Kleinman needs to see me right away.

Time crawls as I cower at my desk. I study my watch, listening to the rest of the department come in around me. Hillary and Carl, the winter interns, then the secretaries, rattling paper bags of coffee and cream-cheesed bagels. I don't hear Duncan, pray for uptown meetings or an intestinal bug. I think longingly of the new office Marsha Moore promised me, willing to trade anything for a door that locks. I pretend to read a press release about the merger of two European pharmaceutical giants and see only the phrase, "a case of the blind leading the crippled," over and over. The blind leads the crippled, the blind leads the crippled, the blind leads the crippledtheblindleadsthecrippled, and then I feel a touch on the back of my neck.

I jump and look up. It is Duncan.

"Darien." He smiles a wide yellow smile. "Hard at work?"

I look down at the press release. Someone has drawn a daisy chain of loopy circles around the perimeter of the page.

"Or hardly working?"

Duncan pushes the paper aside and sits himself down on my desk. His meaty thigh is only inches from my hand and I shudder, pull my hand into my lap. I owe him an apology. I told him off on Friday night. In my peripheral vision, a buckled loafer swings. I notice, as if it matters, that for such a tall man Duncan has awfully little feet.

He holds the press release up for me to see. He leans in toward me and murmurs, "I, too, find myself somewhat distracted today." His breath tickles my ear and neck and I pull my head away to give him a glare, apology or no, what the hell. He winks at me and my stomach goes cold.

"Listen, Duncan," I say. "I think I owe you an apology for Friday night, and I probably should have come and found you straight away, but I had some calls to make, and so I'm sorry about that." I try to laugh. "An apology for flubbing my apology. At any rate, if it's all right with you, I'd rather not do my mea culpas here. Can I buy you a cup of coffee?" I remember belatedly that Duncan is not a coffee drinker; he drinks herbal teas and protein shakes, and I revise my offer. "We could maybe grab a conference room?"

He grins and stands up. "A conference room," he says, his voice still conspiratorial. "What's wrong with my office?"

"I don't—nothing—" I push my chair away to get some distance on him; he's smiling down at me like some kind of circus freak. "Your office would be fine, of course. I just thought—"

"Or yours." Duncan's hand touches mine as he follows my chair across the cubicle. He clears his throat and bends down to speak into my ear. "Unfortunately, though, I don't have time for your, ah, apology right now. I just wanted to see how you were doing. But I

[204]

will take a rain check on that, your *apology*." He straightens up and wipes his hands on the front of his pants. "Don't make me wait too long, though, Darien. I am a patient man. I will surely take a rain check on that."

He twitches out of my cubicle, his broad shoulders, his tiny pelvis, and panic breaks over me in big, prickly waves. I grab my head and pull out two handfuls of hair in short tugs. I snap hairs into pieces, wrapping them around my fingers and yanking fast. It is better than shattering, much better than breaking off my fingers or ripping out my teeth. I want to throw myself at the plate-glass window, fall seventeen floors through merciful air. It is head-trip, pure and simple. I can't take it. I just can't take it. "What a fucking psycho," I hiss to my desk.

For the rest of the morning, I keep my head low and work on my hair. I jump every time the phone rings, sure it is Mr. Kleinman finally working his way around to the "Darien Gilbertson" item on his to-do list. It never is. It's a client; it's an intern; it is Sylvia in the library, calling to tell me my article on New England trends in managed care is ready for picking up. Robert calls once to make sure I'm okay. His voice is neutral and courteous, as if he is not calling his wife but phoning in a government documents request, and I am surprised he didn't ask his secretary to complete the order. At lunchtime, I sneak off to the bathroom when I hear Carl rally troops for the Atrium, and later, I pick the phone up and punch in my own home number any time anyone comes near. After the fourth or fifth time she walks by, however, Hillary comes into my cube and pokes the disconnect button with her thumb, putting an abrupt end to the farce of my own voice in my ear.

"Can I talk to you, Darien?" she says. She leans against the edge of my desk in roughly the same spot that Duncan occupied earlier.

"Uh, sure," I reply, bending down to rifle through a file drawer. "Can we make it later, though? I'm kinda swamped right now."

"Sure." She pauses. There's a scrape of paper as she slides something across my desk. "Why don't you call me when you're free."

I see Hillary's legs uncross as she pushes herself away from my desk and out of my cube. "Okay," I say. "I'll call you later. Tonight."

Hillary's moving feet stop. "I'm only trying to help, Darien," she says, close to my head.

"Help what? I'm fine."

"You're not fooling anyone, Darien. I know you think you are, but you're not."

"I wasn't trying to *fool* anyone, Hillary. Maybe I'd just like it if everyone would mind their own business and leave me alone."

I look up now, wait for the lip curl, the scowl, as Hillary stalks out of the cubicle. Instead, she leans back and studies me, winding a curl around her finger. She shakes her head slowly, affecting matronly dismay. "You can't pull that on me, Darien, no dice. I know you way better than that."

No, you don't, Hil. You really don't. I want to say it but I don't, knowing that to do so would be to add another mistake to an already extensive list. I'm tired, though, of people who seem to think they know me, know how I ought to behave: Robert, Dr. Lindholm, and now Hillary. I don't know myself, don't know the first thing about me anymore, and so there's no way anyone else does, certainly not Hillary. *You're too late for this,* I should tell her. *You're at least five years too late.*

"Push all you want, Darien, I'm not going anywhere," she says. "I'll sit on this desk until you're ready to talk to me."

I sigh and lock my arms across my chest. Suddenly, I crave a showdown. I imagine hysterics and histrionics, and it's a welcome reprieve from Robert's cold silences or Duncan's creepy familiarity. "Okay, you win," I say. "Happy? You want to talk, I'm all yours." I stand up and reach for my bag. "What'll it be? The Back Room? McSorleys?"

Invoking two of our oldest haunts conjures up an instant picture of me and Hillary laughing across cheap melamine, cigarette smoke, the loose-elbow feel of icy beers, and minutely I find myself swaying toward her. Hillary smiles and puts her hand on my bag. "Forget that. I'm treating. I was thinking we could try that new coffee bar down the street."

It has grown colder out since the morning and I soon regret leaving the office without my gloves. Wind blows garbage down Hudson Street and a section of newspaper plasters itself against my legs. I bunch my fists in my pockets and try to hurry Hillary along, but she is in a wandering, small-talking mood, seemingly oblivious to the garbage and the wind and the cold. She congratulates me on my promotion and I thank her quickly. She asks about Robert and my plans for Christmas and I tell her we'll be celebrating in Eastman by ourselves, then going to Robert's brother's house on the twenty-sixth. She asks why all the travel and I explain that David and Cynthia have a newborn, which somehow seems to grant them senior status in the family decision-making dynamic. Hillary smiles, as if this is one of the wittier observations I've ever made.

At the coffee shop, we're the only customers. I order a caramel mocha gingerbread latte, the most ridiculous thing on the menu. Hillary orders a cappuccino, decaf, and a tall glass of milk.

"So," I say, after the waiter has set our drinks on the table and walked away. "Let's have it."

Will it be a comradely lecture, admonishing me not to throw away all the professional advantages I have been given? Or the lament of the onetime fellow-at-arms, wondering where it all went, what happened to my spark? *Remember how close we were, Darien; how happy you were then?* I raise my latte glass to a half-salute, ready to drink to whatever agon Hillary is ready to lay on me.

Hillary smiles nervously. "Mark and I are pregnant."

My drink makes it halfway to my lips and then stops. "You and Mark are what?"

Hillary says it again. "Mark and I are expecting a baby."

[207]

Congratulations, I'm supposed to say. *Best wishes.* "Holy shit. On purpose?" is what comes out instead.

"Not exactly, no." Hillary isn't smiling anymore.

"Shit, Hil." For a second, I feel something of our old comradeship flare. "I'm sorry."

"Don't be. I said we didn't plan it, I didn't say we weren't happy about it."

My cheeks go hot and I glance quickly around the room. "I didn't mean it like that. I meant I was sorry for saying something so stupid about whether it was on purpose or not. Of course it's great news. I mean, a baby. Wow."

"Thanks." Hillary laces and unlaces her fingers quickly a few times around her milk glass. "It *is* great news. I was a little freaked out at first. I mean, can you see me changing diapers? Playing patty-cake? And I didn't have any idea what Mark really thought. But my parents were over the moon, and one day he came home with this little stuffed bear, Mark, that is, and I—" Hillary's guarded expression has lifted with her words, but now in mid-sentence she stops and shifts me a look of sudden and horrible pity.

"Look, Darien." Hillary rests one hand against her abdomen. "I'm sorry. I'm worried about you. Being pregnant has made me see things differently. I love you, and I just want you to be happy. If there's anything I can do . . ."

It's just the hormones talking, the HCG, and Hillary should know it, but I get the message now, loud and clear: the world is moving on and I am being left behind. I was right about the Darwin thing, after all. The piece I hadn't understood was that building a family is the most basic requirement for being a legitimate adult; it is the step required to prove that your life is evolving, your trajectory forward. Without this demonstration of your protogenerative power you're simply stuck in place, or maybe sliding backwards; becoming extinct.

Wanting children is selfish, that much I've understood all along; it's wanting a claim to the world. Actually taking it is proof you were meant to be here. And if Hillary can claim it, anyone can.

I await the burst of triumph I expect to accompany this revelation. After all, here it is, the second sign, what I've been waiting for all along. Heraldic declaration of my slow, sure demise. I told you I was dying. I told you I was grand and glorious, heroic, tragic, Byronic, self-exiled and cast out, I told you I was a warrior, brandishing my broken bones like a banner, a fantastic symbol of my defiance. Told you I was a martyr, self-nailed to my own private cross.

I continue to wait.

Across the table, Hillary's eyes mother me. I open my mouth for my own annunciation. Other words come out.

"Cheers, Hillary. That's really great. I'm very happy for you." I lift my drink and clink it against hers with a satisfying *chunk*. She has tears in her eyes, but her smile is almost rapturous. I smile quickly and look away, because for a stupid, weak second I want that rapture for myself. I look away because for a second it hurts.

I'm sitting in this big, sunny playroom, cross-legged on the floor, doing my damnedest to get this baby to smile. The room is full of children, a waiting room, a nursery, and laughter bounces off the walls with the streams of sunlight and crayon drawings, high baby giggles and happy shrieks, but not from this kid. I smile at him, stick my tongue out, *ppphhht,* and he eyes me calmly, blankly, big cobalt pools locked straight into me. His hair stands out in downy spikes, his mouth turns down like a bloom-blown rose. He is grossly fat, rippled like a hubbard squash, and I hold him propped between both hands like a pig on a bicycle. I cross my eyes, waggle my tongue. "Bay-bee," I trill, dolphin-high, "hello, bay-bee." His gaze goes right through me and I realize too late that there is something terribly wrong with this child, as if he isn't a child at all, a man made of rubber, flattened and compacted, comic-book style, hammered into the earth. Plutonium, uranium, cold carbon steel. I take my hands away slowly, carefully, like someone setting down a basket of snakes, but his eyes won't let go of me.

Duncan walks in and picks the baby up from behind, and now I see the blue felt-marker Xs and hatchmarks that track his fat-folded back in three parallel lines. I look up at Duncan. "What's wrong with him?"

Duncan wears scrubs. A surgical mask dangles around his neck.

"Not a him," Duncan says, "them. Siamese twins."

He turns to take the baby out of the room.

Them.

Oh.

But.

One head, one body.

"One head?" I say. "One body?" The trackmarks down the back divide the baby in three.

"One head. One body. One set of lungs. One penis." Duncan grins and electric blue light dances between his teeth.

"But," I say. "But—"

Duncan turns and stops, halfway across the room, heading for a set of swinging doors. Behind him, I see the cold, sapphire light of a suspended overhead, the stainless sterility of the suite beyond. He shrugs his shoulders, the baby still in his arms. "One of them will die."

The baby looks at me and speaks in a voice I've heard before: "Help me."

Chapter 19

For the first time, I come to Dr. Lindholm without defenses. I count the days, hours, minutes until Wednesday at six. I sit in her waiting room and rock myself anxiously, hating the anonymous patient who comes before me, exits discreetly through the back door, leaves the couch warm. I whisper to myself, inchoate prayers, *Please, please—* When Dr. Lindholm finally appears at the door, I nearly throw myself at her, hurry into the warm cave of her office. As soon as I sit down on the couch, my eyes fill with tears.

"Oh, no." She starts up out of her chair and toward me, arms spread as if to furnish a hug. My own arms flail frantically to wave her off.

"No, please. If you do that I'll never get through this." I pull a tissue from the box at my left elbow and jam it against first one tear duct and then the other, relief in the small pain. I close my eyes. I hear the clock, Dr. Lindholm's breathing. She waits for me.

I rock behind my tissue, soothe the sofa with a gentle, cattle creak. Forehead against palm, warm on cool, I could go to sleep. "I feel like everything's falling apart. There are too many pieces. I just can't hold them all. It's like—it's like I've been running, and juggling at the same time, and carrying on three conversations at once, and I just don't know. I suddenly can't do it. I feel like I'm having a nervous break-down."

Creak, creak, list, rock. Wave, shore. Part of me hates this, loathes me for what I am doing here. *What are you doing, Darien? What the hell is this all about?* But the greater part feels a vast relief. I can just let go. It is not a thought that has occurred to me previously, that would have appeared as a legitimate possibility. I can just let go of all of this, stop fighting, stop screaming. I can just bid my brain adieu. For a minute, I am unable to locate the harm, the hurt in doing so. Send it away like a bad dog or a letter, a helium balloon hurrying skyward after some Truman Capote metaphor.

"Uh-huh." Dr. Lindholm's voice is low and soothing, coming from somewhere outside of her body.

"I don't know." I feel the small spill, a liquid gush and trickle. It is enormously quiet inside my head. I breathe deep the scent of the cave. Wood, wood. Deep and brown. Chewy putty of paint, warm, tallowy leather, icy glass, atticsmelling; the sicky, sticky sweet of an off season flower. I float above a strange meadow. Rolling hills, wheat grass bending in the breeze, clusters of purple heather, red and yellow Indian paintbrush. Shapes transform as I think about them. A field of poppies, the Wizard of Oz. I clatter to the floor in the Boylan bathroom, cold ceramic on a champagne spin. I spin into my dorm bed, vomit in my laundry basket, lose again at quarters, heave vodka and fruit punch. One foot on the floor, proprioperception, safe, a fifties sitcom. Ricky and Lucy. *Leave It to Beaver. The Brady Bunch.* Touralouraloura, alone. Left alone. Fourteen. *Good-bye,* I say to my brain. Good-bye.

"Darien," Dr. Lindholm croons. "Darien. Please, let me help you. Let me do this with you, please. What are you feeling?"

"I don't know." Words find my mouth with effort. "I don't know. Sad, I think, or maybe upset. Scared. I'm not sure." For a moment, I can say: I feel desperate. Desperate to feel something, to understand what I feel, to tie the awful, clenching, shifting pain inside of me to some garden-variety, commonly accepted emotion. Something as tidy as anger or fear.

"What happened, then? What went wrong? Can you tell me about it? Start with something specific."

"I don't *know*," the refrain as wail. "Nothing. Everything. I—I—I—" The metal plate, the ice floe, I can't tell which, has shifted to my throat, blocking off all speech. Glibness vacant, severed, source depleted. Complete sentences impossible. "—just *sit* here?"

"Of course you can," Dr. Lindholm says. "Darien, we're going to get through this. It's going to be okay. It may not feel like it right now, but I promise you, we will."

I take a hard breath, hold it steady against my ribs. I crush both hands tight, trading fists for breath, exhale loudly. Better. Speeding up or slowing down. I look at Dr. Lindholm and realize how badly I have blown it. She is frowning at me, eyebrows down, lips up, her whole face compacted with worry. I comprehend what I have done, the step that has been taken over some unseen threshold, the undoable change in our relationship. I have become the patient now, absolutely. Sick. Needy. Medication imminent, or hospitalization. I will myself into a spartan, barred bed, feel the coils through the thin mattress like a physical craving. I stay there I can't say how long. I come to and get myself the hell out.

"I feel better now," I say minutely. "I'm sorry about all that. I don't know what this is all about." With effort, I wave my hand at the last five minutes, at Dr. Lindholm's frowning face.

"I think maybe I just don't like holidays." My voice seems smaller than usual in the room and I find myself talking loud and hard to fill up the space. I tell Dr. Lindholm about the Christmas party, about being promoted, about fighting—not fighting—with Robert. I tell her about the drinking, confess to everything with something like relief, the words now working, as free as I can remember feeling. *It doesn't matter. You don't have to hide.* I tell her how it hurt to talk to Hillary.

When I finish, Dr. Lindholm is still watching me cautiously, and I want to reassure her, *No, I'm okay,* but I can't. It's not my place.

Finally she speaks, a little unsure of herself, it seems. "Holidays can be hard," she says. I nod yes. She hesitates. "Is this something you feel comfortable talking about? Should we continue with this?"

"Yes." Thank you, Jesus. A chance to redeem myself, to put it back together. Tell that spartan, barred bed, *Better luck next time.*

"Is there anything in particular that you think will be hard about this year?"

"No, I don't think so," I say. "We're going up to Connecticut by ourselves. It's what we usually do. I really don't sit around and feel bad about my family. I'm sure that's what you're thinking."

As if in defiance of my statement, my eyes fill again with tears. These are unexpected, though, as if tapped from an external source, some spigot to the side of my head turned by an unseen hand.

"No?" Dr. Lindholm puts in, coaxing. "What are you sad about?"

"I don't know." I shake my head and feel a tear slide back and forth along the underlip of my eye like a ball bearing on a skateboard ramp. "I don't know!" There is shock there, and betrayal, as if I am understanding for the first time how irreparably severed my brain and body are.

"Can you tell me what it was like, Christmas in your family?"

Yes. That much I am capable of, can do with an ease that surprises me. It's something I haven't thought about in years, something I went through a period of deliberately not thinking about, of banishing, the entire notion of holiday and family, and I expect my archetype for Christmas to be deeply buried, the scents and sounds and images difficult to conjure. Instead, I find that it is immediately beneath the surface, attached between my topmost layer and skin like a blood blister, neatly packaged, whole, something I have carried with me all along.

"Christmases in my family were sort of manic-depressive is probably the best way of generalizing it," I tell her.

"It depends on the year. Some were a lot of fun, like the year we were at my grandparents' house in Iowa. We ate a real holiday dinner and had presents, just like any normal family. I got one of those giant Barbie heads, the ones you could put makeup and earrings on, and style the hair for. Beauty Parlor Barbie, I think it was called. I was really happy about that."

Dr. Lindholm nods at me encouragingly. I feel for wet spots on the underside of the tissue and poke holes through them with my fingernail.

"Another year I remember one of my mother's boyfriends got us kids a whole year's subscription from a place called the Pop Shoppe that delivered soda to your house. Not just any soda, though, but Pop Shoppe soda, in little glass bottles, with flavors like apple and blueberry and chocolate and ginger beer. Every month we'd get a great big flat of sodas and Mac and Ken would hog up all the ginger beer because they thought it was real beer and our mom just hadn't noticed, and they would stagger around and fall all over the place because they'd actually convinced themselves they were drunk. I didn't care. It was the worst flavor of all of them, some cross between cream soda and mouthwash. I liked the apple best. It was a weird fluorescent green.

"And then one year I got this T-shirt that I was so excited about. That was probably my favorite Christmas of all. I'd seen it in a department store over the summer and had bugged my mom about it for months. It was a white T-shirt, one of those baseball T-shirts, with red sleeves. It had a decal on the front and my name in iron-ons on the back. The decal was this kitten, hanging from a tree limb by one paw, with the saying, 'Hang in there, baby, Friday's coming,' underneath the picture, and—"

Abruptly, I am laughing, foaming, percolating hysterical laughter. "I'm sorry," I gasp, eventually. "I have no idea why that's so funny."

Dr. Lindholm smiles at me, sharing in a joke that neither of us quite get. "Why, Darien," she says, lightly teasing. "I do believe that sounds like genuine amusement."

I nod, not quite breathing. "I guess so. I mean—'Hang in there, baby, Friday's coming'? I was like five. What the heck did I need to hang in there until Friday for?"

Laughter overtakes me again for a minute; I again feel wetness spill from my eyes. I sigh, applying the ratty tissue carefully. I see the shirt again, vividly, the scrawny, tiger-tufted kitten, staring out from the decal in mute, helpless appeal. Poor terrified kitten! In the store, my chest had ached for it. I would more than wear it, I would cradle it. When I'd opened the present on Christmas, I couldn't believe my eyes. My mother had remembered.

"But I really wanted that T-shirt." I sigh; a long silence. "A couple of Christmases were pretty bad, I guess, compared to that.

"A couple were pretty miserable, actually. There was the year my mom split up with Tony, I guess that sort of stands out. He was the one who lived outside of Philadelphia, the assistant principal? I don't think we even *had* Christmas that year. It was kind of a case of bad timing. He'd been fooling around with one of his students, and she came by the house a couple of days before Christmas to drop something off, a recommendation form or a paper, maybe. My mother answered the door, and there must have been some kind of scene or something, some behind-closed-doors meltdown. All I know is the next thing, my mother's reeling drunk, locked herself in the bathroom, and Tony's just out of there."

Dr. Lindholm's office becomes Tony's living room. I see the pea green shag of the rug, smell the fuggy mix of mildew and cigarettes that it discharged regularly, like a smokestack chugging out creosote.

Striped light falls from the kitchen, cheap jalousied doors in imitation woodgrain.

"My mother never said a word about it. Not about a fight, not about Tony leaving, not about Christmas. But Dayton and I had given her and Tony this *godawful* Christmas ornament as a present the year earlier—it was this sort of hippie couple, made out of some sort of ceramic dough, naked behind this big toilet paper banner that said, 'Merry Christmas Lenora and Anthony, nineteen seventy-whatever,' seventy-six, maybe, because I think their divorce went through in mid-seventy-eight—and my mother had broken it in half and thrown it in the trash. I found it the day before Christmas, just the woman-half, actually, with the part of the banner that read, 'Merry Christmas Lenora and Ant.' The man-half was pulverized, like she'd smashed it with a hammer or something. She said it was an accident."

The room goes silent again, but this time it seems more than quiet. It seems under the force of some negative pressure, as if all the oxygen in the air were being drawn out, pumped elsewhere, and the air that remains seems thinner, attenuated somehow in the unplanned-for space. I feel the pull, subtly, sucking me back against the wall.

"Darien." Dr. Lindholm's voice is almost a whisper, as if vacuumed out by the pressure, a vibration beneath it, and when I look at her, I know she feels it, too. Her face is scared. "Say again for me what you just said."

I am puzzled, uncomprehending of what I have done wrong, though I clearly have done wrong. "She said it was an accident?" I hear my voice lift up above the humming, a question, a guess.

"No, the whole thing. Tell me the story over. How did you start it? Who bought the ornament for Tony and your mother?"

I look at her small, strange face, bewildered. It is as if, abruptly, we have begun speaking separate languages, languages with different syntaxes, constructions, meanings. I have dropped English like a rope, lank and heavy. It lies before me in a flat, undifferentiated line. I reach back for the story, but the words have vanished from my brain. I know it was something about Christmas, about Tony; something about an ornament. But the words to tell the story are missing, erased, and the harder I pull, the more the letters unravel. The light in the room has gone green, the air still humming. I am having a stroke.

"I don't know."

Dr. Lindholm's voice is so soft it's barely audible. She speaks slowly. "You said, 'Dayton and I bought Mom and Tony this awful Christmas ornament.' Who's Dayton?"

I measure the two small syllables on my tongue. Heavy. Substantial. Suspicious. Day-ton. I say, "You know. Dayton. My sister."

In the strobe pulse of a moment, I am able to comprehend what has happened. For a heartbeat, it is not too big, not impossible, and I am able to grasp the thought wholly, with perfect rationality. That thing that has been drifting around inside of me, the ice floe, banging first one wall and then another, rising, falling, has finally found its opening, a bloodless runnel in the back of my neck, and silently, sterilely come out. Dayton. My sister. The words hang suspended in the air next to me, just to the left of my line of vision, luminous, plain, almost invisible, for a second, a beat, another. Dayton. My sister. And then they fall to the floor and throw a million sticky shards, razors and knifelets, up to my legs, my arms, my face.

Two

Chapter 20

Robert and Dr. Lindholm look at me from funny angles. Right angles, in fact, as if I have caught them fooling, in the middle of a David Copperfield stunt perhaps, their chairs turned ninety degrees sideways on the wall. They are cross-legged and wrinkled, a pair of commuters waiting for the M-31 bus. I understand at once they are goofing for me. "You guys," I want to say, suddenly tickled, suddenly abashed, but my lips u—u—a few times uselessly and the words won't come. Their expressions are relations: Dr. Lindholm, frowning, unhappy, I suppose, about balancing on the wall; the commuter with the place to go. Robert frowning, worried, afraid that I'm the one who will fall onto the floor. He doesn't need to worry, though. I am welded in place.

I am welded in place, and that seems odd, propped in ridiculous upright as if I have been dipped head to toe in epoxy and then left to dry. It occurs to me that I must be standing, because I am straight-legged, and nobody sits straight-legged, it isn't possible, but I wait to feel the comforting weight of gravity against my feet and it doesn't come. I search my body, top to bottom, and I still can't find it, feet, knees, hips. All I locate is a strange pounding at the back of my head.

I will ask Robert, I think, what is going on, still sitting silly, sitting sideways on the wall. He looks at me, but he isn't looking, and when I wave my arm to get his attention, it doesn't move. There is a door on the wall next to him and I am afraid he will use it, walk out sideways like Spiderman before I have a chance to tell him I am here. Only my head is working, not my arms, not my feet, not my tongue. I don't know where I am.

—Robbut?

He leans over and says something to Dr. Lindholm, his voice hollow and bouncy, and then, just as fast as I didn't, I realize I *do* know where I am. Somehow, we have ended up at the bottom of a swimming pool, like that girl Joni I read about who broke her neck diving and couldn't masturbate. She ended up in one of those Stryker frames, her head in a halo like a roasting pig on a spit, but I think she learned to paint watercolors with her teeth.

—RobBUT?

Louder, I try again. I don't so much like his talking to Dr. Lindholm, them excluding me. Sounds slide down the walls of the pool, masking Dr. Lindholm's reply to Robert, her professional murmur, a loud, steady pinging and an announcer's voice, as if a race is about to start over our heads. *On your mark, get set*—There's no way I can race, not glued, not frozen in place like this.

For what reason, I'm not so sure, but Dr. Lindholm is here in official capacity. She has stolen from her office chair; she is wearing her white lab coat, a stethoscope slung sideways around her neck like a doctor on TV. I try to giggle, at first. Who is she kidding? She's not a doctor, not a real doctor, she wears bouclé sweaters and Venetian glass neck-laces and Bergdorf Goodman shoes. But then I think of her chair, her gray leather easy chair, sitting alone and empty in her office, aban-doned, forsaken, stripped naked, and then I start to cry.

I cry and cry, and the world goes all black-green, and the announcer calls the race again, and then Robert is over me, finally, off the wall without falling, his anxious face looking anxious in mine. I feel him take hold of my hand though I can't see it, and he strokes it over and over as he stands on the wall.

"Dairy-Anne?" He tries to smile at me but his lips do the wave instead, trembling like surface tension. I think of poking my finger into a glass of water, what do they call that? Meniscus curve. "Haydee," he says, "hay's wheaty. Oh, sweetie. I'm so sorry. It's okay, Darien, I'm here."

I hear *I'm so sorry* and it makes me cry harder. He understands; he sees about the chair. I think of it again, see it waiting, patient, in the dark of Dr. Lindholm's office, see it hunch its shoulders and cower, not understanding what it has done wrong. It's held her faithfully, softly; so perpendicularly. I wail, "Oh, Robert. Dr. Lindholm—the chair!" I keep sobbing, though I no longer remember what I am crying about; the tears feel too good. Dr. Lindholm's face crowds into the square Robert makes over me.

"Darien?" Her voice is like rulers and Granny Smith apples. "It's Dr. Lindholm. Do you remember me?"

I nod. I am crying too hard to speak.

"Do you know where you are?"

The question inspires new despair, formless, incalculable. Of course I do. I flail my epoxied arms, howl panic, futility. I'm trapped here! "Yuh-yuh-yes," I sob. "I'minna swimming pooe."

Dr. Lindholm gives me one of her kind smiles and reaches out to stroke my hair. "No, Darien," she says firmly. "You are not in a swimming pool. You are in the hospital."

I stop crying. I am? My eyes slide across the rippling walls. Green bends and waves at me, the tinny *ping-pings* sing behind my head. I roll my eye rearwards and make out the corner of a miserly, chicken-wired window, filtering fake yellow light. Not a hospital. A swimming pool. I strain my neck back and see gray cords snaking upwards, climbing the wall of the pool behind my head, reaching for the surface. I travel left and see a thin tube, an IV bag anchored above it, matter-of-factly dripping fluid through a pipette. Farther left, a TV monitor, green grids and orange lines ribboning across the screen. A tiny heart throbs in one corner, counts *98, 96, 92, 89, 97,* my breaths get liquid, jerky, counts *98, 104, 116, 121, 136*— Oh, Jesus. Not a swimming pool. A hospital. The monitor screams at me.

"Darien!" Dr. Lindholm's voice is sharp. She steps over me, reaches in front of my face, and turns a dial on the IV tube. The drip-drip-drips start double time. Her fingers are hard, cold on my wrist.

"Darien, listen to me." Her words turn my face with effort, away from the shrieking heartbeat. "You're at Mount Lebanon Hospital. You're in the emergency room." The emergency room, Mount Lebanon. She speaks deliberately, and I feel myself shrink, melt. I am lying in bed. The monitor quiets. "You've had some medication, and I've just given you a little more. You probably feel a little confused right now, and you're going to begin to get groggy. You might even feel it already." Her eyes leave me, come back again. "Go ahead and go to sleep if you want to, okay? I want you to relax."

The words make sense. I nod, and my head makes a big, ugly *thwi-thwi* across the pillow. It hurts, vaguely. I think to ask her why and then I don't.

Some time passes. A snake sucks tight around my left biceps, hugs harder, and then lets go. Robert stands over me, kneading my right biceps correspondingly. I can't see my hands. I am thirsty. Dr. Lindholm walks out of the pool and then back in.

Clatter-thunk as she pulls a chair over to my side. "How are you feeling now, Darien?"

"Uh-kaye."

"Do you remember being in my office tonight?"

This I have to think about. In principle I do. I have a model for it: I been there plenty. Brown couch, gray chair, printwainscoting, Paris blue. *DSM-IV, The Mutilated Mind.* Tissues, ecru. A-choo. My cheeks move, stay.

"What are you smiling about?"

I raise my arm to touch my face, am I smiling? My arm lifts minutely and then won't move. I remember, this time, to ask.

"Whuzrong wih miarmz?" My tongue is swelled to double size and someone has tied it to the base of my mouth. "Am I paralice?" I think of that Joni girl again, bobbing along the bottom of her swimming pool like a stunned fish. I try to panic but adrenaline is elusive. I am at Mount Lebanon, I am in the emergency room.

"You're in restraints, Darien. You were very upset when you came here." Dr. Lindholm pauses. "Would you like me to take them off?"

I suppose I should. I think about the question, but disinterestedly, the way I used to think about integrals in high school calculus, or questions raised by boys in college I'd screwed and sent away, like, *Why are you so fucked up?* Or, *Have you always been such a cunt?* The question is something I should care about. Restraints are bad; restraints signify bad. I made a crack to Dr. Lindholm about them once. Four-point restraints, I think they're called. Wrist one, wrist two; lift my legs for ankle three, ankle four. For Robert's sake, then.

"Yes, please." And then, because I do, "I have an itch on my nose."

Dr. Lindholm gets up. She walks around the bed, blocking my view of the TV monitor, the TV heart, now bleeping lazily, regular. A creak and a bright metal snap and then my hand drifts up to my nose. Dr. Lindholm smells orange, like face powder, chemical. I lift the restraint toward my eyes. Scarred, heavy leather. Three buckles, grooved straps, for a dog with a triple-wide neck. Yellowing, rusting terrycloth on the inside.

"These yours?" I ask Dr. Lindholm. I think to be concerned about whether the restraints are sanitary. The terrycloth is gathered up in little pills. I sniff my wrist and it smells sour.

"How do you mean?" She makes her worried face and I giggle; I didn't mean like *that*. But then, because she's given me license, I picture it, Dr. Lindholm and her Sotheby's husband, doing dirty with four-point restraints, spread-eagled, sprawled, Dr. Lindholm shackled to the bed.

She sits down again and rakes her hair back with one hand. "Does that feel better? Do you feel okay?"

I nod my head again and feel the vague, burning pain in the back, on the bulge of my occipitus, a ponytail yanked far too tight. "I think I hurt my head."

Dr. Lindholm agrees. "Yes, you did. You have some stitches."

I press my head into the pillow, roll slightly side to side. I try to count the stitches with the pressure; differentiate the knots against my skull.

"Do you remember how you hurt yourself?"

I do not. Dr. Lindholm hesitates, and asks me what I remember about being in. her office. I remember the question; she asked me before. I tell her about the chair, the couch, the ecru tissues, the *DSM-IV*. She frowns.

"Yes. Those are things within my office. But those things are always in my office. Can you tell me anything specific you remember about tonight?"

I try to focus, remember something, but it is difficult. I don't like giving the wrong answer. I try a little harder. A vase of flowers. A new picture frame? The return of *Dr. Susan Love's Breast Book*. My brain slides around on top of memory like a thumb on a cube of chicken fat. It bulges to one side and then the other. It pops out and lies quivering on the floor.

"I don't know." My hand comes up and pats my bandaged occipitus, something like a maxi-pad taped to the back of my head. Tidy. I can feel the whiteness, the cleanliness. I no longer care about right answers. "Can I go home now?" Something reminds me, blandly, that I do not like hospitals.

[226]

Dr. Lindholm and Robert trade looks. "I'm afraid not," she says. "I want to keep you here, in an inpatient bed. For observation. Just for a couple of days."

I finger the bandage a little more, dimly impressed with myself. "How many stitches did I get?"

Dr. Lindholm shakes her head negatively. "Only a couple. Nothing to worry about."

"But how many?"

"Six, I think. Or maybe seven." She takes a deep breath. "Darien, do you remember talking to me about Christmas?" She pauses. "It's important."

I think about it a second. I do remember. "Yes!" My voice is louder than I expected it to be. I feel triumphant.

"Good." She looks relieved and I think I might not have to stay, after all. "What do you remember?"

I remember talking about Eastman. I remember Beauty Parlor Barbie, hang in there, baby, apple soda. I remember that Christmas is coming, that I want to buy an overcoat for Robert at Aquascutum, order Walter a new bed from the Orvis catalogue. I remember that I am not sad.

"Do you remember telling me about the year your mother had the fight with Tony?"

I remember green carpet, jalousied light, *Merry Christmas, Lenore and Ant*— I remember that I am sad. Without permission, my eyes start to cry.

"Do you remember telling me about Dayton?"

"Yes." I sniff. A tear sneaks down to settle between my lips. A bubble breaks in my stomach, fills my abdomen. The walls of my insides go grainy and loose, collapse, wash away. I speak to tense them, for glue. "Yes. I do."

"Who's Dayton, Darien?" Dr. Lindholm's voice comes out soft.

"She's my sister."

A shriek, a long, low horn, chair on floor like a car crash. Robert on his feet.

"Where is she now?"

Flood melts me, becomes me. Shake it off, move, it doesn't exist. Love the pain. Become the pain. "I, I don't know." Hear the words in my head, struggle to make them real, struggle to make them a lie. There is no difference. Saying, not saying doesn't matter. What happened was. Is. "She isn't—she's dead. She killed herself."

Oh. Dr. Lindholm's eyes flutter and close. Long, soft silence, *ping-pinging, ping-pinging,* and then I hear someone crying wild, jerky sobs. I cannot cry like that, the sobs would break me. Rip me into pieces. Dr. Lindholm grabs at my hand and squeezes it hard. The pain feels nice. My head is light, high. I travel down my arm and seek refuge in the crushing grip, the tight security. "We were fourteen."

Dr. Lindholm's eyes open again, s-l-o-w-l-e-e. "You both were."

Pain against the pillow. "Yes. Of course. We both were. I told you I was twins." I laugh, abruptly. "I mean, we were twins. I was a twin."

The eyelids close, shutter and lift, shutter and lift with each breath, come to rest, butterflies. I imagine the delicate blue veins crooking through them, tiny, lacy pink capillaries feeding each eyelash. My heartbeat slows to match the rhythm: one open, two close, *tha-thump, tha-thum.* One open, two close, *tha-thump, tha-thum.* They close, they close, *thump, thum.* Dr. Lindholm must be sleeping. I am sleepy. It must be very late. Hours, then years, then seconds pass. The lids rise up over a matter of weeks.

"Can you tell me what happened?"

I roll my head over my stitches, back and forth, back and forth. I take my time, roll with the thud of my heartbeat, the remembered breath of her eyelids. I have forever to do it and I take my time, because I cannot. Cannot say to Dr. Lindholm. Can you tell me what happened? It is far too big a question for me to answer.

Chapter 21

Dee. Dee-e-e. Dee-e-e-e—" The voice in my head is a feather, light and fluffy and tickly. It rises and falls like breath. Sunlight burns through my eyelids, turning the world invisible orange-red, but if I don't squint I don't see. I don't squint; it is too early. I'm not ready to get up yet. The sheet is hot against my skin and my legs are sticky beneath it. Already, there is no breeze, and the fabric hangs on me. I think of ice cream cones teetering with soft-serve vanilla, chocolate and lime candy topping. I think of Otter Pops and rocket-shaped Popsicles.

"Dee, wake up," the voice complains. It tickles its lips against my ear and breathes a hot, pinky smell against my skin.

I smile, though I try not to, and the voice giggles knowingly. "You're awake!" it cries. "You're awake, you're awake!"

I open my eyes and Dayton is there.

She is wearing the Wonder Woman bathing suit, mine. The yellow crest on the red top is faded and her nipples poke dots in the fabric. The blue bottom gaps around her legs. She has rubber bands around both wrists, bullet reflectors, and the star band around her forehead. She is carrying a towel. One foot reaches up, stork-style, scratches the opposite leg, and thunks back down on purple carpet. She hasn't put on the boots. Sunlight catches white hairs on her thighs. I close my eyes again and pull the sheet up over my head. Wonder Woman's my favorite. The Cinderella bathing suit is hers. Inside the bed, the air is thick and sour.

Dayton claps fat hands at me. "Dee," she pleads, "wake up!" She tries to pull down the sheet, but I am stronger. Light twists and wrinkles over my head. Dayton stops tugging and crawls into the bed from the side. Her hair tickles my legs and stomach as she climbs up my front. Our knees knock and we both whisper giggles. *Getupgetupgetup,* she hisses, digging her fingers into my armpits. Her chin bangs into my collarbone. She gives me hard, pointy kisses a million times and my fingers have to, they let go of the sheet. I push Dayton off and am on my feet in a single motion. "Race you!" I cry. I run to the bathroom and yank Cinderella off the door.

The grass is wet and we make footprints. The big dog next door barks at us through the metal fence, but he's on a rope and we're not afraid. We make two circuits before we climb into the pool. The water is shivery-cool and we scream and *sssh* each other. We hug arms as we scrunch ourselves in. Knees, thighs, bellies, shoulders. We dunk down on command. Icy delight pours out of us in silver bubbles that pop one another as they rise.

We play Marco Polo, we do somersaults and jumping jacks, bottom to surface, we walk on our hands and do slow-motion backflips. We do a seesaw, clutching hands, first one up and then the other. We sit on the bottom, or try to, breathing from each other's mouths until all the air is gone. I open my eyes to the bitter, wavering world and look at Dayton. Her lids are squeezed shut. We laugh at goose pimples and shivering purple lips.

"You're coldest," Dayton says.

"No, I'm not," I shoot back. "You are."

Next door, the big dog keeps barking. A screen door slams and there's the smell of bacon frying. We climb out of the water and fall to the ground and our hands are wrinkled white. Dirt is hot on our knees and palms and the tops of our feet. Bacon rumbles our stomachs. We lick our dry lips and our mouths taste like chlorine.

Mac comes around from the front of the house in shorts and bare feet. A dirty T-shirt is pulled up tight over his rounded stomach and he's holding a soggy-nosed paper airplane. We watch as he loops the plane through the air and makes *bbbb*'s with his lips. He crashes the plane into the ground and it crumples. He gets on his hands and knees to straighten it and we can see his underwear, white peeking above the yellow shorts. He throws the plane and it wobbles to the ground, he tries again and it falls harder this time. He jumps up and down on it and yells, *Dammit!* We giggle at each other, clinging to the pool.

"Suhlilily Muhlulac," Dayton mouths to me.

"Stuhlupuhlilid Muhlulac," I respond.

"He bruhloloke huhlilis pluhlalane."

"He bruhloloke huhlilis bruhlali*lane*."

Mac walks over to the fence and sticks his hand through one of the holes. The sound of barking gets louder. The dog leaps at our brother, but the rope catches it and breaks its bark. Mac kicks the fence and laughs. "Stupidog," we hear him mumble, "caneven getme. Wanna getme?" He puts his arm through the hole till his elbow disappears.

Another door slams and then Jerry is on the back steps, painter's pants and a V-neck shirt. His face is beardy and dark. "Mac!" he shouts. "Get in here! How many times I have to tell you to stay away from that goddamn dog and my pool?"

Mac shuffles away from the fence. His head is bent and his feet kick up dirt. Clumps of brown grass fly around him. "Wasn't near the pool," he mumbles. When he reaches the first step, Tony grabs his collar and yanks him the rest of the way up. They both disappear inside and Mac's whining cry starts up even before we hear the wet slap. Dayton grabs her boots and I grab my crystal slippers and we run.

Nurses come, go, pull the curtain open, shut. A large man arrives, piles me on another bed, follows a rainbow on the floor—red, yellow, green, blue. Red and yellow branch off, and we leave the swimming pool announcer's voice behind. Green goes next and the sounds subside to *ping-ping-ping-ping,* diving deeper, the walls close over us. ROYGBIV, and then blue's the only light wave left in this deep sea. My clothes swing in a bag above my head.

A door and a diving bell, *ding-ding* as it counts the atmospheres. We break through the bottom; a new bed, another door. A tiny pill rattles in a tiny paper cup; pastel yellow. A woman with a mustache stands over me.

"Swallow." Her hands are fleshy moist. My mouth is dry.

I take the paper cup and swallow. I ask for more water.

I climb into a big, blue box and someone shuts the lid.

Morning again, and it is dark and my legs are frozen from the night beneath the bar. Dayton is still sleeping, her mouth hung open in a soft oval, a shiny line of spittle tracking from her lip to her cheek to the rug. Her arm is over my waist so I lift it off slowly and hand it back to her. She shifts in her sleep and her hand crawls toward her mouth, but I push it away; we're eight now and eight's too old to be sucking your thumb. Early light pokes weakly at the crack between the bar door and the wall and Dayton blooms in the band of light that falls across her face. I ease the door open, the slowest *scree-ee-e* in the world, and back myself out into the rec room. Bottles click softly around me and I pull the door to. I leave it open a sliver so Dayton will see me when she wakes.

It is cold. The linoleum sticks to my feet and I can't stand without hopping except in the squares of sun that fall through the windows on the big green door. The room is asleep, the blue couch, the brown chair. Only the Genesee Cream Ale lamp might be awake, rocking in the invisible rhythm of the El down the road. Outside, there are garbage sounds, the clang of cans and the grinding hum of a truck. Inside, scattered drips and steady sleep sighs, the smell of beer and piss and cats. The windows are strung with dirty, panting cobwebs. I walk to the door, leaping painfully across the islands of sunlight, and tug at the handle. It is locked. My eyes travel up to the silver dead bolt; locked, too. My fingers touch the undersides of icy feathers creeping up the panes.

"Locked." My lips move but the sound doesn't come out.

I back away from the door and close my eyes in the sunlight in the center of the room. I spin in circles, taking in as much beer and cat and sun as my arms can hold. My feet make tacky spit-spit-spits on the linoleum, the back of my head throbs, and a jagged pain sinks its teeth in my shoulder blade.

"Slept funny," I whisper to the quiet room. "It's that I slept funny, is all."

I spin and spin, my soggy head back, arms aching, and the sun swings and the Genesee light is there and gone, there and gone. When I'm done, the room spins for me, and I lurch into the big blue couch. The sun makes a stain on the knobby fabric and I fall into its warm, narrow pool and soon I am back asleep. I dream about a cat with teeth like meat hooks, a circus ride that swings me against a wall. We run away, me and Dayton, but nobody cares or looks; they dead-bolt the door. I open my eyes again, and the sun is gone. Dayton is standing over me. Half of her face is scared and sleepy and curious, and the other half has blossomed the biggest, blue-purplest hydrangea you have ever seen.

She looks around the room, then back at me again. Her cheek is so big her mouth hangs open and her words are blurry as she asks the question that's been on my mind.

"Dee, what are we going to do now?"

[233]

We tiptoe up the stairs, hand-in-hand, Dayton's fingers hard against mine. At the top we go straight, step over Phil's cat. The bathroom door locks with an eye-hook. I lower the toilet seat and Dayton climbs up, her legs tucked under her. I kneel in front and empty our mother's makeup bag onto the floor. Tubes and pencils and brushes and bottles roll in every direction. Dayton bites her lip and jerks forward, but I hold up a hand and say, "It's okay, stay there. Trust me."

I line up tubes and bottles and pencils across the edge of the bath-mat. There are liquid and powder blushes, a little vial labeled *Crème Vixen Rouge*. There are three shades of foundations, five black eyeliners, an orange eyebrow pencil, and a dozen lipsticks. I run my fingertips over the head of each container and pick up a triangle-shaped bottle first. I pour a small puddle of orangey foundation into the palm of my hand.

"Hold still, Day," I say, but Dayton trembles in stiff jerks. Her knees knock against her chin. Her lips are as blue as her cheek. I pull a stiff towel off the shower rod and drape it over her.

The foundation goes on in big gluey smears and Dayton is brave. Her cheek shines through the makeup purple and then maroon. Fat tears stand out on her lashes and I say, "You're doin' good, Day, you're doin' good." I unscrew the cap from the *Crème Vixen Rouge* and rub my fingertip in it hard. I smooth a saucer-sized circle of rouge onto her good cheek and say, "There! Let me see."

I avoid Dayton's eyes and study her lopsided cheeks, the Raggedy Ann rouge on one side, the angry sunken glow on the other. "Almost, Day. We've almost got it."

A tear rolls down through the rouge. "It hurts, Dee," she says.

I look at her and think, *I know*. I tell her, "No, it doesn't."

I pencil in eyebrows and stroke on teal shadow in silence. I add another layer of powder. An eyeliner hovers over her eye and I say, "Hold your eyes still."

Dayton's whites roll and she looks at me. I bring the pencil in closer.

"I didn't even do anything," she says. Her voice is grief and wonder.

I grip her good cheek in my hand. "Your eye keeps moving. Try not to make it move."

A new tear swells and spills over. "All I did was look at the record." She doesn't say the rest: *You were the one who played it; you were the one who dropped the needle too hard. You were the one who told him to go fuck himself.*

I look in her eyes and I see she doesn't blame me. Fiery thorns have settled in my shoulder and I jerk my arm hard to make it ache. I reach for the hairbrush. "I know," I say. "I'm sorry. I hate him, too."

When I am finished, Dayton's hair floats around her shoulders like a cape. The naked overhead light catches strings of gold. "You look buhlelalutuhlifuhlul," I tell her. For a second she believes me, and when she smiles, it's true.

I leave the makeup on the floor and we tiptoe back out of the bathroom. There are harsh, heavy breathing sounds coming from our mother and Phil's room now, the fat gasping of somebody struggling for air. "Oh!" we hear our mother say, "Oh!" Downstairs, we look outside and see that it has started snowing, a light, fluffy layer on a weeks-old crust of gray. In the kitchen we find three wrinkly apples, some white bread, a can of deviled ham, and wrapped slices of yellow cheese. There is only beer and sour milk to drink. I fill a mayonnaise jar with water and stack it along with the food in a Kroger's bag. Dayton pulls on her boots. We find our coats but no mittens. The bag is heavy so I hold it with both hands. We walk back through the living room and undo the lock and the silver dead bolt. The door sticks and then shudders free. I close it behind me and we step out into the white, swirling world.

More nurses come, go, pull my new door open, shut. Shoes squeak down the blue hall and then run *bam-bam-bam* the other way. Back and forth, back and forth, over, over again. Lights dim and rise, breakfast smells whine by. A nurse changes my IV and the businesslike drip-dripping slows.

A tray of food arrives. I crack one eye open and then the other. I pick at the clotted eggs, strings of hard yellow and white, a moat of chalky liquid all around. I bring the fork up to my mouth and place a few of the strings in it. Chew. Swallow. Gag. The eggs go away and in comes another nurse, rattling another yellow pill. Fingers clamp down on my pulse, the biceps snake squeezes. My TV monitor has disappeared. I should need to go to the bathroom but I don't. My mouth is still dry.

"Have you slept yet?"

I haven't.

"Try to sleep."

Swish, click, pill nurse goes away, my eyes close and open, my breaths go in and out. Ceiling tiles bear down on me. My heart goes *tha-thump, tha-thum.* At some point, Dr. Lindholm unhooks a chart from the foot of my bed. Her hot hands feel both my ankles for a pulse, but I feel the fur of my unshaved leg and pull away.

We feel the sting of late spring sun and Johnson's Baby Oil on our new-shaved legs and pull our thighs against scratchy brown towels. Our hands are over our eyes and our tank tops are rolled up over the jags of our ribs to the hinting swells of our new breasts. We are shiny and pale and there is mayonnaise in our hair. An extension cord runs from the back of the house to the portable radio at my side. Something tickles my belly button, an ant or a gnat, and a fly buzzes around my mayo head. I scratch at my stomach and fingertips rest in a small pool of wet.

The world stutters in orange when I open my eyes. There are fuzzy white scratches across the empty blue where a plane climbs into the atmosphere. I have never been on an airplane, but I imagine the words on its side: *Delta Air Lines. Pan Am. Cayman Air.* Dayton rolls to the side and lifts aside the strap of my shirt.

"Nothing yet," she says. "Check me?"

I do the same for her. A cigarette burn on her shoulder glows red as new.

I wipe a thin trickle of mayonnaise away from her temple and reach for my water glass. Already, the ice cubes are gone. I stick my fingers into the warming water and drizzle them over my stomach. I dip in again and do the same to Dayton. She bends her legs up and her stomach collapses like a long, shallow bowl. She has bulging racehorse knees and I can see blue veins through the chalky skin of her thighs. She locks her arms behind her head and stares up at the sky.

"Think there's anything up there?" she says.

"There's an airplane." I point to the scratchy vapor trail, a scalpel-thin line that spreads to a thick white blur. There is a shiny flare at the tip, where the airplane must be. I angle my eyes up my arm so the bright gleam is blocked out by my thumb.

We are both silent a minute. A lawn mower drones in the background, the hollow, regular spank of a basketball. Latin music drowns out the staticky Duran Duran coming from our radio. The ground is hard against my spine and I imagine the stinging of a dozen fire ants on my thighs and back. I roll over and raise myself up on one elbow. Dayton lifts both arms to the sky and makes a circle with her thumbs and forefingers, capturing the sun in the center. She carries the circle down toward my head.

"Look, a halo," she says.

"Yeah, right. Wrong head," I reply. "You can keep that for yourself."

Dayton makes angel wings in the dry grass. She holds her breath, cheeks popping, and lets it out with a hiss. "Do you think Nat Helsher likes me?"

I look at her long and hard. Her eyes stare straight up and her face says nothing. Sweat and water shine on her stomach and I scoop up another handful. "Yeah," I say, "I do." I pour the water over her.

"You're lying. You can't ever lie to me. I always know you." She smiles up at me and then she sits and she is glowing and magnificent, and then I lose her in the white glare of the sun.

Chapter 22

I wake up again and the world is different. There is sunlight but no sun, just a general, generic brightness to the atmosphere, a polite sterility to the universe. Flat light falls across a dresser to my right, handleless and mirrorless, and the fake-woodgrain footboard of my bed. It pools in defeated blots among the ridges and contours of my sheets. The sheets are white. The walls are the palest, barely-est green. My arms are brown and white and black and blue. There is evidence of an IV once in residence on the top of my wrist.

I hold still a minute and discover that sound and smell have gone prosaic, too: *pings* and rattles and the bricky smell of bacon all but disappeared. The air hums with only the tiniest of quivers, behind the walls and beneath the floor; the only smells I smell are the hollow stab of antiseptic and the crusty brown of old tape. Far away I hear cars and sirens and the wet sizzle of electricity. My breath sags in and out in wheezy hiffs and whuffs.

My eyes move slowly, in granular jerks, and I hear mechanical clicks as I take a few practice blinks. I try to survey my surroundings without clicking too much. I know where I am, a private room at Mount Lebanon Hospital, on the East Side, Manhattan, United States of America, planet Earth. I have been here for some time. I have hurt my head.

I am sitting at an angle, or lying at an angle, propped up by pillows or some cast of the bed. I can see the lank flats of my forearms and the bony points of hips, knees, toes. I think about wiggling my feet and my feet wave back at me. I stop feet and lungs and heart. I should have to go to the bathroom but I don't, I should feel hungry but I'm not. I look at the light and wonder what time it is. There is no clock on the wall, no watch on my wrist. Tiny hairs tickle my nose as I breathe in the nutty tang of unwashed skin. It is morning; I remember sunrise and cereal, then a nurse with a pill in a cup. I hear voices and shoes in the hall and guess it is around ten-thirty. I count *one-Mississippi, two-Mississippi, three*—until I lose track.

When Dr. Lindholm comes in, she is garish against the room. Her eyes are too blue, her hair too blond. She's wearing lipstick and it seems much too red.

"Okay," she says. "It's time to start talking to me."

"It is?" Her words are a surprise. Our voices sound loud and vulgar, a dirty joke told at a bishop's wake. "I wasn't aware that I haven't been talking to you."

"Well, you haven't. I've been to see you five times over the past three days and you haven't said a word to me, and I've waited as long as I can, but I'm sorry. I can't wait anymore."

"I'm sorry," I say.

"I don't want to hear sorry. We don't have time for sorry." She reaches for her briefcase and pulls out a yellow file. "Darien," she says. "Listen to me. Are you listening to me? This is very, very important."

I nod. Dr. Lindholm settles the file across my legs, opened to a single sheet of paper, a form of some sort. I recognize the seal of the State of New York at the top, Robert's angular handwriting in half a dozen of the boxes. Insurance forms, I think.

"These are commitment papers," Dr. Lindholm says. "For Marshall

Hospital. Do you know what that is? It's a psychiatric facility upstate, in Culver. Three hours north of here. You're scheduled to be transferred on Monday. That's two days from now."

Dr. Lindholm's shoulders heave up and down. "Do you hear me, Darien?" she says.

I look at the form, Robert's writing. The boxes Dr. Lindholm needs to fill out are empty. "Today is Saturday?"

"Darien—" Dr. Lindholm lurches toward me and then stops herself, grabbing the arms of her chair.

"Yes." She lets out a loud breath. "Today is Saturday. You came in here Wednesday night. You've been on some medication. You were heavily sedated when you came in, Haldol. You hit the back of your head against the wall when you were in my office and you were bleeding and I was frightened for you. You've been on Risperdal since Thursday afternoon. I know you haven't wanted medication, but it was necessary. Do you know about Risperdal?"

I nod; I do. I have a file on it at work.

"It's to keep you calm. My feeling is that we can manage you right here, or down at NYU even, if we just keep you on the Risperdal and in the hospital for a couple of weeks."

She takes another breath. "Now, Marshall—Robert wants you transferred, and I—Darien, I'm not sure what that's all about. He and I haven't talked about this at all, and I don't—I'm trying to learn about the facility. They have a large schizophrenia program, and some affiliation with SUNY-Albany, but I don't know the staff or their treatment methods. I assume there's some group, but I doubt they do individual psychotherapy. A colleague told me he knew them for ECT.

"Do you understand what I'm telling you? Marshall is for very sick people. I think it would be disastrous for you. But I'm not going to be able to keep you from going if you don't start talking to me."

The date at the top of the form is Thursday, December 12. I see my name, address, birth date. Robert's insurance information is neatly printed; his income information in sharp, boastful digits. The line for patient's mother's maiden name is left blank.

"Robert's having me committed?"

Dr. Lindholm nods.

"Can he do that? He can't do that. I'm over eighteen."

"I'm afraid he can. He's your husband and your only given relative. Right now, he's also your health care proxy."

For a second, I think about this. I inspect my insides, wait to feel something. I see smooth tubes of intestine, slippery bulges of brain. "That bastard," I finally say, when nothing comes.

"I'm sure Robert's scared," Dr. Lindholm says softly.

"Robert's sick of me." Marshall. *Culver.* Three hours north of the city. I wonder how he ever even found it.

"Robert loves you very much."

I shake my head once, sharp. The words suddenly no longer belong in the same sentence, Robert, love. How could I, how could she think I—"But what about you?" I say. "Can't you overrule him?"

Dr. Lindholm sighs and rubs her forehead. "Robert and I agreed to the health care proxy when I brought you in here Wednesday night, because it was clear you were a danger to yourself and we needed to do it in order to admit you."

"Against my will, you mean."

"Safely," she says. "Darien, I assure you, you weren't able to articulate what your will was Wednesday night." Dr. Lindholm turns my face to hers. "But that's exactly the point, why you've got to start talking to me now. Robert was given the proxy because you were in an extreme manic state. For it to be revoked, either Robert has to withdraw or you have to demonstrate your mental fitness to an impartial third party who can be confident you're no longer a danger to yourself. Impartial third party, that means someone here, not me. Do you understand what I'm saying to you?"

It's quiet in the room. I realize I expect more noises, beepers and wheelchairs and the indifferent chatter of nurses in the hall. Where are the smocked volunteers wheeling around carts of dog-eared magazines? Or the overloud visitors, telling their patients they look just great? But then it occurs to me that this must be the psych ward and my next-door neighbor is probably strapped to her bed and not just down with the flu; the rooms are probably soundproofed, the doors locked. I look toward my own door, and it is closed, indeed. "How do you suppose Robert picked Marshall?" I ask.

"I don't know," Dr. Lindholm replies. "I don't know. All of this—this has all been news to me. I think he's scared, and angry and confused. I think he's frightened about how sick you might be." She pauses. "Robert didn't know about Dayton."

I shake my head.

"That's an awful big thing for a husband to learn. For anyone to learn."

I look at the flat sunlight, the wall. "I didn't know about Dayton." Even I know the words are ridiculous.

Dr. Lindholm's voice comes softer now, and it's a voice I remember. Careful, modulated, maternal. "I know you didn't."

"It's the truth," I say. "It really is. I'm not saying it just to excuse myself. I forgot her. I don't know how that's possible. I mean, she was my twin sister, and we were fourteen—" I can't finish the sentence. I find a brown stain on a ceiling tile and send my brain after it.

"Keep going. Please."

My fingers find a wrinkle in the papers on my lap and begin tracing it, pressing down, rolling side to side like a worm. Roll, press. "No, thank you." My fingernail splits the wrinkle lengthwise.

"Your twin sister." The words are a hammer, and when I don't respond, Dr. Lindholm says them again. "You were only fourteen years old. She meant everything to you. How could anyone have expected you to withstand losing her?"

For a minute, I think of the Risperdal, the tiny yellow pill dispersing its molecules through my bloodstream. It's a tranquilizer, a serotonin and dopamine antagonist used to treat severe anxiety, agitation, and psychotic behavior. In the lock-and-key mechanism neurons use to fire messages to the central nervous system—"I'm scared! I'm angry! There's a rattlesnake next to my bed!"—Risperdal acts like gum in the keyholes so the messages don't get sent: I'm not scared. I'm not angry. The radiant water heater is hissing because it's hot. I picture tiny, tadpole-ended neurons, blobs of pink Hubba-Bubba mortaring over the crenelated surfaces. I see the dopamine-fueled messages racing toward them, bouncing off and tumbling backwards, *Return To Sender, Addressee Unknown*. I'm not sad. I'm not grieving. There isn't a giant hole in the universe opening in front of me.

I breathe through my mouth, big, steady gulps. "I'd rather not talk about it."

"You have to talk about it." Dr. Lindholm's voice is harder again, a note of panic returning. "Darien, listen to me. Look at me. You have to talk to me."

I'm not sad. I'm not anything. "Why?"

"Because you have to get better. I know it's beyond hard, the hardest thing in the world, and I know you're not ready. If we had the time, I wouldn't push you. But the fact is there's virtually nothing I can do to stop your transfer if you won't help me, and if you get transferred to Marshall, I'm awfully scared about what might happen to you." Dr. Lindholm stops.

I look at the commitment form on my lap. *Legal status of admission*, it says, *Involuntary. Person initiating admission: Robert J. Gilbertson. Relationship to patient: Husband.*

Husband. I smile.

I hand the yellow file back to Dr. Lindholm. "Who says I have to get better?"

"I do." She looks stricken. "Of course you have to get better. It's—it's what we're doing here. Just because you know about your sister—it's the same thing it's always been."

"It's not. Before I knew about Dayton, we were trying to figure out what all my lousy behavior was about so I could stop doing it. Now I know why I was doing it and there's no reason to stop. It was what I was supposed to be doing, what I was biologically *programmed* to be doing." Dr. Lindholm opens her mouth to protest and I wave a hand in front of her. "I'm not going to get better. I'm not meant to get better."

"What does that mean, Darien?" Dr. Lindholm's voice is low and grave. "You're going to kill yourself?"

"Not really. I won't have to. I'm just going to die. It's what I was telling you, back in September. All that stuff I do to myself? Little deaths. One day I'll do the right one. I cut my arm and hit a vein, get so puking drunk I have a heart attack or fall in front of a bus."

"But that's not suicide."

"It isn't." It isn't. "Dr. Lindholm, do you know about programmed cell death?"

Her blue eyes don't blink. "Programmed cell death?" she says. "Do you mean apoptosis?"

"Either way."

"It's a controlled process of self-extinction among damaged cells in an organism, as in cancer or stroke. Why do you ask?"

"I'm not asking. I'm telling you. It's exactly what I'm telling you. It's not just cancer cells. All cells contain a death program. When any cell becomes damaged or superfluous, the engine that runs the program for self-extinction switches on. It's there all the time. It's just in healthy cells, the program gets suppressed by signals from the other cells that say, 'It's okay! You're healthy! You're wanted!' "

"Okay," Dr. Lindholm says slowly.

"Okay, what? That's everything. Dayton and I were identical twins. We came from the exact same cell. She was good, I was bad. I was useless, superfluous. She died, stopped signaling."

Dr. Lindholm pushes her chair back and crosses the foot of my bed to the far side of the room. She shakes her head at the window and presses three fingers against the pane. They leave condensation negatives that linger, like the noseprints of three puppies. She turns back toward me and starts to pace.

"As always, Darien," she says, "I have to be impressed with your system of rationalizing. You do understand that what you've just given me is one giant rationalization. Programmed cell death is just that: programmed *cell* death. It happens to cells, not entire people. Not even entire organs. You're not a cell. You're several trillion cells. What you're talking about is a metaphor, not scientific fact. It's a rather elegant metaphor for suicide, but that's where it ends." She rubs the side of her ear. "Your sister stopped signaling you. Maybe your family stopped signaling you, though my guess is you probably stopped signaling them. You say Robert's stopped signaling you, which I don't believe—"

"He's sending me to *Marshall,* Dr. Lindholm."

"I'm still signaling you." She stops at my bedside table and leans toward me. Her face is deadly earnest. "How about that?"

I try to say it kindly, because I can see it really matters to her, and I understand the way these things go. She doesn't like losing; nobody likes losing. I clear my throat. "With all due respect, Dr. Lindholm, you're paid to signal me."

She rocks slightly, but her face doesn't change. "Yes," she says, "that's true, I am. But I'll tell you something, Darien. I couldn't signal you like this if I didn't care about you. And I care about you, very, very much. I can care about you and still get paid."

"Well," I say, "that certainly works out well."

"I'm sorry I couldn't be there to help your sister before things got so awful she had to kill herself. I'm sorry I couldn't be there to help you through it when it happened to you. But I am here now, and I want—I *need,* Darien—to help you. I know I don't even know how painful this is for you, but I do know that I can help you, and that it can get better. Will get better. It's what I do. It will be horrible, but you will survive it."

She pauses, waiting for me.

"You have so many gifts. Your wit, your love for Robert—"

"I had a twin sister. She was the only person in the world who ever mattered. And she killed herself without telling me, for good. She crawled through a window one night and jumped in front of a train and didn't even tell me she was going to do it. And we shared *everything.* So that means something. That's all I know. There's nothing else that matters."

"Okay," Dr. Lindholm says. "Okay." She hugs my file to her chest. "Tell me about what it means to be a twin."

I laugh, a single, short bark. "I couldn't possibly," I say. "There aren't words to describe it. It would be—it's like describing winter twilight to a blind person, or chocolate mousse to someone without tastebuds. It would take a lifetime."

"Well," Dr. Lindholm says, "you and I have two days."

Here is what Dr. Lindholm should be asking me: How did we get here? Not what does it mean to be a twin, not are you going to kill yourself, but just how the hell did we get here? A week ago you were a stereotypical neurotic New Yorker with a husband and a dog and a job and just the slightest tendency toward self-mutilation, and in the blink of an eye you became another person with a cavernous, unexplored past, another life, and just how the hell could that be? You could not have forgotten the other half of your brain, your self, the person with whom you spent the first half of your life. There has to have been too much evidence: letters and photographs, souvenirs, people who knew you and could say, "Remember the time when you and Dayton . . . ?" There must have been memories, pictures burned on your brain as if they were filmed outside of you, singing, roller-skating, eating ice cream. You couldn't have forgotten all of that; it isn't psychologically, physiologically possible. Where would all of that evidence have gone? You must have been lying to me, you traitorous, treacherous bitch.

Dr. Lindholm should slap my face, shake my shoulders so hard my head snaps on my neck like a lead balloon. Liar, liar! Tell me all. Each minute I sit and breathe, a new memory breaks through my skin, whole and minute and unvarnished, a perfect capsule. Me and Dayton climbing the rocks at Wallis Beach in pink-striped halters, the bright scrape of our pails and the hot kiss of the sun. Me and Dayton in kindergarten, dragging paint-loaded toothbrushes over squares of screen to make spatter prints for our mother. Me and Dayton dancing to American Bandstand, scuffing imaginary platform shoes through mustard shag rug. Our big chance for stardom, a gold lamé top and bicycle shorts. Shake and shake and shake all the capsules out of me.

Dayton killed herself on a spring night, May 13, five weeks before the end of school. We lived on Long Island. We had done our homework in front of the TV and watched *Dynasty* until ten o'clock, then brushed our teeth and put our nightgowns on. Before getting in bed, we'd turned on the radio and picked out our outfits for the next day. I had art class, so I chose jeans and our yellow zip-front sweatshirt. Dayton had gym, square dancing. She took our prairie skirt and our mother's white peasant blouse. We'd hung our clothes on the back of the door, left it open just a crack, and giggled and whispered in the dark. We talked about *Dynasty*, I remember. It was the episode when Krystal Carrington's evil clone took over her life and I was glad—Krystal was such a sap! Dayton felt sorry for her. We both had crushes on John James; we definitely would kiss him. Dayton was hoping Nat Helsher would pick her for square dancing again the way he had earlier in the week. We said, *'night, Dee . . . 'night, Day . . .'night, Dee . . .'night, Day . . .* until I drifted off.

In the morning, the alarm clock woke me up. It was next to Dayton's bed, on the dresser, and I screwed my eyes tight as it bleated on. Usually, Dayton slapped it off at the first beep and I'd doze until she jumped on my bed and shook me, and instantly I was annoyed. Dayton always woke up easier. I fell asleep easier. "Day," I groaned, "turn that stupid thing off."

When the clock continued to beep, I fished around my bed for something to throw at my sister. I found a sock, and, eyes still closed, I whipped it at her bed. In the next room, my mother—or someone— banged on the wall.

"Dayton," I howled, "turn the stupid clock off."

I opened my eyes and saw she wasn't there. Her bed was made. The sheet was pulled tight and her stuffed mouse sat on her pillow. My blue sock hung from the side of the mattress. I listened to the *eep-eep-eep* of the alarm for a minute longer, then leaned over and turned it off. The radio emerged: *Shootin' out the walls of heartache, bang-bang*—I turned that off, too, and then the house was quiet. I heard the shifting of bedsprings in our mother's room and the steady roar of traffic on the Long Island Expressway. There were car horns on the street and a dog, the neighbor's pit bull, barked in a constant, low *woof*. But the house was quiet. I listened for sounds from the bathroom—water running, hair dryer—or the clank of dishes in the kitchen. "Dayton?" I said. There was a little trill in my voice already; a panicky echo of the alarm clock in my head. I looked around the room and saw my clothes were missing from the back of the door.

I ran past the empty bathroom and then down the stairs, clutching

Dayton's blouse in my fist. "Dayton?" I yelled. I stood at the foot of the stairs. The chain was off the front door. "Dayton!"

Nearby, one of my brothers' voices responded: "Shut up!"

In the TV room, there were blankets on the windows and the air smelled like marijuana. Ken and Mac were sprawled out on the pullout sofa and I looked for Dayton's silhouette between them in the dark. "Have you guys seen Dayton?" I asked. My voice was loud. "Did you hear her leave for school?"

Ken lifted his armpit and cracked one eye at me. "Get the fuck out of here, D-bag. Shut your mouth and shut the goddamn door." Mac rolled over and Ken shoved him with his foot. "Stay on your side of the bed, faggot."

I stood frozen at the foot of the sofa. My eyes made two circuits around the room: weak, pinky light through the blanket, dark lumps of clothing on the floor, the mouth of the half-opened closet. My stomach rolled. I stumbled sofaward and yanked the sheet down. "It's time for you to get up!" I screamed. "It's time for both of you to go to school!"

When I ran upstairs to tell my mother Dayton was gone, dressed in my clothes, she didn't even open the door. She told me she'd heard me downstairs with my brothers; Dayton had probably just gotten up early and why didn't I just wear her clothes? She and I could switch at school if it really mattered that much. I waited, listening to my breathing, tracing the raw woodgrain of my mother's door with my fingertips, and then I tried again. I told her I'd looked all over our bedroom and the kitchen and Dayton hadn't left a note. My mother was silent, so I rattled the doorknob. My head felt light, and I leaned it against the door and closed my eyes. I was going to throw up. There were conferring murmurs on the other side of the door, and when my mother's voice came again she sounded fully awake, and—now—angry. Why in blazes did I think Dayton would leave a note just because she took my clothes, and if I really wanted to know, why didn't I just go to school and find out for myself? I whispered the answer down between my feet: *Because she isn't going to be there.* That much, at least, my gut already knew.

I put on the prairie skirt and peasant blouse and left the house and then I didn't know what to do. I got as far as the concrete blocks of the front porch. My eyes took in the street without seeing any of it. Garbage cans, garbage. The front tire of a bicycle, chained to a cyclone fence. Cracked sidewalks laced with grass and dandelions, brown leaves, a crumbly pile of dog shit. Next door, the pit bull was still barking; a couple of streets over, a siren wailed.

I made a full circle around the house, the Zapeskis' side and ours, calling, "Dayton?" I went half a block toward school and then changed my mind. I walked all the way back up King Street, past the house, and turned left on Ellwood. Another left on Cedar, past Mrs. Estee's nail salon and the Second Chance designer boutique. Cars honked and I stumbled up onto the sidewalk. Right on Fir, another right on Main, past the post office, the IGA, the Kwik Kopy, and the parking lot for the commuter rail. It was warm, but I was shivering when I made the final turn on Harrison and into the police station. I told the first person I saw that I needed to report a missing person, my twin sister. Her eyes were tired when she looked at me.

A policeman came out, and though he smiled, he looked tired, too. He pointed me toward a wooden bench and sat down. He rubbed big, square hands up and down his thighs. "I'm Sergeant Holter," he said. "What's your name, honey?"

"Darien Gorse."

He nodded his head and pulled a small pad of paper from the breast pocket of his white shirt. "And where do you live, Marion?"

"Darien," I said faintly, "102½ King Street. Just up the road. I woke up this morning and my sister was gone. She was there when we went to bed. She's afraid of the dark."

Sergeant Holter wrote something down. "Older sister, younger sister?

A car is missing? Did she leave a note?" He smiled at me again. His tired eyes crinkled at the corners and there was a line of small black seeds between his front teeth.

"She's my twin sister. She can't drive. We're fourteen."

A phone rang. The sergeant studied me. "Twin sister, eh?"

He smelled like coffee. I nodded.

"Does she have pretty brown hair, like yours?"

Condescension coiled around cold surety at the pit of my stomach and it was all I could do to swallow. I nodded again.

Sergeant Holter's pen hovered over his notebook. "Remember when you saw her last? Early morning? You woke up to go to the bathroom, maybe, and you saw her? Any chance she went out for a jog or got a head start for school?"

I shook my head. "I don't know. We went to bed together last night, at ten o'clock. I woke up this morning and she was gone, and she's never—she wouldn't be. She didn't leave a note. I looked around. She took my clothes."

"Your clothes?"

"My jeans and sweatshirt. My yellow sweatshirt." I pulled at the peasant blouse. "These are hers."

His lips fell over the row of seeds and he didn't look so kind anymore. He just looked tired, beyond tired, like he didn't want to be in the room with me anymore. "Marion, honey," he said, "are your mom and dad at home?"

My mother made Sergeant Holter wait while she put on lipstick and finished setting her hair, pawing through her scarves to cover the fat pink curlers crowding her head. She slid into the front seat of the police cruiser with Logan in her arms and told me to go to school, but then, after a short conference with the sergeant, she opened the passenger door and held Logan back out. "You're already late, anyway," she said. "Stay here, and watch your brother." She thrust a plastic diaper bag toward me. "He needs to be fed, and check his diaper. I just changed him but he usually goes number two right after he eats."

"Mom?" My voice trembled. "Where are you going? Where's Dayton?" *Dayton* came out loopy and squealed.

My mother fixed me with a hard, cold look and then her face switched to blank. "Darien, don't give me a hard time. Not now, if you know what's good for you." She pointed at Logan. "Give him the Cheerios and the grape juice. Put it in his Tommy Tippy cup, don't let him have a glass. There's peanut butter and crackers if he's still hungry. Change his diaper, and—jiminy christmas—stay put. Don't let me come back and find your brother alone."

I don't remember how I passed the hours while I waited, but it was late, after noon, by the time my mother returned. Mac and Ken had gone to school, or left the house at least, and I'd changed Logan's diaper so many times he'd taken to screaming the instant I picked him up and moved toward the stairs. I was upstairs with him for at least the fifth time when I heard the front door. I ran, crying, "Dayton? Dayton?" but it was only my mother, seated at the kitchen table in her gold sweater and red lipstick, slowly removing the curlers from her hair. She rolled one under her fingers, slow motion, as if reading the Braille of its bristly surface with her fingertips. The scarf was on the floor, half-coiled around a leg of the chair. "Where is she?" I said. "Where's Dayton? Where's Dayton? Mom, where is she?"

"Where's your brother?" she replied, looking at the door. "Didn't I tell you not to leave him alone?"

When she came back down, jogging Logan against her shoulder, she told me without looking at me. She didn't even bother with the Groucho voice, that's how bad it was. There had been an accident. Dayton had gone out for a walk last night and she had slipped and fallen in front of a train. She was dead. It was an accident. She'd slipped and fallen and she had died. My mother's face was dumb and blank. It was okay if I didn't feel like going to school.

[253]

The moment, now, is crystallized, perfect in my mind. The capsule cracks and the scene emerges whole. I see my mother sitting at the table, her face slack, as if the skin itself can barely hang on to bone. I see the yellow oilcloth table cover, garish against the Pepto-Bismol pink of her hair curlers. She rolls them with her fingertips, over and over, and her shiny almond nails make skritching noises. I see the avocado green refrigerator behind her, I hear it humming. A jelly jar of dried flowers, on the shelf above the sink. Canisters for flour, sugar, and tea lined along the wall, next to the range top, a dirty saucepan still sitting on a burner. The strange look of sunlight attached to my mother's empty face. And though I don't want to, I hear my mother's words. *She slipped and fell. It was an accident. It's okay if you don't feel like going to school.* And I feel the lurchy, goofy rising as my face breaks into an enormous smile.

Chapter 23

In the morning, Dr. Lindholm arrives with an overnight bag that holds a pair of jeans and a sweater, boots, a turtleneck, and my hairbrush. I thank her, running my hands over the sweater. It is black wool, my favorite, a red-scarfed Scottie dog knit on the front. Robert bought it for me in England. "Traveling clothes?"

"There are socks and underwear somewhere in there, I think," Dr. Lindholm replies. "I'll step out for a minute if you'd like to put them on."

Briefly, I think about it, visualize the entire, tedious task of getting dressed. One leg, then the other, socks, sleeves, zippers, laces, straps—I shake my head at her. "No thanks."

"You sure?" Dr. Lindholm raises an eyebrow. "I thought we might go outside."

"Ah-ha." This is another matter altogether. I look for coat and mittens and see none, but no matter; we beggars can't be choosers, after all. "Not traveling clothes," I say. "You're breaking me out."

After four days in pajamas and hospital underpants, my own clothing feels strange. I haven't been out of my room since Wednesday night, but the hall is as I remember it, somehow: blue and bland, wheelchair-railed, doors spaced at even intervals like missing teeth. I move slowly, dizzy from the Risperdal, and we pause periodically for me to catch my breath. In one open doorway I see an empty bed; in another, a fleshy, peri-menopausal woman with a black pompadour, eating pot roast forcefully. There's a skeletal, teen-aged girl in a third room, head turned toward the window as she performs bicycles in the air.

"I see I'm in with the anorexics and mild depressives," I say.

"There are three wards on the floor, men's ambulatory, women's ambulatory, and the acute psychiatric service," Dr. Lindholm responds. "The APS is a locked ward. It houses the sickest patients. Would you like to see it?"

An inexpert question, beneath her. Will there be balloons, a banner, *Welcome, Darien?* The patients are blank-eyed and drooling, suffocatingly silent; they are howling like coyotes, decanoate esters leaking from their skin. I see it all. It doesn't change a thing. "Plenty of time for that later, don't you think?"

Downstairs, Dr. Lindholm steers me into a small courtyard and I immediately grasp her eagerness to get me outside. It must be close to sixty degrees. There are clusters of people everywhere—clothed and bathrobed patients in wheelchairs, patients pulling IV poles, even one young girl in a hospital bed. Nurses in pink and blue and green scrubs, doctors in suits and scrubs, a small knot of dietitians in white lab coats. There are groups of twos and threes who look just like Dr. Lindholm and me, dressed in civilian clothes, drinking coffee or smoking cigarettes at little wrought-iron tables. I wonder if they are all visitors or if some of them really are just like Dr. Lindholm and me.

"Terrific, isn't it?" she says. She turns in a beaming circle and then points me to an iron table, off in a corner of its own.

"Yeah, tremendous, if you like global warming."

"So you're not impressed?"

"It's the middle of December, almost Christmas. It's supposed to be snowing and twenty-five degrees. When I was a kid, we always had snow by Thanksgiving, never mind Christmas. The snowbanks would be over our heads and we'd build tunnels through them that would last until spring."

Dr. Lindholm cocks her head at me. "That sounds like fun."

"It was." I look off. There's a young woman with a gray complexion and a bandanna tied low to her eyes, holding hands with a man in a blue sweater. They both stare out over the lawn. She is in a wheelchair, hooked to a multi-bagged IV unit. *Cancer patient,* I think. I wave a hand at the sixty-something air. "Just another sign that the world is coming to an end."

"Is it, Darien?"

"For some of these people it certainly seems to be."

"Uh-huh," Dr. Lindholm says. "There are a lot of sick people here. A lot of very sick people." She waits. "What about you?"

"What about me? I already told my sorry story." Three table-lengths away, a woman reads to a little boy on her lap. Snatches of her words carry, nurses' laughter, *That is very high, thought Little Nutbrown Hare*— He is young, three or four. He has a tube up his nose and his abdomen is grossly swollen. He rests his head on the woman's shoulder and even from here, his eyes look old. "Are you trying to make me sound like a self-centered, self-pitying hypocrite? What did you do, pay all these people to come outside? I know my situation doesn't even compare."

Dr. Lindholm doesn't say anything, and for a minute neither do I.

"I know it's selfish. I know it's self-indulgent. I also know I could never make you understand it, and maybe that's reason enough. I mean"—I swing a hand around the courtyard—"not to be really heartless, but take a look at the flip side. None of these people has to justify to anyone what's happening to them. Nobody's out there telling them, 'Stop feeling sorry for yourself just because you're dying. That isn't so terrible. There are starving children in Africa, for God's sake!' I have to think there's a certain comfort in that. They're heroes. They're martyrs. The people around them love them and cry for them and tell them how brave they are. Nobody's spitting on them and sending them off to some nuthouse in Culver."

"That's true," Dr. Lindholm says. "But nobody's letting them choose whether they're dying of cancer, or AIDS, or heart disease, either."

"Yeah, and nobody let me choose if my sister killed herself like that without ever saying a goddamn word."

The words are out of my mouth too fast and I can't take them back or undo the sudden, crazy electricity that jolts from my skull and down my arms. I am on my feet before I know it, my chair knocked backwards with a crash. A table of civilian-clothed smokers glances at me and then away. I right the chair and make myself sit back down. My hands are tingling, and, under the table, my thighs shake. "Aren't the public areas in all New York hospitals supposed to be smoke free?"

Dr. Lindholm puts her hand on my wrist. "Don't stop, Darien. It's important. Please, keep talking. We're getting somewhere."

I shake my head and stare straight ahead. "What if I don't want to?"

"I think you do."

"I don't."

"Why not? What are you afraid of?"

"I'm not afraid. I hate it when you use that word." I look again at the little boy reading about the nutbrown hare. His thumb is in his mouth, his eyes half-closed. "The only thing I'm afraid of is that you'll skew my words and make what I'm saying into something it's not. I'll tell you and you'll tell me what I really mean is I'm mad at Dayton, and I'm not. That's not it."

Dr. Lindholm lets go of my hand. "What if I tell you that I'll just listen?"

Dr. Lindholm stays quiet, but I won't do this, can't do this. My fingertips press against the table.

"You know what the worst part is? The part I can't forgive myself for? The worst part is that I didn't even know. I didn't know when she did it. I was fast asleep, drooling into my pillow, dreaming about Nat Helsher or something."

I swallow. "And I mean it that way. It's that I didn't know, not that Dayton didn't tell me. She shouldn't have had to tell me. I should have known."

Dr. Lindholm still says nothing, but in the silence I hear the questions that she doesn't ask. *Why shouldn't she have had to tell you? How could you have known?* Because I had to know, because we were closer than two regular people ever could be, and because if I didn't, it means—

"I mean, that's the ultimate Hollywood sales pitch, isn't it? Lovers who are so close, such perfect soulmates, that one knows the very second something happens to the other? The GI bride who sits in front of a streaming window with a letter from her beloved and then clutches a hand to her heart the instant he's blown to bits on Omaha Beach. The scene of the sixty-year-old wife sitting down to dinner with friends and thinking, 'Right now, I bet Tom is eating dinner, too. He's having a cheeseburger, because I'm not there to tell him not to, and he's swabbing his French fries in all the mayonnaise he can find.' And then the scene of Tom in the Burger King on the New Jersey Turnpike doing just that. It's the ultimate package, the dream Hollywood wants everyone to be able to have. Reassurance that you're not so far apart, can never be so far apart."

I look again at the woman with the little boy. His eyes are closed now, and hers stare into the distance, and she is rocking him. "But, you know, that's the thing. For regular people it's just that, a Hollywood snow job. No two regular people ever love each other like that, and you get what you deserve for thinking you'd be the one who could. Don't you feel like a jackass when you discover Tom was getting his dick sucked at some rest stop while you were fantasizing about him off eating hamburgers. Fucking serves you right. Aren't you a stupid bitch when you find out you were cuddling your Teddy bear and humming happily while your GI was hemorrhaging his intestines and screaming and crying for you. You fool. You total asshole." I stop and hear my voice, the shaking truth.

To punish yourself, you play the tape over, the way it really happened. You picture your husband, his knuckles white on the steering wheel; your GI on the beach, sand in his mouth, in his hair. You see your knobby-kneed, ponytailed sister at the train station, trembling and alone. You put yourself on the platform next to her.

It is a sweet, cruel night; a warm front moving in on the tail of a rainstorm, and the air is heavy and lush. Dayton lies in her bed listening to street sounds: car horns, the living roar of the expressway, door slams, the slow, steady sigh of my breath. Headlights bend across the wall and disappear. "Dee, you awake?" she asks the darkness, and I am not. She slides out from between the sheets, every nerve cell vibrating, and gathers her clothes silently. She pauses in the doorway, looks at my sleeping form, and blows me a kiss. *Good-bye, Dee,* she says. *I love you so much.*

She dresses in the bathroom, with the light off, ties her hair with shaky fingers. She inches down the creaky, carpeted stairs, turns the dead bolt with infinite patience, steps outside. The crunch of her feet on gravel is the only way she knows she is walking. Her head is light, filled with giddy emptiness as she marches down King and turns onto Ellwood. She doesn't think, she doesn't sweat, she isn't crying. She doesn't even turn her head when a Chevy Malibu inches alongside her down Main, *Hey, baby.* It is far too late for that. She climbs the stairs to the platform, hauling herself up with both hands, catching her sneaker on one of the risers. And then she waits.

I sit beside her as one train and then another pulls in and slowly rolls on, feel the flare of confirmation, the sucking drop of false alarm. She is waiting for an express. She doesn't shake. She isn't scared. She steps toward one of the lights and checks her watch under the foggy orange halo; walks back to the schedule board and runs her finger down the column again. Twelve-forty-eight. Her watch is two minutes slow. Finally, a horn sounds, half a mile off, *coming through*. Dayton steadies herself, walks forward nicely to meet the train, *How do you do, sir*. I stay on the bench, see the nervous flick of her ponytail, the way her fingers curl and release at her sides. I won't do it, I won't, but then I get up and stand beside her. The train's eye separates from the overhead lights strung down the track to its vanishing point, and the vibrations build, shaking the platform and our legs. I take her hand. Liquid adrenaline melts her thighs, boils her lungs, empties her brain as she counts the vibrations, takes a giant step back, then another, and lowers herself into a sprinter's crouch. The thunder builds, closer, closer—and then the train is right there, screaming and snorting, rolling its yellow eyeball, and I disappear as Dayton leaps forward, releasing herself into the night, the air, the obliterating roar.

"Darien, tell me."

Dr. Lindholm's voice comes back to me, and with a jolt I am at the hospital, in the courtyard. The terrace spins around me, *train, hospital, trainhospital*. I put a hand forward to steady myself. "Tell—" My throat closes, and I try again, effortful. "Tell you what?"

"Tell me how mad you are at your sister."

"I'm not. I wasn't, ever, mad at her."

"The hell you weren't. You were mad enough to forget her."

"I wasn't—that wasn't why, that wasn't how—"

"Then what was?"

I shake my head. I don't like this, am not ready for this. The world is spinning, I feel sick.

[261]

"You were fourteen years old. She didn't just slip your mind. What do you remember? What happened after she died?"

"I don't know. I don't remember. We moved."

"Where?"

"To Baltimore. No, to Cleveland. Both."

"Was there a funeral? Did you finish school? What did your mother say to comfort you?"

For a second, I really think I'm going to be sick, and I lean over as if to puke on Dr. Lindholm's shoes. Serve her right; this is bullshit, a trap! She said she didn't care about any of this and now here she is, pushing me, interrogator, mental rapist.

"Stop." I put my hands up. "Stop."

"Darien, please."

"Why are you doing this? I said I want to stop. I won't—I can't—"

Dr. Lindholm slaps her hand down on the table and immediately I am stopped, surprised. Her face is contorted with frustration, panic, fury. "Darien, we're so close," she says. "There's something more in there, and if we don't get it out before you leave for Marshall, I'm afraid."

For a second, a tiny edge inside me lifts, but then goddamn her, there is not. What is it with her? There always has to be something bigger! First, trauma had to be trauma, and now that it is, it has to be better than just losing my sister. An anti-surgeon, teasing open the incision, probing the wound with greedy fingers. No abscess, no infection, nothing there at all? She'll dig her fingernails in shit, wash her hands in piss, and try again. What will it be, a dirty uncle in the closet? I'll take Tony with the screwdriver for two hundred, please.

"Afraid what?"

"Afraid you'll have another episode like the one on Wednesday night and I won't be there to help you."

At that, I can laugh a little bit. I glare around the courtyard, then

[262]

pat my bandaged head with savage satisfaction. "Fat lot of good you did me then."

Dr. Lindholm suddenly looks as if she will cry. She bites on her lower lip, pulling nearly the entire lip underneath her top teeth, and her closed hands curl against the table. Her eyes drop down. Her nostrils flare like seashells. I've never had the chance to study her so closely, so unguarded. There is a small scar on her forehead, at the hairline, just to the left of her part, and a delicate, spidery vein, a broken blood vessel, on the side of her nose. For the first time I can see that her velvet skin is makeup, creases on either side of her mouth. I feel a small, strange stab of something like pity.

"I'm sorry. I didn't mean that."

She looks at me. "Yes, you did."

"No, I just meant I wanted to stop. Can we stop for now? I'm tired. I need a nap." It is a preposterous thing to say. The lawn is nearly shadowless, now littered with sunbathers lying on lab coats or rolling scrub pants to the knee. The courtyard has become a regular picnic central, steady streams of people converging on the dry grass with Styrofoam lunch plates in their hands.

"Of course."

On the ride back upstairs, we both are quiet. Dr. Lindholm walks me to my room. At the door, she takes a step toward me, and then, awkwardly, puts her hands on my shoulders and gives me a light squeeze. "I'm proud of you," she says.

That makes one of us.

"I'll be back to see you later. I need to make a few phone calls, and we need to do some more talking, but . . . You're doing such hard work. Thank you for being honest with me. This is all going to be okay."

I wave my hand, whatever, and turn toward my bed. All I want is to go to sleep.

I can barely kick my boots off or thrash my way out of the sweater before I'm under the covers. My turtleneck is too tight but I don't have the energy to figure out how to pull it over my head, so I just grab at it a few times and roll onto my side. I slide both hands against my stomach and close the flat light of the room inside my lids. Cart and shoe sounds float over me. I see yellow Dayton at the foot of my bed, broken and smiling. I see severed limbs piled across the floor. An arm, a foot. A sneaker leaks blood on my blanket. I see Robert, at home, staring out a rain-streaked window, humming and smiling for me.

When I open my eyes again, I'm not sure at first I'm not still dreaming, because Robert is standing there. He is in the doorway, gripping the doorframe, his body half in the room as if he hasn't made his mind up about entering yet. His fingers worry the jamb like a guitarist feeling out frets. He doesn't say anything, so, for a minute, neither do I. He looks wrinkled and tired, his hair sloppy and his face unshaven. A slab of sunlight falls across the floor and up his body, highlighting the blue and green plaid of his shirt, the unmatching green of his corduroys. I figure I probably look pretty ridiculous myself, lying in bed fully clothed, and before I stop to think about it, I actually care. I spin my legs over the side of the bed and throw out a hand for balance. Robert's mouth moves a few times. Tiny electric lights dance between us and soon the silence feels melodramatic. I look at him, waiting to feel amazed, to feel grateful, furious. It has been four days, fourteen years, and each impossibly dense second stands between us like a sandwich board advertising electrolysis or protesting abortion— somehow sordid and too intimate at once. "Afternoon, Bob," I finally say.

Robert starts. He blinks a few times and wrenches the doorframe. "Hello, Darien."

"In the neighborhood, were you? Just out for a walk? Thanks for

[264]

stopping by." I think about trying to keep my tone neutral but discover I don't need to make the effort. The words come out conversationally, more teasing than adversarial, as if Robert is an old high school acquaintance I have encountered at Duane Reade. "It's nice outside, isn't it? Dr. Lindholm took me out earlier. I didn't even need my sweater." I wave toward the Scottie dog, half-hung from the arm of my guest chair. "It was good of you to send it along."

Robert continues to stare at me, so I lean forward and fetch the sweater from the chair. The room has grown colder and now that I'm upright I can feel that my back is sweaty-damp. I loop Scottie over my shoulders and point to the chair. Robert keeps his purchase on the doorframe. "You can have a seat."

He jerks his head up and down and then enters the room, bent forward in a way that suggests he has to watch his feet to get himself across the floor. He lowers himself into the chair and tips his head back against the blue plastic cushion. He closes his eyes. His hands are folded and clutched against his chest; his knotted fingers work one another rhythmically. I watch his hands and wait for him to speak.

A minute, at least, passes. I feel tired again, and when I ask Robert how he's doing and he sniffs up at the ceiling, I close my eyes and slump toward my pillow. *Two can play at this game,* I think. *I'll just go back to sleep.* Behind my closed eyelids, though, I see Robert's hands, and I look at him again without meaning to; I had thought it was just an effect of the strange, yellow light. The back of his right hand is stained with green-brown bruise and there's a crescent moon of scab on his pointer-finger knuckle. I know what it is, of course. I've just never seen it from a distance before.

"Robert. What did you do—what happened to your hand?"

Robert rolls his head against the cushion. He lifts his right hand to his face and then turns it toward me. "This?" he says. He turns his hand again so his palm is facing me.

"That."

"This is nothing. Isn't it?" He flexes his fist a few times and shakes it in my direction. "Isn't that what you'd tell me? 'Oh, it's nothing, Robert. I'm fine, everything's fine.' Why don't you tell me what you think this is."

His imitation of me is a shrill, Miss Piggy falsetto, and for a moment I feel something like humiliation on his behalf. The bruising is minimal, Robert's hand unswollen, intact, and an old pride reasserts itself to consider the attempt pitiful, a snarly, froggy voice: *That's the best you can do?* This is my fault, what I have reduced him to, a grown man screwing up his courage to girl-punch a wall, and the sorry hopelessness of it all washes across my stomach. Futility rises toward my mouth, but then: no. I didn't ask him for any of this.

"Fuck you, Robert," I say.

"No, fuck you! Fuck you, Darien." Robert is on his feet and over me. His hand on my wrist is hard and his blue eyes are rabid. He isn't yelling, not quite, but his voice is loud and it shakes. He gives my arm a jerk. Sudden pain cramps my hand. I pull back against him and look at the open door.

"You should be careful," I say. "That kind of language could get you locked up around here." I listen for the alarmed squeaking of rubber nursing shoes down the hallway and hear only Robert's angry breath.

"You've fucked me enough for one lifetime and then some, wouldn't you say? Don't tell me fuck you. Fuck *you,* Darien."

He gives my wrist an angry snap. I let the pain roll through my body and drop my head back against my neck. Better. The air vibrates and bandages crinkle against my skull. I hadn't imagined this yet, this reckoning, but at once it seems appropriate, inevitable. I bring my head back up and study my husband's face. His eyes are enormous-pupiled; two days' worth of hard, insectoid razor-stubble breaks through his skin.

"Is that what you came to tell me? Fuck you?" I raise an eyebrow and cross my legs. "What a perfectly Zen little message. And original, too." I rub my wrist. The skin feels hot, a little raw, like an Indian sunburn. "Though you could have saved yourself the trip, if you wanted. I do believe 'fuck you' is a message that's already been delivered unequivocally."

Robert drops back into his chair, and his head falls toward his upturned palms. His shoulders shake and soon I hear the dry sobs that come from him. *"Jesus,"* he whispers. *"Oh, Jesus, Jesus Christ—"*

I slide myself to the end of the bed and step around him to shut the door. On my way back to the bed, I toe a piece of black string like a spider out of my way. I have never seen my husband cry before, not like this, and part of me still understands that I should comfort him, that he would comfort me no matter how cruel or awful or inhuman I had been. His sobs are wild, jerking things; he sounds broken; and watching him now I recognize that this is the worst thing I have ever done. Inside, I still feel something, a graying coal. I picture it forever dead, the anemic trill of white smoke, know what little breath it would take to keep it alive. I try to remember the way Robert held me, back in August, when I first broke my hand. I remember the shudder of his shoulders and the *creak-creak* of our shifting weight against the floor. I stand over him and put my hand out, rest it next to his neck. I pat twice and stare at the top of his head.

After a while, Robert's wails start to hollow, and then he stops hard. He lifts his head and draws his arm across his face and then looks at me. "Thanks a lot," he says. His eyes are bloodshot and liquid, but the hatred they held before is gone. I don't ask him thanks for what.

"I hit a wall, Thursday night," he says. "I thought maybe it might help me understand you."

I nod.

"It didn't, of course." Though he's angry, Robert's tone isn't sneering now. There is something defeated and almost scared underlying his words, and from his face it's clear that he, too, recognizes that something between us has been irrevocably changed. "I'm beginning to think there isn't a you to know at all."

"Maybe not," I say. *Of course not.*

"I got a call from Dr. Lindholm, earlier. That's why I decided to come. I was going to send you off without coming at all, but she said you were incredibly better and that she'd file a court order if I tried to have you transferred to Marshall. How do you like that?" He laughs a little. The sound is dry and harsh, a cat choking on a bone.

I smile at him and he looks away. "She thought that maybe you might be able to come home with me," he says.

"And what do you think about that?"

Robert glares at my dresser. "I think maybe she's the one who needs to be locked up."

I nod and pat his shoulder again.

"I mean." Robert presses his hands together again and I realize he is apologizing. "I'm mad at you, Darien. I'm so goddamn mad I can't even see straight. I don't want to talk about it, or make it better. And if you come home, I don't want to be there." He lets go with a bitter little burst of sobs and dips his head against his arm.

"It's okay, Robert. I don't—"

"It's okay? The hell it's okay. It shouldn't be okay. Don't tell me it's okay with you. It's not one bit okay with me. You're my wife, the woman I—and right now, so help me, if I could I would kill you." He says the words as if they are unutterable, unforgivable. "I've tried not to be angry. I've stayed up nights trying to feel something else, to imagine that you were so sick, or confused, or in so much pain that you couldn't tell me, but I just can't make it stick. I don't think I've slept since Thursday night."

He stops, and I wait. I feel a little stupid, standing over him like a music teacher, and so I climb back on my bed. I want to look out the window, at the starlings and the pools of water on the adjoining roof, but I know that would be rude.

Robert wipes his face again. "Now's the point where you're supposed to ask me what it was I did think. Jesus, Darien," he says, "don't make me do this part all by myself, too."

I look down at the sheets. "What if I don't want to know?"

"Dr. Lindholm tried to tell me that maybe you didn't know—didn't remember, some kind of post-traumatic stress response or something. That's bullshit. I look at you and all I see is someone who's made a joke out of me for the past five years."

I press a wrinkle flat against the bed and see Robert through the sound of his voice. His hands are clenched harder now and his lips have flattened into a thin, womanish line. There is gleeful savagery in the flare of his nostrils and the deep cuts around his eyes and all at once I know there could never be anything redeemable about marriage. Strangers shouldn't ever come to know each other this intimately. For the past few years, when I have looked at Robert, I haven't really seen him, believing instead that I recognized him; that who he was didn't depend on the shape of his face or the color of his eyes. I thought that what was Robert wasn't skin or bones or hair but something kinetic in the air between us, intangible and ineffable. I *knew* him. Change the face but keep the brain and he still would be Robert, no matter what. Now, Robert's inner workings and self-delusions impose themselves on his surface like some terrible disease, and knowing them seems a crime of voyeurism. I see a cleft chin and laugh lines and a thin, shiny line of scar and I don't recognize any of it. I look at the scar and think, *Robert John Gilbertson. This is Robert John Gilbertson.* I have no idea who he is, have never known, and I don't owe him explanations. I don't owe him a single word.

"I didn't lie to you," I say. "I forgot. I banished her. When my sis— when Dayton died, I thought it was me."

[269]

"What do you mean, you thought it was you?"

I lick my lips. I need something to drink, urgently, Bourbon or vodka, cyanide. "Just that. After she killed herself—I don't know. I don't remember what happened. I remember my mother telling me, and then us moving. We moved to Baltimore, and then to Cleveland. I remember lying on my bed for hours, staring at the ceiling. I think it was the only way I could forgive myself for not killing myself, too. I told myself that Darien had died, because Darien was bad. I told myself I was Dayton, and I tried to be Dayton. When Darien kept breaking through, I finally told myself there had only ever been one of us." I think that's right. I think I'm telling the truth.

"And were there?" Robert demands. "Was there?"

"Was there what?"

"Only one of you?"

I close my eyes and feel another sheet of glass in me fall. It is dark and quiet, the deepest, oceanest green. "No," I say. "There were definitely two."

I feel Robert's hand on my knee as he pats me with the same awkward, conciliatory gesture I used on his shoulder. He takes an audible, shuddery breath and says, "Dr. Lindholm didn't tell me any of that."

"I haven't—I didn't tell her."

We both breathe.

"How did she die?"

"She jumped in front of a train."

"Why?"

I shake my head and open my eyes. "I don't know."

Robert gets up and crosses over to the dresser and then stands facing me. His arms are across his chest and his expression is now an odd mix of defiance and confusion. He looks younger; defenseless, somehow, and for an awful second I see him again: in his kitchen on 79th Street, wearing Umbro shorts and an ancient Hopkins sweatshirt; up at Eastman, brandishing his paintbrush like a sword. My chest aches for him, in spite of all I know, and I hold my breath. I cannot. It cannot hurt.

"Everything we went through together," he says. "All those nights we lay on my bed and you cried and told me stories about the things you did and the things that happened to you. What was all of that all about?"

"Robert—"

"Was it just getting off? Has all of this been just getting off?" He opens his arms and gestures to take in all of the room. "I guess it's really all I want to know, when it comes right down to it. Have you just been playing me for some kind of big jerk, one of your mind games taken to some fucking meta-level? Maybe I'm a bigger asshole than that guy in the bar, because all you did was transfer your game to me, and it's taken me five and a half years to catch on." Tears lift up on the wrinkles of Robert's cheeks before they loop around his face and come together on the underside of his jaw. A fat drop dangles at the end of his chin.

I blink and my eyes click wetly but I won't cry. I swallow. "Yes," I say. "I'm sorry. It was all just a lie. Not a game. I lied to both of us." I hold my breath and wait for him to go.

"So you didn't—you never loved me."

My eyes close again and I see the universe against the dark curve of my lids. "No." The syllable sticks in my throat, guttural. "No. I couldn't have. I'm sorry. I thought I really did."

"What is that supposed to mean, you thought you did, you couldn't have?"

I shake my head. "I don't. I'm sorry." I can't explain this to him, not in any way he will understand.

I hear footsteps and wait for the groan of the door. I will the sound away from me even as the *clat-clat-clat* of Robert's loafers closes in. A slap then, or a punch; I draw my shoulders up.

"You are so full of shit." I open my eyes and Robert is right over

[271]

me, the expression on his face so unexpected I almost jump. He is smiling. I smell his shampoo, his musky-warm scent. "You just can't give it up, can you? Tell me that again, right here." He points at his face. "Say, 'I don't love you, Robert.' "

I try a sharp, little laugh. "Say it again, to my face," I say. "You sound like a Danielle Steele novel."

"And you sound like the same stubborn-proud little—*girl* who told me to stop calling her five years ago and then cried into my answering machine when I did."

"Yeah, well." I try to look around him, his strange, crazed face, but he's too close. "It's like you said. It's all just been one big game."

"I love you, Darien. I hate the hell out of you right now, I hate you so much it scares me. I don't even know who you are right now, and I've got to tell you, I'm just not that interested in starting over. But it doesn't look like we have much of a choice."

Robert's smile drops and he sits down next to me on the bed. "I'll tell you something. I thought about divorcing you. I could see the whole thing. I'd sell the house and move down to D.C., really throw myself into my work, get my billings back up to a hundred hours a week. I'd make partner in no time. I would." He shoots me a defiant, vulnerable look. "But here's the kicker: no matter how great I made it sound to myself, no matter how many hours I managed to fill up, there was just this hole at the center, and that was you. Isn't that bullshit? You do all this shit to me, and still I can't even fantasize about living my life without you. I saw myself making partner, and then the first thing I saw was coming home to tell you, and it was like getting socked in the gut because you weren't there." Robert's voice shakes and he stops.

"So that means we have to figure out how to fix this mess, and that means it's time for you to get serious about getting well. You do love me. I know it even if you don't. But I'm tired of guessing what's the right thing, doing things to make you better that don't work."

[272]

For a second, I want to lunge at him and beat my fists on his chest. *You stupid bastard. You stupid, arrogant bastard.*

"I thought it was Dr. Lindholm," Robert says, "but—shit." He looks around the room. "Steve O'Brien told me about Marshall and I just thought—Darien, I'll give you time. Here, NYU, wherever." He grabs my hand and his palm is sticky warm.

Finally, then, I can say it. I pull my hand out of his. "You'll give me time? I didn't know you owned it. How much time is yours to give? A week? A month? A couple years?" Then I lean in and say the words right to his face: "Robert Gilbertson, I don't love you."

I wait until I'm sure Robert is gone, counting the ceiling tiles from one side to the other, before I put on my shoes. I stop into the bathroom and brush my teeth carefully, pushing the stiff bristles of the hospital-issue toothbrush hard against my gums. I spit pink foam into the sink and leave it there. In the hallway, I make a diagonal pattern across the linoleum squares from one wheelchair-railed wall to the other and back for a dozen yards or so, and then switch to a more random zigzag. It always bothered me on standardized tests, SATs, Stanford-Binets, when I'd fill in the columns of little ovals and discover I was making patterns. Orderly processions from A to E and back. Rows upon rows upon rows of letter Bs.

When I get to the nurses' station, a woman in an animal-print smock smiles pleasantly at me. "Hello," I say. "I need the number to Marshall Hospital, upstate, in Culver. Area code five-one-eight, I believe." She adjusts her smile, just a little, and asks me for my name. I tell her, and she punches something into her computer. She looks at me again, surprised, and says, "Oh." Then she picks up the telephone and hands it to me. While the number's ringing, I ask: "Would you be able to tell me how a person would go about getting herself committed voluntarily?"

Chapter 24

"It sounds to me like what you want is a hospice center. A place to die in peace. Do I have that right?"

Across the scarred expanse of a wooden desk, a Dr. Ralph Mintzer looks at me. He is slight, brown-suited, going bald, and I am trying very hard to make myself like him. It is early morning, not even 9:00 A.M., and I feel compassion for his aviator-style glasses and the too-skinniness of his body. There is something pinched and womanly about his chin and mouth, though, his lips too red, and in his eyes I detect the buried licentiousness of a college professor who is pushing fifty-five. I search for something else. It is overcast outside, just starting to snow, and the gray morning throws a muffled brightness into the room and through the dried peach halves of Dr. Mintzer's ears. I look at his sad, battered desk, high school–issue oak, and say, "Yes. Fair enough. I guess that's pretty much what I want."

"Because if I understand you correctly, your whole theory of programmed cell death is that you're physically, physiologically ill, and that what you suffer from is terminal."

"Yes," I say. "No. It's complicated."

"Complicated how?"

"Well, because it's not that straightforward. It's not that I think I have some physical disease where you could draw my blood and see it for yourself under a microscope, like AIDS. You said hospice, and hospice is for people with actual, physical diseases, cancer and multiple sclerosis. It's more—" I search the room, struggle with the words to explain myself. I have been here, at Marshall Hospital, for an hour and a half, in an orange plastic chair, in a cramped, green office where I talked to a social worker. I had answered her questions honestly— my name, why I was here, how I had come—and I'm trying to do the same now. "I don't know," I say, "evolutionary? Genetic. It's like a physical disease in that way, like something like cystic fibrosis. I know you understand the parallels between physical and mental disease, what the interplays and overlaps are. This is the same thing, more or less, a physical illness whose symptoms are mostly emotionally expressed, and whose end result is, unavoidably, death."

"And what are these symptoms that you've noticed?"

"Well—hurting myself. Drinking. Bulimia. A whole bunch of self-destructive behaviors." I hesitate. I have already explained about Dayton. "But the biggest symptom is my sister."

"Your sister?"

"Her suicide."

"Ah." Dr. Mintzer sits back with an air of complacent satisfaction, the man working on the crossword puzzle who has happened upon the answer to sixteen down. "You're depressed."

"I'm not depressed."

"Of course you are. What meds have you been on?" He picks up a pen and clicks it expectantly.

A flash of rage bolts across the base of my stomach. I struggle to stay focused, to stay rational, but it only takes an instant to see something about this Dr. Mintzer, all the Dr. Mintzers of the world, and I know that I have come this far to learn simply what I should have months—years—ago: mental health will never be able to help me. Its practitioners have chosen their profession to deny a terrifying truth other doctors accept—there are ills for which there is no cure. Here I am, giving this man a chance to reckon with something entirely new, and all I can see is the quest for differential diagnosis, neat categorization in his eyes. Paranoia, delusions of grandeur, suicidal ideation; Narcissistic Personality Disorder, *DSM-IV* 301.81, over and out. A little Paxil, a little chat, and we'll be on our way.

"I'm not depressed." With effort, I say it again. "What is it you people find so threatening in the possibility that I'm just meant to die?"

"What is it you find so threatening about living?"

"I don't find it threatening. I'm just not meant to." I gather myself for the spiel I hadn't had ready for Dr. Lindholm. "Plenty of people aren't, and don't. John Belushi, Marilyn Monroe, just about any one of the Kennedys. They hurt a lot of people along the way. I've hurt a lot of people. I'm just trying to do this in a way that won't hurt anybody else."

"Who have you hurt?"

"Well—" I look around the room. "My husband, first of all."

"Mmm." Dr. Mintzer nods. "Tell me about him, your husband."

"What do you want to know?"

"Whatever you want me to know."

"Well, he wanted me admitted here, for starters."

Dr. Mintzer picks up a manila file from his desk and folds the cover back. Upside down, I see what looks like the commitment papers Dr. Lindholm showed me on Saturday, and on top of them a bright pink sticky note. The State of New York seal. I try to read the sticky note. *Urgent,* I see, and *Ralph—*

"I see here that your husband called Friday morning to arrange your transfer from Mount Lebanon, and called again yesterday afternoon to cancel the admission. The second call was confirmed by a doctor Rachel Lindholm, who said she would be handling your treatment." Dr. Mintzer looks at me over the aviator glasses. "Your therapist back in Manhattan, I presume?"

If I had any dignity left, I would get up now and walk out. Every minute of the last half hour—the last fifteen hours—has been a mistake. I'd signed myself out of Mount Lebanon and walked all the way to Penn Station, accompanied the length of Third Avenue by hundreds of other New Yorkers out Christmas shopping in the summer heat. At Penn Station, I'd checked the train schedule; the last one had already left. I moved on to the buses: Greyhound, then Peter Pan. Nothing. A People's EconoLine was leaving at four-fifty. I took a seat next to a sniffling teenager eating salami on white.

Outside Schenectady, an overturned eighteen-wheeler had turned Route 87 into a parking lot, and it was past midnight by the time we reached Albany. At the bus terminal, the cab stand stood empty, the depot was dark and locked. I curled up on an outside bench. When I woke up, it wasn't dawn yet. My neck was stiff and I was freezing; the air smelled like snapped chalk but no matter: I had places to go, admissions to undertake. I'd gotten to Marshall before seven and felt the disappointment form in my stomach like an egg swallowed whole. The Marshall I'd imagined had been a prison, low-slung and gray—a fat hippopotamus crouched on a tuffet. This Marshall looked like a college. The campus was sprawling, Gothic; there were evergreen bushes and ivy walls. Swarthmore with barred windows. Hungry, full-bladdered, I'd rung the buzzer anyway; hoped for the best, the worst. Forty minutes with the social worker, a wait—some papers to sign?—Dr. Mintzer's office. And now all of this.

"Okay, then. Admit me voluntarily."

Dr. Mintzer rears back in his seat and considers me coldly, lips pressed in just the briefest of smiles. I stare back at him. He lifts his pen within inches of his ear, angled as if to jam it into his own brain, and says, "Miss Gilbertson, were you ever in Vietnam?"

"Of course not."

"Well, I was. I spent a good chunk of my residency working with POWs. I saw men who had been tortured so terribly I couldn't begin to describe it to you. Burned. Maimed. Locked in snake-infested pits."

I nod obligingly, though I have the sinking feeling Dr. Mintzer is gearing up for the same sort of post-traumatic stress disorder song-and-dance routine that Dr. Lindholm apparently played for Robert.

"We did studies on these men. I don't need to tell you that most of them were profoundly disturbed. They'd been tortured to reveal U.S. military secrets—encampments, weapons storage, and the like—and do you know what our studies showed? Across the board, the soldiers who were highest ranking, best educated, and scored the highest on intelligence tests were the first to give in to their captors." Dr. Mintzer pauses. "Now, why do you think that might be?"

I shake my head negatively.

Dr. Mintzer's mouth twists scornfully. "No?"

I shrug my shoulders. "Sorry."

"It's because they were the best able to rationalize their actions. To come up with the most complex, emotionally safeguarded justification for a behavior that the lower-ranking soldiers saw very simply: Protect your secrets, right; give them away, wrong. Better to suffer yourself, even die, than compromise the United States Army. The higher soldiers wouldn't let themselves see the choice that way, and they came up with reasons why avoiding punishment was a fair exchange for the lives of hundreds of their comrades. That behavior—that excuse-making—was labeled 'totalism': the more intelligent and better educated you are, the more able you are to construct sophisticated rationalizations for actions society at large would consider unthinkable."

Dr. Mintzer, looking strangely smug, folds his hands. "Now, why do you suppose I'm telling you this?"

Dr. Mintzer is toying with me. I battle fury, snideness, old watch-dogs that now stand in my way. I try to look politely defeated as I say, "I really don't have any idea."

"Because that's exactly what you're doing now, engaging in totalism. Coming up with an excuse for your bad behavior. Programmed cell death, really." His voice is gravelly with disgust.

Automatically, I am on my feet.

"Miss Gilbertson, I'm going to tell you something." Dr. Mintzer's words come fast and thick now, hailstones pummeling the sudden wall of enmity burning through my skin. "Mental illness is not a game. Marshall Hospital is not a hotel. You didn't read our ad in *The New Yorker*. Half my colleagues would say I'm the one who's crazy for turning you away, but I'm not going to admit you because you're not sick. I couldn't be having this conversation with you if you were. The patients we admit here are very, very sick. Schizophrenics and catatonics, for the most part, talking ragtime when they come here. Half of them are in restraints and the other half are so heavily medicated they don't need them. And yet I still have to fight like hell to keep most of them hospitalized.

"You're a very sad young lady, I can see that, and you have lots of reasons for your sadness." Dr. Mintzer's eyes fall briefly to the file on his desk. "Your childhood, your sister. I have every sympathy for you. But you're also a very lucky young lady, with a great many things going for her, including her mental health. You're clearly very bright; you're obviously well cared for. You have a husband who—"

"I have a husband who wanted me sent here."

"You have a husband who didn't know what Marshall was. I could make you a referral to a less intensive psychiatric facility, but that isn't what you need.

"What you need is to get over your guilt about surviving your sister. You don't want to get better because that would dishonor her; you think it's like killing her all over again. But I'm here to tell you that what you want to do can't be done. You can't will yourself to death, and you can't make something up to your sister by deliberately throwing your own life away. You made it, she didn't. It's brutal and awful, but it happens. No two twins are ever the same; they're not the same person. I know you know better than that."

Finally, I find the words I need, the power to put them in motion. "Thank you, Dr. Mintzer," I say, "for your *thoughtful* analysis of my state." Fury and something else make my voice quail and for that, I hate myself more than him. Mistake, mistake. My arm feels tingling numb as I reach down for my bag. "Be sure to send me a bill for your time."

"How do you know your sister's death wasn't an accident?"

Fuck you, I think. Fuck you.

"You say you found out the truth about yourself. Reality is devastating. Unbearable. Myth is what we give ourselves just to survive it. You found out the universal truth. But that's life. What you need to find out now is what you already know, and that is that you're strong enough to handle it and go on."

Two angry strides on shaky legs. My pain, my truth, are not mythical, universal. In a flash of blood, I loathe this man the way I've loathed no one in my life. He's Dr. Zobel, Dr. Flynn, the Swat social worker all rolled into one. My head makes a dizzy swing for the door. Pinky scalp, dried fruit ears, a faint gleam of polish, Mephisphelean, on pointed fingernails. My own fingernails crush half-moons into my palms. Rattle-snick of pen on paper, the bright white sound of something torn free. *Thwip-thwip* as Dr. Mintzer crosses around the desk.

"I want you to consider this." His voice is at my shoulder. "Miss Gilbertson, look at me." He folds a prescription in half and holds it up between our faces.

"Arsenic?" I say. "That's OTC, now, don't bother. A little TPA to stop my silly cell death disease?" The words are clogged, thick; this is all my fault.

"Take a look tomorrow. In a week. Think about it. Think about it honestly." His thumb is against my wrist as he opens my right hand. He places the paper in my palm and closes my fingers down. "Listen to me," he says. From point-blank range, his teeth look like ancient tombstones, grayed tablets creeping with moss. "You're going to be just fine."

My feet clatter down the stairs, my fists close. I glare past the security guard and shoulder the door hard, cracking noise against the metal, not hard enough. Outside, my breath makes white, angry blatts in the air and I stand still, just breathing. Snow whirls in eddies around the closing double doors, the bases of a few skeletoned trees, it blows toward me and sticks to my eyelashes. It is thirty degrees colder than yesterday, at least, and I tell myself that's why I am shaking. I suck in greedy breaths and icicles stab at my chest. I double over, hauling air.

There is a parking lot, nearly empty, and the roar of traffic is muffled by snow and distance. A left, two rights, a left, if I remember, then the highway, a fifteen-dollar cab ride that feels as if it happened days ago. I start down the long, empty drive, furious, crunching steps. At the bottom, I shake out my shoulders and roll my neck and Dr. Mintzer's prescription drops from my hand. It curls up at me, sweat-gray and scalloped in the snow. I kick it once, then stoop to open it. Dr. Mintzer's handwriting is tall and shaky, but the three bullet points on the small rectangle of paper read clear:

• Psychotherapy
• Forgive yourself
• Go back home & live your life

He's even signed it. Dispense as written. I laugh and laugh, loud, honking, rude. I laugh until my eyes are filled with tears.

I walk with my head up through the falling snow. When I left Albany, only the first few flakes were salting down from an iron sky, but now the snow crowds down heavily, a solid three inches on streets undisturbed but for the tire tracks left by residents on their way to work and school. It's residential streets between here and the main thoroughfare. My boots make squeaking noises and already I feel cold creeping in through leather growing damp.

I make the left, two rights, and the second left, carving clear paths through mounds of white on mailboxes and garbage cans as I find the sidewalk and then stumble off again. A car drives by, windshield wipers thunking, another sits in a driveway, running, tailpipe fanning black smoke into white air. The houses are small, ranches and split-levels, side by side and separated by cyclone fences. Giant Santas and plastic Rudolphs leer at me from tiny lawns. The second left spills me out onto the double-lane avenue I remember from the cab ride, low-slung projects and defeated, half-vacant shopping plazas on either side. To the right, the road rolls to Albany, across a bridge, over the Rubicon of the Hudson. To the left, the hill rises into Culver. *The armpit of New York,* Carl called it once, flapping a hand beneath his nose. Discount department stores and bars blink neon messages to the street. Straight across the highway, the Frank Moulin Monument and Headstone Company. There are bus shelters with shattered windows and torn posters; men struggling up the hilly avenue with broken grocery carts or brandishing squeegees at cars stopped at the traffic lights. Lines of aqua blue slush break and reform with rhythmic regularity on drivers' windshields. Farther up the hill, I see a glass storefront, a peeling sign: GIMBEL'S LIQUORS.

I turn left and start to climb.

I pass an International House of Pancakes with plywood over its front door and then a burnt-out motel, its gutted windows like empty eye sockets out on the street. I stop in the Gimbel's and decide on vodka. It's a morning drink, I tell myself, made from potatoes. Hash browns, practically. My stomach rumbles and I collect two packets of cheese-on-cheese crackers at the register. The clerk doesn't card me. I slide the bottle and one of the packets into my bag.

The wind shifts, blowing from the side and front, and I end up eating as much hair as I do crackers and cheese. I watch my feet up the hill, looking up every so often to gauge my progress. I'm out of breath and slow. The snow falls furiously, dulling street sounds and sights, neon now blinks vaguely against the furred sky. At the top of the hill, I think I make out a yellow star. "Hark, a star in the East," I mutter, mostly just to hear my voice. I pull my coat tight around my neck and bow into the wind. I sling my bag forward and squint my eyes, pretend it's a sandstorm and I'm great with child. The star holds steady, then grows brighter. A green sign emerges beneath it; orange lettering, HOLIDAY INN. Is there room at the inn? I walk to the front of the building, find the door marked OFFICE. There is room at the inn. I take a smoking standard with a queen-sized bed, cable TV, and an efficiency kitchenette. I turn the key and drop my bag on the bed. The cap on the vodka bottle unscrews without complaint and I kick off my shoes. Holiday Inn, Hospice Inn, it's all the same.

Chapter 25

When the Gimbel's bottle is gone, there is another, and another, and another and another and another, until the once-fat bill section of my wallet grows thin.

Days, weeks blur as I stumble between the Holiday Inn and the Gimbel's, Culver's three bars, and the gates of Marshall Hospital; I only know it's Christmas when one day all but the first of these are closed and locked. To mark the occasion, I leave a present outside Marshall for Dr. Mintzer—beer and peanuts, scratchy popcorn hulls, cheese-on-cheese crackers that come back up in thick, waxy bars—and find an open supermarket to do my heretofore unpracticed *Leaving Las Vegas* imitation in. Wine and beer, mudslides and hard cider are shrouded with heavy plastic, but I reach in and load 'em up all the same, enough for Santa and a whole workshop of elves, should they decide to pay me a call. "It's room sixteen, feel free to come right by," I tell an ancient matron with a sparse pink hairdo, a bent man haggling with the meat clerk over the discounted price of tongue. "There'll be drinks and plenty of horse-doovers." I sing *"O Holy Night"* right along with the wailing alto on the loudspeaker. At the register, a girl with beet-dyed fingers rings me up. She lets me keep deviled ham and saltines, two cans of Cheez Whiz, the four bottles of assorted pain-killers I throw in just in case.

No one comes to my room, though I wait for days with the overhead thud of feet and perpetual staccato of international radio, the smell of sweetish smoke and greasy fish in the halls. I channel-surf, happy to bide my time: a Hitchcock marathon; *Marnie* and *North by Northwest;* a station that runs eighties B-sitcoms around the clock. I catch up on *Facts of Life* and *The Greatest American Superhero* and *Charles in Charge.* Some big bully steals that little Olson kid's bike on *Full House.* Another week, then the manager stops by; I promise to keep the TV volume low; lower than that, even, looow. Dayton sits down on the bed next to me and takes the remote control from my hand.

"Well, welcome back, silly." She wears Lee jeans, the cuffs rolled over twice, and a bat-winged cowl-neck in a color I recognize. Her hair is mounted high on her head with a banana clip and even sitting down I can tell we're not the same height.

"But, but—" I stammer. "Dayton."

"Yes?"

"You and me." I point between us. "We're twins."

She covers her mouth with her hand. "Oh, no," she laughs. "Not this again."

"What does that mean?" I cross my arms.

"That means, Darien, no duuh."

The ceiling pops with sex and the public access channel. Dayton looks up at it, then around my room. "Come on. Let's ditch this rathole."

I stand and pull her hand. "Shithole. Come on. Say it."

Dayton laughs again and shakes her head, pulling back on me.

I tickle her ribs. "Daytondayton," I croon, "c'mon, Daytondaydee-dee."

"Let's ditch this ratshithole," she says. I grab my jacket and we head for the door.

Outside, it is rainy and cold. We find an open store, and beyond it, a dilapidated square dedicated to President Eisenhower. Behind the sagging fence are an emaciated man in a filthy tuxedo, throwing scraps of something to a dog, another man wrapped in movers' blankets, and a wide black woman with a pyramid of woven hair like a croque-embouche. "*Salve!*" Dayton calls, but none of them turn, and I correct her Latin, a discriminating audience, mad in the classical sense, perhaps. "*Salvete!*" The dog barks.

Dayton elbows my ribs. "Show-off." She hands me a paper bag. "Here. We'll share."

Later, Dayton climbs up on the barstool next to mine, and I order doubles of everything: tequilas and whiskeys and beers, and, to be funny, perfect Manhattans on the rocks. I worry that she doesn't have an ID and tell the bartender, "It's okay. We're absolutely the same. We're twins." He doesn't even look, and together we survey the crowd for the guy with AIDS, hepatitis B. We see denim jackets lined with sheepskin, mustaches, coveralls. Pointy vinyl shoes and rayon shirts; Brylcreemed hair with comb lines running through. Dayton looks at her watch and shakes her head with disappointment, disapprobation. "You're late," she says. "You're very late."

Sudden joy is sucked, rattling and throttling down a drain of despair. "I know!" I tell her. Across the room, a man with messy brown curls and piano-playing hands winks at me. "I'm sorry, Dayton," I say. "Dayton, I'm sorry."

Later still, closing time, she tells me she has to go. I stall her with stories. "Remember how we used to have burping contests in bed?" I ask.

"Yeah." Dayton smiles blandly. "That was fun."

"Or what about the time we put Tabasco sauce in Mom's boyfriend's coffee. What was his name?"

"Gordon. You did that, not me."

"Gordon." I laugh. "That was the best."

"He slammed you against a wall and twisted your nipple. Mom stood in the kitchen and said, 'Oh, dear.'"

"Yeah, well," I say. "Do you remember the time we caught Mac jerking off to his Christie Brinkley poster?" Dayton shakes her head, puzzled; no. "What about the time Ken got so stoned he tried to smoke oregano?"

Dayton shakes her head again. "I don't remember those." She climbs down off her stool. "I've got to go."

"But Dayton," I say, "please. You just got here. I'm lonely." I collapse my head on the bar, pathetic, and whisper to my hands, melodramatic and ignominious. "I'm so, so lonely."

Dayton picks me up by the chin then, and for the first time, looks right into my eyes. Her expression sears me, blank and pitiless as the sun. "I know," she says. She waves a hand around the room. At the bar, men with thick fingers and crew cuts worry their beer mugs and stare up at hockey on overhead televisions. On the dance floor, couples shuffle along to the breaking voice of the jukebox, hands planted in back pockets, eyes glazed with neon and inevitability. At the back of the room a waitress drags a rag across a table, pockets a pile of dimes. "You think you're not like anyone else?"

Back in my room, I knock over the Gimbel's bottles to get to the supermarket bag. A gutted cracker sleeve, an empty Cheez Whiz can; I have a headache, a terrible headache. Motrin, the first box I come up with. I pop the bottle open and put two caplets on the bathroom sink. Then a third, a fourth, a fifth, and a sixth. This is what you learn working for pharmaceutical companies: recommended adult dosages are for shit. About six OTC Motrin equal one prescription pill. The pharmaceutical companies would love you to know that—Take 'em all! Take handfuls at a time, then go back and buy more!—but they can't. What if someone overdoses and the family sues?

"So sue me," I say. I sweep the brownish pills into my fist and toss them in the air. One or two, I think, land in my mouth and I swallow, gagging a little. Candy-coated shells like Ex-Lax. I'd forgotten that about Motrin. Yuck.

Another box, then. Orudis it is, the pills a bright, grasshopper green. A couple of those on the countertop, next to a lonely Motrin that missed the first sweep. I peer at them. The green is lovely, the orange-brown less so, a real drag on that summer day, Skittles bright green. Didn't they get rid of that diarrhea-colored M&M, anyway? I flick it into the sink. Fumble for the other boxes, shake a couple robin's egg blue and lemon yellow pills in with the green, Aleve, Nuprin. Much better. Fun and dandy. Now, something to drink.

Vodka, of course, and the pills go up in the air, cracking against my teeth, bouncing off my nose. Those that make it in go down in the wash, four or five, I don't remember. I try more but my aim is bad and worse, and how many pills is too much, anyway? I weigh a hundred and ten. I pull at my jeans. Okay, maybe a hundred and five, are they all the same formulation, 200 milligrams, 500 milligrams? What's a hundred and five in kilograms, what times two point two? In, bounce, in, swallow, way off. Forty-five? Forty-seven? How old are you when you weigh forty-seven pounds? A little blue Aleve, betrayer, makes a nice arc and then shoots right down, clean down my throat, and for a second I gasp and choke. *Jesushitcan'tbreathe,* but then it clears, and I'm more careful like, on my hands and knees bobbing for pain pills, picking them straight off the linoleum with my tongue.

Ugh. Dust ball.

Got to rest.

Funny thing that, my hand next to the floor, and I reach over to pick it up, but it's tied to something, rooted to something, and it won't let go, plus someone is tugging on my shoulder, and finally I have to give up. Hand? Where are you. Hand? The move is rooming slurry slow and the floor is soft, so soft, the nicest bed I ever had, and I can't—not—want—to close my eyes. I close my eyes. *Beep, beep,* that's nice, *beep, beep, beep,* just wish somebody would turn off that light.

Turn off that light.

Darien?

Turn off that light!

Darien, oh, Darien! My mother standing over my bed, Mom? Mommy? Something wrong with her face, her makeup gone, deep scoremarks on either side of her mouth. Her clothes are wrinkled and food-stained, olive pants and cream sweater, something terrible is going on.

"Mommy?" I feel her grab my hand. "Could somebody please turn off the light?"

She sinks to her knees. Her head comes forward so her forehead is touching the sheet, the hard shell of my chest, and she presses my hand so hard I can almost feel it. Her shoulders jerk and shudder. "Oh, thank God," she says. "Thank the Good Lord Jesus Christ."

But still, there's that light.

That light! It comes toward me through the darkness, a white knife in all that black. I'm moving slow—sore, I have to; it hurts for all my urbane calm, each pedal-turn of the bike connected to a twisting blade between my legs. My thighs are sticky, blood or semen, I don't know which, and they pull away from the seat over and over again with a peeling noise. *Thock. Whirr. Thock. Whirr.* Cars rush by on either side, blowing horns or revving engines angrily when they pass, inconvenienced by my wobbling progress up the road. My mouth tastes metal with beer and there is sand in my hair and my shirt. Out a window, a wadded paper bag turns and tumbles. Exhaust blooms blue in the humid night.

Baby.

I press myself harder into the bike seat, grinding the rigid plastic against my bruised, torn skin. Inseam against bare flesh brings tears to my eyes. Where's my underwear? I had lost my underwear. Baby, stupid baby! Dayton doesn't do that; how can you be Dayton if you can't even get one simple thing right, one little teensy, tinsy thing?

Bay-bee, *I can't hear you.* I said bay-bee. Shut up shutup.

The road is empty for a while, and quiet, but then the light comes again. I knew it was waiting, a motorcycle I think at first, but no, it's just one of those one-eyed cars. What was it she used to call them when we were little, my mother? She had a funny name for it, like davenport and chifforobe, and we had said it over and over, the funniest word in the world. *Padiddle. Pediddle.* Are they good luck? Do you get a kiss or give a punch? What had we done, mushed shoulder to shoulder in the front seat of Tony's pickup, me, Dayton? Me Darien.

I swerve my bike across the yellow line, *thock, whirr,* white light, scream of rubber, brakes. And then *blam!* The loudest sound in the world. My private parts don't hurt so much. And then reddest pain, and blackest dark.

Still it doesn't end. It is too much, unbearable, but it doesn't end. A burning pain in my throat, thick tube, a doctor in sky blue scrubs haloed against that goddamn light. "Breathe," she says. "Blow out. Breathe." The ends of her blond bob peek beneath a surgical cap and she hauls a hose, hand over hand, out through my mouth. *It hurts!* I want to scream, but I can't. *I can't.* "Breathe," she says, "blow." She's ripping me open, turning me inside out, fishing hooks catching, reversing my skin. "All done." She holds out a kidney-shaped plastic cup, her head turned away. "Sometimes they gag a bit when the tube comes out," she explains, but to who, to what, a class? And then I do. I heave all over her wool crepe pants, her *vero cuoio* shoes.

"Hello?"

If she asks, "Who is this? Who's calling, please?" I'll hang up, then find the rest of that vodka and collect the loose pills. It is late, I don't know how late it is, and my head is still pounding. My knuckles are white on the receiver and my voice quavers. Rage, terror, inebriation.

"You were right, okay?" I say. "Happy now? You were right. Smarty fucking you. There was something else. I tried to kill myself."

"Darien?" Dr. Lindholm's voice, groggy-soft, shifts quickly to doctor-alert. "Hello? Darien, is that you?"

"Yeah, it's me. Did you hear me? Dr. Lindholm? I tried to kill my-self."

"Okay. Listen to me. Tell me exactly where you are. I'm going to call 911 on the other line and send someone over for you and you're going to stay on the phone with me. Tell me what you took, what you did." There are scrambling noises in the background, the squeal of an opening drawer.

"No. Not now. I mean then, the night I lost my virginity. The sum-mer after Dayton died. A whole year after Dayton died."

"Okay," she says, "okay. Are you sure? You're sure you're all right now? Because you're slurring your words. I can barely understand you."

"I took some pills earlier, but I threw up. I wasn't trying to kill myself. I had a headache." I laugh a little. "I still have a headache."

"How many pills did you take?"

"I don't know." For chrissake! "I lost count. Listen, aren't you lis-tening? I tried to kill myself after Dayton died, but I didn't."

I hear shifting, sliding sounds, then the indelicate intimacy of Dr. Lindholm breathing against the receiver. "Darien," she says, "I'm get-ting out of bed now to talk to you, but it is almost four o'clock in the morning. I'd like you to tell me where you are, and even more than that, I'd like you to tell me you're coming home so we can have this discussion in person."

"What, you mean like in your office?"

"Is that where you'd like to be?"

"I don't know," I say. "Jesus!"

"Jesus, what?"

I have been sitting on the floor Indian-style, beneath the night table where the phone usually rests, the base tucked between my legs. I don't remember getting here, crawling across from the bathroom; I am still in my clothes from yesterday and my sweater smells like puke. I woke up vomiting, lying on my side, blurting out pretzels and vodka and pills in pitiful jerks. I cross over to the open bathroom, caplets littering the floor like an industrial accident. I pick two blue pills out and swallow them dry.

"Jesus what, Darien?"

"Jesus, all of this!" My voice sounds loud, agitated, and a couple of hard thumps against the wall confirm that it is. "What do I want to talk about, where do I want to talk about it, negotiating. I don't want any of this! I want to be through with it! I want to *want* to be dead. I can't even kill myself. I didn't kill myself because I didn't want to die."

Dr. Lindholm asks me why I didn't want to die, her voice soothing and calm, but I can't do this, I can't, and before I know what's happening, I have started to cry. "I can't," I sob. "Dr. Lindholm, I can't. I'm sorry."

"Yes, you can," she says firmly. "Yes, you can."

For a few minutes, I cry and Dr. Lindholm listens. Then she says, "We can do this one of two ways. I want to know where you are. I can go and check the caller ID unit in my kitchen and have the phone company tell me where you're calling from, or we can skip that step and you can tell me yourself. I'd rather it was the latter."

"Fuck you," I sob. "Fucking phone company. Fucking caller ID!"

"Yes," she agrees.

"I'm in Culver. At some shitbag Holiday Inn. I tried to check myself into Marshall but Dr. Mintzer said I wasn't sick enough."

Dr. Lindholm sighs against the phone and then I see her. She slumps back into a leather chair, her legs crossed at the knee, wearing silk pajamas. I see a headband. Bunny slippers. "Thank you, Darien," she says. "Give me fifteen minutes and I'll call you from my car."

I look at my face in the mirror, brown hair and behind it brown curtains, the dead-bolted door. There is the muffled sound of voices in the hallway, then a door is slammed.

"No."

"No, what?"

"I don't want you to come get me."

"What do you want, then?"

We breathe and I think, *I want nothing. I want all of this to be over.*

"Would you like Robert to come and get you?"

"No," I finally say. "There's . . . a bus."

"When?"

"Every day. Tomorrow. I'll come back."

Chapter 26

The night I fucked Jeff Kaster, I rode my bicycle into a moving car. I had been good all that summer long: not drinking, not eating, not hurting myself. I had been Dayton and I had done a good job of it; nobody had told me that I couldn't. We had moved—twice—since her death, and nobody knew me, nobody knew there had ever been more than one of me. After that night at the beach, trying to kill myself had been inevitable. I'd fucked up, so to speak, and done something that was very bad, very Darien. What did that mean? It wasn't terribly complex: I was Darien, and I was alive. There was only one way to make amends.

When I hit the car, I cracked my skull and bruised my brain and broke four ribs and punctured a lung, and I lay in a coma at the Parkview Clinic for three weeks. I had hit the car at an angle and the driver had swerved away and the doctors had said it was a wonder I'd hurt myself as badly as I did, though it was of course not badly enough. It had been touch and go whether I would pull through and, if I did, whether I would have permanent brain damage: the swelling in my brain had stopped my breathing and I'd been put on a ventilator, and from the ventilator I'd developed double pneumonia. It was enough to kill anybody. It was, in fact, enough to kill anybody three times over, and yet my relentless, predatory body insisted on pulling through. One day I simply woke up. There was no metaphorical thrashing through gauzy nets or golden tunnels: just TV-screen gray one minute and the world the next, albeit a little fuzzy around the edges. My head hurt. My chest and throat hurt. A light was shining in my eyes.

At first, I didn't know where I was. It was just morning somewhere, after a bad night of drinking. But then there was the car, and Jeff Kaster, the mollusky taste of his tongue in my mouth. And after that there was me. Darien.

"Darien?"

A voice, a whisper I recognized. I tried to turn my head.

"Darien! Oh, Darien, oh, thank God!" Something grabbed my hand.

"Mom?" I said. "Mommy?" The words hurt my throat. Something was terribly wrong.

My mother's hand came up and stroked my forehead. It felt funny, furry; my head had been shaved. "Darien?" she said again.

I hesitated—Dayton?

"Do you know where you are?"

"No." No, no. It wasn't—I wasn't—I was dead.

"You're in the hospital. There was an accident. You were riding your bike and a car, some awful jerk, crossed the center line and hit you. He left you by the roadside. Someone called an ambulance. It was an accident."

Inside the dumb shell of my body I was thrashing, fighting off the truth. Darien, Darien, *No I didn't, no I can't,* but instantly, my mother's words made me freeze. I remembered them from another time, *She slipped and fell, it was an accident,* and I felt the flash of light and the blasting scream of my body against metal, a comforting, turgid weight. God, I was tired.

"It wasn't—not an accident," I whispered. "I wanted—to be. Dead. Dayton."

The scraping sound of my mother's chair tore a crescent moon across my forehead. Something inside my skin jumped. "Oh, Dee-dee," she whispered. I could feel her breath on my skin, humid and round, missing the familiar, brittle outline of alcohol. "No. No, Dee-dee. You're the only one in this world—

"Not you," she said. "You're a fighter, sweetheart. Yes, you are. You always have been, just smart and tough. Not like the others. Not like the boys. They'd fall for anything." For a minute, the room was full of sounds, pings and clicks and beeps. Someone was breathing in exaggerated hisses and sighs. I shook my head, or tried to, *no, no.*

"Do you remember the time Kenny got caught for stealing his teacher's purse? Just Tampax and lipsticks, and he tried to give me her keychain for my birthday, with her name and address stamped right on the back!" My mother laughed, and I did, too. I did remember that. Her delight, fumbling with the tissue wrap, *what's this, what's this?* She'd turned the keychain over and her thrilled, animated features had settled, a sinking hot air balloon. *Stoopid Ken. It's lovely; thank you.* The keychain sat on the kitchen table for a week and then one day was gone.

My mother coughed. "Now, this—your sister." Her voice strangled tight. "She wasn't ever like you. She wasn't strong, she didn't have your courage, even from the start." The words shook, clawing and gasping their way around the block in my mother's throat. "Even from the start, I knew. She was never, ever going to make it. If you had seen her, when she was born, so limp and blue and—and—*passive.* Did I ever tell you about that? Let me tell it to you, what happened." For a second my mother's voice went bright and chirpy. "I don't think I've ever told you about how you were born."

And then she told the story that I have carried hung from my neck all these years: the early labor on a Queens-bound subway, the fight with the obstetrician at Bellevue, the confusion, the shock. *Babies— zuh, plural? It was the first time I'd heard the word.* My mother's words burbled and murmured over my skin and for a moment I let myself float away on them, terrible and possible. I was in a river, fish and foam streaming past me. I was in the ocean, riptide.

—"But you were going to be born, whether I wanted you to or not. You were the one who came out first, in breech, yelling and screaming I could swear even before your head came through. You were angry, so angry, like maybe at coming into the world with your bottom first, and I could feel all of that, that *energy* just vibrating through my body. I hadn't wanted you, but how could I not love you? I did, from the second I held you. I did. I did."

My mother stopped, and in the silence, we both believed her. She had loved me, always loved me. The words were soap bubbles, shiny-iridescent in my brain. They mated, multiplied, filled the room. I floated up out of my bed.

"But the other one, she wasn't meant to make it. She was breech too, but when she came out, she didn't make any noise. I asked the doctors, 'Tell me! Tell me! What?' and they lifted her right in the air to smack her bottom. They tried everything, but then they took her away. It wasn't meant to be. She wasn't a fighter like you. She just couldn't make it." There was silence. "Okay? Dee-dee?" My mother whispered *please*.

The bubbles popped. I slammed back against the sheets, mattress coils like awls against my spine. Dayton, oh Dayton, Dayton! For the first time, I felt her corporal loss. Devastation flushed out my limbs, tingling my fingertips, aching my hips. Bone and ligament twisted, torqued, cracked. I saw her tiny, dusky body, her perfect nose, her teacup ears. Her bird mouth opened in an airless *O,* her eyes, deep as slate, rolled back. *We're so sorry, Mrs. Gorse,* someone said. Her legs were drawn in violin bows to her chest.

"Okay." My mother's voice came again, something settled. "There was you, and that was more than enough. Darien, I know I've been a lousy mother to you sometimes, but if I think about that I can't stand it, because there's no way for me to take it back. It doesn't change anything, right? That's what you and—that's what your brothers always said, right? Sorry doesn't help." Her voice shuddered to a whisper. "Darien, don't make me stop moving, please don't make me stop moving. If I do—I can't— This is the way the world works. Things are the way we say they are."

The room pinged and hissed and beeped. Then the sobs opened my eyes. My mother! My poor mother!

Her face was inches from mine. She was beautiful and ravaged; she looked older than I remembered, tracks through the powder on her cheeks, mascara dots on her browbone. She'd forgotten eyebrow pencil, and without it she looked unshielded, surprised. "There's my girl." She leaned in close and stroked my face. "There's my beautiful, beautiful girl."

For a minute, I knew she was looking at me, really looking at me and seeing me. I saw what she held out to me. I closed my eyes again and took it.

"You took what?" Dr. Lindholm sits in the leather chair across from me, one ankle pulled up, unbunny-slippered.

"The bargain. Whatever it was I thought she was offering me."

"And what did you think she was offering you?"

"That's the kicker," I say, "of course. In the end she was offering me nothing. I thought it was"—I can't say this—"some kind of recognition. Love, I guess. Some permanent change in our relationship. That she would love me if only I'd forget Dayton."

Dr. Lindholm nods. "And you did."

"And I did. I just"—I raise my hands—"I don't know. I don't know where she went, how I forgot, but I did it. I checked out of the hospital and went on my merry way."

"Your merry way?" Dr. Lindholm interrupts me, frowning. "It sounds as if you had a very serious head injury."

[298]

"Yeah. Maybe so. But that doesn't explain anything."

"To the contrary, it might explain everything."

I ignore her. "And this, though—here's the really, awful, unforgivable part. I kept on forgetting her even after my mother revoked her part of the bargain."

Dr. Lindholm scowls some more. "That doesn't sound awful and unforgivable to me. For a moment, your mother gave you the one thing you needed your entire life. Why wouldn't you then do whatever it took to get that back?"

"So we're back to the only thing that's wrong with me is that my mommy didn't love me enough? Ugh."

"Worse than that. Your mother dangled love in front of you and then took it away."

"No," I say. "I can't accept that. All this pain can't be about my mother. What about Dayton?"

"Tell me about Dayton."

For an instant, I feel it fresh, feel it new, as brutal as being born, the blown-wide agony of becoming alone. When Dayton died, it was as if the earth itself was cracked open, an egg in the grip of vast, brute hands, all content and meaning shaken out. Something in my brain detonated, liquefied. Without her, I stumbled along, a puppet, a nothing, a tabula rasa waiting for Robert to happen along and find. Why do I endure? That's the question I should have been asking Dr. Lindholm from the start. How do I endure?

"It was"—I look at the familiar print behind Dr. Lindholm's head, the startling pinks and greens and blues of Central Park—"It was the end of the world. It was just black. She was the only person in the world to ever love me, and I loved her back with everything I had, and then one day she just turned around and threw it all back in my face."

Dr. Lindholm says nothing. I fix on the print, a collection of crude slashes, lime green and china blue, a couple spots of white; grass or a pool of vegetable, milky water. I can smell the crushed blades and hear the tiny *lap, lap* of waves. I ask myself the unutterable question: *Am I really that unlovable?*

"What else?"

I shake my head.

"Do you really think it was throwing it back in your face?"

"She had my clothes on. What else could it have been?"

"Well—" Dr. Lindholm draws the word out slowly, carefully. "It could have been a lot of things. Maybe it was about borrowing your courage. Or it could have been her fantasy about taking you with her."

I close my eyes. Briefly, it seems impossible, being here. This morning, I woke up in a room full of brown light, looked around and around at the TV, the light cord, my feet pointing up from the bed. I packed my bag and brought my key to the front desk, a woman with hair the color of lemon curd and surly, bulldog lips. "Leavin' so soon?" The Peter Pan bus smelled like puke and powdered soap; someone had drawn listing Taj Mahal penises on the seatback in front of me, the obligatory arcs of jizz done in green Magic Marker. On Route 87, there had been a water tank with a woman's winking face painted on the side; signs for the Catskill Game Farm. I'd slept, and we'd stood in traffic on the West Side Highway. A hostile shoeshine at Penn Station, another desk clerk, another key. It felt like days ago, as if I had started the morning six time zones back. Where was I yesterday at this time? Four o'clock. Drinking. Passed out on the bathroom floor. "All she had to do was ask me. If she had asked me, I would have gone."

"And what about now?"

I roll my head against the couch. "Whenever I told that story about the way I was born, it was that I crawled over my dead sister. Actually crawled over her, so I could live. I wanted to live. I guess that's the really awful part. I want to be alive, no matter how hideous or relentless or animal that makes me."

"Why can't that make you courageous and strong?"

"It doesn't feel that way to me. It feels—I don't know, cannibalistic. I guess maybe that's really it, the heart of it: I can't reconcile wanting to live with anything that isn't bad."

"So you'll live, but you'll keep punishing yourself for it."

I shrug, and then open my eyes. "I guess so."

Dr. Lindholm stares at me without saying anything. I still hate this, the looking. "Just for the record," she says, "not all suffering is redemptive."

"Mmm." I nod. "Thanks. I'll keep that in mind."

"Do you know what I mean by that? You don't have to suffer to be redeemed, and there's no guarantee that you will be just because you do. If I could, I'd give you permission to live without punishing yourself for it. God knows you've earned it."

"Mmm," I say again. "Thanks."

Dr. Lindholm's eyes shift to the wall. "We're going to have to stop for now. Are you going to be all right?"

I smile grimly. "I'm afraid so."

"I'm glad to hear that." Dr. Lindholm smiles back, and then her face resettles. "There's one more thing I wanted to ask you about before you leave." She takes a deep breath. "What about Robert?"

What about Robert? I look down at my hands, skin red and chapped after weeks of staggering around Culver without gloves. "He doesn't know I'm here yet. I haven't called him, and I'm not—I'm staying in a hotel, the East Side Marriott. I don't know what . . . I owe him a pretty big apology."

"I'd say he owes you a pretty big apology, too."

"Yeah," I say. "No. I don't know. I think he already apologized to me, at the hospital."

Dr. Lindholm angles her head and lifts an eyebrow at me. "But?"

I shake my head. "But."

We both stand, and then, unexpectedly, Dr. Lindholm is over me.

She puts her arms around me and sweeps me into a hug. I smell her perfume and feel her hair against my cheek, the surprising weight of her breasts. Her hands rub my back. "Darien, I'm so glad to see you," she says.

"Yeah, yeah, I know." I push her away just slightly. "You can care about me and still get paid."

Dr. Lindholm pulls me back again. "No, I mean I've missed you." One of her hands comes up to touch my head and then I give in to the maternal warmth of her embrace.

Chapter 27

For the next week, Dr. Lindholm and I meet twice a day, at seven o'clock in the morning and again at seven at night. She says it's the only way in good conscience she can keep me out of the hospital, knowing I am there at each end of every day. I expect to chafe against the regime, the baby-sitting, but the days pass, and instead what I find is that I welcome the sense of purpose to the day. For it seems that what I have learned is that while I appear destined to live my life, I don't have any idea how to do it, where to go or how to spend my time. I don't know what ought to have meaning, make me sad or laugh. I walk and eat, sleep and shower and shave my legs. I decide that what I am missing is the purposefulness of pain. Hurting myself, if nothing else, gave me something to do.

One afternoon I take a walk across Central Park. It's three blocks to my apartment and I head for it, telling myself I'm just going to get some new clothes. My underwear is gray from washing in the sink and all my socks are getting holes. I've worn the Scottie-dog sweater so much it's no longer my favorite. It's three o'clock in the afternoon and there's no risk that Robert will be there.

I open the door and it becomes clear at once that I am right: Robert is not there; Robert has not been there for quite some time. The heat is off. The rooms are cold, and oddly neat beneath a visible layer of dust. In the living room, newspapers are stacked still in their wrappers, and in the kitchen the table is set for a single person, with a knife and fork but no plate or bowl. A faint odor of rot hangs in the air. Garbage cans are empty, and bath towels folded on their racks. The humidifier is full. I open the refrigerator and see composting vegetables, a milk carton dated December 19.

For a second, I get chills. The whole thing looks like a crime scene tidied up by a somewhat fastidious thief. I had hesitated at the outside door before putting my key in the lock: I hadn't been home in a month, an entire lifetime, and what if it looked different to me? What if it didn't? I walk into the bedroom and uncap a deodorant sitting out on Robert's dresser. *Robert!* For a second it is him, so real I can almost taste it. I smack the cap back down and throw the deodorant at the bathroom door.

"God damn you," I say out loud. "Where the hell did you go?" D.C.? I think. Winnetka? I picture him briefly in Culver, hot on my trail. I shake myself. I'm here for clothes. I grab sweaters and shoes and socks, lots and lots of underwear, then hurry past the living room again. The space suddenly seems huge, endless. When did we get this couch, that mirror? In the foyer, I see my housekeys, where I dropped them on the table when I entered. I walk right by them and let the door lock me out.

Another day, I go to work. I can think of plenty of reasons not to—Duncan, dim memories of the Christmas party, the small matter of the promotion I accepted but never showed up for—but none of them, somehow, seems more persuasive than the undifferentiated emptiness of my days. There's only so many times I can window-shop the stores at Trump Tower, only so long I can nurse a cappuccino and the *Times* at Starbucks. Astroland Amusement Park is out, closed for the winter, much as I'd like the ride to Coney Island, and Rockefeller Center is useless to me without ice skates. I pull out the suit that's sat wadded in the bottom of my bag for the last six weeks and call housekeeping to send up an iron. What do I think awaits me? I don't know. If nothing else, I decide, the opportunity to let Mr. Kleinman fire me to my face.

The subway, Hudson Street, then the elevator to the seventeenth floor. Boylan & Westwood, hello. Walking through reception I feel conspicuous, like a person at a cocktail party in a biohazard suit. As I pass through the Foods group, two murmuring secretaries pause and exchange heavy-mascaraed glances, but I don't even know their names, and am not sure they know who I am. I repeat to myself what I heard on the ride downtown, a homeless man counseling his two bickering friends: *Hey, man, no need to premeditate negativity.* The heat is on full blast, steaming up the windows, and as I turn the corner to my cube, I struggle out of my heavy coat, focus on the complexities of the task, buttons, sleeves. The desk is clean and two banker boxes are stacked in the corner. I guess that settles any question about my promotion. "Well, well," I say.

"Well, well." The echo comes over the cubicle wall. "I don't believe it. I don't fucking believe it."

"Oh, go ahead, Carl," I say. I wave my hand. "Fucking believe it."

"I thought you were in the loony bin."

I take in Carl's face as if I have never seen it before: authentically tan and slightly peeling. He's had his hair cut, curls shorn in a Greco-Roman buzz. New contacts, silver-gray. Handsomer than ever, if that's possible. I shake my head negatively at him. "No."

"No? Then where've you been?"

"Where have *you* been?" I swirl my index finger around in front of my own face. "You're tan. Like the haircut."

Carl regards me for a minute and then steps back from the cubicle partition and frowns down at something I can't see. "You know, Darien, when I heard you were sick, I promised we'd stop all the bullshit. But the thing is, you kind of make it tough." He crosses his arms. "I've missed you. We've all been worried."

"Oh, *I* make it tough?" I laugh. "I see. That crack about the loony bin was just meant to make me feel right at home."

Carl scowls, his lips twisted over to the side. He considers his fingernails and then looks up. "You're right. I'm sorry. Ancient habit. I wasn't expecting to see you, especially not at"—he checks his watch—"quarter of eleven on a Thursday. Duncan said you were on medical leave, that you'd had some kind of nervous breakdown or something."

"Oh, he did, did he?" For a moment, I distract myself with outrage: Duncan's smirking face, those puffy lips and porcine eyes. But I hadn't been ready for this, hadn't settled on a plan for how to be someone else, especially not with Carl. I take a breath. "I was upstate, in Culver." I wait for the eyebrow raise. "I went to go to Marshall Hospital. Robert had tried to have me admitted, but when I got there, the little prick who ran the place said I wasn't sick enough and he wouldn't let me in. So I just hung out at a hotel for a month."

"Oh." Carl's eyes widen, and then he looks away. "Is this—was this because of your hand?"

"No. Well, yeah, sort of." I sigh. "I've been seeing this shrink for a while. I had a sister, Dayton. We were twins. She killed herself when we were fourteen, and I—well, I never told Robert about her, not deliberately or anything, but when he found out he kind of freaked."

For a minute, Carl says nothing. Neither do I. The elevator doors chime and we both look hopefully down the hall for deliverance; a phone rings but it is neither of ours. I consider again what I have just said, briefly imagine leaning across the partition and punching Carl's arm. "Just fucking with you, bud. I've been in rehab. You had it right, back in August. I broke my hand when Robert dropped me in the tub." It would be that easy; we both want it. As it is we are stuck, the truth between us, fat and lank as a used condom. Finally, he gives his head a quick shake. "Holy shit," he says. "You were a twin? There were two of you? Jesus, your poor mother."

"Yeah," I reply. "My poor mother."

Carl fires another desperate look around, then reaches down to his desk for a paper coffee cup. "You know what? I've got a meeting with Springer, at Pharmax, and I'm totally late. He's gonna have me bent over a conference table with my pants around my ankles if I don't hup-to. Not that I'd mind that, mind you. But I should fly. I'll see you later. You gonna be around the rest of the day? We'll do—something. Coffee." He kisses his fingers. "Welcome back." He scrabbles around his desk for something to take with him, and leaves without his overcoat. I note his hurried, jerky strides as he heads for the elevator, down to the Atrium probably, for a cigarette, and the sudden, aggressive anger building in my abdomen subsides. I can't blame him, I can't make this his fault. I've come back without a nose, a sunken crater in the middle of my face, and asked him to look at me without staring at the anomaly. I pick up my bag and steel myself to knock on Mr. Kleinman's door.

Chapter 28

In the morning, Dr. Lindholm and I talk about Robert. "Do you remember," I ask her, "back in the fall, when I started?"

"Of course I do."

"I mean, do you remember what you asked me, about if there was anything that had set me off, breaking my hand."

Dr. Lindholm nods. "Your twenty-eighth birthday, I'd say. Living Dayton's life now twice."

"Well, yeah, that," I reply. "Of course. But there was something else. I just remembered it this morning when I was sorting my clothes for the laundry."

"Oh." Surprise. Dr. Lindholm shifts her position on her chair, elbow out, one foot pulled beneath her. Her glasses perch on the top of her head. "Okay."

About a week before I broke my hand, I tell her, Robert was on a trip to Germany, and when he got back I took his suit to get cleaned. There was a huge line at the dry cleaners, so while I was waiting I checked through his pockets. I wasn't looking for anything in particular; Robert was always losing pens and money. That day he had an airline manifest card in his coat. "You know the things I'm talking about?" I ask.

Dr. Lindholm shakes her head.

"They're these little cards you write your name and numbers on and leave at the gate on overseas flights. The airlines say they're to confirm the boarding list, but I always figured they were really like a ready-made Rolodex or something so they can call next of kin if terrorists blow up the plane."

At the cleaners, stuck behind some Lilly Pulitzer–clad woman insisting she hadn't asked for her shirts boxed, I smoothed out the card from Robert's pocket and looked at both sides. *Gilbertson, Robert J. Lufthansa Flight 422, August 13, 1995,* the front said. I flipped it over. Was I listed as contact person? The gray, shaded boxes were filled out with my name, our home phone number. I was satisfied. I moved my thumb. At the bottom of the form, beneath the black line that read, *For Airline Purposes Only, Do Not Write Below This Line,* Robert had slipped in a message: *I love you, Dee, forever. I will always be with you, my angel in blue.*

"Oh, Darien." Dr. Lindholm presses her hand to her chest.

"Yeah," I say, "but don't you get it? I was reading it. He left it in his suitcoat instead of dropping it off like he was supposed to, which means I never would have gotten it if something had happened. It would have been blown to bits with the rest of him. I was standing in the middle of the dry cleaners when I found it and I practically started bawling, right in front of this big Helga the Horrible lady who runs the place. I gave him just total shit that night."

"Oh." Dr. Lindholm's face still looks soft, vulnerable. "Why?"

"I don't know," I say. "So typical Robert, I guess, to do something so beautiful half-right." I stop, shake my head. "No. That's not fair. It scared the crap out of me. I didn't—I've never known what I'd done to earn Robert's love, and it suddenly made me think if I didn't know that, then I didn't know what else I might do to lose it. It was this horrible, exposed feeling, like being lost in Hell's Kitchen with a million dollars in your pocket and a sign around your neck that says—I don't know—'Midwest Yokel,' or something. It made my skin crawl. Better to just trash it yourself so you know for sure when it's going to be gone."

Dr. Lindholm nods.

"And I guess it made me feel guilty. I don't think I *wanted* Robert to love me that completely. I didn't love him that completely, without holding anything back. I mean, I never would have done that thing with that card—I'd have been too worried about whether the flight attendants were going to read it and make fun of me or something." I look down at my hands. "You know, I've come up with a really long list of these, the worst somethings I've ever done, but I really think maybe, finally, that's maybe the worst thing I ever did: going on even though I didn't love Robert the same way."

Dr. Lindholm is quiet. I wait for her to argue, to say we never love each other in the same way, to say we're not responsible for the way other people love us, but she doesn't, and briefly I'm annoyed. What is she here for, after all, if not to perpetually let me off the hook?

"But the good news I guess is he didn't love me quite the way I thought, either. He only loved me enough to want me locked up and zapped back into the good little cocktail party wife I once had been." An enormous ball rises in my throat. "But, hey." I try to smile. "At least we know he would have said good-bye."

"Don't stop, Darien," Dr. Lindholm says. "We've never talked about this, the way you love Robert."

"I don't love Robert."

"Of course you do. You told me so, back in the fall."

"I can't."

"Why not?"

For a moment, I feel my love for him, a metastatic tumor, filamentous. I feel its dull, squeezing presence, its inoperable futility. I shake my head. "Because I can't love him and Dayton at the same time. If I love him, it means I don't love her the way I thought—and don't give me that old you-can-love-both-of-them routine; it's not what I mean. I mean I can't have loved her with the sort of intensity and completeness that I thought, and if I didn't love her that way, then she certainly didn't love me that way back, and if two people like me and her can't love each other enough, how can—what's the point in—" I stop.

"I don't think I follow."

"I mean, I'm not allowed. It's pretty obvious I didn't even know my own sister the way I thought. I didn't even know who she was. In a thousand years, I never would have believed she was capable of killing herself. I mean, Jesus Christ! So I think that pretty much disqualifies me for anything else. I had the best chance of anybody in the world to know, really understand, someone else and I fucked it up, and if I couldn't even know my own twin, how can I know someone like Robert, and if I can't know him, then how can I love him?"

"Maybe you just love him. You don't need a reason, Darien, or a scientific explanation. You just can. You just do."

I look away. "I can't."

"Can't, because Dayton killed herself."

"You don't have to make it sound stupid."

"It's not stupid at all. I'm just trying to understand what you mean." Dr. Lindholm pushes herself out of her chair and crosses over to the couch. She sits down next to me and takes my right hand in hers. Her words, her touch, carry an electric jolt. "Darien," she says, "what would you say to Dayton if you could talk to her right now?"

"What would I *say* to her?"

"Uh-huh. What would you tell her?"

This is ridiculous, I tell myself. *I won't play this.* "I would tell her to go fuck herself."

Dr. Lindholm's free hand strokes our clenched fists. "Uh-huh," she says. "What else?"

"Nothing else. Just fuck you."

"Fuck you," she repeats, louder than me. "Okay. Fuck you, Dayton. Is that all?"

I hate her. I love her. *Why are you still here? Why are you doing this to me?* "I would ask her—I would ask her why."

"Why what?"

"Why did you leave me? Why did you leave me all alone like that? Why were you such a no-good scaredy pussy shit that you couldn't make it through? I did it. I did it!" I am shouting, gripping the sofa's arm, and then I am crying, jerky, vibrating, wrenching sobs ripped off the back of my spine. Crying and crying, I fall through the hole, howl burning my nose, my eyeballs, my throat, my feet. Relief and loathing, I see the black, dripping mass in my lap. How dare Dr. Lindholm drag this out of me? I wonder what sort of prize it represents, if she will mount it on her wall alongside a dozen other such trophies—another credential, another example of her superior emotional strength—or if she will simply dump it in the trash once I'm out the door, today or some day soon. My pain, her satisfaction, that's the true currency of our relationship, but Oh, Dayton, isn't it true that I did that to you, too? Unbalanced, that was the written rule: you good, me bad. I always thought mine was the harder role, the braver, but how much harder is it to fight and scream and fling off all the pain than it is to just lie still and take it all in? I sucked the life out of you, demanded your vulnerability, a parasite. Was it all my fault? Has it always been all my fault?

Compulsively, reluctantly, I see Dayton at the train station again. The Huntington express makes its approach, roaring and snorting, and my sister throws herself against the night, arms flung wide to pull all that chaos and oblivion in. In the split second for which she is airborne, gravity-defying, however, something happens. Time stops. She hangs suspended, and a bubble opens between an instant and forever, granting her leisure to explore the ineluctable act she has just committed from all sides. She feels the awesome might of the train's steel body, inches away from her sneakered toe, feels it blast against skin and bone, the wet way her arms and legs rip free. She sees her brains spat across the trainman's window through eyeballs blown backward through her skull; she feels the speechless snap of agony, death, in every corpuscle. She sees all the future she will never have: her first day of college, her wedding, a squalling, wet newborn placed in her outstretched arms. She sees my sleeping form, silvered with moonlight, waking up alone, and she reaches out for me. It is too much time. It is time enough, too late, to grow afraid. "Darien!" she screams. She has made a mistake, a horrible mistake! "Dee, oh, Dee-dee, please!" she cries. She twists and scrabbles, clawing out at nothingness, pedaling furiously for a foothold, for anything, and the air moves like water through her hands. The night looks on indifferently. The stars are scrubbed chips of porcelain against the dark. Soon, they say, very soon. *"Mommy!"* she screams. It takes a lifetime for her to hit the ground.

Gravel, a wooden railroad tie. Pain shoots up both ankles, she scrapes her palms and she thinks, *Oh, thank God.* She turns and scrambles for the platform, *thank God.* And then the train explodes over her and all is black and gone.

At Marshall, Dr. Mintzer told me that we rely on myth to survive reality; that myth is what makes reality bearable. As galling as it sounds, he may be right, at least in part. I created the myth of my birth to endure Dayton's death. But still, there is no myth that explains Dayton's suicide itself. There's no analogy that, for me, makes it comprehensible, acceptable, lends it heroism or meaning. No Castor to my Pollux, no way to spin it outward from my self to the universal, to attach it to the firmament, to turn it into an abstract, an object lesson, a fable, anything other than my own story, my own loss. My own literal, personal, mean reckoning.

My sister, my twin sister, killed herself. She was murderer and victim both. And I will never, ever know why.

End of story.

Not quite, of course, as much as I'd like to leave it right there. I've left far too many loose ends dangling for having as much as admitted I'm going to continue stumbling along in the world. There are the small matters of my job and my nightly tab at the Marriott, for starters, and having parted ways with the former, I dispense myself of the latter. I think of my empty apartment, picture the lonely table set for one, and so I pack my bags up and ask the concierge at my building to let me in. "You back already, huh?" he asks, and I say yes, and, after I think about it for a second, "Back from where?" He jabs his thumb toward the ceiling and tells me, "You know, Connecticut, the house," and then I know where Robert is. I make my twice-daily visits to Dr. Lindholm, and one morning she herds me into her car. It's a Volvo, just as I thought it was, and we drive out to Long Island. We look at everything: the sagging, soot-fronted house, the high school, the train station with its newspaper boxes and garbage-strewn tracks. A family waits for a train to Manhattan; a fat, glossy rat darts between railroad ties. All of it looks so much smaller and more concrete than I remember.

And yes, there still is Robert, and one empty Saturday I take a cab to the Avis Car Rental at Grand Central and sign on the dotted line for a red subcompact. I don't think about it in advance, don't even know precisely what I'm doing or why. In the end, I'm not sure that that kind of understanding matters. Floss our teeth, apologize, commit suicide. We either do or we don't. Is our decision to act influenced by our awareness of the mechanics? Dr. Lindholm, I suppose, would argue that knowing matters. Maybe if Dayton knew why she wanted to kill herself, she wouldn't have done it; maybe because I know why I hurt myself, I won't do it anymore. And maybe if I knew that I was going to Robert to make something good come of Dayton's death or because I loved him or because I wanted to say good-bye, it would make what happens next happen the right way. But I don't know that, don't know that I believe that. The Avis clerk slides the key across the counter at me, and I just put it into the ignition and drive.

I focus on the roads. FDR to the Whitestone to 95, I follow salt-caked cars along miles of salt-caked pavement. Blackened clumps of snow, eroded like pumice, line the roadsides; tall, ugly buildings stand against the leaden sky. *Ugly, ugly,* I think: New Rochelle, Bridgeport. It is winter at its most unforgiving, everything stark and dead and laid bare.

Just past Danbury, I turn onto Route 7 and New England winter begins to redeem itself. There are fewer cars and more houses. Pine trees line the road. Solitary farms dot the landscape, sparkling hills, church spires. I pass a pasture full of horses wearing blankets, a snow-cleared pond with children in snowsuits, skating. I look for augury and omen: if there is blue sky—if it starts to snow— White signs for New Milford and Kent slip by, the latter still hung with a Christmas wreath. Cornwall Bridge, then Derryton, ten miles to Eastman. A station wagon pulls on in front of me, slow-moving. In the backseat, two children fight. An arm comes up, a ponytail swings. Along the road, barren trees reach their branches down toward me, fluid and eloquent with loss.

When I reach Eastman proper, I slow the car. The town is quiet, closed up, clothing boutiques, antique stores, specialty food shops. Only Hal's Hardware and the gas station appear open for business; in the middle of the road, the single yellow traffic light blinks for no one against the blackening sky. Maybe I'm wrong. Maybe Robert isn't here. The buildings suddenly look flimsy, like cardboard pasteups, the town

[315]

no match for the big, inhospitable world to which it stakes a claim. I hear the rattle in our single-pane windows and feel the perpetual draft that sifts across the floors like a snake. "I have to go to the bathroom," I say out loud. "I'm freezing. This is ridiculous." I pull to the side of the road and think about turning back.

I drive past Brown's Trail and then Ponkapoag Road. An SUV, coming toward me, flicks its high-beams up and then down. Our house is the next left, about a mile and a half up the road.

Walter sees me first. He is in the turnaround, under the overhang of the barn. One of the doors is ajar, and he lies across the opening, working a branch between his paws. When I turn into the driveway, he drops the stick and trots toward me, his ears pricked, tail up, and for a second I am jittery with excitement. *Walter!* I think. He plants himself in the middle of the driveway and barks.

Robert emerges from the barn, a wood-splitter in his hand. He is thin and tired-looking; his clothes are a mess. He puts a hand to his forehead, frowning at the car.

"Hi, Robert." I kill the engine and step out.

The wood-splitter hits the ground with a dull *thunk*.

There is no easy way to do this, no right way to do this, so I let go of the car door and just start to walk. I can't tell from Robert's face or his body language what he feels, and for a second I hope for his anger, easy and obvious, some tiny resentment into which I can dig my fingernails and hold on. But then I realize that this is my moment, my moment to be better than myself, greater, and that our relationship is mine to make a new beginning or ending of, and I have to at least *try,* so if when it's all over I have nothing else, then at least I can have the memory of doing right, for once, to take out and look at for the rest of my life, and so I open my mouth and say, "I'm sorry, Robert. I'm so, so sorry."

For a second, Robert stands frozen. He stares at me, unblinking, his arms down and his hands loose along his thighs, like a sleepwalker caught in mid-dream. Finally, he looks down and stoops to the driveway, reaching a hand forward for the wood-splitter. He picks it up and rubs snow off the angled side. "Darien," he says, like a word he's just learning, too angular and awkward for his tongue. "Darien." He tries it again, surprised and experimental this time.

"I should have called you, or sent a postcard or something, but I was afraid if I let you know I was coming, you wouldn't be here, and really, I didn't even know I was coming myself. I didn't even know if you'd be here. I only found out the other day where you were, and somehow I thought if I just saw you, I'd know what to say, and now I'm here and I don't. I've been horrible to you. I understand completely if you hate me. What I put you through—disappearing like that—it was just unforgivable." I take a big, rubbery breath, then blow it out. "At the hospital, I didn't mean what I said."

I flounder to a stop and raise my hands. My eyeballs ache with a sudden, horrible weight and a million words crowd my throat at once. *Too late,* my heart pumps in my ears. *Too late.* Desperately, I say, "You're probably in the middle of something. Chopping wood, I guess. You're probably busy. Are you busy?"

Robert's head is still bent forward and I watch his hair give a negative shake. His shoulders jerk as if he's fighting to contain his helpless hilarity at a particularly politically incorrect joke, and his voice too, when it comes, seems strangled with laughter. He says, "No, I'm not busy." Just under his breath he adds, "Goddamn you," and then I realize he is not laughing but crying.

I kneel in the snow next to him and press my forehead against his. "Robert, I'm so sorry," I say yet again. "I don't even know where to begin."

His arms come around me. He squeezes me hard, punishingly, my nose against his collarbone. I smell the sharp cold rising off his sweatshirt and beneath it a musky flush. I feel the groove in his back where his ribs slide down to spine. I close my eyes. I hear his ragged, raspy breaths. "Don't begin anywhere," he says.

In the driveway, for a few minutes, at least, everything seemed simple and possible: Robert and I held each other and cried. Robert told me not to begin anywhere and I didn't. I smelled his hair and felt his body and listened to his breathing. I tasted cold and salt and thought, *Robert, Robert.* The wind whistled around us and the world took on a strange, yellow light. But then Robert jerked himself away. He climbed to his feet, brushing his hands together, and squinted over me, at the house. He cleared his throat. "Darien," he said. "Well." He thrust his fists in his pockets. "Why don't you come inside?"

I followed Robert to the kitchen and obeyed his pointing finger as he directed me to the table. "Can I get you a cup of tea, or something?" I nodded silently. He picked up the teakettle and let the sink run, fanning his fingers under the water with his back to me. I listened to the noise, the nasal complaint of the hot water tap, the stutter of the pipes in the basement. "So, what do you want, Darien?" he said.

"What do you mean?" My voice sounded small. I looked for fear, vulnerability, in the set of Robert's shoulders and the angle of his neck. He was still facing the stove, pushing me away because he wanted me back so badly. He set the kettle on the plate and turned back around.

"I mean, what do you want? Why are you here?"

"I came to apologize."

"So you said. So you have."

I swallowed hard. "I don't know. I just wanted to see you." I looked around the kitchen. Blue-tiled counters, cherry cabinets, a fleur-de-lis stencil above the moldings I'd done one winter afternoon.

"Right. To plunge the knife in my heart."

I shook my head at the table. "No."

"Or maybe it was kicking me in the gut you had in mind." Robert stooped to look under the kitchen table. "What shoes do you have on, your steel-toed boots?"

"You know, you don't have to make this hard."

"Yeah, I'm afraid I do." Robert laughed once, short and harsh.

"When did you get so mad at me?"

"You're kidding, right? Oh, I don't know. Maybe it was when you took off on me without telling me where you were going. Or maybe it was when you told me you didn't love me. Or maybe—wait, yeah, I've got it. I think it was when I found out everything about our life was a lie."

"Not everything."

"Oh, really? Name one thing. What wasn't?"

I shook my head.

"You lied about everything, the most fundamental thing about you. I don't even know who you are."

"And therefore you hate me."

Robert looked away quickly. "That's not what I said."

The teakettle whistled. Robert set two mugs on the counter. Tendrils of steam rose and I curled my hands around mine, pressing the heat against my palms. I took a sip, too hot, shocking hot, and coughed.

"You going to tell me where you've been?"

"Manhattan, for the last few weeks, and before that, Culver."

"You were at Marshall?"

"Yeah. Well, no. After you—after I saw you at Mount Lebanon, I tried to check myself in, but the guy in charge wouldn't admit me. He said I was fine and that I just needed to get on with my life."

"But that was like a month ago. Almost two months ago."

"I know." I looked at the window, mirrored already with nightfall. It had started snowing. I couldn't see it but I could hear it, sleety pebbles pinging against the glass. In the breezeway, Walter jangled his collar tags on the floor.

"You know," I said, "when I first left for Marshall, I thought I couldn't love you now that I knew what I knew about myself. I thought what you did: I wasn't the same person anymore. I was this twin, with a capital T. I thought I needed to do something crazy, check myself in, join the Peace Corps or something, go be who I was supposed to be. But I'm here now because I found out I didn't really want to do anything different. I still loved you. Still love you. And I'm sorry. I don't think love has much of anything to do with what we know about ourselves. Maybe it's about what we don't know about ourselves."

Robert turned his mug by the handle, around and around. He shook his head at the table. "I wasn't talking about what I knew about myself. I was talking about what I knew about you."

"But why is that different? I mean, it's not like when you met me you drew up some checklist somewhere and said, 'Let's see, she's got three brothers, she lived in Ohio once, she's a Leo—I think I'll fall in love with her.'"

"You know that's not the point. You lied to me about something absolutely fundamental about yourself, and that calls into question everything else about you I ever believed to be true. How can I trust you? I just—I don't trust you."

"Well, maybe it would help if you'd quit saying I lied to you. I didn't lie to you. I didn't remember. I lied to myself."

Robert stood up again and crossed over to the refrigerator, shimmed against the sloping floor with a wedge of wood. He kicked the shim in tighter against the refrigerator, then used his fingers to lever the two inches or so still sticking out. The wood squealed and cracked as he twisted it, finally wrestling the stub end free. He examined the ragged piece of wood, testing the splintery edges with his thumb. "I can't do this, Darien," he said. "I'm too tired. I mean, I love you. I do. And I've missed you so goddamn much. The first few weeks you were gone, I went crazy. Every day, I woke up feeling like somebody punched me in the guts, and I'd tell myself, *Today she'll call. Today she'll write, or something, let me know where she is,* just to get my body out of bed. I went to work and tried to ignore all those"—Robert stopped, lifting his shoulders and squinching his features into a rude caricature of pity—"faces. And then it was Christmas, and New Year's—Hoyt made me take the time off. Said I was screwing up too much.

"I thought maybe you'd come up here. It was awful at first, so goddamn quiet, and I could smell you. I'd stand in the shower smelling your shampoo and cry. But then one day I actually saw myself, a grown man, bawling in the shower over a ten-dollar bottle of shampoo, and that's when I said the hell with it— She left you. I threw it out, threw all your crap out, hair dye and razors and maxi-pads. I stopped making the bed and scraping all my dishes off. You weren't there to make me, and what difference did it make? I started seeing a whole bunch of things differently. I saw what a pussy I had been, how much time I spent chasing my own tail, being mister Yes, Sir nice guy, worrying about everyone else. You, mostly. I just—" Robert stopped, staring hard at something above my shoulder. "It just took so much energy to be with you, Darien, and now—you being here. . . ."

Robert flipped the broken shim toward the sink. It bounced off the edge and hit the floor. He looked at it, shrugging. From the other room, Walter woofed.

"Right," I said. "I'm here. Apologizing. I did some pretty lousy stuff to you, and I know it, and I know there's no way to undo any of it, and I'm sorry. But you did some pretty lousy stuff to me too, and I don't hear you saying sorry to me."

Robert's face registered disbelief. "Like what? What did I do to you?"

"Like trying to have me committed. Like requiring me to be this helpless, incompetent little fuckup—"

"Uh-uh," Robert said. "Darien, no way. I told you at the hospital. Steve O'Brien told me about Marshall. His sister had been a patient there. I was only—I didn't know what else to do."

"That's bullshit. You can hide behind that story all you like, but we both know it's bullshit. You were mad at me and you wanted to punish me."

Robert made a protesting noise, but I held him off. "You didn't even talk to Dr. Lindholm. She practically had to take out a court order against you! If you really wanted me to get better, why would you do something so totally against her wishes?"

"I came to see you. I apologized. I canceled the transfer. You were the one who said you didn't love me."

"You told me you hated me! You said you wished you could kill me! I mean, of all the lousy things I ever—I never wished you harm."

"You ripped my heart out." Robert pulled both his hands in fast against his chest. "I used to love you so much some days I could barely breathe. Being with you was like standing in the sun."

I looked down at my own hands, at the bluish veins lacing the pad of my thumb. They looked like ink afterthoughts, ballpoint pen drawn on and smudged out. "Robert," I whispered to them.

"But at the hospital, you were so cold. You were cruel. I looked at you and thought I don't even know who this ice bitch is. You looked right into my eyes and said, 'Robert I don't love you.' "

"I was in pain." I shook my head. Stupid words. "I'm sorry. I was scared. I thought—"

"No, I was scared. But I tried to reach out to you, because that's what people do, and then you didn't— All I needed was for you to reach out to me. You sit here and talk like a grown-up about what you know about love and how you love me, but we both know you won't give me the only thing I really need."

If I hadn't looked at him, I could have done it: crossed the room and put my arms out, leaned my cheek against his chest. In my mind's eye I saw him, chewing on the side of his thumb, his shoulders slightly up, unprotected as a little boy clutching his favorite blanket. *Please don't hurt me, please don't tell me no.* Is that how we get by in life and love, these false images, white lies told to ourselves? The real Robert had his arms across his chest and his lips pressed shut. His eyes were cold, assessing, condemning. What he wanted was my abasement: for me not to hug him but to collapse at his feet and throw my arms around his knees, beg forgiveness, accept all the blame. For a second I could do it. I imagined myself walking across the room, hauling concrete legs forward, solidifying with each step. Would I freeze midway, my arms extended, mouth wide? If I made it to Robert, I would have to remain there, the prostitute Mary at the temple, washing Jesus' feet.

"Please, don't make me ask you," Robert said.

The kitchen was quiet. I could hear the electric buzzing of the clock on the stove. The kettle tipped twice on the cooling stove plate. Snow drummed harder against the window. "I won't," I said. "I won't." I spread my fingers against the table. *Get up,* I told myself. "Robert, I'm sorry."

Dishes rattled against the sink as he walked out of the room.

It is morning, the last morning, and I wake up with the sun in my eyes. I have slept poorly—little—in the master bedroom and by myself, unclear as to how I got here or where I should go next. I spent most of the night replaying the argument with Robert and vainly willing myself downstairs and into the guestroom, taking all of it back, and when I'd last checked the clock it had been after three. Snow was still driving hard against the windows. I'd told myself it was a stay of execution from Mother Nature: leaving in the morning wouldn't even be an option, I still had time, nothing to decide. I'd slept, blackout dreams of wind and waves rioting through my brain. Now, however, the world is perfectly clear, a place tailor-made for snowplows and trucks spreading sand. Serpentines of snowflakes rise and subside. I hold my breath—another squall coming through? The windows shudder in their casements and then new bursts of snow blow by, shaken loose from the burdened trees.

I drag myself out of bed and toward the bathroom, as physically tired as if I had walked to Eastman from Manhattan yesterday. I use Robert's toothbrush, then stare at the new shower I have only used twice, not sure I can manage standing and washing my hair at the same time; equally worried that taking a bath instead will come across as some kind of affront. *After all I did for you, and you can't even show me the gratitude to use the shower?*

I turn the taps on, weary, weary, and step in. I lean my head against the wall and try to think. Manhattan? Back to Culver? There was a bed and breakfast in town, but what good would that do, what would that buy? For a minute I just stand and wonder if it's even possible, ever, for two people to agree on a version of reality. After all, if there was anything I had learned over the last six months, it was that there was no such thing as absolute truth. My mother could have seen something one way, Dayton another, Dr. Lindholm still a third, and how could I know if any one of them was really real? My interpretation could only be just that: a fourth version, a scrim imposed upon what someone else perceived. Between me and Robert, now, it seemed, it could be only worse. He was a lawyer, I was a public relations rep. We were two people trained in negotiating the truth.

With my eyes still closed, I fish around the walls for something to wash my hair and come up with a hotel bottle of shampoo and a thin wafer of soap. I rub the soap between my hands and then bubbles squeak against my ears. The smell of Ivory, plain and practical, rises with the steam.

Even our wedding—videotaped, witnessed, the very building block of our marriage—had proved to be something Robert and I couldn't agree upon. The service at St. Mark's had taken place on an Indian summer Labor Day Friday, just Robert's family and a handful of friends from work. I wore a dress I'd bought the weekend before at Lord & Taylor and carried a dripping bouquet of tulips from the Korean deli across the street. My side of the church was almost empty: Hillary and Isabel, my then-secretary; Porter, to whom I winked as I passed. My roommate, Cassandra, sat in a second row, sobbing audibly, and I thought it was no doubt because she was going to have to find another sucker to shell out six hundred bucks a month for a tiny room on West 17th. A photographer scrambled in front of me and I smiled aggressively for him: *Tulips up? Lipstick on my teeth?* I would look happy. I would look real. It was my wedding day.

I watched a cone of sunlit dust motes and thought about how the song the organist was playing always reminded me of *Ordinary People,* and it wasn't until the very front of the church that I noticed Robert. Six o'clock sunlight shone through the tips of his ears and turned his brown hair gold. His eyes were mirrored with tears, but his face was alive with joy and he reached out for my hand. "Oh, Darien," he whispered. "You're the most beautiful thing I've ever seen."

For weeks after, that scene had haunted me. I felt the shame of sashaying up the aisle to marry myself in every minute, and tried harder, acted nicer, to make amends, but I'd forgotten it by the following summer, when Robert and I attended our first wedding as husband and wife. The couple was older; both full partners at Adelstein. The ceremony was lavish and Jewish and held outdoors. The bride had walked down the aisle by herself. The groom waited beneath the chuppah, beaming out at her, and when she got halfway, he went to her, his hands extended. They met the rabbi together, looking into each other as if no one else existed in the world. I writhed in my seat, a child forced to watch her grandparents making love, and felt all my guilt and grief from September coming back.

"Nice ceremony," Robert said that night, on the drive back home, "but not as nice as ours."

I thought before I answered him. Was it a joke? A trap? "Are you kidding me?" I finally asked.

"Not particularly."

"We couldn't come close to that. They were grown-ups. They married each other."

Robert raised his eyebrows at the road ahead. "And we . . . ?"

I turned in my seat to tell him: we were idiots, We were kids! We had no idea what we were doing! But in a flash of passing streetlights, I saw him. His seatbelt was buckled, his door was locked, his hands were on the wheel at ten and two. He looked a little tired but utterly happy, perhaps even eager to sample this latest morsel of his wife's taste for melodrama. For a moment, at least, it hadn't happened: my version of our wedding didn't exist. I looked around the car: coffee cups, scattered CD cases, the little Velcroed clock on the dash. It was after 1:00 A.M. I was tired, too, and suddenly it seemed possible: all you had to do was find a version of reality and stick with it. If you thought something, it became that way. What could be the harm? I saw my mother's face and willed it away. I touched Robert's thigh across the seat. "Our wedding was beautiful," I said.

I'm dressed and dry, sorting through the medicine chest for things I want to take with me, when I hear Robert's voice. It comes from beneath me, on the porch, and at first I think he's on the telephone. He sounds grim, stern, defeated; there's no one I can imagine him talking to like that other than myself. His office? His mother? Maybe he's called Dr. Lindholm. I strain a little harder to hear the words, then press my forehead to the fogged windowpane.

"C'mon," he says. "No fooling, now." *Clap, clap!* He smacks his hands together. "Get back over here, boy."

Not the telephone. Walter.

I clear a small circle on the glass, and then I see my dog, prancing along the frozen perimeter of the lawn, where in summer grass gives way to apple trees. Even from here, I can see Walter's agitation. His tail is aloft, streaming out behind him, and his steps are exaggerated, punching holes in the icy snow. His head points up, swiveling left and right. He looks like a lion, a miniature Clydesdale. Pride shakes his feathers and ripples his coat. I can sense the purposeful, ready trembling of his muscles, the vibration of his nerves. He is dancing, his nose thrust into the wind.

"Walter. Buddy, come over here," Robert says again. "Last time, now." He shifts to a note just shy of threatening. "You know better than that."

Walter tosses his head, a California teenager. I see the radio box on his collar, clipped to the side like a deck of cards.

The wind lifts a layer of snow and circles it around and round, sparkling spindrift in the orchard, and it is out of the moving cloud that she appears. A white-tailed doe, knock-kneed and heavy-barreled. The blades of her ribs rise against her dun coat as she stretches herself upward, stripping the bark off a Cortland tree. Twenty yards away, no more, as oblivious to Robert and Walter as if she was invisible, or they were. She balances a hoof against a branch and pulls the bark in short, sharp jerks.

I leave the window and take the stairs two at a time. Robert's voice echoes through the house, rising a pitch, "Wal-*ter*," exasperation for what he will never understand now warping the notes, and by the time I reach the doorway Walter's already done it, thrown himself through the electric air. He's run himself through with it, white-hot and agonizing, felt the current in twisting lines along every nerve, lost his breath, stopped his heart. When I see him, the moment is over. He is already in the orchard, slowly but matter-of-factly helping himself to his feet, shaking his big, boxy head, shaking it off.

Robert's shaking his head, too. He is outside, in just a T-shirt and jeans that hang far too loosely on him, his arms wrapped across his chest. "Whatever," he says, more to himself than to Walter, now. He stubs his toe defeatedly. "If you say it's worth it. Whatever, man." The doe is already gone.

It is. It hurts like hell, like ripping out a tooth, like ripping out your soul, the sort of flashing, shocking pain that can only last a minute—impossible, inexplicable, ineluctable, but worth it. I open the door and step onto the porch. My breath comes out white with smoke and I think, *Poor Robert! He must be freezing*. I come right up behind him. I reach out for my husband. Just beyond him, Walter is a streak of white and gold, headed for the trees.